Praise for
THE GOOD, THE BAD, AND THE DUKE

"Sparkling . . . a richly engaging romance with a heroine we should all resolve to be more like."
— *Entertainment Weekly*

"Utterly delightful in every possible way."
— *BookRiot*

"Effervesces with lighthearted romance . . . sweet and sultry in equal measures." — *Publishers Weekly*

"MacGregor writes like a warm cozy blanket."
— *Smart Bitches*

"[An] emotionally rich, exquisitely wrought tale that superbly celebrates the redemptive power of love."
— *Booklist*

THE LUCK OF THE BRIDE

"Brimming with family, hope, and tender sensuality, this shrewdly plotted, gently paced romance is especially satisfying." — *Library Journal*

THE BRIDE WHO GOT LUCKY

"Rising star MacGregor once again demonstrates her remarkable gift for effortlessly elegant writing, richly nuanced characterization, and lushly sensual love scenes in the second brilliant installment in her new Cavensham Heiresses series, following *The Bad Luck Bride*."
— *Booklist* (starred review)

"MacGregor has a real talent for developing every facet of a romance."
　　　　　　　　　　　　　　　　　　　—*Kirkus Reviews*

"A heady mix of action, wit, and sexual tension. Readers will eagerly turn the pages to see how this intense story concludes."
　　　　　　　　　　　　　　　　　　　—*Publishers Weekly*

"Deliciously provocative in historical detail . . . There is everything in this novel and more. There is tingling suspense, an intriguing mystery, sizzling chemistry between Emma and Nick, emotional upheavals, and, of course, a scorching romance. This is definitely a keeper! *The Bride Who Got Lucky* is absolutely brilliant!"
　　　　　　　　　　　　　　　　　—*Romance Junkies* (5 stars)

THE BAD LUCK BRIDE

"An enjoyably complex treat. Winningly, although there's plenty of sizzle between the newlyweds in multiple passionate scenes, their efforts to build a meaningful partnership outside the bedroom make this a mature addition to any Regency shelf. An impressive debut."
　　　　　　　　　　　　　　　　　　　—*Kirkus Reviews*

"Debut author MacGregor brings England's Regency era to life in this sparkling launch for the Cavensham Heiresses romance series. This charming tale features a refreshing array of happy families, solid relationships . . . The book's promise of a delicious story is well realized, building anticipation for future installments."
　　　　　　　　　　　　　　　　　　　—*Publishers Weekly*

"Newcomer MacGregor delivers a well-paced, powerfully plotted debut where love and revenge vie for center stage. Here is a romance that reminds readers that love is complicated, healing, and captivating. MacGregor's characters are carefully drawn, their emotions realistic, and their passions palpable. Watch for MacGregor to make her mark on the genre." —*RT Book Reviews*

"Readers, rejoice! We have a new writer to celebrate. Janna MacGregor writes with intelligence and heart. *The Bad Luck Bride* is a full-bodied romance about what it truly means to love, to forgive, and to heal. Plus, it introduces us to characters we will enjoy as they grow and develop. Smart, smart romance."
    —*New York Times* bestselling author Cathy Maxwell

"Delightful! Janna MacGregor bewitched me with her captivating characters and a romance that sizzles off the page. I'm already a huge fan!"
    —*New York Times* bestselling author Eloisa James

"*The Bad Luck Bride* is a stroke of good luck for readers—the intricate plot, arresting characters, and rich emotional resonance will leave you swooning."
    —*New York Times* bestselling author Sabrina Jeffries

"Janna MacGregor's *The Bad Luck Bride* is a seductive tale filled with suspense and unforgettable characters. A must-buy for historical romance readers."
    —*USA Today* bestselling author Alexandra Hawkins

"A diamond-bright debut, with a passionate heroine and worthy hero to root for."
—Maggie Robinson, author of *The Unsuitable Secretary*

Don't miss these other romances in
The Cavensham Heiresses
by
Janna MacGregor

THE GOOD, THE BAD AND THE DUKE
THE LUCK OF THE BRIDE
THE BRIDE WHO GOT LUCKY
THE BAD LUCK BRIDE

From St. Martin's Paperbacks

ROGUE
MOST
WANTED

JANNA
MACGREGOR

St. Martin's Paperbacks

This is a work of fiction. All of the characters, organizations, and events portrayed in this novel are either products of the author's imagination or are used fictitiously.

ROGUE MOST WANTED

Copyright © 2019 by Janna MacGregor.

For information address St. Martin's Press, 175 Fifth Avenue, New York, NY 10010.

ISBN: 978-1-250-295996

Our books may be purchased in bulk for promotional, educational, or business use. Please contact your local bookseller or the Macmillan Corporate and Premium Sales Department at 1-800-221-7945, ext 5442, or by email at MacmillanSpecialMarkets@macmillan.com.

Printed in the United States of America

St. Martin's Paperbacks edition / July 2019

St. Martin's Paperbacks are published by St. Martin's Press, 175 Fifth Avenue, New York, NY 10010.

10 9 8 7 6 5 4 3 2 1

To Nick
Because every single one of William's dining room scenes
in the Cavensham Heiresses series was inspired by you.

Acknowledgments

I'm so fortunate to have such an outstanding team working with me on the Cavensham Heiresses series. My editor, Alexandra Sehulster, is unparalleled. Your ability to draw out the best in my characters and story make me a better writer. Saying thank you isn't enough, but you have my eternal gratitude.

To my agent, Pam Ahearn, thank you for taking a chance on me. You've been instrumental in helping me craft this series and these characters. You're fabulous, but you already know that. Kim Rozzell, I so appreciate all you do for me. You keep me on the straight and narrow while continuing to make everything sparkle! It was my lucky day when I met you. Again, I thank Holly Ingraham and Corinne DeMaagd for all their help and support along the way.

Marissa Sangiacomo, Meghan Harrington, and Mara Delgado-Sanchez, your enthusiasm and support are incomparable, and I'm so fortunate to have you behind me. Thank you. What can I say to the art department at St. Martin's Press, Danielle Christopher, and Jon Paul

Ferrara? You've created the perfect couple for this book. It's an honor to work with you.

Lord Fluff was inspired by Lynne Bannon and Yoda. Thank you both for being there for me from the very beginning.

Thank you, dear readers, for falling in love with the Cavensham family. You make this journey fun.

Finally, I couldn't do any of this without the love and encouragement of my own darling rogue. Thank you, Greg, the author of my romantic life.

The fool doth think he is wise, but the wise man knows himself to be a fool.
                    As You Like It, Act 5, Scene 1

Prologue

Mayfair
One glorious day in May when hope always springs
eternal, 1804

"In one hour, I'm going to be a changed man." Lord William Cavensham, the second child and second son of the Duke and Duchess of Langham, high-stepped down the Mayfair street from his home to the residence of Lady Avalon Cavensham.

"How so?" Mr. Devan Farris kept pace.

"I'm asking Lady Avalon Cavensham to marry me," Will announced. Just saying her name brought a rush of pleasure to him. She was perfect in every single way, from her gorgeous green eyes to her dark brown hair.

Will had finished his last term at university two years ago, and during that time, he'd crossed the inevitable bridge from youth to adulthood. He'd waited for this day all his life, and now, everything he'd dreamed for his future was within his grasp.

"You? Married?" The shock on Devan's face turned the fellow's normally tanned skin to an unhealthy sallow.

It was difficult for Will to determine the exact shade as the sun cast an eerie red-orange glow this morning. It reminded him of the wallpaper from the East his great-aunt Stella favored in her Northumberland estate.

"I've been at Oxford for less than six months. This is what I come home to? My God, you're only nine and ten. That's awfully young to face the hell of matrimony. What about sowing your wild barley?"

"Oats," said Will.

"Oats, wheat, mint—who cares? You understand what I'm saying. Don't you want to enjoy life?" Devan adjusted the brim of his hat to shield his eyes from the sun. "Old man, you're too young."

Will grinned and continued on his chosen path. He was known for his confidence and fast decision-making capabilities, particularly when he knew what he wanted out of life. Those traits ensured he succeeded where other men failed. Such qualities couldn't be learned, in Will's opinion. He had his long line of Cavensham ancestors to thank for those ingrained strengths that resided in every fiber of his being.

Devan twirled his walking stick. "At the age of nine and ten, no less."

"You're repeating yourself. Besides, what does age have to do with it? How do you know that marriage isn't the vehicle for me to enjoy life?" Will's rhetorical questions silenced Devan momentarily. "We Cavensham men are known for falling in love *quickly, decidedly, and thoroughly committed.*"

Devan snorted. "Committed to Bedlam, perhaps."

Will ignored the insult. "We make up our minds and go after the women we're destined to spend our lives with. My grandfather, my uncle, and my father are examples of such a fate. It's a Cavensham man's destiny."

"That's absolute rubbish." Devan stepped over a piece of refuse as they crossed a street and twitched his nose. "How long have you known the lovely Lady Avalon?"

Will stopped suddenly, and Devan followed suit.

"You already know the answer. Since we're third cousins, I've know her all my life. We've seen each other at family events and house parties over the years." Will had never paid much attention to Avalon until last Christmas when they played charades on that first day. With her fair beauty and gentle ways, he'd immediately fallen under her spell and thus, they were inseparable during the entire holiday—proof they were destined to be together.

"Why is it that I've never heard about this grand love affair until now?" Devan swept a hand in front of him, inviting Will to continue their walk. "Under your theory, you should've fallen in love when you first met her. Was that when you were the age of three?"

The feigned sincerity in Devan's tone didn't hide his sarcasm, and Will stopped again.

Like soap bubbles meeting their demise, Will's confidence popped with doubt. What his friend said rang true. If Cavensham men fall in love quickly and completely, why hadn't he felt anything for Avalon when they were growing up?

"What's the matter?" Devan asked innocently.

"Nothing is the matter." He dismissed the disturbing thought, which allowed his self-assurance to again hold center stage. Not anything or anyone—not even Devan—would mar the perfection of the day. "It's easy to explain. We were too young to fall in love."

Devan nodded. "Of course. It's just an anomaly that Juliet was thirteen and Romeo was perhaps fifteen when they tragically fell in love."

"That's fiction. This is life."

"Of course," Devan replied dryly. "Shakespeare is highly overrated."

Will didn't comment further as they stopped outside the large palladium home of Lord Fenton Cavensham,

Avalon's father and the Earl of Calderton. Will extended
his hand to Devan. "Wish me luck."

Devan shook his hand with a firm grip. "You don't
need luck. This is your destiny, remember?"

He frowned as his friend took his leave while whis-
tling a little too merrily. There was no cause to worry.
By the way Avalon looked at him, she loved him as much
as he loved her.

Devan's glib remark was the truth whether he realized
it or not.

This was Will's destiny.

Without further delay, Will walked through the ornate
wrought iron gates with the Calderton coat of arms in the
center, then chuckled. The peacock front and center in
the design always made him laugh. Most coats of arms
featured fearsome or mythological creatures, not some
silly fowl. His family's seal had two rearing lions back-
to-back, symbolizing the family's fierce sense of loyalty.

The butler greeted Will, then escorted him to the all-
too-familiar formal salon. The room was tastefully decorated in green and brown brocades and silks, but it
always reminded Will of a moat around an ancient castle.
But it made little difference what room he was escorted
to, because today he only had eyes for the enchanting
Avalon.

At the sound of the door opening, Will smiled and
turned to greet her.

Instead, the Earl of Calderton whisked into the room
looking a little disgruntled if the crease between his eyes
was any indication. "Lord William, what an unexpected
surprise."

"Good morning, my lord," Will answered.

Lord Calderton waved a hand, offering William a seat
on a puce sofa. After Will took his place at one end of

the sofa, the earl settled his large frame at the other end. "What might I do for you this morning?"

Will cleared his throat in an attempt to tamp down the sudden case of nerves that churned in his stomach. "I'd hoped to have a word with Ava—I mean, Lady Avalon this morning. But your presence is quite fortuitous." Without giving the earl a chance to comment, Will continued, "Sir, I'm here to request Lady Avalon's hand in marriage."

The earl's eyes widened to the size of full moons. "Pardon me?"

"Lady Avalon and I love each other. It's my greatest wish that you'll give your blessing to our union." The words tumbled from Will's mouth. "She and I discussed this last week, and I told her I'd come today and seek her hand."

Finally, Will took a deep breath. It was finished. Once the earl agreed, everything else was a formality. Avalon would glide down the steps shortly. Her father would leave to give them privacy, then Will would pop the question. They'd kiss. And it wouldn't be just any kiss. He'd kiss her with a passion she'd never felt before—one worthy of the woman who'd captured his heart, the woman who would make all his dreams come true.

As if Will had conjured her from his thoughts, Avalon entered the room. The piercing green depth of her eyes resembled a pair of malachite knives he'd seen as a youth in his father's study. An appropriate description as her gaze pinned him in place.

"Avalon, Lord William is here." The earl's brows steeply arched like the perfect vaults in a medieval church abbey. "He's under the impression that you have agreed to marry him."

Will couldn't help but smile like a fool—a fool in love,

and he was glad for it. "My parents are delighted with our match."

The pulse in Avalon's neck visibly pounded, and she swallowed slightly. "He's mistaken, Father."

Will took a step toward her, but with a raised hand, she halted him in his steps.

"Lord William, I'm to marry the Marquess of Warwyk in three days." Her voice trembled ever so slightly. "My family and I will travel to his ancestral seat tomorrow."

"Avalon—" Will wanted to curse when his voice cracked. "What are you talking about?" He blinked twice, hoping this was a bad dream he'd soon awaken from. "Avalon?"

She bowed her head. When she finally met his gaze, her eyes glistened with emotion. "My responsibility is to my family. I made a match with Lord Warwyk." She lowered her voice to a whisper. "I don't have the luxury of marrying a second son of a duke instead of a wealthy marquess."

Unable to speak, Will stood frozen in the middle of the room.

"I'm sorry. If you'll excuse me, I must finish packing." Without another word, she silently left the room.

Everything came to a dead stop. Will's chest refused to expand, his breathing stopped, and his heartbeat stumbled. How could he have misjudged her intentions—even her character?

A deafening silence descended, only broken when Will managed to speak. "There must be some mistake. I've never even heard a mention at White's about such a match." The last visits he'd made to his gentleman's club flooded his thoughts. There was no mention of Avalon or even Warwyk in any of the conversations—not even a single rumor—nor were there any wagers in the betting books.

"Warwyk asked for her hand last March. Her mother has been planning the wedding for weeks." The earl stood and walked to a sideboard with various bottles of brandy, whisky, and other spirits. He poured a fingerful and downed it. Then he filled a second fingerful into his glass along with one for Will.

The earl returned to the settee opposite Will and extended the glass. Without a word, Will shook his head, refusing the drink.

He'd kissed Avalon last Saturday in the silver pantry at Lady Wheaton's house. He couldn't have mistaken the desire in her eyes for something else. She'd said repeatedly she couldn't wait for the day they'd be together.

That night, she'd demanded they do more than kiss, but Will had refused. He's said he wouldn't dishonor her that way. He'd gently explained he wanted to make love with her more than anything else, but as an honorable man, he couldn't. They would wait until the night they consummated their marriage. What a bloody fool he was for thinking she actually cared for him.

He was worse than a fool. He had allowed a woman to gull him into making a proposal, and he'd stupidly fallen in love with her. Hot tears burned his eyes.

He placed his elbows on his knees and rested his forehead in his hands. What was supposed to be the happiest day of his life had turned into a nightmare. Will's heart broke like a crack in a piece of ice when subjected to increasing pressure. Every second that passed magnified his pain. Finally, the hurt became almost unbearable.

The shock that Ava had jilted him made him numb. Slowly, pain leeched the numbness. He stole a peek at the earl.

Lord Calderton met his gaze. The pity in the earl's

eyes forced Will to his feet. He'd not crumble in front of Ava's father. "I must beg your leave, my lord."

"Of course." The earl stood and escorted Will to the door.

Will dug deep inside for words—anything so he could escape.

"Let's keep this between us, shall we?" The earl swiftly shook his head as if coming out of a daze. "I beg you not to disparage Avalon. It would hurt you as much as her if our people"—the earl waved a hand between the two of them as if they were of equal stature—"if the *ton* heard of this. They would tear her to shreds. I have to think of Sophia, Avalon's little sister. You understand, don't you?"

Will straightened his shoulders and stared directly into the earl's eyes. "What I understand is that Avalon jilted me. But never fear, I won't hurt her."

The earl visibly relaxed.

"Nor will I ever acknowledge her again." Will's crisp words echoed throughout the room.

Not waiting for the earl's response, Will exited the room. With every ounce of strength he possessed, he donned a mask of indifference. With his head held high, he counted the steps down the hallway to the entry where the front door offered an escape. All the while he discarded all the memories, hopes, and dreams of marrying for love that he'd crafted over the past several months.

Once outside, he took a deep breath, hoping to cleanse the disappointment and the embarrassment that now colored every thought.

The crack within his heart finally broke open, crumbling into pieces that allowed his hurt and disappointment to bleed freely. Right then and there, he vowed not to let Avalon's jilting define him. He'd learned a valuable lesson—never trust love again—and never allow his heart to be vulnerable to the wiles of a heartbreaker. His entire focus would be devoted to himself and his work.

As if commiserating with him, the sky over London had turned gray with dark, menacing clouds.

The smell of rain permeated the air.

A shower wouldn't cleanse any of the rot that now stained his soul nor would it soothe the ragged and torn chunks of his heart.

But it would baptize his vow.

Chapter One

∿

Ten years later in the late spring
Ladykyrk Estate, Northumberland near the Scottish
border

The new Duke of Ferr-Colby is challenging your right to the Earldom of Eanruig. He plans on moving his staff to the estate within the next couple of days." The old solicitor shook his head. "If the duke were alive to hear this, he'd shoot the man."

Lady Theodora Worth, the new Countess of Eanruig, studied the cup of tea in front of her. Her throat was drier than year-old fireplace kindling, but she didn't dare take a sip. With the trembling of her hands, she'd more likely be wearing the beverage instead of satisfying her thirst. Desperate to calm the rage that ran wild through her thoughts, she clenched her hands into fists.

"If my grandfather were still alive, we wouldn't be having this discussion. He'd still be the Duke of Ferr-Colby and the Earl of Eanruig, and I'd still have my old life."

Six months out of mourning, Theodora stood and smoothed the dull lilac muslin of her day gown. Her grandfather, the old Duke of Ferr-Colby, had been a typical duke, one with an ancient ancestral home, Dunbar on Ferr, and other entailed properties.

But he also held another title, a lesser one but no less noble—the Earl of Eanruig. It was an old Scottish title from his grandmother on his father's side. The earldom's entailed holdings consisted of property in southern Scotland. Thea's ancestors had purchased more property adjacent to the earldom's holding in Northumberland and built Ladykyrk. When Thea's grandfather had died, she'd become the Countess of Eanruig, with all the dignities that came with the title. Such titles were rare, but some of the Scottish peerages allowed women to inherit.

Her grandfather's ducal title and the entailed properties of the dukedom had passed to the duke's heir, Mr. Garrett Fairfax, a distant cousin whom she'd only met twice during her life.

For some odd reason, the solicitor stood now too. "Is something amiss, Mr. Blaze?"

"No, Lady Eanruig. It's custom that if a lady stands, then a gentleman should also stand." His reddened cheeks resembled a freshly stoked fire.

Thea blinked, then waved him to take his seat. She wasn't used to being treated as a proper lady because it had been just her and her grandfather for so long. They tended to prefer informality.

In his sixties, the old solicitor carefully took his seat once Theodora reclaimed hers. "Thank you for sitting. My knees protest all this up-and-down movement."

Thea nodded. There wasn't much call for the rules of etiquette around Ladykyrk. She and her grandfather had led a secluded life since he'd become ill. She'd missed her introduction to society, but it mattered little. Her grandfather had needed her. Though a duke, he employed few servants and acted more like a small farmer. He preferred to live at Ladykyrk instead of his ducal estate, Dunbar on Ferr in Norfolk.

They'd been each other's only family, and she missed

him every day. Though elderly, he'd raised her after her parents had died when she was barely a year old. Ladykyrk was her birthright, and she'd be damned if she'd let some outlier claim it as his.

"Why is the new duke challenging me?" she asked.

Mr. Blaze pulled out a piece of paper from his lap desk. "He's well aware that the dukedom and earldom are two separate titles. The Ferr-Colby dukedom is an English title and passes through the male heirs of the body, while yours is a Scottish title that passes through the general heirs of the body. That small difference in language allows you as a female to possess the title of Countess of Eanruig and all the entailed properties."

"Then I don't see how he can challenge me."

Mr. Blaze scratched his head. "We can't find the charter bestowing your title. The fifth Earl of Eanruig gave the original back to King Charles II in 1681 as a show of allegiance. His majesty immediately wrote a new charter for the title and returned it to the fifth earl. The new duke claims it's an English title, and English law normally dictates that the earldom goes to the male heirs. Since we can't find the paperwork bestowing the earldom, you're going to have to answer his challenge by producing a written history of the title."

Thea moved to the edge of her seat. "He's saying my title is English?"

"Yes. He believes the title should have been enfolded under the Ferr-Colby dukedom when your grandfather assumed both titles." The solicitor swallowed hard. "The new duke wants the title and Ladykyrk and has sent his staff to take inventory of the assets. After the hearing, the duke plans a short visit to Ladykyrk."

"He acts as if he's already won." She tried to swallow the disbelief lodged in her throat, but it was firmly stuck. "He can't have it. This is my home."

Mr. Blaze pushed his eyeglasses back in place after they slipped to the tip of his nose. When he regarded her, his eyes appeared to have grown five times in size. "But the new duke claims he's the rightful male heir."

All she had left in the world was her title and home. "How are we going to prove he's wrong? What are we going to do?" she asked in a flurry of questions.

"It's what *you're* going to do, my lady." Unease etched deep furrows across his brow. "You see, my visit today is my last duty to your grandfather. I now work for the new duke. He's already petitioned the Prince Regent to award the title to him. You need to see this." He handed Thea a broadsheet.

Thea scanned the paper. The title, *The Midnight Cryer*, sat centered at the top. Underneath, an article appeared with the headline: "Lord William Cavensham Proves Once Again He's a Duffer When It Comes to Love."

"What does this have to do with me?"

Mr. Blaze blinked rapidly. "Look below the feature on Lord William, my lady."

Beneath the article about the man unfortunate with love, there appeared another article.

GRANDDAUGHTER DISGUISED AS A MAN-EATER CHALLENGED IN THE HOUSE OF LORDS

Gentle readers, it's come to our attention that the new Duke of Ferr-Colby is challenging the Countess of Eanruig for her earldom. You may remember that the prior duke died under mysterious circumstances. Some say the countess killed her grandfather to inherit the earldom sooner rather than later in order to marry one of her handsome footmen. Reports say the footman has been her lover for years. Could this be the reason no one has seen hide nor hair of the old duke for ages? Thank heavens, the new duke isn't afraid of this viper.

Thea breathed deeply in an attempt to calm her roiling stomach. "What utter depraved nonsense. Is this from London?"

Mr. Blaze nodded.

"Why is my family even a topic of discussion? We're so far removed from society. How can they create such lies?"

Mr. Blaze shrugged his shoulders. "Because they're dukes, my lady. Everyone wants to read about dukes. They sell papers."

She wrapped her arms around her waist. Could any worse luck seem to find her? She had no idea how to find another solicitor. Who would represent her with such rumors swirling about her? Where would one go to find someone well-learned in peerage law? For God's sake, she'd never even been to London. She'd never been anywhere except her grandfather's properties.

She focused on the opened French doors at the north end of her grandfather's study. A beautiful pond shimmered as it basked in the sunshine of a perfect late-spring day. Serene, the scene before her directly contrasted with the turmoil running amok in her heart and mind. With no warning, the biggest fish she'd ever seen broke the calm peacefulness of the water by hurling itself high into the air, twisting its tail. It seemed to defy gravity for a moment as it took command of its surroundings. With a natural grace, it fell back into the blue depths of the water.

Perhaps it was a sign that she needed to break out of the solitary existence she'd known and fight for her rights in London. Indeed, the extraordinary sight was a call to action if she'd ever seen one. Whatever it took, she planned to win.

"Thank you, Mr. Blaze." She lowered her voice. "Will you see yourself out?"

The solicitor nodded and gathered his things. He stood, and she matched his movement.

"My lady, before I leave, allow me to give you the best advice I possess. Your grandfather was a great man, and it was his wish you receive the title of Countess of Ean-ruig and the estate, including Ladykyrk Hall. These types of disputes are rare and will in all likelihood result in the matter being decided by the House of Lords' Commit-tee for Privileges. They're a conservative lot who cling to precedent like a lamb to its ewe." He grinned slightly.

She didn't smile in return.

He cleared his throat, then returned to his earlier grav-ity. "They'll want an interview in London to take your measure. Perhaps you should review a few etiquette books. You should marry or, at least, become betrothed. Quickly. Find some English fop with noble blood. Such a measure ensures that the title will continue once you conceive a child. As important, it'll squelch the rumors. It'll be easier for the House of Lords to make the deci-sion that you're entitled to the earldom. Oh, one more piece of advice."

Thea nodded for him to continue.

"Hire Odell as your solicitor. Good luck."

Thea didn't watch him leave. All her thoughts were consumed by the declaration that the new duke wanted Ladykyrk—her home, her life. Not only must she find a new solicitor, but also a husband. The only man she felt close to was her elderly butler who also happened to be her footman and groomsman. However, he was already married to Ladykyrk Hall's elderly housekeeper. The only local gentry who'd ever visited were old friends of her grandfather. No one was younger than the age of seventy.

She had no clue as to how to find a suitable man. Besides, who would agree to such a union? She couldn't give up her home. It was the only thing that tied her to her family.

Though she suffered loneliness from time to time, she'd become quite adept at pushing it aside and concentrating on more important things, like managing the estate, seeing the tenants were well cared for, and creating the gardens she and her grandfather had spent hours discussing and designing. Now that it was spring, she relished the idea of getting her hands dirty in the rich, cool soil as she planted in the new garden. She never imagined that her life and identity would be challenged by anyone.

Thea stared at the pond, the sun dancing in descent while the evening skies painted the horizon with brilliant blues and purples. The beautiful sight normally captivated her, but not tonight.

The responsibility for Ladykyrk belonged to her. Only she could protect the great estate from the duke. In order to save it, she needed help finding the charter and a husband.

There was only one avenue for her to pursue.

Her neighbor directly to the east, Lady Stella Payne, had been a friend of her late grandfather. She'd always been kind to Thea.

Surely, a woman of Lady Payne's stature would offer assistance and guidance.

After all, any woman who had been married three times should have a world of advice for a countess in desperate need of a husband.

"Madame, the Countess of Eanruig to see you."

Next to the towering footman who resembled a young golden Adonis, Theodora felt foolish and out of place. In happier times, she'd visited Lady Payne's estate on numerous occasions, but always in her grandfather's company. She'd never been in the spotlight—always the companion. With the handsome footman's gaze on her, she didn't know whether to enter the room or wait outside until summoned. Moments like this proved she needed a refresher in etiquette lessons.

"Come in, child," a brisk but cheerful voice called out.

Decorated in a palette of pinks, oranges, and turquoises, the massive sitting room overpowered Thea's vision for a moment. A cornucopia of settees and sofas in corals and blush-pink brocades were spread before her. There was much to admire and study in the light, colorful house, and the sitting room was no exception. But Thea pushed the natural urge to explore aside.

"Over here, Thea." Sitting near a bay window on a tangerine-colored chaise longue, the grand dame waved her jewel-encrusted fingers in the air.

As Thea approached, Lady Payne held her index finger to her mouth, signaling quiet. The biggest emerald Thea had ever seen engulfed Lady Payne's finger.

"Lord Fluff is taking his morning nap. Mustn't interrupt his lordship's routine." With a surprising agility for a lady in her mid-seventies, Lady Payne stood and pointed at a longhaired, cream-colored cat with a gray face. He opened one blue eye and inspected Thea. Finding her of little interest, he closed his eye and continued his nap.

Lady Payne took Thea's hand in hers and led her to another sitting area away from *his lordship*. The grand dame's fingers were cold, but the physical contact with another person warmed Thea's insides. Outside of her grandfather, she couldn't remember the last time she touched a person.

They settled into the cozy sitting area. Before long, an elderly maid presented a tea service. Lady Payne performed the elaborate ritual of pouring the tea and offering the various condiments to add to the beverage while she made idle chitchat. She selected several biscuits and sandwiches for Thea's plate and handed it to her. After she finished with her own tea and plate, she turned all her attention to Thea. "I should have invited you sooner, but I just returned from Brighton. Lovely place. With my husband's passing last year and closing up the other properties, I couldn't come back north until now. I'm so sorry for your loss."

"Thank you." She bit her lip to keep her grief hidden. Now was not the time for tears. "Will you teach me how to do that?" Thea pointed to the tea set. Alone with her grandfather, she'd never learned the proper way of pouring tea. They each had their own pots sitting on the breakfast table, and their butler never poured.

The baroness studied her. Unlike her grandfather's rheumy eyes, Lady Payne's blue eyes flashed with a brilliance that bespoke intelligence, then softened with a hint of kindness. Thea straightened her posture in a poor attempt to withstand the lady's scrutiny. Though it was a nearly hopeless endeavor, she needed Lady Payne's guidance to turn her into a suave and elegant lady, someone who could prove to all of London she was the true heir to the Eanruig earldom.

Lord Fluff decided at that moment to join them in their tea. He'd obviously discarded his disinterest in Thea since he settled on her lap. She touched the soft fur, and the cat rewarded her with a purr that made his whole body vibrate.

"Of course, Theodora. It would be my pleasure," Lady Payne said. Leaning close, she patted Thea on the knee. "Somehow the look on your face indicates there's more that you want."

Thea nodded and studied her lap where Lord Fluff

currently resided. It was beyond humiliating to seek help in acquiring a husband, but she had no other choice, certainly not if she wanted to keep her house and protect her tenants. And truthfully, she'd always wanted a husband and a family. Though she'd felt adrift and feared solitude after her grandfather's death, she couldn't leave. The estate demanded her attention every waking moment since it was springtime. Crops had to be planted, and the livestock sheltered and herded to different pastures. Tenants needed as much, if not more attention.

"Lady Payne, I don't know where to start," Thea murmured.

"*Lady Payne* sounds off-putting for this conversation. Call me Stella," the grand dame coaxed. "Whatever is troubling you, we'll find a solution."

With a deep breath for fortitude, Thea launched into the tale. "Grandfather's solicitor, Mr. Blaze, visited me today and told me that the new Duke of Ferr-Colby is challenging my claim to my title. Months ago, Mr. Blaze submitted my petition to the crown for recognition of my claim as the Countess of Eanruig. I thought everything was in order. But today, he told me he didn't submit the charter bestowing the title because he couldn't find it. And now the new Duke of Ferr-Colby has challenged my right to the earldom."

She glanced briefly at Stella's face and found a frown along with a sudden pink stain painted on her cheeks.

"The new duke disagrees that it's a Scottish title," Thea said. "He claims it's an English one that should only be awarded to male heirs. The solicitor suggested it'll strengthen my claim if I became betrothed and marry someone noble as quickly as possible. At the very least, he recommends an engagement. I must go to London and defend myself in front of the House of Lords' Committee for Privileges. Mr. Blaze thinks . . . the committee won't rule against me if I have an aristocratic family supporting me."

Completely nonplussed, Stella's eyebrows shot straight up. "Where's the charter that bestowed the title? That will have the answer."

"I can't find it, and I don't know what I'm looking for," she confessed. Documents were strewn willy-nilly in her grandfather's study. She'd been through every pile of papers he had squirreled away in his bedroom. "I can't read Latin, and I don't know anyone who does," she said quietly.

Stella shook her head. "It's a hard language. Don't get me started on the horror of conjugating verbs. I never mastered it."

Thea exhaled. "My governess left when I was twelve. She didn't see the need for me to learn any languages other than the *King's English*."

"Good riddance," Stella said. "Foolish governesses are a plague on us all. I'll find someone who reads Latin. Aleyn must be turning over in his grave. Your grandfather was the type of person to have had everything organized perfectly when he passed. That estate is rightfully yours, along with the title."

Her grandfather was the type of person to throw his clothes out the second-floor window, then run naked through the house. The poor dear had been mad as a proverbial hatter. Thea had little doubt he'd hidden the charter to keep it safe. Unfortunately for both of them, he never remembered where he hid anything. She'd spent the afternoon pulling up the floorboards in his bedroom searching for hiding places.

"Stella—" Her voice broke, but Thea tamped down the unruly emotion. "There's more. The duke sent his servants to throw me out of my house. They'll arrive any day. Mr. Blaze suggested I hire a solicitor by the name of Mr. Odell to help with the challenge to my title. I don't know if he is trustworthy or if it's a trick."

"Some dukes think they're in charge of the kingdom and can do no wrong." Stella wrinkled her nose as if smelling something rotten, then leaned forward and patted her hand. "You come stay with me for as long as you like. I'm acquainted with Mr. Odell. He's the best in the business. Bring all your papers here."

"Thank you." Thea exhaled in a struggle to keep her frustration from exploding in anger. "If you want all my papers, we should start with this one." She handed Stella the copy of *The Midnight Cryer.*

Stella's gaze scanned the paper, then looked up with a smirk on her face. "What rubbish."

"I don't even know what to say." Her cheeks heated that she even had to address such nonsense. But she couldn't let it sit there like an uninvited guest in the room whom everyone ignored.

"There's nothing to say except the *Cryer* must be desperate to grow its readership," Stella said. "At least there used to be some truth to their reporting. Now, they're lower than dirt." Stella caught Thea's gaze. "Don't worry over this babble."

Thea quickly nodded, but it was something she would worry about every day. Her reputation would be ruined before she even set foot in London. "Mr. Blaze is now in the employment of the new duke and can't help me. I need a husband quickly. When I appear in front of the committee, I must have all my evidence in order." She lifted her gaze to Stella's but continued her gentle stroking of Lord Fluff. Touching the feline offered a comfort she'd sorely needed. "I've never been to London . . . or really anywhere except Ladykyrk and Dunbar on Ferr. I know no one. I have no friends or family to guide me and prepare for the interview. I have to fight those untruths. It's inconceivable to ask, but would you help?"

An affectionate smile broke across the baroness's face. "When you receive the summons, I'll take you to London."

"Thank you. You'd be a great comfort to me."

Stella stood and patted Lord Fluff on the head before going to an ornate side table by the massive fireplace where a turquoise-jeweled screen stood in front of the hearth. Stella measured a fingerful of brandy in two cut-glass tumblers.

Thea's sliver of trepidation grew into a mountain of doubt. How could anyone help her accomplish the unattainable? She didn't know a single soul in London. How would she even propose to a man, or for that matter, how would she propose a short-term engagement? How could she make herself attractive as a marriage prospect when she didn't know the ins and outs of society? She'd have a better chance of acquiring a husband by posting solicitations in every paper in the kingdom.

She defiantly tipped her chin—she was an heiress, but more importantly, the Countess of Eanruig. She'd find someone to marry.

Stella returned to her side and handed her a glass. "You probably need this more than I do, but as the old adage says, 'Age before beauty.'" She downed it in one gulp, then stared at Thea and waited.

Thea mimicked Stella and gulped hers in one swallow. The strong spirit lit a fire from her mouth to her stomach, but she didn't allow herself to cough.

Stella rested against the chairback. "You've come to the right place. I love solving puzzles and fighting injustices. I can help you prepare your defense to the title. Odell is in London, and Mr. Blaze gave you good advice.

Odell is perfect to represent you in front of the committee. I agree you need a husband. I'm an expert at the sport." She whipped open an ornate coral-colored fan that perfectly matched her gown and feathered turban. "My first husband, Archibald, was fifty years older than me, but he left me a wealthy woman. My second husband, poor Henry, died within the month of our honeymoon. But my darling Payne and I had fifty lovely years together. I'll help you find the man of your dreams."

"How?" Thea asked. It was incredible that she'd find any man, let alone the man of her dreams here in Northumberland.

"I'll ask my best friend since childhood, Lady Edith Manton, to come stay. She always loves *projects*. The tougher the better for Edith's tastes."

"I don't have much time. I need help with etiquette and the ways of society. Any day, I expect to receive the summons to London for the committee appearance," Thea said. "It's hopeless."

"Nonsense, child. I'll help you. Besides, I already have the perfect man for you, one from an excellent family with powerful political connections in London that none can rival." Stella leaned forward as if ready to confide a secret.

Thea's confounded hope started to rise, knowing the veritable driving force in front of her was her champion. Now, the impossible was probable. "He sounds divine. Who is he?"

"Trust me when I say he's superb, handsome, and utterly charming." Stella laughed, the sound pealing through the sitting room like ringing church bells run amok. After her laughter died, she regarded Thea with an artful smile. "He's my great-nephew, Lord William Cavensham."

Let us put the rumors to rest.
There are no "wedding bells" ringing for the perennial
bachelor Lord William Cavensham.
Dear readers, it was the fire brigade.
Respectfully yours,
The Midnight Cryer

Chapter Two

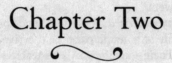

A bsolutely, not. I will not marry her." Will raised an eyebrow as he delivered his refusal to the two elderly women before him. "You'd have more luck marrying me to the devil."

"Imagine the local vicar reading the banns. Would he refer to the devil as Beelzebub or Lucifer? What about a last name?" Lady Edith Manton, Will's great-aunt Stella's best friend, mused as she arranged the myriad of papers that lay in front of her.

The latest copy of *Debrett's Peerage* along with ancient books and outdated prints on the histories of England and Scotland's peerages were strewn across the massive bird's-eye maple library table. Great-Aunt Stella sat across from Lady Edith with her always-present artist pad in front of her.

"Lucifer Beelzebub or Satan Beelzebub, I would presume," Great-Aunt Stella answered while sketching another family tree of some obscure family. Suddenly, she looked up with a startled expression that could only be described as a revelation. "They couldn't marry in a church. The devil would never be allowed inside."

"Special license, then. They could marry anywhere and anytime in London," said Lady Edith.

"Perfect." Great-Aunt Stella chortled. "You always have the answers."

Dirty, dusty, and tired, Will ran a hand down his face. After traveling at a hectic pace, he'd arrived in North-umberland within four days. All he wanted was a bath and bed, not a confrontation regarding marriage. He sat in a wingback chair at the head of the library table. He'd rather chase a feather in a windstorm than continue this outlandish conversation.

Stella turned to Edith. "Will came straight from Fal-mont to see us. He's been there for the last two weeks building a barn. His father purchased Lord Culder's sta-bles and put Will in charge of the new breeding pro-gram," she announced proudly.

"How marvelous and educational," Edith exclaimed. "You'll have to share that with Thea. She'll be im-pressed."

Stella clasped her hands together in glee. "Another thing they have in common."

There hadn't been a single mention of emergency or catastrophe since he'd arrived. His aunt and Lady Edith could only chatter about the neighbor directly to the west of Payne Manor. Will tamped down his temper but swore he'd get to the bottom of the *urgent matter* his aunt had summoned him to manage. When he'd received the mis-sive that he attend Aunt Stella immediately, he'd put aside his work on the account books for Falmont, his father's ducal estate, and raced to her side. He pulled the letter from his coat pocket and reread it.

William,
  My boy, I need you to handle a very dire
emergency on the estate.
  Hurry.
  Crop failure.

                              Yours always,
                              Aunt Stella

Will slowly stood, then walked to his aunt's side. With one outstretched arm resting palm down on the table, he leaned close to stare her in the eyes. "What exactly is the emergency that required I drop everything and attend you, Aunt Stella?" He slid the letter in front of her. "In your summons, I believe you used the words, *dire emergency* and *crop failure.*"

Stella's wrinkled brow added a few lines as she considered his question. "I think the hay and clover in the north field look a little puny."

Lady Edith nodded vigorously. "It could be excess rain. The grasshoppers are plentiful."

"There is no emergency that requires my presence, I take it?" He'd laugh at their antics if it wasn't so ridiculous. His workload had exploded within the last month. He was thankful as it kept him sane, but he was behind in evaluating the proposed costs for several expansion projects for Falmont. His father had wanted them completed last week. "Matrimony is the real reason you called me up here?"

The ladies regarded him with wide-eyed innocence.

"We always have your best interests at heart." With her five-foot frame, Will's great-aunt Stella sat up straight in her chair in a blatant attempt at authority. "Think on it a moment. You wouldn't have come if I'd said I had the perfect woman for you."

"There is no such woman." Why couldn't Stella and the rest of his family see he wasn't interested in marriage? "Besides, I haven't seen a woman whom I'd want to share my life with."

"You'll want Thea." Stella dismissed his comment with a wave of her hand. "She's a countess in her own right, and she's trying to behave responsibly. And you've met her before."

"Because I met her that makes her a perfect candidate for my bride?" he asked. Remarkably, his tone had remained civil. "When did I meet her?"

Great-Aunt Stella slowly tapped one perfectly powered cheek with her forefinger. "You were five, and she was just under the age of one."

"I've visited Payne Manor yearly since I was seventeen, and I don't recall ever meeting her. For the last four years, I've stayed the summers, and this woman has been nonexistent. And where has this paragon resided the other twenty-four years of my life?" Will asked, deceptively calm.

"For years she resided at Dunbar on Ferr with the late duke. For the last seven years, she's lived at the Ladykyrk estate. Hidden away from the world. It's a sad story, my boy," Stella said.

"Isn't it always," he said under his breath.

"What did you say, young man?" Lady Edith challenged. Her hearing had the most amazing power to ferret out sarcasm fifty feet away.

Stella waved her hand in the air. "Edith, over the years I've discovered it's best to ignore his comments. He'll give in faster that way."

Their conversation reminded him of an out-of-control Greek chorus. He had little doubt now. His great-aunt's house had been turned into Bedlam, and the patients were in charge.

Great-Aunt Stella turned slightly in her chair to gaze at him. Her face beaming. "She's lovely."

"And the sweetest temperament," Lady Edith added. "When I met her, I thought her an angel, a perfect lady for you."

"Did I mention it's a marriage to a woman with her own title, a countess?" his great-aunt asked.

"Several times." Like that was all he ever dreamed of in life—a marriage of convenience to a supposed title-hungry elusive countess who needed a husband to secure her title? He let out a deep breath. He had a massive amount of work in London waiting for him. He'd promised his brother, McCalpin, their father's heir, that he'd perform the quarterly audit on the tenants' rents. He was already three weeks late on that project. Instead, he sat in the wilds of Northumberland fending off marriage plans that his great-aunt had dreamt up.

"Since we're speaking of churches, where would you prefer to marry, William?" Stella turned another page in her sketchbook and started to draw something. Her gaze flitted repeatedly from the page to him.

Edith stood slowly as her bones creaked in protest and moved to Stella's side.

"We weren't speaking of churches. But to answer your question, no place since I'm not marrying," he instructed. He rose from his chair and made a straight path to the ornate Etruscan-style side table where Aunt Stella kept the brandy.

"Don't move, young man," Lady Edith commanded while she studied Stella's sketch over her shoulder. "Stella, you've always been an incredible artist. But you've outdone yourself with this. You've managed to capture his fury as well as an intriguing vulnerability hidden in his eyes. Are you going to paint him nude?"

"Of course not. He's my nephew." Stella thought for a

moment. "I could paint him as a knight on a great black steed with a shield and jousting lance waiting to wear his fair lady Thea's ribbon around his wrist as a token of good luck."

"Wouldn't it be a delightful wedding present for Thea?" Edith's voice had risen an octave with unbridled excitement.

"Can we return to the subject at hand?"

Completely ignoring him, Stella nodded to Edith. "Remember the one I painted for Ginny of Sebastian?"

A wicked smile graced Edith's face. "The one you painted with Sebastian facing forward while taking off his shirt?"

"I was especially proud of that portrait." Stella nodded. "I hated to give it up. I hung it on the wall in my bedroom until they married. Sebastian was a gloriously handsome specimen."

"Still is," Edith said.

Stella nodded while still concentrating on her drawing.

"Will you stop discussing my parents?" Will growled.

"Certainly, my boy," Stella said with a conciliatory tone. "Now, what were we discussing?"

"This Theodora person," Will answered.

"Lady Theodora Eanruig—pronounced *Yahn-reek*," Stella admonished. "Stay on the subject at hand, William."

"That wasn't it," Lady Edith announced. "We were discussing poses. Perhaps Will could be taking Thea's hand after he's won his challenge?"

"Edith, you are simply brilliant," Stella exclaimed.

Will closed his eyes. This couldn't be happening. Great-Aunt Stella was his mother's aunt, and she was kindly regarded as eccentric by their family. His parents, the Duke and Duchess of Langham, even credited her with their loving marriage. To call his great-aunt unconventional or unorthodox didn't adequately describe her.

But Will adored her and loved every odd inch of her—completely. She was more like a grandmother than a great-aunt. Simply put, she was a precious gift he appreciated every day.

But sometimes his *precious gift* didn't know when to quit *giving*. What she was asking was out of the question.

"Aunt Stella, I will not marry this countess." He lifted a brow and delivered his most serious gaze, the one he reserved for ensuring he had the last word of any argument. "Understand me. I'm not marrying Theodora. I'm not marrying anyone."

Clearly taking his chastisement to heart, Lady Edith swallowed hard, then returned to her seat at the table and busied her hands with the papers.

The sudden silence in the room made Will feel like a scoundrel. He didn't want to upset the two ladies, but he also wanted to make it clear where he stood on the idea of marriage.

Stella slid away from the table and came to stand by his side. When she took his hand, cold permeated her skin, a sign of her increasing fragility and age. More than anything in the world, he wanted to make her happy. If she was worried, he'd drop everything to help her.

That's why he was here.

But not to help by marrying the next-door neighbor. "Don't doubt my word, Aunt Stella, I'll not marry her."

"Will, darling," she soothed. "You're always so suspicious of everyone."

"I'm not suspicious. I'm just not interested." Which begged the question of why he wasn't at least curious about the woman. Probably because he hadn't been interested in any woman—much less anything else—except his ever-increasing pile of work for years.

"This girl has been alone for months. She needs friends. All I ask is that you go talk to her. She's a lovely person who's had a tough time of it." Stella handed him the latest issue of *The Midnight Cryer.* "Besides, don't you think it's time you settle down with a wonderful woman? It's what you were born to do. Marry and have children. Plus, if you marry Thea, it'll put these articles to rest about the two of you."

Will didn't spare the gossip rag a glance. Why should he when he knew what it said? His irritation started to boil into a raging ire when he threw the paper onto the nearest table. That damnable *Midnight Cryer* haunted him—even in Northumberland. Regularly, it featured him in some incredible story of how he had no luck with love.

He didn't want love or marriage right now.

All he desired was a hot bath and a good night's sleep.

But even he would admit living alone wasn't as satisfying as it used to be. Perhaps it was time to find someone. Recently with all his siblings and cousin married, he had no one to share his life with. But what would he share? He received a generous allowance from his father, but besides that, he brought nothing else except a mountain of responsibilities to the duchy.

He exhaled loudly. "For you, my favorite aunt, I'll talk to her. But, fair warning, it's a wasted effort."

"I'm your only aunt, you rogue." Stella pulled him down for a gentle kiss against his cheek. Her rose fragrance wafted to meet him. "I love your brother and sister. I love your cousin Claire like she was one of Ginny's own. But you are special. You favor your mother, who just happens to be my favorite niece, and you act like my brother William. That's who you're named after."

"I know, love," Will answered affectionately. She was a dear sweet soul, and he'd never hurt her. He'd do as he promised and talk with Theodora—but nothing more.

"I just want what's best for you and Theodora." Stella

smiled, and the lines around her eyes crinkled into neat rows. "Now, get some rest, and you can visit her tomorrow."

"You're incorrigible." Will leaned down and kissed her cheek in return. "Thank you for your hospitality. After traveling all day, I'm ready for bed. Don't stay up late."

Stella slyly glanced at Lady Edith, who winked. "We won't. We've just a few more things to do before we retire." Stella patted his arm.

"Good night, young man," Lady Edith chirped.

Though he was about ready to fall over with fatigue, another half hour wouldn't kill him. "Do you need my help with whatever it is that you're doing?" Will offered.

"Of course not." Stella waved a jeweled hand in the air. "We're just planning your wedding."

With her new clocked stockings, slippers, and the elegant formal morning gown she wore, Thea actually felt pretty for the first time in ages.

Would Stella's nephew consider her new clothing pleasing? She had little doubt that her one hundred-thousand-pound fortune would be attractive.

Though Stella suggested marriage to Lord William, Thea had decided another course of action would better suit her. She wasn't going to marry the first man she met. But it was fortuitous that Lord William had sent a note that he planned to visit. She needed his help with Stella and a few other items.

His great-aunt had invited her to come to dinner this evening where they'd make plans for travel to London and the marriage ceremony for her and Lord William. Poor Stella would not be pleased when Thea announced that she would not marry him. Undoubtedly, he was a perfect gentleman, but this was her journey, and she had to do what was right for Ladykyrk, her tenants, and herself.

Thea stood behind the door as Miles, her elderly butler who wore many hats in the household, stood ready to greet their visitor. Outside of the weekly deliveries of goods and sundries necessary for running the estate, she had no other callers.

The brass knocker tapped against the door plate.

"My lady, are you ready?" Mr. Miles asked softly.

"As ready as I'll ever be." She nodded, and Mr. Miles opened the door.

"Lord William Cavensham to see Lady Theodora."

She couldn't see him, but the deep raspiness of his voice caused her heartbeat to trip in her chest. She smoothed the skirt of her pink muslin gown in an attempt to calm her nerves. If his voice was an indication, he was as handsome as Stella had promised.

"There is no Lady Theodora here." Miles' monotone pronouncement held a hint of reprimand. "If you're referring to the Countess of Eanruig, I'll see if she's accepting callers." The butler caught her gaze as he handed her the calling card and winked.

Thea smiled in return. With renewed hope that her luck would change, she stepped forward to greet her guest, then slammed to a halt.

The man on the other side of the threshold wasn't just attractive. He was breathtakingly masculine. His sable-colored hair caught the late morning rays of sunshine, causing the almost black locks to shimmer in reflection. With a square jaw, high and perfectly angled cheekbones, along with a straight patrician nose, he was striking. But it was his eyes that made her rudely stare. Blue sapphires would pale in comparison to their color. His eyes were huge, but faultlessly proportioned with the rest of his features. Piercing in intensity, he studied her as she studied him.

Heat bludgeoned her cheeks, and her gaze darted to his lips.

That was a mistake.

His full lips were as perfect as the rest of his face. If she pressed her mouth against such perfection, would they be as soft as they appeared? She exhaled deeply to compose herself.

Her musings quickly faded like wisps of smoke when his perfect mouth lost its pleasant shape only to be replaced with thin, pursed lips.

He was scowling at her.

Quickly, she recognized her error. She had more important things to concern herself besides kisses. He must be put out that she had left him standing at the door. Was he to bow first, or should she curtsey? What was the order of precedence Stella had tried to teach her? Did a second son of a duke come before a countess? What about the only granddaughter of a duke? Did it make any difference if he was coming into her home as a guest? She shook her head slightly. Best to get him inside before he left in a fit of pique.

"It's lovely to meet you, Lord William," she offered. She stepped aside and waved her hand inviting him in. Her heartbeat slowed from a gallop when he elegantly swept his beaver hat from his head then bowed slightly. He wasn't leaving.

"*Lady Eanruig*, it's my pleasure." Though pleasant enough, the words caused a gaggle of goose bumps to explode across her exposed arms. Like the lick of a cat's tongue, the roughness in his tone surprised her, but the slightly lopsided grin put her at ease once again.

She waited until he entered the brightly lit vestibule,

then proceeded to escort him to her favorite sitting room. Plain and simple in design, the brownish-gray walls, Roman sculptures, and intricate wooden molding in the neoclassical style gave the room an airy but sophisticated appeal.

She chose a sitting area that provided a lovely view of the grounds. After she'd received his note that he'd visit this morning, she'd instructed her housekeeper, Mrs. Miles to have the tea service prepared. Not only was serving tea the neighborly thing to do, but it would allow her to practice the ritual. Without asking, she poured the tea. Silently, he placed his hat on a side table, then sat near her.

Her hands trembled to such a degree that she spilt tea with her first pour. Her reaction could only be attributed to the fact that she hadn't served tea to a guest ever before. It had nothing to do with the handsome man sitting across from her.

None whatsoever.

Liar.

She took a deep breath to calm the butterflies swirling in her chest. Instead of handing him that cup, she poured another. This time she accomplished the feat successfully. When she handed him the beverage, the cup rattled in the saucer betraying her fraying nerves.

For the first time, she saw him really smile. The sight caused her breath to catch. It only enhanced his attractiveness.

"Nervous, are we?" he drawled. "There's no need to be. My aunt asked that I call on you, but I'm afraid my visit will be short."

"Oh, I hope not. I have several matters to discuss." She reached for a plate to serve the apricot tartlets and small cucumber sandwiches. With a quick glance at Lord William's tall physique, she could tell he'd probably eat at least six dainty pastries and three sandwiches. "Let me first say, I'm sure you're a very nice man with a charming disposition." She carefully arranged the delicacies on the plate then handed it to him.

"What a lovely compliment." Completely at ease, he chuckled as he set the plate on the table before him. "Yet I think there might be a *but* coming."

She nodded in answer, then took a bite of her own tartlet and chewed. They were still warm, and the sweet apricot filling melted in her mouth. At the taste of heavenly perfection, she moaned. Before she could take another bite, she noticed a dab of rich apricot filling had landed on her thumb. It would be a waste, not to mention a sin, to wipe it off with her napkin. With the tip of her tongue, she licked it clean.

His wide-eyed stare enhanced the blue of his eyes.

"I didn't want to waste a drop of goodness." She smiled and shrugged.

He blinked twice as if coming out of a trance. "You seem to be a person who loves her sweets."

Thea nodded as she pointed to his plate. "You should eat yours while they're still warm. As I was saying, you seem to be a lovely man"—she smiled slightly—"but I'm not going to marry you."

"Pardon me?" He leaned back in his chair.

"Your aunt graciously offered you as my groom, but I'm not going to marry you." She said it a tad louder this time so there was no misunderstanding. "I hope that doesn't hurt your feelings. I don't want to hurt hers either, but truthfully, I haven't met many men. If I *must* find a husband, it's best that I wait until I arrive in London and see all the available choices. Not that you wouldn't fit the bill nicely." She smiled in reassurance. "But this is too important a decision for me to rush into." She exhaled her frustration at her predicament, then tried to soften the blow of her rejection. "If my hand is forced and I can't find anyone that I want to marry, then I'll accept you as my fiancé. Of course, only if you're so inclined."

He leaned forward close enough she caught a whiff of his scent. He smelled of expensive soap, sunshine, and the outdoors. Without hesitation, she leaned forward to match his movement.

"You don't want to marry me?" His voice held a hint of humor interlaced with a tad of disbelief that she was rejecting him.

She nodded slowly. The poor man. She'd shocked him with a refusal before he even popped the proposal.

"I've thought quite a bit about my situation over the last several days." She fisted one hand in her lap to keep her anger at bay. "The Duke of Ferr-Colby is challenging my right to the Earldom of Eanruig. The Committee for Privileges isn't expecting him to find a bride. But I'm expected to find a groom. He's still unattached, and they're allowing him to go on his merry way and throw me off my own land." She forced herself to breathe deeply and slow down. "It's simply unfair that I have to marry quickly for the committee and propriety's sake. Wouldn't you agree?" The look of utter astonishment on his face sent a pang of regret through her chest that she'd caused him any discomfort. "I'm sorry."

She shifted her gaze to her hands. When her grandfather was well, he'd instilled in her a sense of pride for their heritage. It was why she was so passionate about her circumstances. Her fight to protect this title and property from the new duke would succeed. She would carry on the line of rugged, proud descendants from the Eanruig line. It would be her memorial to her grandfather.

"Lady Eanruig?"

Thea returned her attention to her guest.

"We're in complete agreement. I don't want to marry

you either, and it's completely unfair that you're being forced to marry. The Committee for Privileges should follow the goose-gander rule."

"Goose-gander rule?" she asked.

"What sauce is good for the goose is good for the gander. Whatever you have to do, Ferr-Colby should have to do." He rested his elbows on his knees and studied her with a smile that made her insides tingle. His intense regard sent frissons of awareness through her, and she couldn't look away.

"You remind me of my sister, Emma." His deep voice dipped even lower. "She would say the same thing about the position you're in."

"I would like her." Thea leaned a little closer until she could see the flicks of gold in his kingfisher blue eyes.

"And she would like you," he answered.

"Thank you," she said softly. Though he didn't know anything about her, her heart had skipped a beat at his kind words. More than anything in the world, she wanted friends and family. He was truly a nice man to say that his sister would welcome her friendship. Plus, he was taking his rejection extremely well.

"If I can help you in any way, please ask." He picked up his plate and popped two tartlets in his mouth at the same time.

"Excellent. I was hoping you would say that," Thea said with the warmest smile she could muster. "Do you by chance read Latin?"

*For those of you demanding to know how to pronounce
Lady Eanruig's name, it's not "Yahn-reek" but "You-reek."
For instance, Lady You-reek, I suggest you bathe.
Respectfully submitted,
The Midnight Cryer*

Chapter Three

Will almost choked on his apricot tartlets. He cleared his throat twice before he ventured to say a word. Not that a question about his Latin prowess was shocking, but he hadn't seen such an odd query coming.

Really, who would ask about someone's Latin skills?

Only the enigma who stood before him. When her tongue had gently darted out to capture that spot of jam on her thumb, he'd almost fallen out of his chair. It was the most sensual act he'd seen since . . . well, he couldn't remember.

Concern flooded Lady Theodora's—Will corrected himself, *Lady Eanruig's*—cheeks with color. Her worry delighted him immensely as it swept away the recent look of forlorn misery that tinted her unusual eyes.

He'd never seen such eyes as hers. They weren't green or blue, but something in between, a mysterious color that seemed to change hue based upon the light. No words could adequately describe her hair color either. The first time he saw her, he could have sworn that she had blond hair. But in the salon, it appeared red with strands of gold braided through. Light freckles dotted her straight nose, and her lips appeared flawless. Plump and lush with the perfect pink color, they demanded attention.

He bent his head so he wouldn't continue to gawk at her. She was uncommonly becoming.

What was he doing? Mooning and cataloging her every feature.

With a swipe of her hand, she brushed a runaway curl behind her ear.

His gut tightened when the loose curl bounced back in defiance. His fingers itched to brush it back for her. It'd give him the opportunity to see which was softer—her hair or the delicate skin of her cheek.

Completely unaware of the effect she was having on him, she scooted to the edge of her chair, and that blasted curl bounced again, taunting him.

"Would you care for another cup of tea?" she asked.

To refer to it as tea was stretching the truth a bit as the liquid tasted more like hot water. But he didn't want to offend her, so he drank the entire cup in one swallow then held it out for more. "Please."

"Oh, lovely." She smiled and poured him another cup.

Will could have sworn the sun shone a little brighter in that moment as if delighted she was happy.

"You were asking about my Latin prowess? Yes, I read it."

"Would you come upstairs with me?" Suddenly, she grew very serious. Her breathing had accelerated which emphasized the smooth and creamy expanse of her chest. The bodice of her gown was modest, but it revealed enough cleavage that he had little doubt her breasts would fit quite nicely in his hand. With her hair color and complexion, he'd wager the color of her nipples were a delightful shade of rose.

He bit the inside of his cheek to quiet his runaway musings. He was only here as a courtesy to his aunt. Why would he even have such thoughts? He'd seen other beautiful women and never had the urge to fantasize about their nipple color.

Though frankly, he could easily see them a perfect shade of coral.

Enough.

His only purpose was to call on her, then take his leave. Hopefully, he'd be on his way to London tomorrow.

"Please, lead the way." He swept his hand toward the door.

With a brisk nod, Thea brushed past him, then glided out of the room like a woman on a mission. Without a word, he followed. When she ascended the staircase, her hips gently swayed side to side as she kept two steps ahead of him. The subtle movement could charm the snake out of the Garden of Eden.

He gently shook his head. What had happened to him? When and how did he lower his guard around this woman? It must be some type of Northumberland magic that had him in its clenches. He'd help her, then take his leave. With his resolve back under his somewhat tenuous control, he continued until she stopped outside a door.

With her back to him, she faced the door with her hand on the handle. A good eight inches shorter than he, Thea's head reached his shoulders. For a moment, she was so still, he thought she might be saying a prayer. She exhaled deeply, the sound poignant, then threw open the door.

In that instant, the sun disappeared behind a cloud blanketing the room in semidarkness. He took a step forward, but Thea placed her hand on his forearm to stop him.

"Wait for the sun. It's too dangerous otherwise."

"Dangerous, how?" he asked. Her clean, light floral

scent wafted toward him. Indeed, it was too dangerous, particularly with her so close to him and all of his senses on high alert. In response, he took a step to increase the distance between them.

She didn't have to answer when slowly, sunshine crept back in the room revealing a massive bedroom tastefully decorated—except for the piles and piles of papers that were scattered hither and yon across the floor. Parts of the floorboard were uprooted and laid to the side like fallen soldiers. An apt description as it looked like a battlefield with holes in the flooring where wooden planks had been removed. If a person didn't watch their step, they'd fall through the gaps.

Thea inched her way into the room, then lit a small candelabra. She placed it on a side table where a chair also resided. "If you'll sit here, I'll bring you the papers."

"For what purpose? What are we doing here?" An appropriate question since he seriously doubted her sanity for a moment—and his, for following her upstairs.

"I can't read Latin." She took a step back.

Instinctively, he shot his hand to stop her. "Careful."

She stopped, then studied his hand on her arm. Her skin underneath his palm radiated heat which made it completely unexplainable why the hairs on his arms stood straight at attention as if suddenly on alert.

He released his grip, then wondered if he'd made the right decision. There were holes everywhere that she could fall in.

"I know my way around the room and around the mess. You asked why we're here. I'm trying to find the charter granting my title. These documents are in Latin, and I'm hoping one of them is the charter." Briefly, her eyes clouded with something before she tilted her chin up an inch. The agitation in her alto voice was unmistakable. "I must find it before I'm called to London to appear before the Committee for Privileges, and I'd hoped you'd help me."

"Of course, I'll lend whatever assistance I can. But why don't you sit, and I'll retrieve the documents."

"That won't be necessary." Before he could say another word, she stepped carefully in a pattern as if she were playing hopscotch around the openings in the floor.

Cautious of the holes, Will followed her.

Gracefully, she sank to her knees with her gown billowing around her, then sat beside the largest pile of papers in the room. When she glanced up at him, she motioned him beside her. "It's safe here."

"We hope." Will smiled, then sat beside her.

"You're probably wondering what happened." She picked up one paper and sighed. "While my grandfather was ill, he hid things that he thought were important. Sometimes it was something inconsequential like a quill or a penny. For a while he liked to hide the fresh eggs that I'd gathered in the mornings. When one of them spoiled and I couldn't find it, I decided it was time that I *hid* them from him." The gentle smile on her face turned bittersweet, and her eyes grew misty. "I think he might have hidden the charter."

"Was this a game you two played together?"

She didn't answer.

"Lady Eanruig . . ." What could he say that would bring comfort to such a sweet but strange memory he didn't understand.

"Call me Thea," she said softly.

"Will, then," he answered. "I'm sorry for your loss."

"Thank you." As if dismissing her grief and him, she turned her attention to the first page on the pile. "I think this is a possibility. It looks like an old parchment."

She handed it to him without looking at him directly which must have meant that she still grieved and didn't want to discuss her grandfather. Without a word, he read the paper she handed him.

"It's a deed to a parcel of property." He returned it to her, and she gave him another. This time when he read it, he shook his head. "A proclamation that the Duke of Ferr-Colby is an honorary member of the Ladies' Auxiliary of the Ladykyrk Parish. It's dated 1779."

She pursed her lips and handed him the rest of the stack. "These are every piece of paper I could find in Latin."

Within moments, he'd scanned the pages. "There's no charter of title here. It would be easy to see as it would have the monarch's large seal at the bottom."

She narrowed her eyes and regarded him. "Are you certain you read Latin?"

"I beat out my brother for top marks at Eton." He waggled his eyebrows, and she rewarded him with a laugh. It was a lovely sound, one that seemed to warm the room. "Are there any more documents?"

"These are all that I've found." She straightened the papers, then captured his gaze. "My butler, Mr. Miles, and his wife, Mrs. Miles, helped me scour the rest of the house for hiding places."

"I'll be leaving for London soon. If you find any more and I'm not here, ask the local vicar to call. He should be proficient in Latin also." He reached over and returned the documents to the top of the pile. "But while I'm here, I'll help you."

The hope in her eyes enhanced the unusual color of her irises.

"Will—"

"Ahem. Lady Eanruig, I hate to interrupt." Her butler stood in the door entrance with two letters. "These just came by special courier."

Without a word, Thea rose and carefully made her

way to the butler's side. She accepted the letters. Her fingers visibly trembled when she broke the seal. Stoically, she read the missive, then repeated the same for the second letter. She turned to Will. "The first is from the House of Lords."

"My lady?" Mr. Miles asked. "Is it the summons?"

Worry marred her face, and all her earlier courage and fight seemed to wither before Will's eyes.

"I'm to appear three weeks from now for the hearing to decide if I'm the true heir of the Earldom of Eanruig." She turned to Mr. Miles. "The second is from Mr. Blaze, the duke's solicitor. The duke's men will be here the day after tomorrow. I don't have much time left."

Wanting to bolster her courage, Will stood and carefully made his way to her side. "What can I do to help? Shall we discuss this downstairs?"

Thea shifted her gaze to his as if he were an unwanted interruption. Her eye color had turned into a hazy gray, that reminded him of a brewing storm. "This is rude and ill-mannered, but I'm sorry, you need to leave. I need some time to gather my thoughts."

He didn't want to leave her here, particularly not in a bedroom with pages strewn about and wooden planks pulled from the floor. Though Mr. Miles stood close, Thea needed more help than a butler and a housekeeper could offer. She needed political clout. Someone who would fight for her.

It would be beyond foolish to become involved with her troubles. He heaved a breath and dragged his hand through his hair. Devil take him. He was a Cavensham, and his family had taught him not to walk away from an unfair fight even if it wasn't his. "Are you certain? It wouldn't be any inconvenience."

She shook her head. "Please tell Stella that I regret the late notice, but I'll not dine with her this evening.

Mr. Miles will see you out." Without a goodbye, she turned, then headed down the hall.

It took every ounce of restraint for Will not to follow her and find out more. But she didn't want him. He took one last glance around the room, then nodded at Mr. Miles, signaling he was ready to leave.

Thea's butler slowly examined Will as if taking his measure. After a moment, he nodded as if coming to a decision. "My lord, I hope you don't find this presumptuous, but if you really want to help Lady Thea—I mean, Lady Eanruig, take a walk about Ladykyrk and talk to some of the people who live here. The Daniels' farm is straight down the road. He'll share what Lady Eanruig means to us."

"That's an excellent idea. Thank you." Perhaps he'd find out more about Thea's grandfather and how dire her situation was if he visited some of her tenants.

After receiving directions to the Daniels' farm, Will cut through the field and found a beautiful farmhouse meticulously maintained. With smoke rising from the chimney and flowers planted out front, it welcomed visitors and proclaimed that the tenants at Ladykyrk were prosperous. In the small enclosed yard, two little girls played with their dolls.

As Will strolled toward them, they both looked up and smiled. He waved in greeting. "Is your father home?"

Before he could blink, they were by his side.

"I'm Fern." A little girl with brown curls regarded him. "This is my sister, Ivy." She motioned to the girl on the other side of Will.

Ivy waved a hand but stayed silent as she studied the doll in her hand.

"We'll take you to him," Fern said confidently. "Ivy doesn't talk much except to me."

"That's not true," Ivy protested. "You never give me a chance to say a word."

By then, his two escorts had opened a side gate that led to a barn.

Ivy glanced up at Will. "Who are you?" she asked softly with a lovely Northumberland lilt.

"My name is Lord William. I'm visiting my aunt over at Payne Manor."

Fern's eyes grew big. "Our lady told us that it's beautiful."

"Do you mean Lady Eanruig?" he asked.

Ivy nodded. "She visits us every week and always brings us something. Last week, she brought honey."

By then, they'd reached the barn where a man in his mid-thirties cut wood.

"Da, you have a visitor," Fern called out.

Their father looked up. He pulled out a clean handkerchief and wiped his hands, before he made his way toward them. "What can I do for you, sir?"

When he reached Will's side, he extended his hand.

As they shook hands, the farmer's eyes widened a little at Will's strong grip.

"I'm Lord William Cavensham. I wonder if you might have a moment to discuss Lady Eanruig." A chilly silence met his introduction. "I'm Lady Payne's great nephew," Will added.

He must have said the right words as the man's demeanor instantly warmed. "Ah, well, that's good. I thought you might be a friend of the new duke. I'm Robert Daniels, but my friends call me Robbie. Girls, why don't you go help your mother."

As the girls scampered off, Robbie motioned for Will to follow him. "While we're talking, you can help me fix the barn siding."

"Gladly," Will offered. At least he'd be able to help someone at Ladykyrk today.

After shrugging out of his morning coat, Will rolled up his sleeves. Robbie offered a hammer and nails, then picked up the boards. Shortly, they both stood in front of an exposed beam that supported the barn's structure.

"What would you like to know about Lady Eanruig?" Robbie held the board against the side of the barn while Will pounded it in place.

"How long has she been managing Ladykyrk and the tenants?" Will pulled another nail out of his waistcoat pocket.

Robbie hoisted another board and secured it against the previous one. "Roughly the past seven years. Ever since she and the duke came to live here."

"Anyone help her?"

"No," the farmer said curtly.

They ceased their conversation when Will pounded the new board. The pattern repeated without additional words spoken. When they finished the repair, Robbie nodded his head. "You're stronger than I thought you'd be."

"Still waters run deep." Will grinned. "I'm no stranger to farm work. I do whatever needs to be done on my father's and brother's estates." He dug the extra nails out of his pocket and handed them to the farmer. "I'd like to help Lady Eanruig."

Robbie took his cap and slapped it against his leg. "I'm not certain how." He regarded Will as carefully as Will studied him. "She's an excellent landlord, and always helps when we need it. Last month, she personally helped all of us bring the sheep up from the lower pastures. For three days in wind and rain, she walked the fields with nary a complaint. Not many landowners would help like that."

"Rough work. I've done it myself a couple of times," Will said in agreement. The fact that Thea would work in such harsh conditions was impressive and a testament to her commitment to the estate and her tenants.

Robbie nodded. "Two years ago, she shared her portion of the harvest with all of us as the crops didn't yield much." Robbie narrowed his eyes as his gaze swept over the fields. "Many of us wouldn't have been able to feed our families that year without her help."

"That's very generous," Will agreed. "Many estate owners don't share their bounty as they'd need to sell their surplus for the upkeep and maintenance of the estates."

In his family, they always had a reserve to help their loyal tenants. It was mutually beneficial as the landowner and tenants relied on each other's successes. Sadly, not all landowners understood that concept.

Somehow, it didn't surprise him that Thea accepted the challenge of managing such a great estate with such kindness and true concern for the welfare of those who depended upon her. Mr. Miles' fondness for Thea became apparent when he told Will to visit the Daniels' family. Both Stella and Edith held Thea in the highest regard.

"Our lady also ensures each house is repaired when needed. She visits all of us at least once a month." Robbie smiled and his eyes brightened with affection. "She's here weekly because of my girls." He flicked his hand over the scraps of wood that remained on the makeshift worktable from the repairs on the barn. "She visits each tenant after every winter and asks what needs to be done to keep our houses safe and sound. She supplies the materials, and we supply the labor."

"Why do you call her *our lady*?"

With a faint smile that bespoke true affection, Robbie

studied the barley field in front of them. "She's one of us and always will be." He caught Will's gaze. "She's ours."

That type of loyalty couldn't be bought in Will's opinion. These people loved Thea. "What about her grandfather? Was he well-regarded?"

"Aye. A kind man who cherished this land. But you should ask Lady Eanruig about his involvement with us." Robbie's lips pursed into a tight line letting Will know they were done with the subject. "The new duke?" He spit on the ground, not hiding his disgust for Ferr-Colby.

"A man held in high esteem, I see."

Robbie chuckled slightly at Will's jest. "You want to help our lady? Then find a way to send the new Duke of Ferr-Colby to the wilds of America and abandon him. He cares nothing for Ladykyrk."

"Trust me. I'll volunteer to dump him on the first ship that sails out of the closest harbor." Will turned slightly so he could gaze on Thea's home, Ladykyrk Hall. She may not want to marry him, but after everything he'd learned today, he'd do everything in his power to convince her to accept his help.

Ladykyrk needed her.

He might need her too.

Shocked at such a thought, he took a step in the opposite direction of Ladykyrk Hall. It was pure nonsense. His contentment required he continue to focus on his work, his ever-increasing responsibilities to his family's estates.

Lady Eanruig's summons to the House of Lords has been sent. When she arrives, this intrepid reporter plans to cover her every move. Such evil will not taint our fair city. Will she bring her favorite footman or some other poor sap? She does like her playthings.

Honest reporting as always.

The Midnight Cryer

Chapter Four

After an hour of pacing in the salon and compiling lists of tasks in her head, Thea had changed into her old riding habit, then saddled her bay mare, Follow. With the assistance of a mounting block, she and her horse had torn out of the stable. Without much direction on Thea's part, Follow had taken their daily trail.

Angry didn't begin to describe Thea's mood. The summons to appear in front of the House of Lords unleashed all the resentment and worry she'd experienced since the visit from Mr. Blaze. Perhaps if he'd told her earlier the Eanruig title wasn't secure, she'd have done things differently. Perhaps she should have left for London on her own months ago to secure her title.

There were a lot of *should haves* in her past, but now she must concentrate on the *should dos*. Whatever she had to sacrifice, she'd secure her right to Ladykyrk.

But the challenge became increasingly tougher since Ferr-Colby's servants were practically at her doorstep.

With a nudge from Thea's knee, Follow took the jump

over the stone fence wall with ease, and landed with a
gentle thud. They tore through the pasture, then changed
course to the Daniels' home when two little girls waved
at her.

She slowed the horse to a trot, then gently stopped in
front of Fern and Ivy, the eight-year-old twins of Robert
and Bess Daniels, one of Ladykyrk's most loyal tenants.
These two always brightened her mood. "Good day,
girls."

"Good afternoon, my lady," Fern answered.

Ivy, who had a tendency toward shyness, simply
dipped a curtsey Thea's way.

"A fine man named Lord William visited us today. Do
you know him?" Fern didn't possess an ounce of reserve
as a huge smile lit her face.

"I do," Thea answered pleasantly, but instantly wondered why Will would visit one of her tenants. "He's
Lady Payne's great-nephew.

Fern carefully approached Follow. The horse bent her
long neck for a gentle pat. Ivy sidled next to her sister and
stretched out her hand. Follow lifted a hoof, then gently
set it down. At the slight movement of the massive beast,
Ivy scooted back a few feet.

"She won't hurt you, Miss Ivy." Thea bent down and
patted her horse to show that the horse was gentle and
well-trained.

Ivy nodded. "Sometimes, I'm scared. But I wasn't
when that nice man came by. Look what he gave me."
The little girl extended a cloth bag. "It's filled with can-
died jellies."

Fern extended a similar bag and giggled. "He gave me
peppermints. We're going to share."

Ivy approached Follow again, and this time, she patted the horse. "He wanted to talk to our da. He said that
two sweet girls deserved two sweet treats."

Fern nodded. "He's very handsome. Don't you think so, my lady?"

"He is handsome and charitable with his time." He truly seemed to care about her circumstances.

Fern tilted her head and regarded Thea. "Our da likes him. The candy man helped Da with the broken beam on the barn. He's very strong."

"He's not a candy man, Fern. He's a candy lord." Ivy patted Follow one last time before clasping hands with Fern. Gently, she pulled Fern away from the horse's head.

Without a protest, Fern moved back with her sister. "Da says he couldn't have done the job without him."

"He's very nice," said Ivy. "You should marry him, my lady. I bet he'd give you candy too."

That ship had already left the harbor when she'd informed him she wouldn't marry him. Unfortunately, if she *did* need a groom, Stella didn't have any other unmarried great-nephews waiting in the wings.

She was letting her imagination run wild. The *candy lord* didn't want to marry her either. Before Thea could answer Ivy, the girls' mother waved to Thea, then motioned for the girls to come home.

With a little encouragement, Follow turned and walked sedately back to Ladykyrk. There was only one explanation for Lord William's visit to one of her tenants. Perhaps he wanted to see for himself what kind of a woman she was. Information about her character and the success of the estate could be easily gleaned from her renters or by simply inspecting the fields.

Mayhap he'd changed his mind about wanting to marry.

She pulled her horse to a slow stop at the crest of a hill overlooking the fertile, green valley.

What if it was the opposite? He could be gathering ammunition for the new duke to use in the upcoming legal battle. She tried to dismiss the thought. She was letting her imagination run wild.

The urge to ride Follow across the valley until the sun set took hold. She'd be so exhausted she'd forget her frustration at her circumstances. But even that luxury was forbidden. Every minute that passed, she was falling further behind in her bid to present herself as the true Countess of Eanruig. Ferr-Colby's determination to push her out of her own home proved that. Even finding the charter now wouldn't halt his plans. She had to go to London to stop him.

She never liked to be on the defensive, but there was little choice at this point except to wait and see what evidence was presented in the battle to take her home. She prayed nothing was discussed about her grandfather.

If anyone outside of Ladykyrk had suspected how he'd suffered, they'd have insisted he be locked in an asylum like a piece of refuge—thrown away and out of sight. Thea would never have allowed that to happen.

Her grandfather had protected and nurtured her throughout her youth. When his illness struck, it had become her turn to become the protector and nurturer. He was her family—truthfully, her only family.

He'd had been utterly helpless the last seven years of his life. Instead of him managing the great estates, the entire responsibility had fallen on her shoulders. She had determined the priorities for the upkeep and maintenance of Ladykyrk, along with the ducal estate, Dunbar on Ferr, including the necessary but mundane tasks that had to be assigned to the various personnel.

How many of the great lords who would decide her fate had borne that duty at the age of eighteen? Probably a few, but not enough to understand the massive worries that went along with that duty.

Thea had ensured that everything she decided had

bore the duke's signature—more for his protection than hers. He'd needed help with running his estates as he was incapable of making a decision. She had taken the vast responsibilities of managing his affairs by writing the missives to the duchy's solicitors, steward, and estate manager while her grandfather took his afternoon naps. She'd wait until the next day before she'd present the documents for signature. After a good night's sleep, he always appeared happier and healthier in the mornings, not to mention more lucid. The fact he didn't even ask what he was signing broke her heart. Her grandfather would just look at her, then with meticulous care, he'd scribble his name across the paper. Toward the end of his life, she had to reteach him how to sign his name, as he'd forgotten.

Thankfully, no one really knew the extent of her grandfather's illness and how important decisions about the dukedom had been made for the last seven years. Singlehandedly, she'd kept those secrets safe without sharing anything. Of course, she couldn't keep everything hidden from the two loyal servants that remained by her side, Mr. and Mrs. Miles. They'd helped her immensely in keeping the duke's illness a secret. In league with them was Mr. Miles' older brother, who was the butler for the duke's ancestral home. He'd also helped keep the duke's secret by having all the ducal estate servants report directly to him. No one ever questioned why the duke stayed at Ladykyrk and never made an appearance.

Once her grandfather had passed, she thought the nightmare would be behind her, but now it was rising from the proverbial grave like a ghost haunting her with the insinuations from *The Midnight Cryer* that she'd killed her grandfather.

Would she ever be free from the guilt and the responsibility that constantly dogged her?

Her traitorous thoughts drifted to Lord William Cavensham. Would he have been a man capable of handling the trials of caring for her grandfather with her?

She couldn't dwell on such thoughts.

She had to secure a title and quickly before all of her secrets were discovered.

Will straightened his cravat in the hallway mirror, then smoothed his claret-colored waistcoat. Great-Aunt Stella had informed him via one of her numerous blond-haired, blue-eyed giants who posed as footmen that dinner would be a formal affair.

After helping Mr. Daniels with the repair of his barn, Will had no desire for a long drawn-out dinner. His time would be better spent reviewing Payne Manor's estate books then preparing his return trip to London. But he enjoyed Payne Manor and relished getting his hands dirty working in the fields. At his father's ducal estates, he'd discovered his love of the land by working alongside his best friend, who just happened to be his brother, the Marquess of McCalpin, and the heir to their father's dukedom. Their father expected them not only to become intimate with the land, but to take an active interest in their tenants.

Since McCalpin had married the love of his life, the former Miss March Lawson, Will's brother still needed Will's expertise in managing McCalpin Manor estate. March was simply brilliant with numbers and bookkeeping and kept meticulous records of the vast operation. But McCalpin and March spent more and more time in London after McCalpin had taken a seat in the House of Commons. Their social obligations were endless.

Like time, relationships and needs always moved forward. Will had been restless in London over the past several years. As his siblings and cousin had married and started their own families, he'd discovered the need for new challenges in life to replace what had been family time.

That's why he spent so much time at his family's estates including Ladykyrk.

Ladykyrk?

Will stopped abruptly before he entered the salon to greet his aunt and Lady Edith. *Where had Ladykyrk come from?* He'd meant Payne Manor.

He chuckled at the slip. No doubt, it was due to his work this afternoon with Robbie Daniels. It'd been Will's pleasure to help the man and had nothing whatsoever to do with a certain countess.

When Will entered the salon, he expected to find Stella and Lady Edith enjoying a sherry cordial before dinner. Instead, he was greeted by a lavish swirl of blue-and-green silk with a matching turban trimmed in peacock feathers. Otherwise known as his great-aunt Stella, who appeared to be guarding the French doors to the meticulously groomed inner courtyard garden.

"Good evening, madam."

She turned to face him, and the fabric of her gown followed in a hurried *swoosh*.

When he reached her side, he took her hand. Before he could execute his best bow, she snatched her fingers away.

"No time for pleasantries. Tell me what happened, and don't leave out a single word." Stella lifted her sapphire-encrusted lorgnette to her eyes then examined him from head to toe twice as if looking for something different about him tonight.

"Shouldn't we wait for Lady Edith?"

"Only you and I will be dining. I'm afraid Edith became overexcited. The anticipation of the good news about your upcoming nuptials with Thea caused the poor dear to break out in a rash."

The best course required Will tell her the truth quickly, but he wanted her sitting down. Her blue eyes twinkled with excitement. Once he dashed her dreams, he didn't want her collapsing from the disappointment. "I'm sorry Lady Edith isn't feeling well. But I'm delighted to have your undivided attention this evening, madam. Shall we sit?"

He delivered his best and most wicked smile, the one that always made her laugh, and he was rewarded for his efforts.

In no time, he had Stella seated on the Dutch-orange sofa, then settled next to her. "I'm sorry, but Lady Eanruig and I will not suit." He reached for her hand, but with a speed that belied her age, she stood.

"What happened?" she demanded.

"I know you're disappointed, but—"

"Disappointed? Young man, you have no idea." She planted her hands on her bony hips.

Inwardly, he flinched at the harsh words. "I only promised to talk to her. Nothing else." Will rose and walked to a side table where he poured a glass of sherry for his aunt and a brandy for himself. When he returned to his seat, she took the glass without a protest and downed it in one swallow.

He'd have to use his best reasoning skills and hope that his wily charisma worked on her this evening. "Darling, it wouldn't have worked. There are strange happenings in that household."

"*Darling,*" she sarcastically mimicked, "I'm aware of that. I sent you over there to talk to her. I thought you were a charmer not a clodhopper. It was your job to visit and find out exactly what that poor child faced over the years." Without a look back, she walked to the side table and refilled her glass. "Did you refuse to marry Thea? Did you even give her a chance to be your bride?"

"No," he said.

"That's what I thought." Stella shook her head like a governess disciplining her charge.

"She doesn't want to marry me."

Her face fell at the announcement, and she released a soulful sigh. "I'm so, so sorry, my boy. I know you must be heartbroken." With a sympathetic grin, she continued, "Leave it to me. We'll find a way." With a decisive nod, she returned to her seat.

"There's no need for help." He couldn't help but compare the spry woman in front of him to a pug with a bone. Both were relentless when they wanted something.

"Of course not, dear. You're embarrassed. I understand." She studied her hands, then mumbled, "They say lightning doesn't strike twice in the same spot, but you've proven that wrong."

"Aunt Stella, you misunderstand." William lifted a brow, then relaxed against the back of the sofa. Lord Fluff sauntered to his side, then jumped on his lap.

"I understand perfectly. You just need a little help. It's important you know everything about her before you start to woo her again." Stella smiled. "Remember, when you fall off the proverbial horse, you must get back on immediately or you'll be scared all your life."

Will shook his head. "Aunt Stella. . . ." The endearing anticipation on her face made his chest tighten, and he silently sighed. What harm would it do to listen? "Please, tell me what you think I need to know."

"Of course, it's her story to tell, but I'll share what little I know." Stella smiled sympathetically. "It's not a secret. She lost her parents when she was a baby. The duke raised her and decided to reside at Ladykyrk instead of Dunbar on Ferr, the duke's ancestral estate. He sent most of the Ladykyrk servants to his estate. It was all very odd. Everyone wondered why the Duke of Ferr-Colby would prefer to live at Ladykyrk instead of his own home."

"Why did he?" Will leaned forward. Lord Fluff mewled his disgruntlement before jumping down. Will's black pantaloons were covered in ivory fluffs of hair, souvenirs from the master of the house, his great-aunt's feline.

The damnable cat only sought him out when he wore black or blue. If he wore his doeskin breeches, the cat ignored him completely. He preferred them anyway. He had no use for formal clothes as he couldn't remember the last society event he'd attended. He brushed off the offensive tuffs of fur as best he could.

"Why would a duke leave his home for a lesser estate, particularly late in his life?" It didn't make sense unless Thea's grandfather was trying to protect someone. Like a granddaughter. "Let me guess, it's something out of a gothic novel. A madman was after her virtue, and the duke hid her away. Before he passed, he solicited your help in keeping her safe until a suitable groom could be found, and thus, I'm the sacrificial lamb?"

Stella delivered a look designed to flay him alive.

"Something much more mundane like a secret baby perhaps?" he offered.

"Sarcasm does nothing for you, my boy," she said. "Of course, not. You can't hide a baby if you're out every day managing an estate."

The chastisement in Great-Aunt Stella's voice was unmistakable.

Now the puzzle pieces were starting to fall into

place. "The duke brought her up here to teach her how to care and protect her title and holdings. That's your theory?"

"Part of it, but not everything. Thea hasn't told me everything that happened, but she shared her grandfather had trouble remembering things. I also know his illness caused her to miss her introduction into society. She's been isolated for years." Stella shook her head slightly.

"If you were such good friends with the duke, how come you don't know the rest of the story?"

"My boy, it's as if everything came to a standstill like a run-down pocket timepiece over at Ladykyrk. The invitations to dine with me suddenly stopped being accepted. He no longer visited the nearby village altogether. Theodora wasn't seen either. It was as if both of them disappeared."

"Did you try to visit?" he asked.

"Several times. I wrote invitations, and they were always politely declined. I even called on them unannounced, but the butler always said neither the duke nor Thea were accepting callers."

Unease weighed heavy in his chest. "Do you think her grandfather was cruel to her?" he asked gently.

"Heavens, no," she exclaimed. "Her grandfather doted on her when he was well. Years ago, he spoke frequently about taking her to London for her Season. He was excited to introduce her to society. He was so proud of that child." She pursed her lips, then shook her head gently. "*The Midnight Cryer* says she killed him. We need to help her, my boy."

Will exhaled. He was well-acquainted with the poison that damnable paper spewed.

He reached over and took his great-aunt's hand in his. "I agree she needs help more than ever. The summons from the House of Lords arrived while I called on her."

When Stella squeezed his hand, Will returned the affectionate gesture. "Other than reading a few documents in Latin for her, she doesn't want my help. Thea hasn't found the charter."

"Oh dear," Stella cried softly. "We don't have much time."

"Thea told me she doesn't want to marry me. You have to accept that." He leaned back in his chair. "She wants to meet other men when she reaches London."

"You aren't afraid of a little competition, are you?" Great-Aunt Stella tilted her head and regarded him. "The situation is far from hopeless."

The sound of the pug gnawing on its bone grew louder. "Thea is not for me."

"Thea's not like that so-called Cavensham woman who taught you to believe all women are nothing but female versions of rakehells and scoundrels in chemises."

The poignancy of her regard made him squirm in his seat, but he held tight like a ship about to capsize before it righted itself. Under no circumstances would he allow his third cousin, the Dowager Marchioness of Warwyk, to enter into this conversation. "Avalon means nothing to me."

"Of course, she doesn't," Stella said sympathetically.

He meant every word he said. It was true that for a year, particularly after London's biggest gossip rag, *The Midnight Cryer*, had carried story after story of his jilting and had labeled him a dud, he had pined away, thinking his heart was broken forever. But, in the normal ebb and flow of life, he healed, and his heart healed. Better than healed actually. It hardened, which allowed him to concentrate on relationships more important—his family and closest friends.

Frankly, he was happy he hadn't been saddled for a lifetime with the former Avalon Cavensham, now the

Marchioness of Warwyk. If she could so easily dismiss
him when they were in love, he could only imagine what
their married life would have entailed once she became
bored with him. He'd heard that Avalon and Lord
Warwyk's marriage had been unhappy. The late marquess didn't hide the fact that Avalon liked to spend to
extremes. Will had little doubt that he'd have lost her regard if they had married.

But after all these years, why hadn't he found anyone
yet to share his life with? All of his siblings including his
cousin Claire had married wonderful spouses, and he
personally believed his own parents' marriage was a sterling example of what the institution should be. Truthfully, he wondered if there was something wrong with
him.

He found no enjoyment in the opposite sex's company.
It's not that he disliked women, but they were all mundane like a rainbow without any color. Mayhap, the fault
lay with him. The lens through which he saw the world
was monochrome. He wanted to shrug at the dreariness
of it all. He simply found more enjoyment in his family
and work than in women.

He took a sip of brandy as he stared into the fire designed to keep the cool spring evening warm. Yet something had sparked an interest outside of his work, and he
could attribute it to an unconventional countess he'd just
met.

Thea reminded him of a determined fox cornered by
baying hounds ready to tear her to pieces. She knew the
odds were against her, but she'd fight to the death.

He'd not let a fox suffer just as he'd not let Thea be
hounded by society, *The Midnight Cryer*, or Ferr-Colby.
Such a challenge might heat his blood and send it roar-
ing through his veins again.

Enough of such thoughts.

Just as he'd explained to his aunt, if Thea didn't want his help, then he'd abide by her wishes. Though a part of him longed for a good fight.

Will stood and extended his hand. "Shall we go into dinner?"

"Not yet." She took his hand between her smaller ones and gently coaxed him to sit beside her again.

Immediately, a ball of unease started to bounce in his belly because she only held his hand when a reprimand was in his future. Sometimes, she patted gently right before she lowered the boom with some demand for action. Like the time she made him escort her and Lady Edith to Cheltenham to take the waters. He still cringed when he thought about that month squiring the two grand dames through the resort town where they ogled every man under the age of fifty.

The remorse in her eyes reminded him of all the times his nurse would force him to take a vile medicine, then add *it's for your own good*.

"Everyone sees you avoid society. Hiding in the card room when forced to attend a soiree or a ball isn't the answer to finding happiness in life."

He didn't say a word as they both knew for years he avoided any *ton* event that might hint he wanted to marry. Yet as the days and years tumbled by with the members of his family happily married, he had thought about marriage. But he had plenty of time to find someone. For God's sake, he was only twenty-nine.

"I expect more of you than anyone else in the family. You're going to have to find a way in your heart to marry Theodora." His great-aunt dropped his hand and straightened her spine. "It's the right thing to do, not only for the girl but for you."

Will leaned forward slightly. "She doesn't want me or my help. You have to accept that fact."

"Convince her. Use some of that charm locked away in there." She tapped him lightly in the middle of his chest.

He caught her hand in the air and held it. He doubted he had anything inside that resembled charm.

"She'll lose her estate if we don't help her," the grand dame said. "We shouldn't let her be taken advantage of. Besides, she needs me."

Will leaned over and kissed her cheek. "It's nice to be needed. We all need you, Stella."

"Thank you, dearest." Endearingly, she grinned. "Truthfully, I need her."

"For what?" Will asked.

"For you," she answered. "You need her."

"I don't need her." Will softened his voice in hopes that she would understand. "No amount of persuading on your part will change the circumstances."

The blue-steel of her gaze tore straight through him. "If you don't marry Theodora, then I'll disinherit you."

Will lifted one eyebrow in challenge.

"Don't give me that expression." Suddenly, Stella bit her lip, then looked at their clasped hands and laughed. "I can barely keep a straight face saying such a thing but don't tempt me." When she settled her gaze on him, her eyes were lit with humor. "You both need each other."

"You, madam, are irredeemable," Will said affectionately.

"William, if you don't marry, then where would Payne Manor go?" she asked, turning suddenly serious. "My dearest Payne and I didn't work for years to build something we intended to give you and yours, then have it lost at the end of your life. This is a home where you should raise a family." She shook her head slightly.

"Thea doesn't want to marry me." A slight ache took up residence in the middle of his chest reminding him that another woman didn't want him. "And I don't want to marry her."

Saying the words didn't alleviate the pain.

Stella narrowed her eyes in disbelief.

"Remember, Cavensham men fall in love quickly and completely." He'd been saying this mantra for years as a way to fend off any type of well-intentioned but wayward matchmaking from members of this family, particularly Stella. "I should wait until the right one comes along."

"That is an excuse you foist as a shield to protect yourself from hurt," she countered.

"It happened to my grandfather, uncle, and father. I daresay it happened to McCalpin too. Perhaps it'll happen to me someday." Will fought the need to fidget. This entire conversation was treading in waters too deep for his tastes.

"You should try harder with Thea. Woo her a little. She's beautiful and loves her estate, like you love mine. Life is slipping you by, my boy." She shook her head. "You're so busy protecting your heart, you're letting opportunities of a lifetime, or shall I say *your destiny* pass you by."

"Mocking doesn't become you." He tamped down the urge to snarl. This was his darling aunt, and they hardly ever quarreled, but this was not something he'd capitulate to.

"I'm not mocking, you precious but utterly aggravating young man." She became even more animated. "Whatever it takes, I'm prepared to do. And you need to let go of your own foolish idea that Cavensham men fall in love at first sight. That was something you created out of whole cloth years ago."

Will stood and reached for her hand. "Let's not argue."

"Don't." She held her palm out to stop him. "If you'll excuse me, I'm not really hungry anymore. I must tell

Edith what's happened. She's simply brilliant at maneuvers and stratagems of this type. I'll take a tray in her room." She stood slowly and stared at him like a general overseeing a parade of troops. "Don't worry, my boy, we'll fix this yet."

Without another comment, the grand dame swept through the room with the force of a hurricane.

An apt description as her words had leveled him. How could he make her understand that Thea didn't want him?

Late Edition!

Word has it that ~~the Damp Squib~~ Lord William Cavensham
is on the hunt for a wife.

Some compare him to a firework ready to light up some
lucky woman's life.

This humble reporter wagers he'll never ignite.

Why do you think we call him the Damp Squib?

Fair reporting is our motto.

The Midnight Cryer

Chapter Five

Thea strolled to the maze that lay on the outer edge of the formal garden that bordered Stella's estate. The garden, the last project completed by Thea's mother before her death, was Ladykyrk's jewel. She slowed her pace once she entered the massive puzzle, then meandered through the intricate labyrinth of boxwood shrubs until she found her favorite bench. The soft gurgling of a fountain in the background lent a lovely musical effect.

Whenever her solitude became too great to bear, Thea headed to the maze. A sense of belonging always surrounded her as if her father and mother stood silently by and counseled her. Though she didn't remember her parents, she felt close to them here, and for some reason, she could clear her jumbled thoughts.

But not now. Tomorrow, she'd leave Ladykyrk for London. The idea that it could be forever weighed heavy. With everything, including her life, tangled into tight knots, Thea feared she'd never find her way free. She needed someone strong to stand beside her when the new duke challenged her title, someone not afraid of conflict.

She had enough experience in her small glimpse of the world to understand she suffered a disadvantage as a woman. Though a peeress in her own right, men could easily dismiss her claims. The House of Lords' committee expected that she'd marry was just another example. The idea that Ferr-Colby could force her from her property was another. Faced with an interview by the committee, she needed to present her best arguments and have support behind her.

An image of the Daniels' family loomed before her. Their family and the other tenants who worked and toiled the land depended on her success, not to mention Mr. and Mrs. Miles' security were her responsibility.

She could not fail. Too much was at stake.

With a sigh, she closed her eyes, and the warmth of the sun enveloped her. Slowly, she relaxed against the bench. Fantasies of a lover, a husband, rose to the forefronts of her musings. The heat of one body against another filled her with longing. It would be a blessing, a gift even, if she could share the responsibility of her great estate with someone. But that wasn't why she needed a husband. She needed a partner, someone with enough gravitas that just by his mere presence, her standing would be secure.

Her traitorous thoughts drifted to Lord William Cavensham. She couldn't necessarily blame him for his response to her refusal to marry him. He didn't even know her. Also, why would a sophisticated—not to mention a gloriously handsome—man want to be saddled with a country bumpkin, even one who possessed a title and a great estate along with a fortune?

Suddenly, a sound drew her attention to the pathway.

The scrunch of gravel signaled she wasn't alone. It was probably a dog or cat, or an adventurous chicken too far from its coop. Perhaps she'd magically summoned her very own knight-errant who would help her save the title and estate.

A shadow crept over her, blocking the sun. When Thea turned, she had to shield her eyes as the setting sun surrounded a man in a brilliant fire of light. Her heart accelerated at the sight. As if she conjured him from her imaginings, he stood before her. He wasn't a knight, nor the devil. Quickly, she stood when he approached.

"Lady Eanruig, I didn't mean to startle you."

At the rumble of his voice, her heart skipped a beat.

"Will, what a surprise." She lowered herself to the bench again. "I didn't expect to see you this evening." She didn't add that she never expected to see anyone in the evening, as no one ever intruded upon her sanctuary.

"May I join you?" He closed the distance between them. When he reached her side, he bowed elegantly like she was a proper lady.

"Please do." She scooted to the end of the bench, and he settled next to her. A hint of orange and bergamot wafted through the air. She inhaled the fragrance, then held her breath, hoping to memorize it. His essence layered the clean crisp scent, a reminder he was sophisticated in ways she'd never be. He must have come from dinner as he was dressed in black pantaloons, a dark red waistcoat, and a gray broadcloth evening coat.

She struggled to find something witty to say. London women probably had formal training in how to converse with other members of society. Another lesson to add to her ever-expanding repertoire she must master before she appeared in front of the committee. "How was dinner?"

He shifted slightly and regarded her. His dark sable hair contrasted perfectly with the brilliance of his blue eyes. He shrugged, then smiled like a child who didn't care a whit at being discovered with his hand in the biscuit jar.

"Sadly, without your company, it lacked any appeal." The corners of his mouth curved upwards. "I'm afraid I dined alone as my great-aunt and her friend chose to dine in their rooms this evening. They're busy packing for London."

She'd dined alone too. Mr. and Mrs. Miles had eaten with friends in the village. It was as if they sensed she wanted the estate to herself for one last night. It was a sweet gesture so she could say goodbye to the great house and the beautiful fields in case. . . .

No, she'd not lose it. She'd not allow herself to think of any other outcome.

"What were you doing at the Daniels' farm?" The question burst free, betraying her fear. Good God, she had wanted to appear sophisticated while she wove that question into their conversation.

He simply stared at her.

In response, she dropped her gaze to her clenched hands. She shifted slightly toward the end of the bench as if to escape his intensity.

"After I left your home, Mr. Miles suggested I talk to some of your tenants. I saw Robbie Daniels struggling with a repair to his barn and offered my assistance."

She peeked at his face and wished she hadn't. His gaze pierced hers as if he could see inside where all her doubts and insecurities resided. "His twin daughters told me of your visit. You made quite an impression with them."

"I never could resist captivating ladies, and those two are quite the charmers." He chuckled, and the sound reverberated within his chest.

In response, she found herself leaning closer. "That was all?"

His brow crinkled into neat rows, reminiscent of the newly planted fields at Ladykyrk. "What are you asking?"

"Nothing," she responded.

Their conversation quieted, and the buzzing of spring beetles and the warning cry of a crow were the only sounds that broke the stillness of the early evening.

"Are you suspicious of me?" His simple question made her cringe.

"A little," she responded without hesitating. "I don't know you, and I don't understand why you would help Mr. Daniels, unless . . ." The words lay suspended in the air. She closed her eyes and begged the heavens he'd leave well enough alone.

"Unless what?" he queried.

So much for her prayers being answered. She straightened her spine, then twisted so she could see his face. "Are you here to gather information against me for the new duke?" She tightened her stomach for the blow.

"Where would you get that idea?" he asked softly, the sound soothing, but the empathy in his voice made her feel two inches tall for doubting him.

"That was a horrible thing to ask. I'm sorry." She twisted her fingers together, a nervous habit. "My first and only thought every day is how to protect Ladykyrk." Tears welled in her eyes, but she drew a deep breath to squelch them. "I haven't had many confidants in my life, but I should have trusted you. Your aunt thinks the world of you, and that should have been enough proof for me."

He shook his head quickly. "No, you did the right thing by asking. I would've too. I think perhaps we're both skeptical creatures." One of his adorable half smiles tugged at one side of his mouth. "That's why we rub along so well together. But, it's apparent we've misunderstood each other. I want to help you."

This was what Ferr-Colby's challenge had done to her. She couldn't even accept the kindness of the man before her without doubting his actions.

Her heart pounded against her ribs, and she took a deep breath to calm the riot of emotions that threatened to overwhelm her. "I'm sorry I sound suspicious. It's just that the people I thought I could depend on failed me."

"Who?" he asked.

"Just people." She didn't want to share that her grandfather had failed her in hiding the charter. Though he was a sick man, he should have given her the charter before his memory had failed to the point where he couldn't remember what he'd eaten an hour before.

But the true failure was Ferr-Colby. In his quest to take her home, the new duke ignored the fact they were third cousins and the only family each other had. Though she'd only met Will once, perhaps he was someone she could consider a possible friend. The idea that he'd betrayed her now seemed ridiculous. He had nothing to gain.

He shook his head quickly as if to chase away a gnat. "I spoke with Robbie to learn more about Ladykyrk. Your estate is beautiful, and your hard work is apparent in every square inch of land. Your tenants greatly admire you. I'm of the same mind." He lowered his voice until it rumbled. "Your estate is impressive and so are you."

For the first time that evening, she smiled. Her heart beat a little faster at such a lovely compliment.

He leaned close as if divulging a secret. "I know those truths because of Mr. Daniels' praise, not to mention that your face beams when you talk about Ladykyrk and the people who work here." A slight smile lingered on his lips. "When I returned home, I spoke with my aunt. I've come to understand your situation better."

He leaned against the granite bench, obviously at ease.

When he contemplated the maze before them, she wanted to protest and ask him to look at her. With his lovely words, he'd woven an enchanting spell around her, and she wanted it back.

"I also understand you've been living alone since your grandfather died," he said.

She nodded. The cadence of his words soothed, but the meaning stirred painful memories. In truth, she'd been living alone for years.

"Will you please take pity and forgive me?" Thea said. "I shouldn't have thrown you out of my home after you were so kind and read the documents for me. Nor should I have asked you about the Daniels family."

"There was no offense taken." He turned slightly on the bench and faced her. "Have you found any more documents?"

"No." Her stomach tightened in protest rather than admit defeat, but she had no other choice. "I've looked everywhere. There's nothing else."

He took her hand in his. Suspended in time, she could only stare at the gesture. His fingers dwarfed hers, and the rough calluses of his fingers against her skin tickled, and frankly, surprised her. She'd have thought such a man would have soft, perfect hands. The roughness of his indicated a man who was accustomed to work.

Without tearing his gaze from hers, he lowered his voice. "My family will help you through this."

"They don't know me." To her own ears, she sounded pathetic, but she had to accept the reality that faced her in London. Besides Stella and Lady Edith, she was truly on her own.

"It makes no difference. You see, I believe in you. And for my family, that will be enough to stand beside you and fight on your behalf. I'd like for you to stay at my father's house with Stella and Edith."

"Truly?" She stared at him. The sincerity in his eyes made her desperate to believe that she might have real help when she faced the committee. "I wasn't expecting such a kind offer. Your aunt and Lady Edith have been everything warm and lovely. How will I ever repay you?"

He stretched out a leg. The tight cut of his breeches emphasized the well-defined muscles of his leg. Though the sight was more proof that he was accustomed to hard work, it held her spellbound. She'd never seen anything like it, or more accurately, anyone like him before.

Eventually, she took a breath and caught his gaze. Something unrecognizable smoldered deep inside those blue orbs. Slowly and with great care, he brought her hand toward his lips. When his warm breath brushed the skin of her hand, an immediate chill raced through her body. Never had she felt so unsure, and frankly, she enjoyed it. He was actually compassionate, not to mention kind.

She couldn't read anything into his action. It was simply an offer of comfort in the moment.

"No repayment needed. It'll be my pleasure. As a matter of fact, I should be the one to thank you." He gently let go of her hand.

The loss of his warmth was almost unbearable. "Really?"

"Yes. My life is nothing but work and family. I think I've grown stale." An endearing smile tugged at his lips. "A good fight might just put me back to rights. Perhaps you'll allow me to help you with the *ton* and others in society."

She nodded. "I'll need all the help I can muster. But why are you out of sorts?" His honesty in revealing this glimpse of himself thrilled her. It made her want to share more with him.

"I think I've allowed myself to become too insulated." His brow slightly furrowed as he contemplated what to say. "I don't go to *ton* events. But when we take you to London, I'll escort you. Who knows? Maybe I'll become interested in city life again."

"Or perhaps a woman?" As the words escaped, she wanted to recall them. For some odd reason, she didn't like the idea of Will squiring around a woman. Such a silly idea as she had no claim to him. But, she reached for his hand again, then pulled away as if burned. What was she thinking? Thankfully, she hadn't touched him, but the damage had been done. His eyes had widened at her action, but since he was a true gentleman, he didn't react or say anything otherwise. Such action was more appropriate for some besotted schoolgirl, not a countess.

"Not likely. I don't ever see myself falling in. . . ." He shook his head gently, then turned, and his attention drew to the maze. "Whenever I'd come for visits here, I'd find myself walking in your maze. Inevitably, I'd become lost. It's quite an ingenious design."

"My mother designed it." She stood to escape his overwhelming nearness. "She completed it right before she gave birth to me."

"Tell me about her." He stood in response with a warm smile that could have melted the snowcaps in the Arctic.

"There's not much to the story." She trailed her hand across the prickly, but meticulously manicured boxwood stems.

"Humor me. I'm in the mood for a story," he said.

"My younger brother died in childbirth along with my mother. I had just turned one. Shortly thereafter, my father was thrown from his horse and didn't survive the fall. My mother's father, the duke, raised me."

"I'm sorry," he said quietly.

She forced herself to hold his gaze. Loneliness and hurt for all she'd lost in life welled in her chest, but she'd not show any weakness. "Thank you."

"Will you escort me through your mother's maze?" Like a rare vintage port wine, his voice soothed away the awkwardness between them. "I'd like to see it again. If I remember correctly, there's an extraordinary fountain in the center."

As if in a trance, she walked to Will's side and took his arm without reservation.

Will could only draw one conclusion.

He had little doubt that any question he'd asked, she'd answer with a rare candor, one that if exposed in London society would likely have all the paragons and grand dames of the *ton* swooning in shock. But only if it didn't involve the hurt she'd experienced in life.

They meandered through the maze without a word. When a root boldly protruded from the ground, he took Theodora's hand to help her over the branch. She stilled, and her questioning gaze darted to his.

"I thought you might need assistance," he said. "It's customary for gentlemen to help ladies over obstacles."

"Thank you." All earlier traces of unease disappeared, softening her face.

Maybe there was a way he could help above and beyond what he'd offered.

The more time he spent with her, the more intrigued he found himself.

Deep down, he felt sympathy for her plight. She'd been raised by an elderly man, then most likely become his caretaker. Her childhood must have been lonely—stuck out here in the country without any other relatives.

Except for his aunt's misguided help, Theodora was alone in this fight to save her title and estate.

And his lovely, brave aunt wanted him to marry Thea. Last night's conversation with Stella still haunted him today. Thea had experienced unbelievable hardship already in her life. Whatever help he could offer her, he'd do it in a heartbeat. He despised that Ferr-Colby intended to strip Thea of her title and her land.

They strolled through the maze, and Will caught himself glancing down at her every few steps. With the setting sun, her silky hair seemed to glow with an iridescence reminiscent of butterfly wings. The subtle shades shifted between a pink that matched her gown and the slightest hue of coral.

Theodora tilted her head. Those amazing eyes absorbed the purples and blues of the sky and reflected a light shade of indigo. He leaned closer, fully expecting her eyes to change color again. Abruptly, he pulled back. What was the matter with him? Never in his life had he felt a pull as powerful as the tempest that surrounded her.

He'd do well to remember not to stare too deeply at her eyes again. Much too dangerous for his tastes.

"Will?" she asked.

"Pardon me. I'm just woolgathering," he answered.

"We should turn left here to see the fountain." She slowed to a stop at a break in the hedgerow, and he allowed her to take the lead.

"Do you know the new duke?" he asked.

Thea's grip tightened on his arm briefly. "Yes. As my grandfather's heir, he visited several times when he was younger. Once he finished his university studies, he moved into one of my grandfather's lesser estates."

"I'm acquainted with your cousin," Will offered. "We don't socialize together."

"What's your opinion of him?" She led them through a turn to the right.

"Honestly, he reminded me of a prize mule. Particularly, when he constantly mentioned to everyone within five feet of him that he was the Duke of Ferr-Colby's heir."

Theodora giggled, then stopped when her adorable chortles of pleasure blossomed into full laughter. The sound reminded Will of wind chimes. All too soon, her humor lessened, but the most glorious smile lit her face. *Good God, she's beautiful*. He took a step closer to bask in the warmth that surrounded her.

"You're calling him an arse," she announced.

He feigned a shocked look and placed his hand over his heart. "Me? I'm everything civil and affable."

She lifted an eyebrow in challenge, but a grin graced her ruby lips.

"Some say I'm debonair," he teased. He inched closer. She matched his movement.

"There's not much call for that skill here in Northumberland, I'm afraid," she countered as another winsome laugh escaped.

He slid closer until only a foot separated them. She gazed up, and the movement elongated her neck. From nowhere, a wild urge slammed into him and demanded he run his lips up the length of her sensitive skin.

"You might be surprised how valuable it can be." His voice deepened. "Shall I show you how charming I really am?"

"You're simply incorrigible." She focused on his lips before her eyes darted to his. Instantly, her laughter dissolved. She glanced behind her. Somehow, they'd entered a row that led to a dead end. "How did we end up here?" she breathlessly whispered.

He stood still, not daring to move closer to her and her enchantment. "You led us here."

Her gaze searched his. "I never understood why there are dead ends in mazes."

"They're here for a specific reason," he said softly.

Her rapid breathing fanned across his lips like the beating wings of a hummingbird. "What's that?" Her voice quivered slightly.

The slight pout of her lush mouth called to him, and the urge to rub his thumb across her lower lip grew in strength. Her lips were perfect like delectable pillows—plump, soft, and lush. "Kisses. They're made so couples have a place to hide when they want to steal a kiss from each other."

He almost fell to his knees when she licked her bottom lip as she considered his words.

"I wouldn't know. I've never been kissed." Her words barely made a sound.

Instantly, he wanted to be her first, the man who won the honor of kissing her.

What was he doing?

He made the mistake of glancing at her lips again, full and red and ready for his kiss. His conscience screamed no, but a desire with the devil's own strength urged him to take what he wanted. Thankfully, he'd always been a reasonable man and listened to all sides of an argument.

Immediately, he rethought his position. His conscience had never steered him off course, but his heart had blindly led him down the wrong path all those years ago when he'd convinced himself he'd fallen in love. It had nearly destroyed him.

He wouldn't inflict that type of pain on anyone else, particularly someone as vulnerable as Theodora.

"Theodora." He wrestled the urge to kiss her under control. He'd not take advantage of her. But then that same rebellious curl that had taunted him yesterday diverted his attention to her face. Without thinking, he reached over and caressed the lock between his fingers. He caught her gaze. "It's even softer than I had imagined."

Her eyes widened, but she didn't look away.

Gently, he brushed his fingers across her cheek, lingering against the warm skin before he tucked the curl behind her ear. "I should return to my aunt's house."

"May I show you something first? Years ago, my grandfather built it for me. This might be the last time I'll visit it." Her smile turned nostalgic. "I've never shown it to anyone outside of Ladykyrk, but I want to share it with you."

Beware, Gentle Readers!
The Countess of Eanruig's mysterious eyes are said to
possess a magic that
paralyzes men with a single glance,
then turn them stupid.
You've been warned.
The Midnight Cryer

Chapter Six

Thea led William past a small stream to the crest of a hill that overlooked a large valley of green pastures. Deer and sheep freely mingled below a darkening blue sky decorated with white clouds.

The bucolic scene was breathtaking by itself, but the majestic folly sitting regally before them demanded center stage. The stone pavilion had four separate entrances under elaborate porticos, each guarded by Boreas, Zepher, Notus, and Eurus, the gods of the four directional winds. A small dome centered in the middle of the building was topped with a weather vane in the form of a welcoming Aeolus, the King of the Winds, with an outstretched hand.

"What is this place?" The awe in William's voice was unmistakable. "It looks like a miniature palace."

"The House of Four Directions. It was my birthday present when I was eight years old. My grandfather built it for me as a playhouse." It was one of Thea's fondest childhood memories. Each time she came across the building, her sense of excitement became acute. Her grandfather had loved her when she was younger, and she'd never felt so cherished. Not that he didn't continue to love her, but when he became ill, the memories of their time and what they meant to each other disappeared like evening into night.

William smiled coyly. "It appears that somebody was their grandfather's favorite."

Thea nodded and smiled. "The day of my birthday, he brought me up here and spent the entire afternoon playing games and pretending we were galloping horses and gallant knights. That day was perfect."

"It's amazing." William walked around the structure, and Thea followed. "Is there a purpose to the building besides an elaborate playhouse?"

Thea gazed at the king who slowly rotated with the southwesterly winds. "My grandfather told me he built this folly so that whenever I needed comfort or if I was unable to find my way, all I had to do was follow my heart. It would lead me here, no matter what direction I found myself lost."

William stepped close, and his nearness blocked the gust of winds that blew across the hilltop. "That's lovely. You were lucky to have him in your life."

"I was. Come, each side points due west, east, north, and south. It's perfectly situated." She led him up the steps into the folly. It hid the lone tear that escaped. She had little doubt it was due to the wind gust instead of her emotions. She'd cried all her tears years before her grandfather died. "When he became ill, I wondered if he ever remembered that day and if he'd remembered his words of wisdom."

"What happened to your grandfather?" he asked.

"Later." She clenched a fist at her uncouthness, then stole a peek at his face. The tenderness of his regard surprised her. Immediately, she felt unbalanced and in danger of falling.

"Thea?"

The rough resonance of her name on his lips set everything within her vibrating like a tuning fork. Her heartbeat pounded out in warning that she was in danger of losing a part of herself to him. She swallowed slightly but refused to turn away. His steady gaze pierced hers as if he could see inside where all her doubts and insecurities resided.

"To handle the responsibilities of this great estate is amazing for anyone," he said gently and took her hand. "But to carry that burden while grieving is truly an accomplishment." The sincerity in his eyes startled her, and she blinked. "You don't have to share anything with me. I don't want to cause you more distress. I just want to help." Before she led the way, he entwined their fingers together. "Everyone needs a little help sometime," he said.

Such a kind gesture robbed her of speech. Instead, she nodded gently.

Holding hands, they climbed the stairs. At the top, she released his hand, then opened the double doors on the south side of the folly. Brightly painted red walls and cheerful pink-and-blue antique Savonnerie rugs greeted them. A fireplace with pink-and-red mosaic tiles stood on the north wall, and a plush brocade sofa overlooked a small lake to the west. A pink marble French rococo table with gold overlay legs and matching chairs stood in the middle of the room.

"If my sister were here, she'd fall in love with this place," William said with a hint of wonderment and a smile. "She adores follies and parks. She spent half of her childhood in the park next to our London home."

"Tell me about her." Thea walked to the pristine

windowed doors that faced west. Will followed and stood by her side.

"Well, Emma is married to the Earl of Somerton and they just had their second child, a boy named Sebastian. They have an older daughter, Laura Lena." When he smiled, the love for his family was readily apparent. From the windowsill, he picked up a miniature lapis globe where each country was represented by some type of pavé jewels.

"Are you close?" Yearning leaked into her voice, and she didn't try to hide it.

William nodded. "Extremely so. My brother and I were inseparable when we were younger. Our cousin Claire, the Marchioness of Pembrooke, came to live with us when she was ten after her parents died.

"Claire sounds just like me."

Will nodded, and his eyes were warm with sympathy. "She's more like a sister than a cousin." He carefully placed the globe back on the windowsill.

"You're very fortunate." She desperately wanted what he had with his family. The folly was undeniably beautiful and worthy of a princess, but she'd give up everything to share life's simple moments with someone.

"My grandfather gave me something else besides the folly." She swallowed and forced herself to continue. "I'm an excellent rider. My grandfather always said my father's death was senseless, and he wouldn't let the same happen to me. That's why he made certain I could ride." The words drifted between them, but Thea couldn't stop. "See that swing hanging from that massive oak tree?"

He nodded as he studied the impressive tree outside.

"My grandfather built it for me. He picked that tree because he said it was like his love for me—strong and ageless. I think he knew I was lonely and wanted playmates, but there weren't any other children around. He told me I could share anything with that tree, and it'd keep my secrets."

Will's affectionate grin warmed a place inside her that she didn't even realize needed such attention. "That's lovely."

"My grandfather became ill about seven years ago." She lowered her voice. "He started napping more, and he would have trouble with his correspondence. I started to act as his secretary."

William turned from the view outside to face her. His gaze cut through her layers of reserve.

She had to tell him everything if she wanted his help. It was a risk she had to take. He needed to know the truth. "When he started to wake up in the middle of the night and roam the hallways then the grounds, it became a tremendous amount of work to convince him to come inside and retire. Mr. and Mrs. Miles suggested sending the Ladykyrk staff to Dunbar on Ferr, and I agreed. We couldn't risk any of the other staff learning about his illness. I was always afraid my grandfather would walk out one day and we'd never find him. With just the three of us around, we could keep him contained, and no one was the wiser." She shook her head to keep her anger at his illness under control. "I didn't want him to be the subject of horrible rumors."

"When the staff left, what did they tell the other servants at the ducal estate?" Will asked.

"The butler for the ducal estate is Mr. Miles' brother. He helped us keep the rumors from spreading. I'm so thankful that Mr. and Mrs. Miles convinced me to send them away. Soon thereafter, my grandfather started talking at all hours of the night, having conversations with his dead relations. He was particularly fond of conversing with his sister. She died at the age of ten. That's why

I never had a lady's maid. I couldn't risk rumors being spread about his health."

His long black lashes flew open. He took a step closer, then gently pulled her into his arms. "I'm sorry. Truly, so, so sorry."

His warmth and strength surrounded her like a lazy, soft dream that she never wanted to wake from.

He tucked her close and gently rested his head atop hers. "He was senile?"

"Probably. Up until seven years ago, he was as sane as you or me. Then gradually . . . my grandfather . . ."

For a brief instant, Will tightened his arms around her. But neither said a word.

Thea rushed to fill the awkwardness that had settled between them. "It would have been unspeakably cruel to put him into an asylum. I was concerned the new duke would have my grandfather committed." She stepped away from the comfort of his arms, then clenched her fist against the middle of her chest in an effort to thwart the pain. "Each new day stole some part of my grandfather's memories. His entire life just vanished. He didn't remember my grandmother or my mother." She drew a deep breath to stifle the numbing pain. "He didn't remember me."

"Oh God, Theodora," he softly exclaimed. He clasped her other hand as she still clenched her fist against her heart, desperate to control the onslaught of emotion.

"The night he gave me the House of Four Directions, he tucked me into bed. I was exhausted from all the excitement, but I remember what he whispered in my ear. He told me that I was his forever."

She'd kept those solemn words locked in a special place in her heart. Never did she think she'd share them with anyone.

"Since he'd taken ill, I told him every night that he was forever mine. At the end, he'd just look at me with a faraway gaze, and I knew he didn't remember, and that memory had been heartlessly stolen from him, and also from me, in a way." She squeezed his hand, and he squeezed in return. "He'd become so distraught with himself for his inability to remember. I'd calm him by repeating the words 'I'll remember for you' over and over. Will . . ."

"Thea, I want it all." His voice was so low, she wasn't certain she'd heard him correctly. "I want everything you can give me."

She faltered in the moment of silence between them, then rallied with the strength she'd gained over the years taking care of her grandfather. "Will, you see . . . he always impressed upon me that this was my home, my family." She searched his eyes, desperate he'd understand. "I can't lose this, Will. I can't bear to think there's a chance I'll lose it. I need this folly. I need this land. I need Ladykyrk."

"Of course, you need it. It's your home." A gentle smile tugged at his lips.

"It's more than that." She managed a slight grin in return. Her grip tightened until her knuckles turned white, and she was fearful she was hurting him.

He squeezed her hand again in reassurance.

She had to find a way to explain that failing her grandfather at the end of his life made her more determined to prevail and succeed after his death. Wishing to be relieved of the responsibility, the sheer weight of his care, she'd failed in her love to him. Whatever it took, she'd preserve his love for her the best way she could—by protecting Ladykyrk.

"If it's mine, then my memories and my efforts are his.

He'll know I truly loved him." She dropped his hand and stepped away. "I can't blame you if you don't understand. But I can't lose Ladykyrk."

"Even if he wasn't aware of your care and regard, I'm sure deep down, he trusted you. He knew you loved him. You won't lose Ladykyrk, I promise." The cast-iron strength in his voice offered a comfort she wasn't certain she deserved.

"You don't know that. The solicitor told me to be prepared," she challenged.

He leaned close until they looked each other in the eyes. "My father is very powerful in the House of Lords and carries a tremendous amount of influence. I'll ask for his assistance, and he'll be delighted to help you." There was not boastfulness in the words, just certainty. "Believe it or not, Stella is not without her own allies in London. You'd be surprised by her influence at some of the highest levels."

"Thank you. I'll take all the help I can gather to solidify my claim." She took a deep breath and prayed for courage and a little luck to come her way. "May I ask you a question?"

He nodded.

Never before had she revealed so much of herself or her grandfather's tragic plight.

Or made herself so vulnerable.

"All right, then." She stood straight and stared into his eyes. "Will you . . . be my friend?"

The songbirds' warbles, the rustle of the breeze through the leaves, and every other sound slipped to silence, and all sights faded the moment Thea asked him to be her friend. He couldn't move as the air grew heavy and locked him in place. All his concentration centered on her. Finally, the spell she wove around him lessened, and Will tilted his head and stared at the folly's ceiling.

Cupids and cherubs frolicked in glee as if laughing at him. For the life of him, as Thea hesitated in asking her question, he'd thought she would propose to him. In those mere moments, his emotions had run the gamut from trepidation, relief, happiness, and finally, to disappointment.

Why he experienced disappointment was a complete and utter conundrum that he couldn't navigate. They'd both agreed they didn't want to marry the other. But something deep within him had sparked to life, like a flint against a piece of steel, igniting a hope she might want him. When Theodora had shared the tragic circumstances of her family's demise, he'd become lost—in her and the extraordinary challenges she'd faced on her own in Northumberland. It was as if they were physically joined in some manner, and he'd never felt that tied to another woman.

The only explanation could be that he'd never met anyone like her before.

Theodora possessed a refreshing honesty and fierceness at times that belied her underlying vulnerability—much like his own. But the more time he spent with her, the more intrigued he found himself. When she'd approached Aunt Stella with her reason to marry, she'd been brutally honest, and he respected her for that.

Well, he was a Cavensham, and a Cavensham never shirked from duty or tough questions or even simple requests such as friendship. "Thea, I'd be honored to be your friend." He slowly smiled. "But I was under the assumption we already were."

She huffed a breath of air to blow that elusive curl from her face. "Thank you. You would not believe how much courage it took me to ask you that. I wasn't certain you'd want my friendship after I'd practically demanded you leave my home when I received the letter from the House of Lords."

"Don't worry. I didn't take offense, as you had important matters that needed your attention. Besides, I've been summarily dismissed many times before. That's not what you did to me."

"If there's anything you need from me, all you have to do is ask." He leaned against the doorjamb and regarded her. "Are you ready to go to London tomorrow?"

"No, I dread it." Thea smiled and leaned close. "However, do you know what's lovely about all this turmoil in my life?"

"No," he answered.

"I have my first real friend accompanying me. We can chat and gossip on the way. You'll help steer me through the muddle of London society." She cleared her throat, then focused her gaze on him. "You're helping me, and I'd like to help you. I hope whatever you need or want, you'll ask for my help. I'll do everything in my power to see it happen."

The swirl of emotion in her eyes reminded him of a kaleidoscope, and it captivated him. Determination, loyalty, generosity, plus a myriad of others combined into a pattern that showed her true strength of character. Thea would fight with her last breath to save her home, and she'd love a husband with the same potent power. Whoever won her hand would never doubt her heart was true.

"Shall we save what you can do for me until later?" He extended his arm in offer for her to take it. She didn't see the gesture as her gaze roamed over his figure. When her eyes found his, he winked. It marked the first time she'd ever really looked at him. "I'd rather concentrate on you. Come, let's sit down."

Her cheeks turned a marvelous shade of dark pink as she hooked her arm around his and led him to the sofa that overlooked the lake.

"As your friend, I'll help you prepare for your entrance to the *ton*. We'll organize dance lessons, an etiquette refresher, and whatever else you'll need. I'll arrange to help you ease into society as you make your claim in front of the committee. My parents will be your hosts and will introduce you into the highest echelons of the *ton*. You want to make an excellent impression every time you're out in society."

"Your aunt is already helping with the etiquette, but"—she blew out a frustrated breath—"I don't know about the rest."

Will rested his ankle on his other knee. "Everyone will want to meet the elusive Countess of Eanruig. I'll have you ready."

She wrinkled her nose and stared out the window. "Would you introduce me to some of your friends?"

"Absolutely." He nodded.

"I might have to marry quickly." She caught his gaze. "I trust your opinion. If they're your friends, maybe . . ."

"There is no cause to worry yet." He leaned close as if divulging a secret. "I'd like to introduce you to some of my closest friends. I think you'd like them. Plus, I'll teach you the latest dances, how to greet other peers, and most importantly, how to stay out of trouble. After all my years as the second son of the Duke of Langham, I'm an expert at it."

Her brief look of relief melted into an expression reminiscent of deer caught by a hunter.

"Come now, it won't be that horrible. You'll get to dance with me. That in and of itself will be worth the effort," he teased. "Besides, it will make your task of taking your place in society—"

"I've never danced." Her voice wobbled, a crack in her veneer of confidence.

"You mean at a ball? Never fear," he said. "Country assemblies are practically the same, only a little smaller."

"I've never been to a country assembly. My grandfather didn't go out much in society after he became ill."

Her skin glistened with beads of sweat that had popped up across her brow.

"You've never danced?" It was incredible that a young woman, the granddaughter of a duke and a countess in her own right, had never danced.

Thea stood and shook her head. "Well, my grandfather twirled me around in a circle a time or two. But you really can't call that dancing." She walked to the door and pretended to be interested in the lake again.

He immediately tamped down his shock. She was embarrassed, and every instinct within him wanted to comfort and protect her.

He rose, then walked to her side. "You have an innate grace and athleticism that will lend itself to mastering the steps in no time. Trust me."

She clutched her arms around her waist. Immediately, she looked like a little girl unsure of her place in the great big world.

"As your friend, I'll help you be ready for the *ton*." He leaned closer, daring himself to offer comfort without touching her. "It's all right. I won't let you fail."

She didn't acknowledge his promise. Instead, she turned toward the opposite exit. "We should head back. We have an early start for London tomorrow."

For a moment, he physically ached to hold her and soothe the worry from her brow, but then he thought better of it. Thea and her mysterious eyes could make a man surrender everything.

She'd have no difficulty finding a husband if she

wanted one, and it set him on edge. He'd never experienced jealousy in his life. That couldn't be what he was feeling.

The thought made him wonder if he were going mad.

The quicker they arrived at Langham Hall, his father and mother's residence in the city, the sooner Thea could secure her title, and the sooner he'd gain his sanity back.

Chapter Seven

Theodora's exhaustion vanished as soon as their coach entered the city of London. Never before had she seen such sights. The buildings crowded each other as if pushing their way to the front of the streets. The calls from the street vendors and the clop of horses pulling carriages harmonized into a symphony of sounds she'd never heard before. Shop windows were decorated with fashions and goods, tempting her to investigate all their treasures. Several bookstores littered the shop fronts as they traveled down Bond Street. Silversmiths, jewelers, and exclusive haberdasheries added to the spectacle. She could shop for weeks and never see it all.

But the most startling sight was the sheer number of people. Never in her life had she seen such a gathering. From all walks of life, the citizens of London fascinated her. They all seemed to be in a hurry, except the nobs and fops dressed in their finest as they strolled the streets with various servants and attendants in tow.

When Will peered out the carriage window, his shoul-

der brushed hers. She drew a deep breath of his bergamot scent and held it as long as she could. Slowly, she
exhaled. "Perhaps you'd recommend a perfume shop. I've
never been in one."

A crooked half smile creased his full lips. "I have the
perfect establishment. It's become a family favorite ever
since Claire's father, the previous Duke of Langham,
shopped there the first time."

"Do you think I could have a fragrance made"—her
gaze caught his, and the laughter in his eyes made her
suddenly shy—"for me?"

"I like the way you smell." He leaned close and sniffed.
He closed his eyes as if judging her scent. "You smell of
Northumberland, clean, fresh, a hint of floral, with a
hefty dose of wild beauty."

An uncontrollable heat licked her cheeks. He smiled
in that cocky way of his, but she relaxed at the warmth
in his eyes. It was a lovely compliment as Northumberland
was known for its exquisite splendor.

Lord Fluff jumped from Stella's lap to Thea's. Stella
tore her attention away from the book she had borrowed
from Theodora's library, a treatise on the history of
Thea's family. The grand dame had read it religiously for
the entire five-day journey as they made their way to
London. "Will, every woman wants to be unique with her
own signature fragrance." She straightened her seat, and
a sly grin graced her lips as if she were enjoying a private joke. "Perhaps something light like a blend of rose
water and peonies."

Will arched one perfect brow. "How mundane. I think
something more interesting. Perhaps gardenia or something with a base of *melograno*."

"*Melograno*?" Thea asked. "Is that a flower?"

"Italian for pomegranate," Stella answered. She narrowed her eyes and critically examined Thea. "With her

coloring, it would be perfect. An incomparable scent for an incomparable beauty."

Will's gaze never strayed from hers. "My thoughts exactly."

He turned slightly and winked. The intimate gesture was hidden from Stella and Nancy, the grand dame's lady's maid who sat between Stella and Lady Edith. Another blast of heat assaulted Thea's cheeks.

"You're gorgeous when you blush," he whispered. The words were so quiet that for a moment, she imagined she hadn't heard him correctly.

Lady Edith's eyebrows shot up.

Thea would melt into the bench of the carriage if he continued such teasing. To preserve what little composure she had, she returned her attention out the carriage window. Without looking at Will, she could sense him drawing away. As if some vital link had been cut, her chest felt hollow.

Soon the coach arrived at a massive mansion in the middle of Mayfair, a gorgeous home that bespoke grandeur the likes of which she'd never seen. Her sharp intake of breath gave away her excitement at arriving at Will's home.

"Welcome to Langham Hall, Lady Eanruig," Will announced before he departed the coach. Handsome liveried footmen and groomsmen met the carriage. Will greeted each by name, then held out his hand to Stella who was the first to depart the carriage, then Lady Edith, and finally, Nancy with Lord Fluff in her arms. Thea waited inside and hoped the brief interlude alone would calm the nervousness that rumbled through her with the force of a runaway carriage.

Will returned and leaned into the carriage, his tall body framed by the doorway. The simple act emphasized his fit and lean build. Instantly, Thea's heart raced at the sight, but she scolded herself at her response. No good would come from allowing him to unsettle her at such an innocent action.

She smoothed the wrinkles that marred her traveling gown and spencer. Though the design lacked any frills, the cerulean brocade shimmered in the sunlight that had broken through the clouds and now graced them with its presence. She'd wanted to look her best when she met his family.

"Are you ready?" He extended his hand, and she placed hers in his. The soft leather of his glove caressed her. "Put on your gloves. It's customary when you're introduced to others that your hands be covered."

"Oh. I apologize." She fumbled with her kid-skinned gloves that were dyed to match her gown.

"No need for that. We all must learn these lessons. They're not inborn in any of us." The gentleness in his voice did little to calm her unease.

"Do you think your family . . ."

His stare burrowed deep inside her. "Will they what?"

She did her best to tamp down the sudden onslaught of apprehension. "Like me?"

Will took her hand to help her down. The heat of his fingers warmed her skin through the leather. "They'll love you."

Her eyes watered at his simple statement. He had no idea how much that meant to her. To be welcomed by a family and accepted as one of their own was her greatest desire. To belong to someone was a gift, and if she ever possessed enough luck to be accepted by a family, she'd cherish it forever. Determined to make a favorable impression, she had peppered Stella with questions about her expected behavior around such an illustrious family, late at night when they'd stopped at an inn or stayed at one of Stella's numerous friends' homes along the route.

"I hope they'll like me," she answered quietly.

"They will." He squeezed her hand with his, then gently tugged her to exit. Will led the way and escorted Stella and Edith to the front of the house. Thea and Nancy followed behind.

An elegant older man perfectly attired in a lovely wool suit with an embroidered blue waistcoat that matched the liveried servants' dress opened the door. "Lord William, welcome home," he beamed.

"Thank you, Pitts. It's good to see you. Are my parents home?" Will smiled as he stood aside so Stella, Lady Edith, and Nancy could pass. When Thea stepped forward, he took her hand and wrapped it around his arm.

"I'm afraid not. They had a social engagement before dinner. But luck is with you. Tonight is the weekly family dinner. With you here, the entire family will be attending this evening." Pitts helped Stella with her spring pelisse.

Stella clapped her hands. "How lucky for us all."

Pitts turned his beaming smile to Stella. "My dear Lady Payne, may I say that it's always a brighter day in London when you grace us with your presence."

"You old conniving rascal," Stella retorted as she held up her lorgnette and examined the man from head to toe. "You're still as wily as ever. How long has it been? A year?"

"Indeed, my lady." Completely unfazed with her rebuke and thorough examination, Pitts laughed, and Lady Edith joined in their frivolity.

"I'd like to introduce Lady Eanruig." Stella turned to Theodora. "Lady Eanruig, this is Pitts, the most pretentious butler you'll ever meet."

"It's a pleasure to meet you," Pitts offered. The warmth

and affection in his eyes was a refreshing balm to Thea's travel weariness. "Welcome to Langham Hall." He turned back to Stella. "Madam, if your and Lady Edith's schedules allow, perhaps we can finish that game of whist from the last time?"

"It'd be my pleasure to take your money," Stella retorted. "May I add, once again."

"Perhaps your ladyship will recall that at the end of our last play, you owed me"—Pitts counted on his fingers—"ten pounds and forty shillings."

Stella grinned playfully. "Old man, we shall meet after dinner and finish this for good."

Will leaned over and whispered in Thea's ear, "They do this every time they meet. It's like a ritualistic dance."

"I've never heard of a butler wagering with a baroness," Thea whispered in return.

"As you may have surmised, Aunt Stella is a little unorthodox, and so is Pitts. My parents don't mind their play. It's a penny a hand, and Pitts always wins."

"My lady, shall I escort you to your usual room?" Pitts asked.

Stella nodded. "Escort Lady Eanruig to the Iris bedroom. That's where both William and I would like for her to stay."

Will stiffened beside her as Stella regally ascended the steps with Pitts in tow. A handsome liveried footman bowed slightly to Theodora. "My lady, may I show you to your room?"

"I'll take her." Will grinned in good humor, then gently tugged her arm. They ascended the stairs following Stella, Edith, and Pitts, who were engaged in a rollicking bout of laughter with one another. "They've put you in the bedroom that connects to mine."

"Is it inappropriate?" Good heavens, she didn't want

to make a bad impression before she'd met his family. "Shall we ask for another room?"

"No. It's just my darling great-aunt outmaneuvering me in hosting responsibilities." He patted her hand, the one gently wrapped around his arm, and continued their upward ascent. "If I were you, I'd get some rest. You'll need every ounce of strength to survive the evening," he said dully.

"Why?" she asked.

"You, my dear Thea, will be the center of attention tonight."

After changing from her traveling clothes to a plain muslin gown, Thea lay under the huge canopied bed and studied the intricate patterns of irises and tulips above her. The room was everything lovely, decorated with delightful florals in blues, indigos, and purples. It practically sang a song of spring. She'd never seen—much less stayed—in such an opulent room.

Instead of resting, her mind whirled with thoughts of her last conversation with Will. How would his family react to hearing the news she was a houseguest and the notorious Lady Man-Eater? Though she was the Countess of Eanruig, she had no experience being a worldly woman of society—let alone London society. She was well aware of her limitations, growing up so isolated, but it mattered little in Northumberland. But London was a different beast altogether.

Stella had shared so much about her niece and nephew-in-law, the Duke and Duchess of Langham. They were lovely people who put their family first. Tonight, with her introduction to the Cavensham family, Thea vowed she'd shine. Whatever she had to do, she'd ensure that Will was proud of her, and as importantly, proud to announce her as his friend.

Tonight, she would wear an evening ensemble in the loveliest shade of blue for this special evening. The brilliant marine color reminded her of Will's eyes. She'd tried it on several times back at Ladykyrk, and each time she slipped it over her figure, she'd felt like a princess in a fairy tale. Tonight, it'd give her confidence.

A knock on the door broke her reverie. Nancy stood outside ready to help Theodora dress. The lady's maid offered to help her disrobe and bathe, but ever modest around strangers, Theodora undressed behind a bathing screen and slipped into the tub on her own. From the noises around the room, Nancy busied herself with straightening up Theodora's clothes and unpacking the remaining items.

"My lady, do you need my help when you're finished with your bath?" Nancy's voice called from the other side of the screen. "I help Lady Payne all the time with her bath and dressing. You don't have anything that I haven't seen before." The maid faintly chuckled.

"There's no need," Theodora answered. As she quickly rose from the rose-scented bath, the water sluiced from her body. She grabbed the toweling Nancy had laid out and wrapped her body in the softest cotton she'd ever touched in her life. Comparing it to wool was like silk against steel. She dried quickly, but her hand lingered and caressed the luxurious material. Gingerly she stepped around the screen.

Ever efficient, Nancy had laid out her undergarments, shoes, and finally her dress. She had another new pair of kid gloves for the occasion, but as this was a formal dinner, they were ivory—a perfect accompaniment for her gown. The gloves' length would cover her forearms and elbows.

Which begged the question, how did one eat with such elegant gloves covering one's hands?

She could ask Nancy the proper etiquette, but how foolish would it make her appear? On the way to London, Stella and Lady Edith had been relentless with etiquette lessons. Some Thea had easily remembered from her governess. Others were like a foreign language. There was no rhythm or reason to the madness of rules. But Thea had never thought to ask about gloves.

She clenched her eyes shut and tried to dredge forth the memories of the few formal dinners she and her grandfather had shared. She recalled little of the actual customs of removing or eating with gloves.

Her grandfather and her governess had instructed her about conversing with the guests who sat on the right and the left. For the life of her, she couldn't remember a word either of them had said. At the time, she'd didn't see how it could be important because she and her grandfather were the only two who ever dined together at Ladykyrk. Tonight, she'd be expected to participate in conversation. Suddenly, she suffered from the same affliction as her darling grandfather. There were rules about whom one could and could not speak to at a formal dinner, and she couldn't remember a single one.

What if the committee, who would decide her fate, discovered her ineptness with even the simplest rules of polite society? Her hands started to sweat, and she clenched her fists. If she didn't get her unruly emotions under control, she'd stain her dress. Any moisture would ruin the delicate and fragile silk of her evening gown. All her worries combined into a maelstrom she couldn't wrestle under control. Suddenly, each second that passed foretold a disaster that loomed in her future.

"My lady, are you all right?" Nancy stood with Thea's delicate chemise in her hands and studied her. "You look like the devil himself has taken a shine to you."

Thea notched her chin up and tried to dismiss her

unease. It wouldn't do to be nervous tonight. She vowed not to concern herself with any tangled thoughts of etiquette tonight. The Cavensham family would warmly welcome her as both Stella and Will had assured her.

Besides, she was the Countess of Eanruig and would rule her own world.

*Lady Man-Eater enjoys a fondness for small children and
darling lapdogs
for the first course of a formal meal.
Faithful in our quest for the truth,*
The Midnight Cryer

Chapter Eight

Thea smiled to herself before the full-length mirror. A creature from another world, one who was familiar but at the same time unrecognizable, stared back at her.

The dress and the evening would launch her into London society. She prayed for success as this day brought her one step closer to appearing in front of the committee. A niggle of unease, almost a foreboding wrapped itself around her. She tried to dismiss the thought as nervousness, simply a typical reaction to her new circumstances.

"My lady, you look beautiful," crooned Nancy. She stood behind Thea and straightened her skirt, adjusting the train that gracefully draped to the floor.

A quick knock at the door signaled that a footman had arrived to escort Thea to the family gathering before dinner. Nancy adjusted the train once more before answering the summons.

Thea forgot to breathe when she first saw Will standing on the other side. Resplendent in a silver-threaded gray waistcoat, black wool evening coat, and matching pantaloons, he reminded her of Hades come to abduct Persephone. Unlike the Greek myth, Thea wouldn't fight him, but would gladly take his escort anywhere, including the underworld, if it meant she could avoid this dinner.

"Good evening, Nancy." He turned to Theodora, and a roguish smile tugged at his lips. "And who might this beautiful creature be?"

Nancy dipped a slight curtsey. "Good evening, my lord. Lady Eanruig is a delight, isn't she?"

"Indeed," Will answered.

Her eyes locked with his, and time seemed to stop its relentless pace. Everything within her stilled, reminding her that this would be a moment she'd remember for a lifetime. A strange eagerness like a hunger flashed in his eyes. It caused a molten heat to explode in her chest and slowly sink lower into her body. She couldn't look away nor did she want to. For the first time in her life since her grandfather died, she felt tied to another person.

"Will you be needing anything else, my lady?" Nancy asked. "If not, then I'd best go help Lady Payne."

The simple question broke the magical moment.

Thea shook her head to clear the remaining wisps of desire that floated around her. "Thank you for everything, Nancy. You've worked miracles."

The lady's maid blushed. "You're too modest, my lady. Enjoy your evening."

Will stepped aside, and Nancy took her leave. Without a word, he held out his arm for Thea to take. Drawn to him like a bee to nectar, she lightly placed her hand upon his forearm. His warmth wound around her and, powerless to resist, she leaned close.

"You look beautiful tonight," he whispered as his gaze lingered.

"I feel beautiful."

"Good." He led her toward the stairs but stopped at a hallway mirror.

His gaze flew to her lips, and his eyes softened with some undefined emotion. Whatever this was that swirled between them, she didn't want it to stop. If they stayed in this hallway for eternity, Thea would consider it a blessing. Then, the outside world couldn't intrude, and her disquiet would melt away like winter frost when it's ravished by the spring sunshine.

"There will be so much interest in you tonight from my family. I wouldn't be surprised if you run from Langham Hall, vowing never to return." Will smiled.

She answered his smile with one of her own. "It sounds like heaven to me."

"Ah well, the Cavenshams' infamous teasing, cajoling, and merriment make even the bravest tremble. I've seen it before with my own eyes." He held out his arm again. "Shall we go into the lion's den—I mean, heaven?"

He winked and a new rush of desire hit her square in the middle of her chest. He was charming in his attitude toward his family.

Without another word, he led her down the steps where laughter and murmurs of conversation joined together in some harmonic joie de vivre that invited her forward. The closer they came to the salon where everyone had gathered, Thea found it hard to keep her excitement and frankly, her nerves under control. Her heartbeat accelerated as if rolling nilly-willy down a hill.

They stood outside the entrance, and Will drew her aside. "You have nothing to be afraid of from my family. If I've given you cause to be alarmed, I shouldn't have. They'll welcome you unconditionally and shower you with kindness."

"How are you going to introduce me?" Her stomach

roiled as visions of *The Midnight Cryer*'s headlines of "Man-Eater" and "Northumberland Nemesis" taunted her. Seeking comfort, she stroked the cool strand of pearls against her neck. They were her mother's, and this was the first occasion she'd ever had to wear them.

"As my friend." He held out his arm. "Are you ready?"

She smiled gently as she wrapped her hand around his arm, then nodded. Together, they walked forward.

Pitts nodded at their entrance and stood aside.

Never before had Thea seen such a gathering. Handsome men and beautiful ladies, all elegantly attired, graced the room. In the center of the gathering, a middle-aged couple held court. When the woman turned to her husband, she placed her hand on his chest and laughed, an act so endearing that Thea had to remember to breathe. The man caught the woman's hand and held it to his heart. His hearty laugh enveloped the whole room in affection.

"Who's that couple?" Thea asked.

"My mother and father."

At the sound of Will's voice, the woman looked their way. There was little doubt she was Will's mother, the Duchess of Langham. He'd inherited her smile. Will's father, the Duke of Langham, followed his wife's gaze, and the smile that broke across his face was simply stunning. Will had definitely inherited his father's height and handsomeness.

"William!" His mother made her way toward him with her hands outstretched in welcome. "It's so good to have you home."

"Hello, everyone," Will called out in greeting. "I'd like to introduce Theodora, the Countess of Eanruig. She's my friend and guest."

"Friendship is a start." Stella's voice rang from behind. "We're hopeful for more."

"Cavenshams fall in love thoroughly"—Lady Edith turned to Stella—"and what was the other?"

"Decidedly," Stella chimed in.

"How could I forget?" Edith chuckled. "We're certain these two are well on their way. Lovely news, isn't it?"

At that pronouncement, the duchess's face fell when she stumbled forward. The duke caught her elbow before she tumbled to the floor.

The entire room fell silent as every head swiveled toward them. This was an examination like no other. If only there was a side door, then Thea could escape and run from the house as Will had predicted she'd want to do. What was she supposed to say to Edith and Stella's pronouncement? Tell them all that it was a lie and that she'd told Will she wouldn't marry him?

A beautiful blonde in an emerald green dress dropped her fan at the announcement. "Oh, my word, Will. What have you done?"

A handsome man who resembled Will and the duke had the audacity to laugh. "Emma, I'd say he's done the unthinkable and has done it remarkably well. The day of reckoning has arrived for our brother. Who is that charming creature beside you?"

"Don't stand there dawdling, you two," Stella chided. "Go face the pack of hounds."

Before his family had noticed their arrival, Will stole a glance at Theodora and had been struck by her expression. It reminded him of a child staring into a candy shop window wishing for the world without a penny in her pocket. Then when his family had turned their attention to them, and Aunt Stella had blurted her hope for their engagement, he'd felt her physically retreat. She had moved away and turned as if deciding to run. Without a second thought, he'd squeezed their fingers together, then tugged her closer to his side.

"What are we going to do?" Thea whispered, her voice laced with panic. "I don't want to mislead your parents."

"Leave it to me," he answered. His stomach dropped as if he'd been thrown from a horse. Stella and Edith had made things more complicated for Thea and for him.

A tumble of confused thoughts and feelings assailed him. It was more than problematic, though. Unintentionally, Thea's words created a latent ache he thought long since dead. A vulnerability that he despised crept to the surface. Just because another woman had spurned him as a suitable groom had nothing to do with Thea. She'd never been anything but candid with him.

Yet for once, he'd wondered what it must feel like to have a woman look at you as if you were the only man in the universe. At Thea's folly, he'd thought he'd experienced it. Perchance, he'd foolishly mistaken what he'd seen.

Before he could consider it more, his mother and father reached them. With tears and a joyful smile, his mother took his other hand in hers.

Immediately, he'd leaned over while never breaking contact with Theodora and kissed his mother's cheek. "Madam, you're a beautiful sight to behold."

"Thank you, William. So are you." Her attention immediately switched to Theodora. "Hello, my dear."

For a second, Theodora stood frozen, then dipped into the expected curtsey. "Your Grace, it's a pleasure to meet you."

Will automatically relaxed. With his mother and father smoothing the way, Theodora would soon feel welcome. That was the beauty of his family. They might charm and badger each other, but at the same time, there was never any doubt they loved one another. Deep down, they stood together united in a force that no one could break. It was the Cavensham way.

Will squeezed Theodora's fingers once last time, then dropped them to shake his father's hand. "Father, it's good to see you."

His father growled in response and ignored William's hand. Instead, he took Will into his embrace, and when he let go, he clasped Will's shoulder. "And the same here, son." His father turned, then blessed Theodora with a smile worthy of a rogue. "Welcome, my dear, to Langham Hall."

Thea bobbed a hasty curtsey. "The honor is all mine, Your Grace." Her voice had cracked with nervousness, and it punched Will in the stomach.

Never had a woman's emotions caused such havoc in him before.

His father tugged his mother into a side embrace. The couple beamed at them.

"Congratulations to you both," his father said, then smiled. "On your *friendship*."

The rumble of amusement in his father's tone meant only one thing—Stella's offhanded remarks had awoken his curiosity.

His mother held Thea's hand, refusing to let it go.

"Hello, my dearest Ginny." Without waiting for a response, Aunt Stella pecked her niece's cheek, then crowded next to his father. "Sebastian, Thea is the Countess of Eanruig, an old Scottish title. She lives next door to me at Ladykyrk."

His father nodded once. "We're honored you'll stay with us, Countess."

"Theirs is a match made in heaven, if they can just see

it," Stella said under her breath. No one else heard it as it was meant for Will's ears alone.

He wanted to roll his eyes but kept his demeanor cool and calm. He loved Stella dearly, but sometimes her hyperbole became a bit too much.

"Thea and I are friends." His voice sounded a little too forceful, but he didn't want Thea any more nervous than she already was.

Aunt Stella smiled, then monopolized his parents, and it didn't take long until his siblings approached with their spouses. Never shy, his youngest sibling, Emma, beat everyone to the introductions.

Emma held out her hand for Theodora. Once his sister had a firm grasp, she gently tugged Theodora toward her with her green eyes blazing with laughter. "One can never have enough friends. I must share a little secret about Will." Emma leaned close, and Will leaned along with her. "He's a scoundrel at times." Emma winked at Theodora as if sharing the location of the family jewels. "But he's loving and fiercely loyal. He'll be a good friend."

"Emma, don't," Will scolded as heat crept up his neck. He turned to Theodora where a smile that reminded him of a sunset slowly spread across her face. "My sister has a weakness for the dramatic. She hasn't shown it yet, but soon will."

"Then we shall be fast friends too. I'm sure of it, Lady Somerton," Thea said.

"Call me Emma. I want you to meet my husband, Nicholas, the Earl of Somerton."

Somerton swept forward and offered Thea one of his notorious smiles, the kind that had women from the age of one to one hundred and one melting at his feet. Then, the devil sketched a perfect bow. "Lady Eanruig, the pleasure is mine."

Will chanced a glance at Thea expecting her to become putty in Somerton's hands. Most woman usually had that response because of his perfect looks and athletic physique, but she just smiled. "Pleased to meet you, Lord Somerton."

Will's brother, McCalpin, and his wife, March, waited patiently for their turn to greet Theodora. Emma brought March forward and made the introductions. As the women started to chat, McCalpin bent close to Will. "She's the one I heard about at White's. She faces a challenge from Ferr-Colby for the title and entailed properties?"

Will nodded. "It's a complicated and convoluted story. But I want the family's assistance to make her feel welcome and help her introduction to society."

The bland expression on McCalpin's face was devoid of any empathy. "I take it there was no emergency in Northumberland?"

Will shook his head. "Because of Stella's summons, I'm behind in my work now more than ever."

"I know how you hate that," McCalpin answered. "Don't worry about my estate books. March finished the accounting for you. But I need you to go to McCalpin Manor soon. I'd like your opinion on something."

Will lifted an eyebrow.

"The roof. March is concerned that it may need repairs again," McCalpin said with a half grin, then turned his steady gaze to Thea. "You always were Stella's favorite. I used to be envious of her regard for you, but now, I'm so thankful you were her chosen one. You deserve special treatment for all you do for this family. I must say the grand dame has done you an amazing favor. Theodora is lovely."

"Indeed." Will studied Thea as she spoke with March and Emma. The simple chignon didn't hide the splendor of Thea's hair as each strand glowed in the candlelight. Her cheeks were flushed with excitement rather than nervousness. She wasn't just lovely.

She was beautiful.

Will turned to his brother. "But she's just a friend."

Fair warning, London! Do not, we repeat, DO NOT get between
Lady Man-Eater and the orange cream.
It's been reported that several Langham Hall footmen made that mistake
and are now reported missing.
Truthfully reported,
The Midnight Cryer

Chapter Nine

The duke had escorted Thea into the dining room and had insisted she sit next to him. He sat at the head of the table with Thea to his left. Across from her, Will's beautiful auburn-haired cousin Claire claimed the seat.

The duke reached over and clasped Claire's hand. "I'm glad you and Pembrooke could come this evening. Let me introduce you to Theodora, the Countess of Eanruig, Will's friend and a guest at Langham Hall."

The woman's eyebrows shot straight skyward as if a highwayman held them up.

The duke's generous smile did little to calm the swarm of butterflies in Thea's stomach.

"Theodora, this is my niece and Will's cousin Claire, the Marchioness of Pembrooke."

"I'm delighted to meet you, my lady," Thea offered. Another decision of etiquette loomed before her. Should she stand and offer a proper curtsey or just sit and nod?

Before she was forced to make a choice, Claire took

the decision from her hands. With a *swoosh* of her skirts, the marchioness rounded the table. Once she reached Thea's side, Claire leaned in and hugged her.

Startled and unsure what to do, Thea stood. Claire pulled away and took her gloved hands in hers. "I'm so happy to meet you." She leaned and whispered in Thea's ear, "There's no one like William." Before Thea could ask her meaning, the marchioness continued, "When did you arrive in London?"

"Today," Thea answered.

Claire turned to her uncle. "I would have rushed over here sooner if I'd known Will had invited a friend." She squeezed Thea's hand. "He's never invited anyone to dinner before, much less asked them to stay at Langham Hall."

The duke leaned back in his chair. "Ginny and I met Thea right before you and Pembrooke arrived."

The auburn beauty's mouth formed a perfect *O* in surprise. Then the most breathtaking smile lit her face. "I'll come for tea soon. You'll have to tell me all about how you and William became friends."

"That would be lovely, Lady Pembrooke." Denial sat on the tip of her tongue. What would she be refuting? That they were friends? If she were brave, she'd announce she didn't want anyone to be disappointed but she and Will had no plans for marriage. Instead, she took the safe route and kept quiet.

"Call me Claire." She winked at Thea.

"Would you call me Thea?" she asked softly. "It's a pet name my grandfather gave me. It's short for Theodora."

The smile that graced Claire's lips bespoke kindness, and Thea's hopes rose that they'd forge a true friendship. This was the woman Will said she'd have a lot in common with.

A handsome man with raven-colored hair stood at Claire's side. The marchioness affectionately placed her hand on his arm. "Alex, this is . . . Will's new friend and mine, Thea, the Countess of Eanruig." Still touching the man's arm, Claire turned to Thea. "This is my husband, Alex, the Marquess of Pembrooke."

Whereas, the Earl of Somerton was handsome in a light, brilliant way with his blond hair and turquoise eyes, the marquess's dark, rugged beauty derived from his perfect features and aquiline nose. His startling gray eyes flashed with humor. "It's lovely to meet you, Thea." He took her gloved hand and bowed over it.

"Likewise, my lord," she answered. Her gaze swept down the table to Will, who was staring at her. She swallowed her unease. Hopefully, she hadn't done anything to embarrass him or her, but it was difficult to know precisely how to act and what to do. Suddenly, he grinned in his familiar impish manner, and she relaxed.

The men in his family were fabulously attractive, but when he bestowed a grin like that her way, he was the most handsome man in the room.

"We should sit," Claire said. "The first course is about to be served."

Behind each chair, a handsome liveried footman stood waiting to serve them or retrieve their dirty dishes. She'd never seen such a huge number of staff whose sole purpose was to ensure that every person had a plate of food in front of them or a full glass of wine. Even though her grandfather was a duke, they never dined in such a formal fashion. Once he became sick, their eating habits had become routine. Mrs. Miles would place the dishes on the table, and Thea would serve the duke. In his final months, Thea would feed him like a toddler since he was incapable of holding a fork or a spoon, let alone cut his own meat.

Conversations erupted around the table. McCalpin, Will's brother, sat to Thea's left, but his attention was devoted to Stella who sat to his left. The duke became enthralled in a discussion with Pembrooke about an upcoming vote in the House of Lords, and Claire listened intently. Every few moments, she'd glance Thea's way and smile.

The duke and duchess and their hospitality were all so welcoming, and they were kind just as William had promised. Warmth and affection surrounded the family. It reminded her of all she'd missed growing up with only her grandfather.

But tonight, Thea couldn't shake the feeling she was truly an outsider. A better description might be an imposter, since she doubted she'd deserved to be a part of such an illustrious group of people.

Immediately, those ever-present feelings of shame and remorse flooded her. Many a day, she wished she'd spent more time with her grandfather, even if he didn't remember her. He was the only family she'd had, and when he'd passed, she hadn't grieved like a normal granddaughter.

Selfishly, she'd only felt relief that it was finally over. Discreetly, she glanced around the table. The family's regard for one another was apparent in how they spoke and laughed with an ease that was astounding. If anyone within the Cavensham family had fallen ill, she had little doubt that the entire clan would rally and support one another in the care for their loved one.

The bond they shared slowly surrounded her like a fog rolling in from the sea, and she'd never felt so alone. She wasn't a part of this family who had deep ties to one another.

She came from another world—one without anyone to call her own.

As if Will sensed what she was thinking, he caught her gaze and that charming lopsided grin appeared, making her forget her loneliness, at least for a moment.

The footman served the first course of a carrot and leek soup. Her gaze flew to Claire's hands to gauge whether she should remove her gloves or leave them on. Unfortunately, the marchioness's hands were tucked in her lap, and the long sleeves of her gown were the only part of her arms visible. Thea chanced a glance down the rest of the table. All the women's hands were hidden from view as they each waited to be served.

Heat assaulted her cheeks. Once the duke raised his spoon, they would commence eating. She had an even chance of getting this piece of dining etiquette correct. She glanced at her table setting, and her stomach fell. She'd never seen so many spoons, forks, and knives, some in the oddest of shapes and sizes. What purpose did a spoon laid sideways at the top of the plate have in the course of a meal? Her heartbeat accelerated, and she placed her hand over her heart in a futile effort to calm herself.

"Is something wrong?" the duke whispered as he leaned close.

"Y-yes. . . ." A slight shudder of embarrassment tore another piece of her confidence.

"What, my dear?" The faint glimmer of amusement in his eyes evaporated.

"I've never attended such a formal dinner, and I'm not certain what to do." She waited for the look of disdain to twist his face, but the duke's brow furrowed into neat lines. "Do I take off my gloves to eat?"

As she waited for his answer, the room grew deathly quiet. They all were waiting for him to lift his spoon. He bent toward her until mere inches separated them. "What would you like to do?"

She bit her lip. There was little doubt now. She was a complete ignorant goose. "I want to do what's right and not embarrass Will."

With a discreet nod, he answered, "Watch my Ginny. She'll teach us both."

Slowly, he drew away and lifted his glass. "Duchess, will you raise your glass with mine? I want to give you, *and only you*, a toast."

The duchess lifted her glass with a *gloveless* hand and smiled endearingly at her husband.

"To the woman who rules my heart. May we never forget what's worth remembering, and may we forget what is best forgotten." His words of love flowed like silk across the room.

With a blinding smile, the duchess dipped her head in acknowledgment. They both took a drink, and the collective sighs around the table were a clear indication the rest of the family was as affected as Thea at the loving words.

Afterward, the duke lifted his spoon and took a sip. Renewed conversations obliterated the earlier quiet at the duke's toast. Thea quickly slipped off her gloves and laid them across her lap.

Like a hawk, she had discreetly watched which spoon the duke picked up, then followed suit. As long as she watched him eat, she would not embarrass Will or herself.

After her first sip of soup, she whispered, "Thank you, Your Grace."

"You're most welcome, Theodora," he whispered. "It'd be my greatest joy to make a toast at the end of the meal for you, only if you're comfortable with it."

She glanced at Will who was deep in discussion with his sister and his mother. He appeared comfortable, happy even. Thea's spirits flattened. If she felt unease with Will's family, then she shuddered to think about the *ton*. It took years to teach children the manners expected in society. She only had a week.

"I'm not certain that's for the best." She didn't say it aloud, but deep down, she was terrified she'd have to stand in response and say a few words. She didn't want any more attention drawn to herself, not tonight. She simply wanted to enjoy the rest of the evening, then go to bed.

"I see." The duke's deep voice lowered to the softest whisper. "Of course, whatever you wish. Perhaps after all this nasty business with the committee is over, you'll feel differently."

Surely, she'd just imagined the sympathy that tinted the duke's words. McCalpin turned slightly in his chair and asked a question of his father. The hum of their voices floated in the air, but all she could concentrate on was the silverware while stealing glances down the table. The entire family enjoyed themselves with an ease she longed for but doubted she'd ever attain.

As the meal proceeded without any other faux pas, Thea allowed herself to relax and joined the conversation. Claire kept her entertained with stories of Will as a boy. Soon, the handsome footman assigned to serve her placed a dessert plate filled with Shrewsbury cakes, fresh sliced strawberries, and orange cream. The whole dish was elegant and decadent at the same time.

Thea stole a peek at Claire who picked up the spoon at the top of the plate, leaving all the other silver untouched. Delicately, she took one bite of the pudding.

Thea mimicked her movements and scooped up a small spoonful of the orange cream. As heaven melted on her tongue, she fell head over heels in love with the dainty delicacy. It reminded her of blancmange only with a more sweet and citrusy flavor. She took one more bite and groaned. Her eyes flew wide open at the sound.

The duke winked at her. "Theodora, you suffer from the same affliction that I do."

"What's that?" she asked.

Claire leaned forward as if divulging a state secret. "He possesses a notorious sweet tooth."

The priceless twist in the duke's mouth revealed his contrariness. "Since you've married Pembrooke, you're such a telltale." The admonishment in the duke's voice was muted by his affection for his niece. "I'll sneak another serving, and Theodora will share in the conspiracy. Connoisseurs of sweets must band together when under attack."

Thea giggled and Claire joined her. The marchioness's laughter echoed like the merriest of bells ringing through the room.

For the first time that evening, she felt truly as if she belonged.

Thea finished her last bite of cream and instantly wanted more of the light but decadent dish. It had been years since she'd ever had anything so fluffy and unique in taste. She glanced behind her and discovered the footman who waited on her had disappeared.

As the other footmen collected the dirty plates, Thea rose and took her plate to the buffet table where a bowl of the delicious cream rested. A huge mound of orange fluff loomed like a tower before her in a silver bowl, inviting her to take more. She spooned a dollop on her plate.

The liveried footman assigned to her approached and cleared his throat. "I apologize, my lady, but I had to remove the plates. If you'll sit, I'll see you have another serving."

The gentle clatter of the footmen collecting plates disappeared entirely. Slowly, the lively conversations around the table stopped. Only deadly quiet, the kind that foretold disaster smothered the room and eerily surrounded her. She kept her gaze fixed on the footman. Thankfully, he was tall enough that he hid her from sight. She prayed no one saw her, but the sudden heat on her neck gave her ample warning. Indeed, they all—the duke and duchess and their family along with the servants—had to be staring at her.

"I . . . I thought it easier if I served myself." She cringed at the defensiveness in her tone.

"I'm . . . not really certain what to do, my lady." The footman's gaze darted to the butler Pitts as if seeking direction.

Perhaps if she looked at Pitts, he might direct her how to get out this predicament too.

What was she doing?

Her stomach knotted at the thought that the Langham servants would spread rumors she was wild and uncouth. What if *The Midnight Cryer* printed what had happened here, and the committee read it? Every lesson she'd learned from Stella had disappeared the instant she set foot in the city.

She glimpsed several other footmen standing awkwardly by with dirty plates in their hands.

How could she have been so stupid to get up from the table for another serving of dessert? That's why everyone had a footman standing behind them. Ducal families and their guests didn't serve themselves food.

If she couldn't master the simple rules of dining with a family who welcomed her with open arms, then how in God's name could she manage a committee of white-wigged men who would decide her future and more importantly, the future of Ladykyrk?

If a meteor fell from the sky that second and swallowed her whole, she'd declare it a simple mercy.

From nowhere, a man's hand gently took the plate from her hand. He placed it on the buffet, then gently tried to pry the spoon from her hand.

"Theodora, let go," he whispered.

At the sound of Will's voice, the vise clenching her chest broke free, and she could breathe again. Instantly, she released the spoon, then fisted her trembling hand to hide her humiliation.

He turned slightly until he faced the footmen before her. "There's nothing to be concerned about." His deep voice echoed around the room. "We're perfectly capable of serving ourselves." He lifted an eyebrow as if he considered the matter closed to discussion. "We have two feet."

Stella turned in her chair and nodded. "And two arms."

"Plus, two hands," Edith added.

By now, Will's attention had returned to her. "It's all right." His comforting tone did little to tide her embarrassment.

It was anything but all right. She'd made a fool out of herself, and she had no escape except to turn around and face everyone. Finally, she stood a little straighter and tilted her chin. There was little else she could do but make a quick exit, then nurse her self-inflicted wounds by herself.

"Thea, come sit," Stella coaxed. "One of the footmen will bring you another serving."

She slowly turned to face the entire room. It was worse than she expected. The footmen stared at her with wide eyes like she was some hideous creature rising from a dark Scottish loch.

"I find I'm not hungry anymore. Please pardon my lack of decorum. I should have known better." She focused on a Greek statute of Hermes in the corner of the room. Without making eye contact with any of the family or Will, she dipped a slight curtsey. "Thank you for your hospitality. If you'll excuse me?"

Thea didn't wait for a response. As if Hermes had lent her his winged feet, she ran from the room with a speed she'd never possessed in her life.

Will's teasing of his sister, Emma, died to nothing when the room quieted, and everyone's attention turned to Theodora helping herself at the buffet. The footmen were the first to notice, since it was their job to help the Langham guests with anything their heart desired. It was his mother's edict, and the footmen followed it without question. Slowly, like a wave rolling toward the shore, the family, one by one, noticed the footmen staring, then turned their attention to Thea.

When her cheeks grew redder, everything within Will locked in place, and he couldn't move. He could only stare as her humiliation became apparent to everyone. Finally, whatever force held him broke, and his heart pounded for him to save her. His family might not know of her penchant to blush when she was embarrassed, but he was well aware of it. At that moment, her entire body seemed to be radiating a scorching heat from her mortification. This was exactly what she hadn't wanted to happen.

Will stood, and his mother briefly grabbed his hand. The empathy in her eyes encouraged him to hurry to Theodora's side. When Thea ran from the room, Will didn't take his leave from the others. He simply followed.

She had such a speed in her step that he had a hard time catching her. Thankfully, Pitts stood guard at the dining room entrance leading to the massive hallway of the main floor.

When Will reach his side, the gentle butler pointed down the hallway. "The library."

In seconds, he stood next to the bird's-eye maple table that commanded the middle of the room. "Thea?"

Only silence greeted him. As his gaze swept the room, Will found her escape. The floor-to-ceiling French doors to Langham Park, the extensive garden and acreage attached to Langham Hall, stood open. He quickly crossed the room and stood outside on the stone balcony overlooking the park.

Creatures serenaded one another in a cacophony of buzzes and chirps, while the sweet songs of male nightingales filled the night with notes designed to seduce their mates. But through the noise, he heard another sound that didn't belong.

"Bloody hell." The words tripped over a voice husky from tears. A hiccupping sob followed a sniffle. "What a fool and an oaf."

He'd found her. Relieved, he inhaled then let out the deep breath slowly. Like a thief, he silently but swiftly descended the marble stairs and turned right where a recessed alcove lay partially hidden from view. He stood at the entrance. "Thea?"

Hidden in the shadows, she leaned against the wall with her arms wrapped around her waist. The defensive gesture broke his reserve, and he stepped forward. As if coming out of a trance, her gaze flew to his, and she stepped away from the wall.

"I take exception to the words *fool* and *oaf* to describe my friend. I'll have you know her character is sterling, and she's of the highest caliber in society." He closed the distance between them but didn't touch her. Not in her current mood, though his arms itched to hold her and soothe away the pain.

"Go away," she said.

"No, thank you. I don't like to see you upset. Let me stay here in your company?"

"You obstinate man," she murmured as she gently shook her head.

"Perhaps I'm more of an *assiduous man*. I prefer persistent rather than obstinate man."

"Have it your way," she said. A full moon cast a glow around her that caused her hair to shimmer as if strands of fine gold had been woven through her locks. The remnants of tears on her skin glistened in the moonlight.

"Then I can stay?" he asked softly.

Without looking at him, she nodded.

"Let me tell you a story, one that doesn't paint me in a good light." He took a step closer. "When I was eight years old, I was roundly chastised for eating the icing off a strawberry torte the pastry chef had made for an important dinner my father and mother were hosting for the Prince of Wales."

Theodora's eyes widened. "The Prince Regent?"

Will nodded. "I'd never seen my mother so angry with me. But do you know what caused my utter embarrassment?"

She shook her head.

"My parents made me apologize to the chef in front of the whole kitchen staff. My parents' disappointment in me was nothing compared to the distress I saw in the chef's eyes. He'd always been kind to me and had special treats for me and my siblings." Will bent and studied his boots. This story still caused him to feel uneasy. "He'd worked on the torte for two days, and in a matter of ten minutes, I'd ruined all his efforts."

"You were eight, and I'm an adult," she said, then turned and looked out toward the park. The moon's glow kissed her profile, making her skin radiant. She tilted her chin defiantly, but her hands clenched into fists betrayed the shame that still haunted her.

The urge to take her in his arms didn't diminish, but he shouldn't—no, couldn't act upon it. She was not destined for him, and they'd both be happier for it. His duty as a Cavensham was to make certain that she felt welcome. That was all this conversation meant between them. "Thea," he said kindly. "I daresay that I had more etiquette lessons by the time I was eight than you've had your entire life."

At that, she whirled around with the skirt of her gown trailing behind. "I'm well aware of my lack of education of all the things expected of someone in my position."

"Theodora, stop." To hell with not touching her. She misunderstood what he was trying to impart. He closed the distance between them and placed his hands on her upper arms. Her gaze flew to his. "That's not at all what I'm saying. I should have known better. But my actions hurt someone in my parents' employ. It felt like a hundred needles pricking me when I had to apologize to the chef. That apology cost me more than any I had to give my parents."

"Why are you telling me this?" she whispered. Trails of tears stained her cheeks.

Without any thought to his actions, Will ran the back of his forefinger down one wet cheek. Her softness was a beacon to him, and he trailed it down her cheek once more, wiping away the remnants of tears.

"Because I saw your face in the dining room when you looked at the footmen. You were mortified. I knew what you felt in that moment as I'd experienced it before."

She leaned against him, and his arms automatically encircled her lithe body. Gently, he ran his lips over the top of her head. That mystical red hair tickled his skin, and she smelled of sunshine and pureness. He took a deep breath and held her scent as long as he could.

"Your parents were everything lovely, and your entire family was welcoming. They're all elegant and handsome, and I'm a bumpkin. The title of countess doesn't hide my flaws, and I'm powerless to change them with the short time I have left before I appear in front of the committee." Her hands rested against his chest, and she burrowed her forehead against him. "What am I going to do? How will I ever manage to make my claim believable in front of that committee when I can't even manage a friendly dinner?"

"You'll be yourself. Everyone will recognize your strength as you tell them who you are and where you come from. You are the Countess of Eanruig. Never forget that."

She didn't lift her head and talked into his chest. Her words seemed to vibrate within him.

"What mortified me more than anything is that I . . . I embarrassed you."

"No, you didn't." He continued to rub his lips across her hair, soothing her. Her breathing calmed, and eventually, she relaxed in his arms.

"Even before Stella announced our *friendship*, I wanted to be perfect for you and your family. Wasn't that the definition of a friend, someone who values what you value?" She lifted her head and studied him. "I want your family to like me because I know they mean the world to you."

His chest tightened at the sentiment. He'd had people in his life who claimed to be a friend, but they didn't have any idea what was important to him—and frankly, didn't care. She understood how much he loved his family. And she wanted them to like her because of him.

"You're perfect the way you are." Will's voice turned

guttural, but he studied her. This moment he'd remember for the rest of his life. She truly was special and didn't deserve to be tortured by Ferr-Colby. He gently pulled away and took her hand in his. "Come, I'll escort you back to your room. You have a big day tomorrow. I understand that Aunt Stella and my mother planned an afternoon of shopping."

She heaved a sigh. "Wonderful. Another opportunity to show how inept I am."

"Another opportunity to show how magnificent you are." He raised her gloveless hand to his lips. Reluctantly, he released it.

"I truly appreciate your concern and attention." She straightened to her full height and squared her shoulders like she was ready to face the enemy in an epic battle.

That was Thea's true essence—kind and lovely with a hint of diffidence that was replacing her earlier Northumberland brashness.

She sighed gently.

"Come, Thea." He held his hand out for her. She studied it as if debating whether to return inside or not. Finally, she made a decision. With a nod, she gently slipped her small hand into his. Without their gloves, the touch of skin to skin was as intimate as a kiss. He entwined their fingers together, not wanting to let her go.

Thankfully, they didn't meet one of the family or any servants as Will escorted Thea to her room. It was as if everyone realized he needed to find her and comfort her in privacy. After he wished her a good night, he proceeded downstairs for a brandy.

He deserved one.

Pitts waited for him at the bottom of the steps. "Sir, the duke and duchess would like a word before you retire."

God only knew what the summons meant. No doubt,

they wanted to find out more about his *friendship* with Thea.

He only hoped they weren't helping Aunt Stella with her plans and setting a wedding date.

It was all a wasted effort, but no one would listen to him.

Nancy had Thea's bed turned back and her nightgown laid out when she entered her room. Without waiting for the maid to return, Thea undressed herself, then unpinned her hair from tonight's elegant styling.

As she ran the brush through her locks, she couldn't help but think of the happenings of the evening. She was still mortified, but with Will's kind and considerate words, perhaps it wasn't as bad as she'd thought.

Tomorrow she'd start dancing lessons, and she prayed they'd be easier than dinner. She glanced in the mirror on top of the dressing table where something caught the reflection of the candlelight in her room. Sitting on a side table, the glint of a silver dome covering a serving tray caught her attention. She went to investigate and found a note beside the tray.

> *Dear Theodora,*
>   *I decided to have another serving myself and thought you'd like one too. I personally prepared it for you. I hope it brings as much enjoyment as the first serving we shared.*
>   *Just remember, those of us who enjoy the sweet things in life and deserve such goodness must follow our instincts when it comes to securing our heart's desires, particularly orange cream.*
>
>   *Langham*

Thea already suspected what was under the silver dome, and when she lifted it, her thoughts were confirmed. A beautiful serving of orange cream sat in the middle of the tray with an orange slice and a perfect green mint leaf decorating the plate. The first bite was as delicious as her earlier one, and she had the duke to thank for the kind gesture. On her last bite, she licked the spoon clean, and reread the short note.

She completed her ablutions and cleaned her teeth with tooth powder.

When she finally settled into bed, the truth couldn't be denied. The Langham family had completely charmed her.

But their son, William, might have just stolen her heart tonight.

*We're simply giddy with the news. The Northumberland
Nemesis has moved into Langham Hall where we have an
intrepid reporter assigned outside the premises.
We dare think we'll soon have double the content to report.
Neither Lady Man-Eater nor the Damp Squib can seem to
stay out of our papers.
Humbly reporting from Mayfair,*
The Midnight Cryer

Chapter Ten

"Will, come in. I've got a brandy poured for you, or would you prefer whisky?" Will's father asked.

"Brandy," Will answered.

His father walked back to the sitting area of his study and placed three glasses on the table. He gave one to Will's mother, then settled in beside her on one of the two blue velvet sofas that faced each other. Will sat in the one opposite his parents.

"Your mother and I are delighted with Theodora." His father nudged a copy of the latest copy of *Debrett's Peerage* across the table for Will's attention. "She comes from good stock. I met her grandfather several times, and he was always on the right side of decisions in the House of Lords. Of course, he never came to London in recent years because of his age. The challenge for her title is all Parliament can talk about."

"The Duke of Ferr-Colby should be strung up by his heels," Will practically growled.

"Son, I agree with you." His father shook his head as he studied his glass. "Back when my father was alive, another Scottish countess had a similar problem claiming her title."

"What happened?" Will asked.

"She defeated the challengers." His father's gaze caught his. "However, she was only a year old, but she had powerful peers as her guardians who took up her challenge."

Will nodded in acknowledgment. "That's what Thea needs."

In so many ways, it felt right to be at home with Thea where his family welcomed her with open arms. Their love and comfort were constant, and truthfully, when he was surrounded by them, he felt renewed with an energy he couldn't deny. Thea would feel the same way once she became more comfortable.

"How did you meet her?" His mother took a sip of whisky. The flash in her eyes did little to hide the wheels that were gaining speed in her thoughts.

"I called on her at Ladykyrk. It was all Aunt Stella's idea." He took a sip too, for fortitude. "She wants me to marry Thea and help her. In that order, I might add. Thea hasn't had, how shall I say this, an easy time since her grandfather's death. The duke's old solicitor works for the ducal estate and won't help Thea secure her title and dignities. But he told her she should marry before the committee hearing or at least, become betrothed."

His father leaned forward and rested both elbows on his knees, a signal that his attention was completely devoted to Will and his story.

"Plus, Aunt Stella has the idea that if we marry, the two estates will be joined. She's pushing hard for this marriage and told me that she'd disinherit me if I didn't marry Theodora. When I didn't say a word, she must

have felt guilty. Immediately, she changed the subject."
But he'd still remembered the lecture that she didn't want
him to end up alone.

Neither did he. But somehow, he had to escape this inability to move forward with his life. Sometimes it felt
as if he were stuck waist deep in a muddy bog.

"I see." His father leaned back and put his arm around
Will's mother. A sign that whatever decision happened
this evening, they'd be a united force, one that Will
would find hard to buck against. "I'm generally not in
favor of Stella manipulating my children and their
futures, but she's looking out for your interests. If you
marry Theodora, you'll enlarge the estates by combining them. It'll give you more political clout as you'll be
her representative in all legal matters. Frankly, I think
it's brilliant."

His mother turned into the embrace, and a smile
tugged at her lips. "Aunt Stella does have a way of bringing couples together."

His father kissed Will's mother on the forehead.
"Ginny, I had the hardest time convincing you to marry
me. Without Stella's help, I'd probably still be a lovelorn
calf. That's why she's my favorite aunt, even if she did
paint that portrait."

"She wants to paint one of me for Theodora," Will
added. Both of his parents shot their gaze to his.

Oh God, why did he share that?

"Really?" His father started to play with one of his
mother's loose curls. "That's serious, son. Not many
women can resist a Cavensham man's portrait by Stella."

His mother laughed.

His father joined in his mother's mirth.

Will didn't join in their merriment. He should share
that Thea didn't want to marry him, but he felt uneasy—
almost prickly—and didn't trust himself not to reveal too

much. It was difficult to admit that another woman didn't want him.

His mother grew serious and took his father's hand with hers. "I feel terrible. Pitts and I were training several new footmen. I thought that it would be a perfect opportunity since it was just family. If there were any mistakes, no one would mind. I never thought it would turn out to be such a torturous event for Thea. We should have told you before dinner."

"Where did you find her after she left the dining room?" his father asked softly.

"She ran into Langham Park and found refuge in one of the alcoves next to the house." Remembering how wounded she was that a simple dinner had caused her so much pain, Will clenched his teeth. When his jaw protested, he forced himself to relax. "I should have sat by her. I think I managed to take most of the sting out of it, but I'm not really certain. But she possesses more problems than just a minor slip of etiquette rules, like the Duke of Ferr-Colby."

"What do you know about his challenge to her title?" His father pulled Will's mother closer into his arms.

Will exhaled. "Probably as little as you. Ferr-Colby claims he's the legitimate heir to the Earldom of Eanruig. Theodora just came out of mourning for her grandfather and hasn't done much to proceed with her claim to the title. I was hoping you might inquire on her behalf with some of the committee members the House of Lords has assembled. They've asked her to make an appearance. Thea retained Mr. Odell as her counsel. He'll appear in front of the committee with her." Will leaned forward and lowered his voice. "No one can find the charter."

His father's eyes widened. "That's serious, but Odell is the best at this sort of legal challenge. Anything I can do on her behalf, consider it done."

Will nodded his thanks. "Mother, could you help her also? Perhaps make her way into society a little easier. She's been . . . well, there's no other way to describe it. She's been isolated at Ladykyrk for years. She'll have a rough go if we don't smooth the way for her."

"Of course, William." His mother smiled, but the twinkle in her eyes was the real answer. She'd relish introducing Theodora into the *ton*. "We'll have a small gathering to introduce her to important members of society."

"That's perfect, Ginny." The lighthearted grin on his father's face melted into genuine concern. "Will, let's get back to Stella's announcement. Is there any affection between you and Thea?"

"We're simply friends." Will held his father's gaze, determined not to reveal anything else.

"I half think she's in love with you already," his father murmured.

His mother's eyes softened.

"I think you're confusing gratitude and friendship with love, Father." Will shook his head gently. "She doesn't have anyone except Stella, Lady Edith . . . and me. Her grandfather had been ill for seven or eight years. I believe he suffered from senility. Theodora took the responsibility to care for him, with the result that she's been locked away in the remote outreaches of Northumberland with no one. *The Midnight Cryer* has taken advantage by spreading vicious rumors about her. You both have taught me not to allow that to happen to anyone, whether I have an interest in them or not."

"Yes," his mother agreed hesitantly.

"I offered to arrange a dance instructor, plus Stella and Edith are helping with etiquette lessons. I want to introduce her to people in society so that when she interviews in front of the committee, she'll be ready. But that is all."

"I hate to think that poor young woman has been alone all this time. By the sound of it, I'd say you're invested in her." The lift of his mother's eyebrow was a warning shot across the bow.

He could already tell his mother had grown attached to Thea.

"Do not break her heart," his mother said gently.

"Of course, I won't break her heart. What Thea and I share is friendship, and I would never hurt a friend."

The duke leaned back against the sofa. "I'll do what I can to help her, but you can't walk away. Even if she secures her title and all that goes along with the entailment, she'll need your support more than ever. The gossip will overtake London. She'll either be the darling of society if she wins or a social pariah if she loses. She'll be ripe to be taken advantage of."

"Your father has the right of it." Hardness, like well-forged steel, laced his mother's normally sweet voice. "It would be akin to you forsaking her, and if she's emotionally invested in you, she'll be wounded."

"Mother, she doesn't want to marry me."

There. He said it.

He took a deep breath, then exhaled silently. The simple statement should inform his parents of Thea's true regard for him.

"Perhaps not." His mother's gaze grew tender. "Just protect her. The *ton* loves to feast on stories like Thea's for weeks or even longer. Look how all those broken engagements damaged your cousin."

"I plan to protect Thea." Will ran his hands through his hair. He'd do his damnedest to protect her from the *Cryer*. What they'd done to Claire was a travesty.

He and Claire were as close as siblings. When she suffered through four broken engagements, Will had wanted to fight the injustice of every rumor about his darling cousin, but there were so many lies being told about her. *The Midnight Cryer* had called her cursed. Then Pembrooke had swept in and rescued her from total devastation in front of the *ton* at a ball. Will had been livid at the rogue, but when Claire fell in love with him, the entire family accepted their union. Now, they were the proud parents of three children.

In his growing years, Will had always thought that same path would be his future, a wife to love and children to spoil and raise. But love wasn't for everyone.

Him especially.

But now, that old urge for more in his life stirred like a bear waking from its winter nap.

"Will?" His mother took his father's hand and entwined their fingers together. "Have you thought about marriage? Your father and I don't want you to be alone. We have little doubt you'd give your heart to a wife and family. You'll be wonderful with your own children. The way you dote on Emma's and Claire's children—"

"Mother, I don't need to marry to enjoy children. As is evidenced by my regard for all my nieces and nephews. Besides, I'm too busy with my work for a courtship now," he added.

His mother's eyebrow shot straight up in challenge. "If you don't have children, then who will inherit your estate if Aunt Stella leaves it to you?"

"Liam."

"Pembrooke and Claire's youngest?" his father asked incredulously. His tone hinted that Will had lost his mind. "Liam will probably receive Claire's Lockhart estate in Edinburgh. Wouldn't you want your own son or daughter to share what you and Thea build together?"

The room turned suddenly silent. Will stared at his father.

"Pardon me." His father's cheeks turned scarlet, a

sight so rare that Will couldn't recall ever seeing it before. "I meant your future wife."

Will leaned forward and rested his elbows on his knees and regarded both of his parents. He had to make them understand without eviscerating himself in the process. "All I'm doing is escorting her to society gatherings and other functions. Thea wants to meet my friends, and I'm inviting over a few. She may have to marry to appease the committee. I pray that it won't come to that." He released a silent sigh. "If she's forced into it, then hopefully, she'd be happy with one of my friends."

Both his parents regarded him as if he'd grown a horn in the middle of his face.

"You'd best be careful, son," his father said slowly. "I'd hate to see either of you hurt."

He dismissed them both with a wave of his hand, then took a sip of his brandy. "Thea and I are in agreement. I'm simply helping her prepare for her fight against Ferr-Colby. If she's not careful, he'll have her wrapped up in court for years, and I want to make sure her future is settled. That's the only reason I'm invested in her."

His father took a drink of brandy. He discreetly smiled at his duchess before turning his attention back to him. "I think you have a lot more interest in Thea than you're admitting. More than what you're allowing yourself to believe. My advice? Just don't do anything rash."

"Indeed, I agree with your father," his mother said. "This is too important for you to just casually dismiss. People marry for the combination of estates, fortunes, and political power all the time. You may have received the greatest gift you'll ever receive."

"What is that?" he drawled.

"A woman who wants you for you." His mother's soft lilt filled the room. "Not for your money, not for prestige, and not for power."

"Mother, she doesn't want me. What else can I say to make you see the truth?" He stood to exit. "I think I'll retire. I must start on the McCalpin Manor estate journals tomorrow."

His father nodded once. "Son, while you're home, I'd like your advice on the finances we'd need for a new expansion at Falmont. Would you have time tomorrow?"

"Of course," Will answered.

After he said good night, he made his way to his bedchamber. With each step a yearning, a want to fill the emptiness that had steadily grown through the years, took root. What if he wanted to marry sooner rather than later?

What if he wanted to marry Thea?

If he did want Thea, what could he do to make himself her first choice instead of last?

He *humphed* to himself at such a ridiculous thought. He was much too busy for marriage. He didn't want a wife, and Thea didn't want him.

His gut twisted whenever he remembered her words that she'd choose him if she couldn't find anyone else. Rationally, he was well aware that Thea didn't mean it as an insult. In her stalwart way, she'd told him what she wanted out of life. She didn't want to marry either but would do so in order to save Ladykyrk.

If only he knew what he wanted. It would be so much easier on both of them.

The Damp Squib has turned into a ~~Lame Horse~~ Dance
Master. Rumor has it that Lady Man-Eater can't dance a
lick and repeatedly steps on Lord William's toes.
Is anyone certain she's of noble blood?
Humbly reporting from Mayfair,
The Midnight Cryer

Chapter Eleven

The next morning, Thea had received a summons
from Stella which meant another deportment lesson.
Nancy had helped her dress in a simple but elegant yellow morning gown made of satin that tied in the back.
The gown gave her confidence which she sorely needed
today. After her etiquette lessons, she was scheduled for
her dance lesson with an instructor who came highly recommended.

Within minutes, Thea entered the blue salon where
she found Stella and Lady Edith chatting away.

"Come in, Thea. We've been waiting for you." Stella
absently stroked Lord Fluff who was curled beside her.

Lady Edith rested in the sofa directly opposite Stella
and patted the seat next to her. "Sit by me."

Once Thea settled, her hostess poured the tea and
served the most exquisite biscuits, seedcakes, and fairy
cakes with butter frosting. Thea took a bite of a delicate
fairy cake, and it melted in her mouth.

"Theodora, how is your preparation coming for the
hearing?" Stella asked.

Thea shrugged, then smoothed her hands down her dress. "I have the family history memorized, along with all the papers of marital and birth records I could find. But I'd feel much more confident of my chances if I had the charter in my possession. It would prove my right to the title without a doubt."

"It'll be nice to have all this ugly nonsense settled." Edith patted her hand.

Stella scooted to the edge of her seat. "Have you given any more thought to marrying?" she asked softly.

"I don't want to be forced to marry," she answered. "Honestly, Stella, I shouldn't have to, and Will shouldn't have to be the sacrificial goat."

Edith wrinkled her brow. "I wouldn't call it a sacrifice, nor would I call him a goat."

Stella nodded in agreement. "I don't think either of you should consider it as such"—she tapped her finger against her lip as if deep in thought—"but perhaps you could think of Will as more than a friend." She nodded decisively. "Yes, that's it. A best friend."

A warmth settled over Thea as her cheeks heated. She'd never had a friend close to her own age before Will. Suddenly, memories of last night took control of her thoughts. Will had been the definition of a staunch and loyal friend who treated her with respect and kindness. When he'd held her in his arms, it'd been heaven.

"He is my best friend," Thea admitted.

"Excellent, my dear," Lady Edith said with a knowing smile. "Shall we review precedence again?"

Stella gently set her cup and saucer on the table in front of her, then regarded Thea with a look reminiscent of an army general lecturing the troops. "If you're standing with a marchioness and another countess preparing to enter the dining room for a formal dinner, who of the three of you enters first?"

Thea took another sip of tea before she answered. These things were always tricky. Such a question appeared simple, but nothing was as it seemed when it came to the rules of the peerage and their love of standing with another. "Since the marchioness stands in place of her husband, meaning she's higher in rank than an earl or in my case, countess, she goes first."

This was where everything became a muddle. What to do with two countesses, one a peer in her own right and the other married to a peer of equal rank? It was this minutia of detail that drove her batty. Really, who cared? They would all eat at the same time with the same food at the same table.

With no earthly idea the correct answer, she put forth her best guess. "It would depend upon the ladies' ages. Whoever was oldest would proceed first." Whether that principle applied or not, Thea believed it should. No matter what rank, if Stella and Edith waited with her to enter dinner, she'd allow the two elderly ladies to enter first. It was good manners in her opinion.

Stella shook her head. "No, Thea. The order of precedence between the two countesses will be based upon the year the title was created and where. English peerages created before 1707 precede peerages of Scotland created by 1707 like yours." She nodded decisively like a strict governess. "Those peerages precede the peerages of Great Britain created between 1707 and 1801. Then we have the ones from Ireland and their dates of creation. Are you following, dear?"

Swimming with titles and dates that she'd never master, Thea shook her head.

"It's all right, darling." Edith patted her hand. "But you should try to learn all the earldoms and when and where they were created. That will help."

"You're right." Though she wanted to roll her eyes

at the monotony of it all, she sat without further comment. How lovely for her—more inane information that she'd never use after she returned home—if she returned home.

She promised herself no negative thoughts today, and she would keep that pledge.

"Let's go to another topic. Fan lessons." Stella picked up three fans for each of them.

As Edith and Stella swooped and fluttered their mother of pearl confections, Thea sighed. At their last lesson, they'd tried to teach her how to have a conversation with a man while holding her fan.

She bit back a laugh.

It was the definition of silliness. If she wanted to talk to a man, she'd just walk up to him and start a conversation. She didn't need to twirl a whimsical piece of lace to talk to someone.

But the expectant looks on the two grand dames' faces were alight with glee. They cooed and twitted about while pretending they were at some ball flirting with their mysterious beaus. They were charming, and Thea wouldn't hurt their feelings or their pride by saying it was a waste of her time. But she couldn't go through another lesson in nonsensical frivolity.

"Perhaps there's something else you could teach me today? There's so much I have to learn, and we've already covered the fan basics."

"Excellent idea, Thea." Stella beamed while still managing a flutter or two of her fan.

"I thought you could teach me about gossip and *The Midnight Cryer*. I should be prepared if anyone asks about my grandfather." In no way would she allow anyone to slander her grandfather or for that matter, her.

"The best advice is to deny everything." Stella defiantly lifted her chin in the air. "That's what I've told William, and the same applies for you."

Edith waved her hand, and the light from the wall of windows on the south side of the room illuminated the jewels around her wrist, creating little rainbow prisms that danced around the room. "Have you heard about William?"

"I'm afraid not," Thea said softly.

"When he was a young man, he thought himself in love and ready for marriage. He proposed to a girl, a third cousin named Lady Avalon Cavensham," Edith said innocently. "She accepted."

Stella shot a look of censure at her friend.

In response, Edith lifted an eyebrow. "If Theodora is to have half a chance with how to navigate the *ton*, she needs to know what her *best friend* William experienced. She needs to know *everything*."

Stella nodded her reluctant agreement, then took a sip of tea. "I need a little fortitude to tell his story." She sighed deeply. "She jilted my William in front of her father. Practically destroyed my boy. Because of his jilting, *The Midnight Cryer* rubs salt in the wound by calling William a 'damp squib.' He's tried to ignore it, but it hurt him deeply. He's been wary of the *ton* ever since. I'd even say he's skeptical of love."

"Cynical is a better word for it," said Edith. "His suspicion practically caused a rift between him and his brother when McCalpin fell in love with a woman who was embezzling from him."

"With a woman who McCalpin *thought* was embezzling. Edith, are you going to air every stitch of dirty laundry the family possesses?" Stella challenged.

"It's not dirty laundry if there's a happy ending." Edith turned to Thea. "Once William realized he'd judged

March unfairly, he was the first to make amends. Now, he and the marchioness are the greatest of friends and even work together on the Langham duchy's estate books. He's really very talented with numbers and such. A great catch in my opinion." She took a sip of tea. "Of course, his handsome visage and perfect physique don't hurt the eyes."

For the first time this afternoon, an affectionate smile graced Stella's face and reached all the way to her eyes. "Thank you, Edith. He comes from good stock. You couldn't find a better family to marry into, Theodora."

Thea raised her hand to get a word in edgewise. "Lord William and I have no interest in marriage. I'll only marry if I have to."

She'd not give up the hope she'd fall in love and marry when she wanted to—not when some committee of men dictated she should.

"Thea?" Edith gently asked. "Perhaps, maybe"—she pinched two fingers together—"you're a smidge interested in our William?"

By now, both elderly women were leaning forward in their seats, enough that it appeared they would fall while waiting for her answer. Even Lord Fluff had forgone his meticulous ablutions to give Thea his undivided attention.

"No, you misunderstand. I told him I didn't want to marry." Thea couldn't sit any longer. She stood and started to pace. "I'm hopeless at all this."

Stella rose and joined her, then took her hands in hers. "Oh my lovely girl, you are a jewel, a very precious one at that. You just need a little polish, and your brilliance will be blinding. It's far from hopeless."

Edith tapped her index finger against her cheek. "Besides, it's just a matter of time before you catch him."

"I don't understand." Thea had a hard time following the grand dame's jump in logic.

Stella tugged Thea back to the sofa. "It's simple, dearest. If you feign disinterest, then Will might become interested in you. Cavensham men always like to think they're in control." Stella patted her hand again.

"Such smart thinking on your part, Thea. I wager he'll soon be smitten," Edith declared.

"Oh, how clever, Edith," Stella said. "You're correct as usual, my dear."

Edith regally tilted her head acknowledging the praise.

"I don't want to be rude, but you're both wrong. He's not smitten." Thea leaned back in disbelief at what they were saying. "He doesn't want to marry me, and I don't want to marry him."

"Don't make any hasty decisions." Stella squeezed Thea's hand. "Let me explain something. You can lead a horse to water. The horse being William."

"Though you can't make him drink, you can encourage him," Edith added helpfully.

"By adding treacle to the water," Stella said.

"Pieces of apple would work as well," said Edith. "Or both."

"Could someone explain?" Thea asked softly.

Stella turned to her. "Your new wardrobe is the treacle or apple pieces. You, my dear, are the bucket of water."

Thea did indeed feel underwater, drowning in confusion.

"He's seeing you in his native environment. It's something he's familiar with. I'm afraid all that Northumberland fresh air rattled his senses," Stella added. "Just wait until he sees you in the new dresses from the Duchess of Langham's personal dress designer."

"Mademoiselle Mignon." Edith sighed. "Perfection. You'll be the toast of London." Her wrinkled brow crinkled even more.

Thea's heart beat a little faster as if approving of this entire conversation. Could she be falling a little in love with Will? He was incredibly kind, and when he was in the room, she couldn't seem to take her eyes off him. Never had she felt so interested in another before. When she saw him, everything inside of her seemed to soften into a pool of want for him.

The longcase clock chimed the hour.

"Finish your tea, dearest. It'll soon be time for your dance lesson," Stella said.

"Thank you both for everything, including these lessons." Thea smiled as both ladies beamed at her. "I can't believe you've gone to this much effort on my behalf."

"It's no trouble. In fact, it's our hobby," Edith said with pride. "It's like treasure hunting. We've even thought of starting a business."

"Teaching etiquette lessons?" Thea asked.

"No," Stella answered. "Matchmaking services for peers who have no clue how to find an appropriate spouse. We like to look at estates and fortunes or lack thereof, then we think of couples who would suit. It may seem a little old-fashioned, but this has always been a popular avenue to bring couples together. In certain situations, it's the best way. Both Edith and I believe that with our superior matchmaking capabilities, love will follow."

"You're our first project," Stella offered. A hint of pride with a healthy dose of affection colored her words.

Thea slowly shook her head. The two ladies in front of her were unruly and everything delightful at the same time.

Without giving a glance in Thea's direction, the

women started a lively discussion of the best colors to highlight Thea's coloring and what materials and trims would be best for her new wardrobe.

Thea's thoughts returned to Will. He'd been unceasingly loyal to her ever since he first met her. He understood her views on marriage and would keep her from becoming involved with the wrong men. By what she heard this morning, Will needed friends just as much as she did, along with his confidence bolstered too.

She would be the best friend he'd ever had.

The only challenge?

What if she wanted to be more than best friends?

The Langham Hall library had always been one of Will's favorite rooms in the house. Airy and bright, it lent itself to many an afternoon and evening of pleasurable reading. Today, it was a room of torture. Will ran a hand down his face in a desperate attempt to clear the running rampage of numbers from Falmont's account books that danced in front of his eyes.

A ruckus of heated words and hot tempers exploded in the hallway.

With quick steps, Will left the library to investigate. Two doors down, a major battle had erupted outside the smallest of the two Langham Hall ballrooms.

"I don't care how much you pay me." The dance master, Mr. Jeremy Pinabell, stood practically nose-to-nose with Aunt Stella. His hands were clenched into fists. "She cannot grasp the steps of the simplest dances. Every dance I try to teach her is a fiasco. My feet are perfectly ruined."

"My ears are *perfectly ruined* by the howls that erupted from your mouth," Aunt Stella scoffed. "I find it inconceivable you are deemed the most sought-after dance master in all of London. You can't even dance two steps without yelling at her. How in the world is she going to learn?"

Aunt Stella's scarlet turban sported twin ostrich plumes. With each nod of her head, they bobbled in tandem and poked at Pinabell's eyes. If Will knew his greataunt, the grand dame was deliberately taunting him.

The battle wasn't the only thing that grabbed Will's attention. Theodora stood several feet away from the feuding duo with her arms wrapped around her waist. He couldn't see her face, but if she suffered because of that bloody dance instructor, Will would personally rectify the situation by throwing the man out of the house.

As if privy to his thoughts, Aunt Stella announced in a crisp voice, "We don't need your services anymore." With a snap of her fingers, Pitts miraculously appeared. "Would you please do the honors, Pitts, and see Mr. Pigabell—"

"Pinabell, madam," the dance instructor corrected.

"As I was saying, Pigabell needs to be escorted out— the—door."

With a brisk nod, Pitts extended his arm. "After you, Mr. Pigabell."

With an outraged huff, Pinabell followed Pitts, leaving Will with Stella and Theodora.

Finally, Will had a clear view of Theodora, and the tension in his body didn't relax. She blew an errant curl from her face, then regarded him. Immediately, her gaze shifted to her feet. Though dressed as a fairy ready to cast a spell on all around her, she was a woman withdrawing from the world.

Suddenly, Aunt Stella whirled around in his direction. "That man was horrible."

Thea wrinkled her nose as if smelling something rotten. "I really don't see the need for dancing lessons."

"Nonsense, *Thea*." Stella shook her head in disapproval, the plumes sailing in the air like a flag on a clipper ship. "A countess must dance at least a waltz. Come, William. I'll play, and you dance with Theodora." Without waiting for a reply, his great-aunt returned to the ballroom.

Thea shrugged, then followed Stella.

Will exhaled. He had to think about the future and not about the piles of work that waited for him in the study. Dancing with Thea would instill a sense of poise and self-assuredness she'd need when introduced into society and when she appeared in front of the Committee for Privileges.

Plus, he'd have the honor of holding her in his arms again. Frankly, the idea of Thea possibly finding someone left a hole burning in his gut.

The cause had to be the restless sleep he'd suffered last night. Several times, he woke with swirling thoughts that demanded his immediate attention. He recalled his earlier conversation with his parents encouraging him to tread carefully with Thea and her grand plan to find someone to marry.

When he entered the ballroom, Aunt Stella sat at the pianoforte with Thea by her side. Thea's iridescent yellow gown, the color of a goldfinch's feathers, shimmered in the sunlight that shone through the windows surrounding the room. The rays converged at the exact spot where she stood as if vying for her attention.

Bloody hell, he was making himself sick with such silly thoughts. Best to get the dance lesson over with so he could return to work.

"Come, William, don't dawdle. Thea needs to be ready for Ginny and Sebastian's soirée. Lord Howton will attend and is in charge of the committee. He's low-hung fruit. She'll have him eating out of her hand within a half an hour, I predict." Aunt Stella placed one hand on the keyboard and waved the other at the empty dance floor. "The morning light won't last all day."

Will did as instructed. He extended his arms in a proper waltz form, and gracefully, Thea stepped into his arms and took his hand in hers. When his other hand settled on her waist, she released a heavy sigh.

"Am I that tiring?" he teased. The urge to draw her close grew acute.

"No." She straightened her shoulders and tilted her gaze to his. The round cut of the gown's neckline emphasized her neck and shoulders. Barely visible freckles danced across her skin. When his eyes met hers, the smile on her face punched him in the gut. He had to be careful around this woman. How could one look from her have the power to force him to his knees while vowing to dedicate all his days to her? He'd promise his fealty to her forever if she'd continue to smile at him that way—an expression that conjured all sorts of whimsical wishes to make her happy.

"Dancing instruction is a waste of time," she said.

"Remember?" He lowered his voice. "You promised I could teach you to dance. A friend doesn't renege on a promise."

She nodded curtly in response.

The music flooded the room, and he pressed his hand to hers signaling the start of the waltz. With a sure step, he took the lead. She matched his movement with one of innate grace, no doubt acquired from all those days riding her horse.

"Why are dance lessons a waste?" He kept his voice low so Aunt Stella couldn't hear. From the pianoforte, the grand dame nodded her approval as he made their steps more precise.

"I'll never dance in Northumberland."

Suddenly a vision of the folly appeared. Will held her close and swept her in a full waltz pattern as he hummed the music. Her eyes sparkled, and she laughed in pleasure.

"Will?" Thea tilted her head back and regarded him.

His musing evaporated like mist on a summer morning. "Pardon?"

"My dress," she whispered.

Bloody hell. He was practically disrobing her as his left hand had pulled the sleeve of her gown down, baring one of her perfect shoulders. Her skin appeared to glow with a silken softness. "Excuse me." The words felt thick in his throat as he straightened the sleeve. "I was holding you too tightly."

"No." A blush kissed her cheeks. "I liked it."

The softness in her mellifluous voice reminded him of honey. He'd always known she was attractive, but when had she become exquisite? He'd never held perfection in his arms before, and the urge to tighten his arms around her grew fierce.

Suddenly, she stumbled slightly.

"I've got you." He gently pulled her back into position. "Just think of moving with me like you do with your horse when she takes a jump. She moves, and you trust her completely. It's the same with me."

She lifted one brow. "You want me to compare you to my horse?"

The huskiness in her voice created an intimacy between them, a world where only the two of them resided. He studied her eyes, the mystical orbs that seemed to change color with her dress, sometimes her mood. Now they were a light green that reminded him of the start of spring. In response, he drew her closer. "Yes. You can ride me all day, and I'll not allow you to fall." He didn't hide the innuendo of seduction that colored his voice.

What was wrong with him? He wasn't supposed to be seducing her.

She wrinkled her nose in laughter, causing her freckles to become more prominent, then a wicked smile graced her lips. "What if you fall? Won't you bring me down with you?"

With a smile designed to match hers, he gently twirled her in an elegant circle. All sounds and sights disappeared from his notice. She relaxed in his arms, her stance more natural, as if the two of them were a couple who'd done this sequence of steps before.

"Imagine the journey down if we fell together while you were riding me. Wouldn't it be worth . . ." He cleared his throat.

For God's sake, they were friends.

What in *bloody hell* was he doing?

Whatever had he been thinking to tell her to imagine riding him? His cock had thickened at the thought of her astride him, riding them both to completion. He blinked fast, hoping to clear the image of all her glorious hair covering her beautiful breasts flowing down her back as they rolled their hips in tandem. It did nothing to tamp down the hunger that flooded every inch of him.

"I finished the piece several moments ago," Aunt Stella announced, not hiding the glee in her voice. "Since you both have continued the dance, you must be enjoying yourselves. Shall I play it again?"

"Shall we?" There was an invitation in Thea's eyes that challenged him. For a few brief moments, he waited as he wrestled with what he wanted. He couldn't deny he wanted nothing more than to sweep her away and kiss her until they both shut out the world in each other's arms.

Then like a cloud of smoke, the desire in Thea's gaze disappeared.

"No, thank you, Stella. I have work to attend to."

He'd hesitated too long.

Will didn't want to let her go. His cock was still at half-mast. That was the problem with pantaloons and Thea. Every inch of him was exposed in a manner that showed her effect on him.

"Will, are you all right?" She kept her voice low, but that distant look as if he'd disappointed her still flickered in her eyes.

"I've much on my mind. Work never ends." *What a lame excuse.*

"Your family depends a great deal on you, don't they?" She studied him as if trying to divine the answer for his unusual behavior.

"Yes, they do, and I'm better for it. If you'll pardon me." After a quick bow to Theodora, Will turned on his heel and exited through the floor-to-ceiling French doors behind them.

At the moment, the most pressing work was learning how to keep his body under some semblance of control.

But a nagging doubt wouldn't leave him alone. Thea's effect on him wasn't lessening as he'd expected.

It was growing in strength.

Gentle readers, you can dress a badger in silks and jewels,
but it's still a ~~Man-Eater~~ badger.
Respectfully yours,
The Midnight Cryer

Chapter Twelve

❧

Thea didn't have much of an opportunity to consider Will's strange behavior after her waltz lesson. Immediately, Stella had collected her, Lady Edith, and the duchess for the shopping excursion that she'd promised Thea.

But Thea had a suspicion it was more for Stella and Lady Edith than it was for her.

The first and most important stop was the duchess's favorite seamstress, Mademoiselle Mignon's dress shop. As Lady Edith and Stella perused the endless rows of velvet, silk, crinoline, muslin, printed cottons, and the accompanying matching trims and accessories, the duchess helped Thea pick out a few dresses that were close to completion but had not been commissioned by anyone.

Besides two gowns, one evening and one day dress, a lovely but elegant riding habit in an iridescent peacock green caught Thea's attention. After discovering from Mademoiselle Mignon that it was available, Thea added it to the list of purchases along with a matching hat that mimicked a man's tall beaver hat, only this one was made of wool felt in a brilliant ruby red with several perfectly placed peacock feathers.

If there was one thing in this world that Thea had a weakness for, it was riding habits. If her grandfather were alive, he'd have insisted she purchase the beautiful garment. With a silent sigh, she let the thought slowly fade away. He wasn't here, and even if he was, the poor man would have been scared out of his mind with all the seamstresses who were busy attending the shop's customers. If he'd seen the yards and yards of material laid out before her, he'd have run in the opposite direction. Anything new and different had startled him.

"Theodora?" the duchess asked serenely.

The duchess's blue eyes were as crystal clear as the lake outside her study window at Ladykyrk, and the smile on her face was tender and open and affectionate. Thea dared herself to look deeply into the duchess's gaze to see if she was misunderstanding the duchess's concern.

Before she could decide, the duchess hooked their arms together, then drew her to the front of the mantua maker's shop. With a look over her shoulder, she addressed the shopkeeper. "Mademoiselle Mignon, will you have those delivered to Langham Hall tomorrow afternoon? Also, if you could accompany the delivery in case Lady Eanruig needs an extra fitting? The peach silk will be perfect for the Prydwells' soiree. It matches her complexion beautifully."

"Of course, Your Grace." The shopkeeper and her employees all curtseyed as the duchess reached the door.

"Aunt Stella and Lady Edith, would you meet us at the perfumer?" the duchess asked. The strength in her demeanor belied the mellow sweetness in her voice, telling everyone that behind the gentle manners, the duchess was a force to be reckoned with.

"Of course." Stella waved her hand without looking up. Both she and Lady Edith were studying some bolt of fabric hidden in the corner. "We'll come over shortly."

As they walked out the door, the duchess leaned her head close. "Those two are up to something. They always find the most exquisite fabrics, and somehow manage to convince Mignon to sew a new gown for them immediately."

"I'm not surprised." Thea squeezed the duchess's arm gently. "They're everything charming but have an innate way of convincing everyone to do what they want. They seem to weave a magic over everyone."

"Have they weaved their magic over you?" The duchess's gaze was direct but warm.

"I'm not certain what you're asking, Your Grace."

"Don't let my aunt talk you into something that you don't want to do," the duchess said before she softened her voice. "Do you want to marry my son?"

Thea bit her lip and looked away for a moment. She'd answer honestly. "I don't think so." She paused for a moment before she continued. "Stella is everything dear. I asked for her help when I first heard there was a challenge to my title. My grandfather's solicitor thought it best if I marry before I appear in front of the committee, so your aunt suggested your son would be the perfect man for me." She released a breath. "But I want to marry on my own terms."

"Meaning?" The duchess tilted her head.

"I wanted to fall in love and have a family like yours, one that is loving and committed to one another. I don't want to be forced into anything." Thea studied the duchess for any reaction.

She smiled slightly. "Go on."

"I shouldn't have to marry just because a group of men

believe it'll make their decision easier for them. It should be in my best interests, don't you think?"

"Of course." The duchess wrapped her arm around Thea's once more as they continued down the street with one of the Langham liveried footmen two steps behind. "Marriage is a lifetime commitment. You have to choose wisely." She smiled slightly. "However, I must say what's on my mind."

For a moment, Thea tensed, wondering if the duchess would address Thea's behavior when she helped herself to a second helping of dessert.

"I think you and William need each other as friends," the duchess said. Her face glowed as if kissed by the sun. "I'm very happy that he has you in his life."

"He's an honorable man, one I greatly admire." Thea said the words softly, but there was no hesitation in her voice. "He's helping me immensely with my preparation for the committee. He's unselfish with his time." More important, he listened to her guilt over losing her grandfather without judgment. He's the first person she'd ever revealed any of it to.

The duchess sought her gaze as they continued toward the perfumers. "May I share something with you, my dear?"

Thea's reserve vanished at the term of affection. She was intrigued by the duchess's warm but serious demeanor. "Please. I'd like that."

"William can be . . . stubborn at times." They stopped walking, and the duchess took both hands in hers. "He's a typical Cavensham man. They're loyal, protective, and once they give their heart, it's always true. But he got his obstinacy from me, I'm afraid."

Thea had seen that in abundance last night, when he stayed by her side as she fought her humiliation.

Thankfully, he had been tenacious and wouldn't leave her until she found comfort in his words. Because of that, she'd been able to put the matter *mostly* behind her.

"You see . . . he's entirely too cautious." The duchess looked at their clasped hands and squeezed. Slowly, she lifted her gaze to Thea. The hurt in her eyes caused Thea's breath to catch. "There's no easy way to say this, but he's loath to allow himself to be vulnerable."

Thea nodded in understanding. "Your aunt Stella told me that long ago he'd given his heart to another, but the matter ended badly."

The duchess's eyes glistened, and she pursed her lips as if in pain.

"Though my manners aren't as polished as one would expect from a woman of my position, my commitment is true. I would never hurt your son or allow him to be hurt by another." Thea smiled gently.

"Darling girl, comportment and manners are easily learned from others, but how to value another and be a great friend are sterling qualities that a lot of people don't possess. They're only learned from the people that surround us. I can tell from your bearing that you were loved and in turn, you learned how to love." The duchess took a step back and examined Thea from head to foot, then smiled. "I think my son is very lucky to claim you as a friend."

Her kind words pierced Thea's heart. How would the duchess consider Thea's worth if she knew the true regard she'd had for her grandfather at the end of his life? What kind of a family member wished for the suffering for all to be over with? What kind of a person felt relieved when the only family they had finally passed and allowed them some rest?

The duchess's brow furrowed. "He needs someone with patience and fortitude. You have that in abundance."

The duchess clasped her hands again, and the smile on her face showed true affection. "I'm sorry you felt uncomfortable last night. I don't know if William told you what was occurring, but Pitts and I were training a few new footmen. We thought it best to make the dinner as formal as possible. I hope, Thea, you'll forgive me and Sebastian."

"Your Grace, there's nothing to forgive. Truthfully, last night I was horrified, but after speaking with Will last night and now you, I can put it behind me. The next time I have an urge to do something, I hope you'll allow me to consult you first on the proper etiquette."

"Of course. However, I expect you'll be the one setting the *ton* on its head. You're lovely and most importantly, kind." The duchess exhaled and smiled. "Enough of this type of talk. Let's go to the perfumers. Mr. Ainsley is known throughout London for his miraculous magic with fragrances. He's provided scents for my family and the previous duke's family for years. Believe it or not, Mr. Ainsley makes the previous duke's personal favorite for Claire to wear, and he only makes it for her. If you like, he'll make you an exclusive scent too." She smiled. "Something as unique and beautiful as you."

"Thank you, Your Grace." Heat crawled up Thea's cheeks at the duchess's kind words.

As the Langham footman opened the shop door, the duchess swept Thea through the entrance. Immediately, she was transported into another world. Aromas of flowers and herbs gently wafted in welcome. She inhaled deeply. The perfumes didn't overwhelm her nose. If anything, they teased Theodora's senses. She wanted to pick up every bottle and investigate the treasures inside.

"Good afternoon, Your Grace." A handsome elderly man bowed deeply. He managed the feat without upsetting the mop of snowy hair that crowned his head.

"How delightful that you've come to visit today." He turned to Thea and smiled.

"Mr. Ainsley, I'd like to introduce you to Lady Eanruig, a dear friend"—the duchess announced as if daring a challenge—"of the Cavensham family."

The pride in the duchess's voice was unmistakable, causing a sudden heat to lick Thea's cheeks. It was simply glorious that Will's kind mother thought of her so fondly. She couldn't help but think the entire Cavensham family had come into her life to ease her loneliness. She straightened her shoulders and smiled at the shopkeeper. Earlier, she thought a shopping trip was unnecessary, but now, she wouldn't have missed this afternoon in the duchess's company for anything. "Good afternoon, Mr. Ainsley."

He smiled warmly. "I'd hoped you ladies would stop by today. I have it on good authority that Lady Eanruig is looking for a new fragrance."

Thea tilted her head in confusion. "How did you know?"

"Lord William sent a note earlier saying I should expect you and Her Grace to visit." He picked up a tray and set it on a mosaic tile table surrounded by two chairs. "I have some fragrances that you might like to sample."

Thea and the duchess seated themselves as Mr. Ainsley pulled a stopper from a bottle. The subtle scent of roses filled the air. He waved the stopper under his nose. "This is a classic scent, one that Lady Somerton favors. Dab your wrist. You'll see how it smells against your skin."

Before he handed it to Thea, she shook her head. "I'm sure it's lovely. But I was wondering if you might have something made with pomegranates?"

With a perceptive smile, he inclined his head. "Indeed. I was going to save it for last, but I can tell you're a woman of discriminating tastes." He pulled an antique bottle from a tray and repeated his ritual of pulling the stopper and waving it under his nose. Only this time, he closed his eyes as he inhaled. When he finished, he turned his attention to Thea. "Would you like to smell it first before you try?"

Thea nodded. He slowly held the glass stopper at an angle in her direction. The scent gently floated through the air, and Thea breathed it deeply. "*Melograno*," she murmured.

"Indeed, my lady. My favorite and a very rare scent. I have it imported from Italy." He held the delicate glass top between his fingers. "Try it on. Lord William suggested this might be the perfect fragrance for you."

Thea's eyes widened. "He suggested this?"

"My son?" The shock in the duchess's voice perfectly matched Thea's astonishment.

Mr. Ainsley nodded with a smile. "His missive said that only a woman with Thea's strength and character could do justice to this fragrance."

Thea dabbed the fragrance on her wrists. Immediately she knew the rich floral scent was hers. "I adore it."

"Shall I prepare a bottle for you?" Mr. Ainsley asked.

"Please," Thea answered. She sniffed her wrists again and immediately thought of Will.

When Mr. Ainsley went in the back room to prepare her purchase, the duchess gracefully reclined in the chair and regarded Thea.

"I wonder why Will wrote such a note?" Thea mused aloud.

"Friends looking out for friends, I suppose," the duchess said then leaned over, her small hand covering Thea's. "William wants you to succeed and enjoy London."

"He's been everything kind to me already. But as far

as London?" She shook her head. "I'm not certain if I can enjoy it."

"Try for your sake, at least?" the duchess asked gently. "Along with Will's?"

She'd do her best in London under the careful tutelage of Stella, Lady Edith, and of course, Will. She had to remember that her journey here was just a moment in time, one that she hoped to enjoy with Will. But she had every intention of returning to Ladykyrk.

Immediately, the large fish that had jumped out of the pond, popped into her thoughts. If she caught such a mighty creature, she'd admire him, then release him back to his own world.

Just as if she caught William for her own, she'd release him too. He was too magnificent to tame or keep contained. He belonged to his family and to London with all its finery and pomp—not the wilds of Northumberland.

All of this was rather fanciful thinking, but the truth couldn't be denied.

She was the real proverbial fish out of water.

Even the Damp Squib's illustrious siblings and cousin doubt
if he's capable of "rising" to the challenge of matrimony.
Would you, gentle reader, if you were contemplating
nuptials with the
Northumberland Nemesis?
Puts a new meaning to "life sentence" in this humble
reporter's opinion.
Respectfully yours,
The Midnight Cryer

Chapter Thirteen

W ill inhaled breakfast, which was completely normal since he was dining at McCalpin's home in
the formal dining room. His brother employed an excellent chef who had the rare talent of knowing how to prepare a perfect English breakfast. The man cooked enough
food to satisfy the entire English army with enough left
to last the week. Since Will attended today's breakfast,
the chef had prepared his favorites—sausages, ham,
mashed potatoes, kippers, eggs, rashers of bacon, flaky
pastries, and crusty bread with fresh jam and honey.

He and his siblings, McCalpin and Emma, and his
cousin Claire, shared the private breakfast every week
whenever they all were in town. No spouses, parents,
children, or friends were invited. It was the only time that
the siblings and Claire—who everyone thought of as a
sister—could talk freely with one another without any
parental fallouts.

Will took another sip of tea and relaxed in the chair.

"March and I plan on telling Mother and Father about the baby this evening, along with March's sisters and her brother." Joy seemed to vibrate in McCalpin's voice.

Emma smiled and placed her hand over McCalpin's. "Congratulations to you and March. That's wonderful news."

"Indeed." Claire nodded. "You'll make excellent parents."

"Well, since March raised her siblings, this will be like second nature to her." McCalpin drew a deep breath. "Frankly, I'm terrified."

The bemused look on his older brother's face was charming. Will immediately thought of sharing the news with Theodora.

"Please feel free to share this information with your spouses with the proviso of complete privacy until tomorrow." McCalpin turned his attention to Will. "You may tell Theodora also. After all, if Stella has her way, she'll soon be your wife."

His brother's simple statement sent a blistering stab of guilt through Will's chest. He had to tell them the truth about his arrangement with Theodora.

"There's no need." He swallowed his trepidation and continued, "She and I won't marry."

In unison, the three of them swiveled their heads to stare at him, much like a trio of owls. McCalpin's attention darted to the two footmen in attendance. Without a word being spoken, they left, closing the door behind them.

"How can you be sure?" McCalpin asked.

Emma gently laid her serviette on the side of her plate and crossed her arms. He loved his sister dearly but recognized her shift of mood. Emma only did that when she was preparing for one of their epic arguments.

"Pray, tell us your thoughts." Claire's gaze never strayed from Will's.

McCalpin leaned forward with his elbows on the table and a dark scowl crossed his face. "Did she jilt you?"

"No, she didn't jilt me." Will cleared his throat. "I'm inviting a select group of gentlemen to Langham Hall this week to meet Thea with the precise purpose that she might find one of these upstanding men as a suitable husband."

"I don't understand." Claire's dulcet voice had grown a tad sharper.

"It's simple. Aunt Stella thinks Thea and I should marry. She even told me she'd disinherit me if I didn't. To appease her, I called on Thea at her home. Thea doesn't want to marry unless forced by the committee. I'll introduce her to some of my friends in case she needs a groom quickly." Will clenched his stomach in preparation for the barrage of questions that would surely be forthcoming. "I want her happy and secure. Whatever she needs, I'll help her."

He didn't want to share that Thea would only consider him as a last resort. It would rip open a new hole in his chest.

A frown creased Claire's brow.

"She's my friend." Will quickly added, "As such, Thea will have me beside her when she makes her first appearances in the *ton*, and I'll even appear in front of the committee by her side if she asks me."

"You are going to *ton* events?" Emma asked incredulously.

Will nodded. "I'm going for Thea. After the challenge to her title is finished, she can find someone to marry if she wishes. I'll have satisfied Aunt Stella's desire that I marry Thea."

Emma's green eyes flashed. "That's the most illogical sentence I daresay you've ever uttered."

McCalpin leaned back in his chair and smiled. Trust his brother to enjoy his grilling by Claire and Emma.

Will held up his hand. "Allow me to explain. After Thea secures her title, she plans to return to Ladykyrk. I'll continue with my work for the family. Aunt Stella will come to realize that Thea and I would never have suited. I'll be out of the doghouse and back in our great-aunt's grace once again."

"Exactly how are you going to arrange this parade of potential paragons to Theodora?" With his earlier amusement fading, McCalpin regarded Will dubiously.

"It's simple. I'm inviting three friends to Langham Hall for Thea to meet. If forced to marry, hopefully she'll find someone whom she wants." As Will said the words, his cousin's eyes narrowed. A sure sign that her rare anger was about to make an appearance.

"That will never work, particularly as *The Midnight Cryer* mocks her every chance they get." Claire shook her head vehemently. "I know what it's like to be treated as an object of money and position while not being taken seriously." Her voice cracked with emotion. "After four failed engagements, I understand what it feels like to have men look at you but not really *see* you. What you're doing to her is unspeakably cruel."

"Claire," he spoke softly. "It's not like that. I know you were hurt deeply by how the *ton* treated you. I would never treat Thea that way. This is what she wants. It's a plan she can fall back on if the committee forces her hand."

His cousin simply stared at him with a look that didn't conceal her pain. "What about you?" she asked.

"It's what I want too." Even to his own ears, the words sounded lame—even weak.

Heavy silence descended in the room, reminding him that all the women in his family were strong and steadfast, like cornerstones of a building, always ready to bear the weight of keeping the structure sound.

Theodora possessed such strength forged from the trials she'd had to shoulder when her grandfather became ill. In a similar fashion, she'd support her family and husband. An image of Thea with their children flashed before Will. He pushed such thoughts away. Whoever was lucky enough to marry Thea would receive those gifts, but it wouldn't be him.

"May I make an observation?" Emma asked. "You've always been admired by your friends. A natural leader who they emulate. With you escorting Thea to society events, it'll appear you're interested in her. But if *The Midnight Cryer* finds out you're introducing her to potential marriage partners, it'll hurt her. If there is even a hint that you're jilting Thea or find her wanting, then your friends will also."

McCalpin nodded. "She makes an excellent point."

"Nonsense," Will argued. "Everyone will think there's something lacking in me. Once people meet her, they'll see that she's intelligent, warm, and generous. She's a lovely woman who anyone would be lucky to marry."

"With a fortune," Claire added.

Will nodded once in agreement. "She just happens to have an ancient Scottish title with an accompanying grand estate and fortune."

"Humph." Claire brushed a loose lock of hair behind her ear. "How will you determine who wants the person you described and not her fortune? Remember how men treated me until Alex came along? He loved me for who I am, not what I owned."

"The same applies to me," Emma agreed. "Every man evaluated my value by the size of my dowry and the fact that I was the daughter of the Duke of Langham." She sighed as if releasing a weight from her chest. "Until Somerton, no one believed in my ability to build a bank. Now, because of him, it's a financial success that rivals the most prosperous financial institutions in all of London."

"And your point, Em?" William drawled.

"Don't be dense, William." Claire's retort sailed through the room. "We both found men who believed in us and, most importantly, looked beyond the trappings society tried to bind around us. Our husbands fell in love and married us for who we are, not what we own." She held his stare as if challenging him. "How are you going to find a man worthy of her, and not someone who is only interested in her fortune and title?" She softened her voice. "I can't help but think you do a disservice to yourself to not even consider marrying her. You deserve love, Will."

McCalpin lifted an eyebrow in challenge. "Bad form, Will. You're so worried you'll get hurt that you don't give happiness a chance. Be careful, Brother. This smacks of turning into an epic disaster, one of your own creation."

"It's not like that," Will protested as he fisted his hands under the table. If he shared the humiliating fact that it was Thea who didn't want him, it would cut him open and expose his failings. Was it a failing or just vulnerability? Perhaps he'd likened it to a twice-shy horse. He didn't want to pursue Thea and experience rejection again.

It was simply easier to lose himself in his responsibilities. There was never a danger of a jilting or rejection when work waited for him with open arms.

Completely ignoring Will's unease, his brother continued, "Aunt Stella isn't squiring Thea around. You are."

"Cavensham men fall in love—"

"We know the litany by heart. *Quickly, thoroughly, and decidedly.*" McCalpin waved his hand through the air. "The only one who believes that drivel is you. I didn't love March until I came to know her as a person. How she thought. What she valued."

"Though I'm not a Cavensham man, Cavensham blood runs in my veins," Claire said. "Alex and I fell in love over the months after we first married."

Emma smiled. "I knew Somerton for years before I realized we were destined for one another." She wrinkled her nose. "I thought you were smarter than that." She leaned close and stared him in the eyes. "I don't think you truly believe it either. I think it's an excuse."

"Now see here," Will protested. He pierced each of them with his gaze, though his defenses were weakening. "Thea and I will not suit."

The bitter taste of bile rose in his throat, and he forced himself to swallow. God, he prayed they'd leave his affairs alone and not ask anymore.

"How do you know?" Claire's eyebrows shot up, then she leaned forward slightly and narrowed her eyes.

"Claire, you know me. I'm not husband material." He tried to take his cousin's hand in his, but she drew away.

Will swallowed. He valued Claire's opinion since she was one of the most levelheaded members of their family. However, her cheeks were stained scarlet, and the slight pursing of her lips gave him pause. He'd never seen her so angry—at least, never with him.

"Do you remember your eighth birthday?" Claire bit out.

McCalpin and Emma's gazes bounced between the two of them.

Will shook his head.

"You asked the new cook to make you cherry tarts, knowing full well we weren't supposed to eat cherries." Claire shook her head slightly. "You *knew* that cherries didn't agree with you, yet you proceeded without any thought to anyone but yourself."

Will suppressed a shudder. After that birthday, he had never craved another cherry in his life. He'd been an itchy, miserable mess for days.

"Took full advantage of the cook, as I recall." McCalpin chuckled. "Afterward, you resembled a swollen boiled lobster. Redder than the cherries you ate."

"You were covered in hives." Emma's laughter joined McCalpin's.

"Everyone except for the new cook knew you couldn't tolerate cherries, *including you*," Claire scolded. "Yet you proceeded to do as you wanted to the detriment of everyone else. The entire family had to postpone a trip to Falmont for a week. The cook almost quit, she was so upset."

"I really don't want to discuss it further." Perhaps it'd be best if he just got up and left. He didn't want to listen to his cousin's litany, nor did he want to share anymore.

Claire stood also, then poked him in the chest to get his full attention. It wasn't a hard poke, but the mere fact that she disapproved of his actions and thought to reprimand him was completely disconcerting.

"Be." *Poke.* "Careful." *Poke.* "What." *Poke.* "You." *Poke.* "Wish." *Poke.* "For." Claire squared her shoulders. "I'll ensure that she has men following her like she's the Pied Piper of Hamlin." She turned, and the swirl of her silk skirts slapped his boots. With her ire high, she glided to the door, then turned and faced him. "Once I'm done, you'll feel as if you've eaten a bowl of cherries."

"Whatever she's planning, I'm going to help her." Emma stood and followed Claire out the door.

McCalpin shook his head. "What are you doing, Will? I've never seen you this out of sorts."

"I'm not doing anything. It's what Thea wants."

McCalpin lifted a single brow in disbelief. "Oh, really?"

"She doesn't want to marry *me*!" The sharp words ricocheted through the room.

There, he'd said it.

A beautiful, kind woman who he thought the world of didn't want him. *The Midnight Cryer*'s words taunted him—he was a failure, a damp squib—and he'd finally admitted it. The pain in his chest threatened to bring him to his knees.

His brother simply stared at him.

"I apologize for my outburst." He exhaled, wishing he was anywhere but McCalpin's home. He threw his serviette on the table like a gauntlet. "Theodora's an intelligent, affectionate, loyal, not to mention, lovely young woman. She deserves the best."

"And you're not the best?" McCalpin asked. His voice was low as if he were scared he'd poked the sleeping bear. "You have feelings for her."

"It makes no difference." He forced himself to hold his brother's gaze. "She told me she doesn't want to marry me." He chuckled but it held no humor. "The first time I met her, she made it clear her thoughts on marriage to me."

He'd never shared anything so personal with his brother or anyone else in the family.

"You can't tell Emma or Claire. Let them continue to be angry with me. Perhaps they'll be able to find someone whom Thea will love. But he needs to be a man worthy of her hand."

McCalpin walked to Will's side and clasped his shoulder. "Will, I'll say it again. Admit it. You do have feelings for her."

Will tried to tamp down the foreboding, but his heart was pounding in alarm.

He wanted to deny it, but he simply couldn't.

Indeed, what had he done?

Will wonders ever cease?
Word has it that Lady Man-Eater can pour a cup of tea
without spilling.
Amazing that it's a fait accompli for most ten-year-olds.
Respectfully yours,
The Midnight Cryer

Chapter Fourteen

Later that afternoon, Thea poured the first cup of tea without incident. With a deep but silent sigh of relief, she gently handed it to Lady Pembrooke. With her confidence mounting, Thea didn't hesitate to pour her own.

Unfortunately, she held the teapot a little too high, resulting in a tiny spill on her own saucer. At least the spill was on her saucer and not the lady sitting in front of her. Another week of practice in pouring tea, and she'd be serving it perfectly in no time. Instead of a defeat, Thea considered it a success. There wasn't a hint of rattling china.

Or spilt cream.

"I'm so pleased you had time for me today." Without even looking, Claire gently set her cup on her saucer. "Emma sends her regards. She wanted to come, but with two little ones and her bank, she couldn't come today." Claire smiled sheepishly. "But truthfully, I'm glad it's just you and me."

Her mood instantly brightened at the thought that the beautiful woman in front of her would be her friend.

Someone she could visit and shop with. Someone she could share the everyday stories of her life as well as her troubles.

A sudden warmth welled in her chest. Will was her friend.

And now she could consider Claire a friend too. But her friendship with Claire would be a different type of friendship than what she had with Will. The bond she shared with him was something she'd never thought she'd find. It was deep and true.

"Thea, I'll come right to the point. We Cavenshams are known for being direct." Claire sat ramrod straight, and her soft musical lilt didn't fool Theodora. The woman was made of steel.

"Please, I want you to be frank with me." Thea matched Claire's posture.

Claire's gaze lowered to her hands that were neatly clasped in her lap. When she finally looked Thea's way, her green eyes were gentle and kindhearted. "I took William to task for his ludicrous idea that he wants you to jilt him in favor of one of his friends. I'm here to offer you support and advice."

Heat licked Thea's cheeks. She swallowed in hopes that it would prevent her mortification from being recognized. She struggled to find something to say but finally responded. "I won't jilt him."

Claire let out a sigh. "I'm so happy to hear that."

"We're not engaged," Thea said softly.

"Well, I know. But. . . ." Claire studied her with such an intensity that Thea was convinced she could see through her.

It was increasingly difficult to discuss what exactly her relationship was with Will. Never had she felt closer to another. There was a part of her—a big part of her that wanted Will. But she had no idea if it was friendship or if she wanted something deeper and more intimate.

She bit her lip. How to explain it when she wasn't at all certain she grasped what they were to each other.

"Is Will planning to jilt you?" Claire asked.

"No." Thea shook her head. "I want him to introduce me to his friends. Though I don't want to marry unless it's for love, I'll do what is necessary to protect my estate and the people who live there." She studied her clasped hands, then raised her gaze to Claire. "I told Will I didn't want to marry, and I didn't want to marry the first man I met. As luck would have it, Will just happened to be him."

Claire elegantly stood, then rounded the small table between them. She sat next to Thea and took her hands in hers. "I have a plan."

Claire's soft skin belied her underlying strength. Thea squeezed Claire's hands, hoping for some of the marchioness's fortitude. "I don't see how a plan is going to help me."

Claire tilted her head and peeked at her. "Do you want to marry Will?"

Thea shrugged once. "Truthfully, it's difficult to say. I admire him. He's honorable, and more importantly, he's my best friend."

"I see." Claire stood and pulled Thea to a standing position. With a gentle tug, Claire led Thea to a mirror in the sitting room that extended from the floor to the ceiling. Standing in front of it, Thea could see the entire room. She stood there without any idea what the marchioness wanted.

"It's important to be able to recognize the right man when he comes along. I want you to be prepared, so I'm going to teach you society lessons," Claire announced.

"Stella and Lady Edith have been helping me." She

blew a stray wisp of hair that had fallen down her forehead.

"And I'm sure they're fine teachers. I'm only going to enhance the training a bit." Several inches taller than Thea, Claire moved behind her and held Thea's gaze in the mirror. "Think of it almost as flirting but more general. You need to communicate your interest in a man while showing your charm. If done in a playful manner, it's completely harmless and amusing while teaching you confidence in talking with others." Claire lightly rested her hands on Thea's shoulders. "You learn how to engage another person's interest. Think of it as a way to enrich how you talk to others." She leaned close and whispered in Thea's ear. "You, my dear, are going to drive every man invited to Langham Hall wild, including William."

"I have no idea how to capture a man's attention." Thea shook her head. "I have no experience. Outside of Will, I haven't had much contact with any men except my grandfather. Besides, *The Midnight Cryer* has made me out to be a murderer." She let out a soulful sigh.

"*The Midnight Cryer* doesn't care about the truth. They only care about making money. Trust me. I've had plenty of experience with that gossip rag. This is a way to rectify your reputation. You must practice your movements and sayings. Now, I've arranged for my husband, McCalpin, and Lord Somerton to come to the house tomorrow morning for a demonstration. Of course, Emma and I will be there to steer you and address any concerns you might have."

"*I can't do that in front of them.*" Thea shook her head vehemently. "They'll see what a colossal fool I am."

"I have the utmost confidence in you, Theodora. You're a brilliant, not to mention capable person who happens to be beautiful on the inside as well as the

outside. You just need a little practice. Shall we try?"
The marchioness caught Thea's gaze in the mirror and
grinned. The slight smile bespoke a woman who was
confident this plan would succeed.

"I suppose." If this exercise held the promise of helping her with Will's friends and others within the *ton*, then
why not try it? It might also help her gain the approval
of the committee if they see her self-assuredness and
confidence.

"Excellent. The first thing you have to do when you're
introduced to a man is make eye contact and smile. It
shows you're interested enough that you'll engage in a
conversation with him."

"Outside of discussing the expected yields of the various crops at Ladykyrk and the weather, what would I
say?"

"You could start there. Most of the men you'll meet
have estates they're responsible for. Tonight, I want you
to make a list of things you could talk about," Claire instructed. "Talk to your mirror as if it were a man or a
stuffy society matron. You'll grow more comfortable
with hearing your voice and the words."

"I'm responsible for an estate and approximately one
hundred tenant farmers. I could debate the necessary
qualifications of the new land steward I plan to hire." She
straightened her shoulders and smiled at the mirror. "I
could tell them how beautiful Ladykyrk is."

"See? You have more in common with these people
than you think you do. These men face the same challenges and receive the same rewards as you do." Claire
gently squeezed her shoulders. "You're a countess in your
own right. Pick out your gown tonight. If you have the
scene planned in your mind, it'll be easier tomorrow."

"Don't you think it's a little ridiculous that I stay in
my room and talk to my mirror? Would you do it if you

were me?" Completely bemused, Thea waited for Claire's answer.

"In a heartbeat." The marchioness grinned. "You'll soon learn that people do whatever it takes to secure their heart of hearts."

"Claire, I might have made a mistake," Thea whispered. "Within the first five minutes of meeting, I told Will I wouldn't marry him."

She closed her eyes as the hot sting of tears burned her eyes.

"How did Will answer?" Claire asked.

"That he didn't want to marry me either."

Claire blinked twice as if trying to take it all in.

Thea glanced out the window to gaze at Langham Park hoping for clarity in her regard for Will. She had to concentrate on securing her title. Only then, could she consider marriage with a lifelong partner and a houseful of children. It would be in her best interest not to dwell on Will and her feelings. Truthfully, Thea had hoped for love, but she couldn't expect to find a man who would fall head over heels in love with her while she was in London for this short visit. She also knew that no man would measure up to Will. His kindness, teasing, and comfort had made it so easy to share her past and its secrets along with everything she wanted in the future. She couldn't imagine sharing so much of herself with another man.

Why did she even need to meet other men?

Claire gently turned Thea around until she faced her. "Be brave. Some men, like William, are afraid to risk their hearts. That is why you must be strong. Just remember, people change their minds, Thea. Do you think you changed yours?"

"I don't know." She let out a sigh. "Perhaps it's best if I accept our friendship without wanting more." Maybe she should accept that love wasn't something she could attain.

Claire immediately hugged her.

"We all can change our minds." Claire swept back that errant curl that refused to stay pinned in Thea's chignon. "I did after I decided I didn't want Alex." Claire smiled ruefully. "I thought I'd lost him, but I didn't."

"I don't even know what I want at this point," Thea said gently, as mixed emotions seemed to swirl throughout her thoughts.

"You have plenty of time to figure it out," Claire said. "Only marry for love not because a roomful of men in white-powdered wigs think it's good for you."

"All right. If I'm going to learn how to make a man interested in me, I should probably spend some time in my room. I believe I have an assignation with my mirror."

The optimism in Thea's voice belied the doubt that rooted deep inside her. Perhaps she didn't deserve love.

"See. You're already polishing your skills." Claire laughed, but then returned to her earlier seriousness. "Never forget you're a remarkable woman, Thea. Anyone would be fortunate to be married to you. I'll teach you how to act in society, and in return, life will reward you an abundance of friends."

She took a deep breath and slowly released it. There was no sense in wanting more. But she had one consolation. At least she had Will's friendship.

But why did her obstinate heart insist on more than just that?

After taking tea with his mother and father the next day, Will descended from the second-floor family quarters. He found Pembrooke and Somerton strolling through the entry toward the blue-and-yellow salon, aptly named the Duke's Salon since it featured the favorite colors of the previous duke, Claire's father.

"Where are you off to?" Will called out in greeting. "I didn't know you were coming this morning."

Both turned with what could only be called roguish smiles on their faces. "Morning, William," Pembrooke said.

"Morning." Somerton nodded in greeting. "We're meeting our wives and Thea this morning."

"We'll catch up another time, William," Pembrooke said with a smirk.

Without another word, the two men approached the salon where their wives awaited them outside. Claire grinned at her husband, and Pembrooke took her hand and brought it to his lips. A dreamy-eyed Emma took Somerton's outstretched hand.

Will stood in the entry. Before he could investigate further, his brother, McCalpin, and his wife, March, entered the house.

After the appropriate greetings, Will asked, "Why is everyone here?"

"Claire asked if we'd all meet this morning," McCalpin said. "She's seeking our assistance with a project."

March nodded. "I was invited too, but first, I'm meeting with the duke and duchess to discuss last month's financials for McCalpin's estate. Would you like to join me?" Without waiting for Will's answer, she continued, "I think it's a ruse for the duke and duchess to coo over our recent news about the baby."

"Indeed." McCalpin pulled his wife close to his side and kissed her cheek. "As they didn't invite me."

Such an act of intimacy shouldn't have bothered Will, but for a brief instant, a pang of envy coursed through him, much like a pain in his chest.

"They're beside themselves in celebration of another grandchild," McCalpin added.

March scooted closer to McCalpin, and his hand visibly tightened against her waist.

"Are you feeling well?" McCalpin murmured in her ear. He leaned close and kissed her cheek.

She blushed and nodded at the same time. Both stared into each other's eyes completely oblivious to Will's presence.

They fit perfectly together in temperament, talents, and most importantly, in their love. Will glanced at the ceiling of the atrium and pretended to study the chandelier while the two continued their moment of privacy.

McCalpin finally tore his gaze from his wife, then waggled his eyebrows at Will. "Imagine the possibilities for your future. You could be married with children on the way if you put your mind to it."

That sinking feeling Will experienced when any of his family discussed marriage and babies took hold like a rabid dog. Truly, he was happy for them all. Claire and Pembrooke, Emma and Somerton, and now, McCalpin and March deserved every happiness that life had to offer.

Times like these, he'd always wondered if he'd fallen in love with a different woman, if it would have made a difference. Perhaps if he'd been older and more experienced in the ways of life. An image of Thea walking into their bedroom with a baby propped on her hip popped out of nowhere. Instead of dismissing it, Will allowed the vision to linger. He held out his arms to welcome both into bed. Warmth and contentment rushed through him, and it felt right.

A sound of a deep baritone laugh interrupted his musings. Somerton emerged from under the staircase holding Emma's hand. The blush of her cheeks and her swollen lips revealed that those two had been sharing more than a private conversation.

Watching his siblings and cousin and their happy state of matrimony caused that sinking feeling again.

The sound of feminine laughter garnered his attention. Pembrooke was bending over Claire's hand. His lips touched the top of her hand, and Claire audibly sighed.

"So, that's how it's done." Dressed in a vermilion-colored gown with a gold lace overlay, Thea practically glowed. The smile on her face turned from attractive to breathtaking. The sparkle in her eyes and the slight flush of her cheeks enhanced the amazing sight of her. Mesmerized, he couldn't turn away even if a coach-and-four were barreling toward him.

Her gaze caught his, and her eyes flashed briefly as if genuinely happy to see him. With a dip of her head, she acknowledged him. Believing he'd be included in whatever she was doing, he took a step toward her. Abruptly, she turned on the spot and moved toward the entrance of the Duke's Salon. The others had already made their way inside.

"Thea, wait."

Gracefully, she turned and came to a stop. The tenderness in her expression surprised him, but it was quickly replaced with a secretive smile. "Hello, Will."

He smiled at the pure pleasure of seeing her and having her undivided attention. "Good morning. What are you doing this morning in the Duke's Salon?" He leaned in close until a mere hand's width separated them. He lowered his voice. "Did you forget to invite me?"

She laughed softly, then looked him directly in the eyes. "Of course not. I'd never forget you." An enchanting half grin tugged at one corner of her lips.

"I can't tell you the overwhelming relief I have at hearing those words cross your lips." He reached toward her, then gently brushed his fingers over the silky skin of her cheek. It was as delicate as he remembered. "You have a loose curl," he murmured.

It was the perfect excuse to keep on touching her as he pushed the loose wispy curl behind her ear. The sweet scent of *melograno* and the essence of Theodora rushed toward him.

Her incredible eyes warmed at his touch.

Good God, he could stay here all day if she kept on looking at him like that. He cleared his throat then swallowed in an attempt to find his sanity—which had strolled away on its own. "What are you and the others doing in the salon?"

She slowly batted her eyelashes as if awakening from a dream. "They're teaching me how to . . . present myself in society."

"McCalpin, Somerton, and Pembrooke volunteered to teach you deportment lessons?"

"No." She laughed. "A little instruction in flirting just might be involved."

The lighthearted sound tugged at something deep in his chest. He took a long-drawn-out breath to slow the rhythm of his pulse.

"They're teaching you how to flirt? What could they possibly know about the subject?" Seeing the amusement in her eyes, he laughed. "They're married men."

"Proving they're accomplished in the craft. Wouldn't you say so?" The sweetness in her voice reminded him of midsummer honey.

"It's fortunate I'm here." He deepened his voice. "Let me help."

"I'm sure you're an expert at communicating everything you desire," she purred.

Her gaze penetrated him, and for a brief moment, he could feel her inside him, invading and conquering his defenses against letting a woman get near him. In some ways, it was a perfect moment, one he'd remember always. Her hand tenderly rested on his arm, the touch a private communication between them.

Unaware of his surroundings, Will wanted to take her into his arms and kiss her until they were both lost in each other. "Thea," he groaned.

"Yes, Will?" She leaned closer, and he bent his head. The distance between their lips was inches apart. She tightened her hand on his arm, indicating she felt this perfect interlude between them also.

He wanted to roar in triumph.

"Let me escort you in, and we can continue the lessons. I'd like to teach you." His gaze never strayed from hers. "Everything."

She studied his face as if memorizing every feature, then her gaze slowly captured his. The serene look on her face held him spellbound. "Will."

The breathless sigh of his name made every organ inside of him tighten, particularly his cock.

"I'm terribly sorry, but you weren't invited." Without another word or explanation, she turned and walked into the salon. The gentle roll of her hips would entice a man to follow her anywhere. But the click of the door proved he truly wasn't welcome.

He exhaled a painful but silent breath. The truth was she certainly didn't need flirting lessons. By what he'd just seen, he'd consider her an expert in the art.

What he didn't expect was the pain from learning he wasn't wanted.

It bit into his pride with a savage chomp.

The Northumberland Nemesis is husband hunting in London. Such news, gentle reader, has thrilled scientists around the world since it renders an entirely new biological classification
to the mate-eating black widow spider.
Just the truth as usual,
The Midnight Cryer

Chapter Fifteen

Hours later, Thea entered the library with a confident smile on her face. Will looked up from the books spread before him.

Will stood, and a grin tugged at his lips. "Lady Ean-ruig. How delightful to see you."

Before Thea could pull out her own chair, Will did the honors for her and helped her get comfortable. He leaned close—close enough Thea could smell the fresh scent of his soap.

"How was your lesson? Perhaps after we're finished here, you could give me some pointers," he murmured. Without waiting for her to answer, Will straightened and closed the books in front of him.

"Of course." Heat pummeled her cheeks, but a smile tugged at her lips. The Cavensham family's lessons were everything spectacular. She'd never felt so welcome in true friendship. But what thrilled her was that he'd been thinking about her the same as she'd been thinking about him.

"How did you find Pembrooke, Somerton, and McCalpin as teachers?" he asked.

She picked up a writing quill and twirled it in her fingers as she struggled for the right words. *They were lovely, but they weren't you.*

"*Charmant messieurs?*"

A tinge of apprehension coursed through her. She'd never had a French lesson in her life. "What did you say?"

He leaned toward her. "I asked if you thought the men in my family charming." He lowered his voice. "Would you include me in such illustrious company?"

Another wave of heat hit her. His teasing could only be called affectionate.

Heaven help her.

"We'll save *that* discussion for later." He lowered his voice, then reached over and squeezed one of her hands. "Is my family overwhelming you?"

"On the contrary. I feel quite comfortable with them." The duke and duchess's kindness toward her was another example of the Cavensham family's charity. Stella's and Claire's friendships were treasures she'd never dreamed she'd find.

But her recalcitrant heart yearned and demanded for more. To have Will care for her would be a gift she would cherish forever. But there were more important matters she needed—the charter for one.

"You need to see the latest." Will pulled a copy of *The Midnight Cryer* from his papers and gave it to her.

Immediately, she straightened in her seat in preparation for the blow. A sudden bout of nausea made her dizzy, but she forced herself to read the headline.

HOW EXACTLY WILL THE DUKE AND
DUCHESS OF LANGHAM INTRODUCE THE

COUNTESS OF EANRUIG AT THEIR
SOIRÉE LATER THIS WEEK?
MY LADY MURDERESS OR THE
NORTHUMBERLAND VILLAINESS?

Thea closed her eyes in hope that the vile words would disappear. The sharp pain in her chest was a reminder that she had a long battle in front of her. "Everyone thinks I'm evil."

"I don't, and neither does my family. But perhaps this would be a good time to discuss the hearing." He studied her thoughtfully for a moment. "I don't want you to be surprised by anything they might ask you. I thought if I asked you questions, you'd feel more comfortable."

"You mean coming from a friend instead of a group of men I don't know?" She tried to relax.

"Yes. Think of it as a way of preparing for the hearing. I think we should discuss your grandfather and you." Without a hint of censure, Will asked, "Why did your grandfather allow you to take on such responsibility for the duchy? You were how old?"

"I was barely eighteen, and he was barely in his right mind then." How to explain the situation without belaboring her grandfather's ineptitude to carry out the simplest tasks. "One day, I read a directive he wanted me to post to his solicitors. In it, he instructed them to sell the duchy's ancestral estate, an entailed property that belonged to the dukedom. Such a demand would have been a warning that things weren't quite right in my grandfather's thinking." She pursed her lips. "From that day forward, I took over." In an effort to eliminate her unease, she cleared her throat. "And . . . you see, it was just easier . . . because we lived together. He needed me. I didn't trust anyone else to protect him."

His smile was genuine, but empathetic. "Your grandfather's estates are almost as complicated as the Langham duchy's holdings. Why you? I'm not asking these questions to pry into your relationship with your grandfather. But I don't want you to be caught unaware by the committee if they ask such questions."

She swallowed in a bid for time, as she wondered how much to share. This was Will and he was trying to help her. "Ferr-Colby wants Ladykyrk because there's a fortune in minerals under the land, specifically coal. He'd evict my tenants just in the name of money. Before my grandfather became ill, he'd expressed that concern. I couldn't let it happen under my care."

"That's a sound reason to keep it quiet. But you missed out on so much that life has to offer a young woman such as yourself. Are you sorry you never had a Season?"

"No, because I didn't know what it was." She'd never really thought much about not participating in a Season. But now being in London, she had some idea what she missed. She would have found friends and perhaps a husband along the way. But would she have ever met Will? Probably. However, she was certain they wouldn't be close like they were now.

Will turned to her and placed his arm on the back of her chair, the movement so protective that she wanted to lean closer until he held her in his arms.

Will's fingers gently caressed the back of her neck. "You are a brave woman, Thea."

She leaned into his touch. It was so hard to share her grandfather's misery. But if she wanted to be successful in front of the committee, she needed all the help she could muster. With each stroke of his fingers against the nape of her neck, she gathered an extra speck of courage.

Without a word, he placed his other hand over hers. "You did a marvelous job of protecting your grandfather and his wealth. You make my own estate management skills pale in comparison." He lowered his voice. "You're remarkable, and the duke was very lucky to have you as his champion."

Thea gulped a tremulous breath as her eyes blurred from unshed tears. A tiny sob escaped, and she sniffed to hold it in. "He was an incredible man, and I was very fortunate that he was my grandfather."

"I'm sorry, Thea," Will murmured.

"I'm just sorry I wasn't a better granddaughter." A watershed of grief hit her, and she fought not to lose herself in the sadness. She straightened her shoulders, but Will kept right on stroking her neck.

"Why would you say that?" He withdrew a handkerchief and gave it to her. "You protected him."

"Sometimes it was so hard." She let out a tremulous breath. Outside of Mr. and Mrs. Miles, no one knew the vile secret that ate at her soul. "I didn't honor him as he deserved," she whispered. Another tear fell, and she brushed it away. "At the end, I thought he hated me. He'd become angry at me over nothing. He'd rail at me repeatedly and call me horrible names."

His mouth curved with tenderness. "If this is too painful, we can stop."

"No, I want you to know everything." She bit her lip to keep from sobbing. The black memories still scalded her. "He'd dismiss me from service as if I were a servant. I'd stay outside his room for five minutes, then return. He'd never remember firing me."

"How often would this happen?" Will stroked her neck again.

"Sometimes three or four times a day." Her body stilled as her heart broke into a million pieces. The cavern inside her chest stood empty except for a crippling pain that gripped her. Desperate to gain control of her grief, she clenched her fists so hard that her nails gouged her palms. "I don't think he loved me at the end. It was excruciating to listen to the venom that spewed from his mouth." She turned to Will and searched his face. "Perhaps *The Midnight Cryer* is telling the truth."

He studied her face, feature by feature, until his gaze rested on hers. His deep blue eyes reminded her of a serene pond, one that offered peace. "Tell me."

"I—I was with him for two days straight before he passed. He'd fallen asleep and didn't wake up." She forced herself not to turn away. Once she told the tale, he'd see how despicable she really was. If he called her pure evil, it would be no less than she deserved. "I tried to wake him, but he wouldn't respond." She took a deep breath for fortitude. "So I let him sleep. He was dying, and I didn't even try to save him."

Will didn't flinch at her words. His eyes softened as if he could tell how much her confession was costing her. "How could you have saved him?"

He continued to caress her neck, and if she really wanted to atone for her sins, then she would push his hand away. She didn't deserve such comfort. But selfishly, she didn't want him to stop. Her grandfather hadn't hugged her in years since he had no idea who she was. No one had touched her in so long. She craved this physical connection with another, and because it was Will, it was all the more poignant.

Once he discovered the depths of her depravity, he'd draw away in horror. As selfish as it was, if she didn't tell him anymore, then hopefully, he'd continue to touch her. But that was cowardly, and she needed his help. "I tried to make my grandfather as comfortable as I could. I stroked his lips with a wet cloth, and I tried to feed him. He wouldn't eat. He just slept." She shook her head as if daring him to confront her. She deserved no less. "I should have called for a doctor."

"What do you think a doctor could have done that you didn't do?" he asked. There was no judgment in his voice, only true concern.

"I don't honestly know." His quiet attention encouraged her to tell him everything about that night. "But I didn't want anyone to see how frail and weak he'd become. If the doctor would have somehow managed to wake him, I didn't want anyone to witness how he truly was." She released a deep breath, but it didn't lessen the pain. "The last time he was awake, he kept asking me who I was. Then he'd turn and have a conversation with his dead sister." She gasped but forced herself to continue. "I couldn't . . . I just couldn't let anyone see him like that, and I couldn't risk anyone seeing how much he hated me."

With those last words, a sob escaped, and she pulled away from Will. "He didn't love me, and perhaps I deserved his loathing."

"No, you were fearless and kind." The certainty in his eyes comforted her. "He didn't mean it, sweetheart. His mind was gone." Will gently tugged her into his embrace. "It's all right. The amount of responsibility you bore for his welfare and the estate was amazing. You did everything you could for him. You have nothing to be ashamed for."

She didn't respond for a long while. She just allowed him to hold her and comfort her. His tenderness fed a part of her—the longing to belong to another that she didn't realize was starving.

"I wish I could have been there with you. No one should have to grieve alone." He rested his head on top of hers and pulled her tight.

"No. You misunderstand." She drew back until she faced him.

He cupped her cheeks with his hands. The warmth

and strength in his fingers encouraged her to continue. Gently, he brushed his thumbs across her cheeks and wiped away a tear she hadn't realized had escaped.

"I didn't grieve. All I felt was relief that it was over." She clenched her eyes tight in hopes that Will couldn't see how despicable she really was. "That's why I can't lose. It's not just about the tenants and my livelihood, but also the only way I can make up for my failings to him."

"Thea, look at me," he commanded softly. His words laced with infinite compassion. "You didn't fail him. He was lucky he had such a strong, supportive, dedicated caregiver." He pressed his lips to her forehead. "Not many in your position would have lasted a year, let alone seven years."

She released a breath.

"You're stunning, Thea." He smiled, and for a moment she thought she saw a deep emotion in his eyes for her. He brushed his lips gently against hers. "You'll get everything you want. Everything will be fine."

She forced a nod, but she didn't have the heart to tell him he didn't speak the truth. She wasn't going to get everything she wanted.

Because she realized in that moment all she wanted was him. The real truth couldn't—no—wouldn't be denied. She didn't deserve a kind, loving man.

Which meant she didn't deserve him.

Gentle readers, "showing one's cards" has a whole new meaning
since the Northumberland Lady Nemesis is in town.
She really is desperate.
One would almost feel pity if she wasn't a murderess.
Respectfully yours,
The Midnight Cryer

Chapter Sixteen

〜

The yellow salon, the most formal sitting room within Langham Hall, made the perfect venue to introduce Theodora to Will's friends. He'd sent out invitations to the three men, and immediately, acceptances were sent in reply.

Out of the three Will considered two were his best friends. Mr. Devan Farris, the brother of the current Earl of Larkton, and Julian Raleah, the Marquess of Grayson. He'd also invited Lord Frederick Honeycutt, a viscount in his own right, and a man of high moral standards, who would inherit an earldom one day.

Will had stayed in close contact with Devan throughout the years. As the fourth son of the previous Earl of Larkton, Devan didn't have any choice but to join the church as he had no money for a commission in the military. As a vicar, he'd been assigned to various parishes throughout the countryside and special assignments from the church bishops. But his latest position had been in

Northumberland, not a great distance from Aunt Stella's estate.

The Marquess of Grayson had been Will's friend since they were young boys. However, Will didn't have the opportunity to see the marquess as often as he'd liked. Grayson's time in London had been limited. He'd inherited an ancient and well-respected title, but one that had been poorly managed for the last fifty years under the previous marquess's supervision. Unfortunately for Grayson, the coffers of the marquessate were practically empty. He needed to marry an heiress quickly to keep the estate viable and out of bankruptcy.

Will's friendship with Honeycutt grew from their years at university. His friend's loyalty was second to none.

If Thea chose any of those men as a suitable husband, she'd have a happy and contented life. He was sure of it.

Will fisted his hands as if preparing for a practice match at Gentleman Jackson. He admired his friends, but what Thea planned to do this afternoon still didn't sit right with him. It was nothing more than if she were on display like a prime haunch of venison in the butcher shop's window. All afternoon, he'd tried not to dwell on such thoughts, but it'd been impossible.

He wanted Thea safe and happy, particularly after she'd shared so much with him earlier this morning. It was becoming impossible to keep his distance from her. She didn't see what a kind and generous person she was. All she saw were her failures. In direct contrast, all Will saw were her strengths. Her dedication to her grandfather was heartbreaking and loving.

Who was he fooling? The truth refused to be denied. He was deeply attracted to her, even as he knew that nothing could come of it. He exhaled his frustration. Even if she didn't want him, he'd do his damnedest to ensure that only the best man would win the honor to be her husband.

As she stood between him and Grayson, Thea could only be described as resplendent in a shimmering spring-green silk gown with black satin ribbon around her waist, bodice, and hem. The gown's skirt was slightly fuller and gave her the appearance of a regal queen holding court. Devan and Honeycutt stood facing them.

"Lady Eanruig, it's my understanding your estate is right next to Lady Payne's in Northumberland," Lord Honeycutt said. "That means you and Lord William are next door neighbors."

"Indeed," Thea answered as her gaze locked with Honeycutt. "I expect our friendship will continue to grow closer. He'll undoubtedly need my advice on farming and managing such a great estate. I plan to spend as much time as necessary to see him succeed." She slapped Will's arm with her silk fan. The crack of the mother of pearl frame across his arm was a little harder than necessary.

Though the men around them didn't notice or understand the meaning, he did. Her outward poise indicated a calm demeanor, but he sensed her nervousness. In her hand, she clutched several folded papers which crumpled in protest against her tight grip.

Will tilted his lips in a feigned smile. Nevertheless, Thea's flirting prowess continued to improve. Honeycutt kept glancing at her, and Thea kept grinning at him.

Honeycutt took a step closer to Thea and caught Will's gaze. "Are you throwing your good fortune in our faces, Lord William? You only invited us to gloat."

She lightly touched Honeycutt's arm and smiled. "I'm not at all certain what you mean."

"He has the pleasure of your company here at Langham Hall while you're in London," Devan said in a silky voice. "He invited us over to meet you, knowing full well we'd be envious of his unrestricted time with you."

"Lord William would never be *crass*. He's hosting this event as a favor for me." The soft lilt in her voice caused Will to tighten his torso for a direct punch. "Lord William invited you all here today so I could see for myself who the finest men in London are. I think that's always appropriate if a lady might be looking to marry. Wouldn't you agree?"

Will's stomach roiled in protest once again. The men laughed in answer, but Will felt the color drain from his face.

She smoothed the wrinkles from the papers she held in her fist, then efficiently distributed a copy of each to their guests. Her gaze darted from the lone page she'd held in her hand to Will.

For a moment nothing existed except the two of them, and she searched his eyes as if looking for an answer or approval. He smiled gently in encouragement. She returned his smile briefly, then nodded once.

"This might explain my situation better." With a deep breath as if collecting all her courage, she turned her attention to the men. "I prepared a summary of my assets along with the privileges and positions that come with my title." She glanced at the paper in her hand once. "You see here a complete listing of my lands, estate, and my dowry. With my title, there are certain appointments my husband would receive. After Scotland and England united, the king appointed the Earl of Eanruig the Assistant Constable of the Royal Horses. It's a ceremonial position, but my husband would appear by the Prince Regent at every opening session of Parliament. He'll be the local magistrate on my lands in southern Scotland. As a woman, I can't be appointed to those, but my husband would. They're very prestigious positions."

As the words tumbled from her mouth, the shock of what she was doing hit Will with the full force of a battering ram. Instead of allowing the men to be charmed by her delightfulness and intelligence, Thea thought she needed to persuade them she was suitable for marriage by what she'd bring to their union.

"You can even call yourself Earl Eanruig like my ancestors did when their wives were the titleholder." As the last words of her speech faded from the room, silence descended.

Devan's eyes widened as he read the list. Usually, he'd be the first to say something if there was any sense of awkwardness. Instead, Will's friend remained quiet.

Grayson stared at the paper, then slowly he raised his gaze to Will. The marquess cleared his throat as if to say something, then shook his head, clearly flabbergasted.

Thea released a pent-up breath, then folded her paper. "I'll be more than happy to address any concerns you may have. Perhaps it'd be efficient for all of us if you share whatever questions you might have in front of each other. That way everyone will be on an even keel in a manner of speaking."

"Hmm, yes. Good idea." Honeycutt lifted a brow. "This is an impressive list. But there's no mention of your stables? I'd be interested in the number of hunters and hounds you have available. For hunting parties, you understand."

"Honeycutt," Will growled.

"I don't understand." She tilted her head, the movement accentuating her long neck. The pulse at the base of her neck fluttered, betraying her unease.

"William, no offense meant." He turned his attention to Thea. "My lady, normally, these things"—he waved a hand at the list—"are negotiated through solicitors. I'm afraid my glib comment was an inept attempt to hide my . . . surprise." He bit his lips to keep from smiling.

Devan finally lifted his gaze from the sheet of paper he was holding. "This is unbelievable."

Thea nodded curtly. "I forgot to include the trust my parents created for me."

"Thea." Will cleared his throat. "Perhaps we should discuss all this later after you have an opportunity to talk with my friends more."

She trained her beautiful eyes on him. "Emma made mention that courting would be easier if women wore a card with their dowry pinned to the front of their gowns, meaning that women should be more forthcoming of their worth." She clutched her paper to her chest. "I thought there was practicality in her idea, considering how quickly I need to find a husband. Yet, gentlemen, I'm sure we all agree that a woman is worth so much more than her dowry. But I want to make one thing clear, this is just a contingency plan if I'm forced to marry. But if any of you have another opinion. . . ." A deep crimson colored her cheeks when she noticed Honeycutt laughing softly.

"I'm envious. Contingency plan!" Honeycutt announced with a chortle. "No, a better description is that I'm green-eyed." He turned his full attention to Will. "You've pulled one over on us, haven't you, William? But I don't understand the list explaining the wealth Lady Eanruig brings to you? Are you rubbing your good fortune in our faces?"

"That's enough," Will warned. He didn't care for the smug look on the viscount's face. "I'll not tolerate anyone besmirching Thea."

"Careful there, my friend. No insult intended. I'm referring to today's lead article in *The Midnight Cryer.*

It reported that at your parents' soirée, you'll be announcing your betrothal."

Devan's eyes popped wide. "Is that true?"

Grayson shook his head and smiled ruefully. "Why didn't you tell us? Congratulations."

Thea blinked twice as if trying to get her bearings. "That can't be."

Will's own smile vanished. "What?"

"Felicitations on your happy news." Devan smiled in relief, then clasped his hands behind his back and rocked on his heels. "Lady Eanruig is simply enchanting. Perhaps I'll steal her away from you."

Thea recovered more quickly than he did. "Perhaps I'll jilt him for the right man."

Will cringed at the word *jilt*.

Thea glanced in Will's direction. The smile on her face didn't reach her eyes. Normally, they flashed in brilliance when she was happy.

"Be careful what you wish for, my lady." A charming grin tugged at Grayson's lips. "I take that as a challenge."

Will smiled blandly, but blood pounded in his veins.

"I quote the article's headline, 'A Match Made in Heaven.'" Honeycutt chuckled.

A storm was brewing in Thea's unusual eyes as they'd darkened to an emerald green. "What else did it say?"

Things were going from bad to ruinous in the blink of an eye. Suddenly, her face paled considerably. Without a second thought, he took her hand, willing her to look at him. He inched his way closer to her side. She straightened her shoulders.

That damnable *Midnight Cryer* would not upset her again. Even if he had to personally tear apart the paper's offices.

"Well . . . nothing of import," Honeycutt stammered.

"My good man," Devan crooned, clearly trying to change the subject. "Love has finally found you. The lovely Lady Eanruig has charmed you silly with her extraordinary cleverness. That's why you called us over today."

Thea's gaze shot to Will's, and the grin on her face turned wooden. "I wouldn't call it a love match," she murmured.

Before him, her magnificent eyes faded to a light green as if her confidence from earlier was slowly being extinguished. "Thea, shall we stroll around the room a bit?"

She either didn't hear him or refused to acknowledge him. She dropped his hand, then turned to Devan. "Mr. Farris, it's not what you think. Will invited you today so I could meet you and hopefully persuade one of you to marry me if I need a husband," she stated calmly.

Will slowly blinked. This was the Thea from Northumberland. All of her earlier polish from her society lessons had evaporated into thin air. He had to stop her before everything exploded into chaos. "Thea—"

She waved him off. "You'll find that my charm doesn't lie in my wit or even my conversational skills or even the rumors that swirl around me. My appeal lies in my estate. All totaled, it's worth well over one hundred thousand pounds. My grandfather, the previous Duke of Ferr-Colby, provided a sixty-thousand-pound trust and a twenty-five-thousand-pound dowry. I also inherited an additional fifty thousand from my parents." The strength in her voice belied the hurt in her eyes. "I hoped it'd be enough to interest one of you in marriage."

"Thea," Will murmured. "Perhaps we should discuss such details later?"

"Why?" She turned to Will.

"Because it's not a suitable subject for women to discuss," Honeycutt said as he flushed a brilliant red like a hothouse rose.

"Women don't discuss money?" She shook her head slowly as if coming out of a dream. "Of course, if I secure my title, I won't need to marry . . . but I'd like to have a family." She offered a tentative smile. "I can pay if any of you are interested. . . ." She let the words trail to nothing as another blast of heat colored her cheeks.

Will took a step between Honeycutt and Thea. "The idea that women don't discuss finances is provincial thinking. My sister, the Countess of Somerton, discusses money every day at her bank. Why can't women discuss it? It's their future."

How could he have thought the viscount suitable for Thea? Honeycutt would not insult her in Langham Hall or anywhere else as long as Will was by her side.

"Well . . . I—" Honeycutt stumbled with a response.

"He's right, Will." She turned to his three friends. "I apologize for my vulgarity to speak of money. You now see who is the crass one between Lord William and me." Her pulse throbbed at the base of her neck. "Gentlemen, I'm in desperate need of some fresh air." Without a glance his way, Thea gracefully walked to the French doors that led to Langham Park.

He closed his eyes. How could everything have gone awry so quickly? He wanted her safe and happy with a good man. Instead, with Honeycutt's stupid retorts about her lists and *The Midnight Cryer*'s words, she'd been gutted—her humiliation plain across her face. Never in his life had he seen a woman hurt this way. The throbbing pain inside his chest threatened to knock him to his knees.

Before he could chase after her, Grayson had exited the same door as Thea.

"Sorry, old man." Honeycutt bowed quickly, then left as if the hounds of hell were nipping at his heels.

Devan stood staring at him with disbelief plainly written on his face.

To make matters worse, Aunt Stella entered the room as Honeycutt reached the door. "Out of my way." She scolded the viscount as she waved several editions of *The Midnight Cryer* in the air.

"What just happened?" Devan asked. "Is what she said the truth? Is that why we're here?"

"I'm not really certain what happened." Will could only answer his first question. The rest of his inquiries would have to wait as all clarity in his thoughts turned into a murky muddle.

"Is this some sort of a joke between you and Lady Eanruig?" Devan asked.

"No, you misunderstand. She wanted to meet you." Will shook his head to object.

"What I understand is that she was mortified." Devan glanced at the French doors while gently shaking his head. "You're her friend. Go to her." He turned back to Will. "She'll need you."

Will nodded. He had to find her, then deal with his friends later. If he could hold her hands and look into her eyes, perhaps they both could talk through what had happened.

"William, you need to see today's *Cryer*." Aunt Stella's voice rang through the room as she came to stand by his side. Without another word, she handed him a copy.

The House of Langham's perennial disappointment, who we affectionately call the Damp Squib of Love, Lord William Cavensham, has finally found romance. His notorious reputation for failure in the matrimonial market has finally come to

an end with his own "match made in heaven." Un-
fortunately, he's betrothed to the Nemesis from
Northumberland. One piece of advice for the spare
heir—don't fall asleep in Lady Eanruig's presence.
You might never waken.

"Where's Thea?" The lines around Stella's eyes tensed. "She needs to see this before anyone says something to her."

He wanted to drive his fist through the wall. He should have never agreed to introduce his friends this way. "I'm afraid it's a little too late for that, Stella."

Gentle readers, you need to read the latest.
Somehow Lady Man-Eater possesses a plethora of suitors.
It's like a piranha fishing in a barrel.
Always truthful in our reporting,
The Midnight Cryer

Chapter Seventeen

Thea's heart pounded as she sped through the park, desperately trying to hide where no one could find her. The haunted look on the men's faces as she blurted out her financial worth was a sight she'd never forget. Her cheeks still felt as if they were on fire. A small rectangular garden of boxwoods lay to her left, and she made her way into the cool shade. Tucked away from view, a seating area of several granite benches beckoned her forward.

She plopped down on the closest seat with her skirts billowing like clouds around her. With her elbows on her knees, she hid her face in her hands. It was nonsensical, but if she kept her face hidden, perhaps she could get her mortification under control. Whether she could ever return to Langham Hall was a question she couldn't answer at this point. She had nowhere else to go.

However, Claire might allow her to stay until the hearing in front of the committee was finished. She'd face the committee alone. If she had any luck at all, she could return home and back to her old life.

"Lady Eanruig?" Lord Grayson's deep masculine voice echoed around her. "May I join you?"

Without lifting her hands from her face, she nodded.

The rustle of clothing meant he'd sat next to her. For the next several minutes, they sat in an uncomfortable silence. Finally, she forced herself to look at him. She was a titled lady in her own right and needed to act as such.

Inwardly, she cursed at the sympathy in his eyes, but she forced herself to hold his gaze. "Well, that was awkward, wasn't it?" Her voice wobbled a smidgen. "You probably know what it all meant."

Lord Grayson studied his clasped hands in front of him. "I take it to mean that William hasn't changed his position on the idea of marriage."

She let out a sigh. "No, he hasn't. But it's not what you think. I told him I didn't want to marry him either. His aunt wants us to marry." She turned slightly toward him. "I've received advice that I should consider marriage before I answer the challenge to my title."

The marquess lifted his gaze and regarded her. "You need to marry?"

"Or an engagement." Thea nodded. "The new Duke of Ferr-Colby is challenging my claim. My grandfather's solicitor says the Committee for Privileges is conservative in nature. If they see that I'm connected to a powerful family, then they'll likely decide in my favor if I can prove my lineage."

A kind smile broke the severe features of his face. He was tall with dark hair and deep brown eyes. There was an inherent strength to him that most women would find appealing.

But her silly heart protested he wasn't Will.

"Farris, Honeycutt, and I were invited here today to see if one of us might suit you." His words lingered in the air.

"And if in return, one of you found me likewise pleasing."

"You are a true original, Lady Eanruig. I like your candor. Now tell me, did you find one of us pleasing?"

His words made her a bit wary. "Of course. I'd consider myself very fortunate if I garnered any of your friendships."

"Like your friendship with William?" He lifted his hand to stop her from protesting. "Though I'm not a romantic, I saw how the two of you looked at each other. I had expected him to announce you were his before Honeycutt brought up *The Midnight Cryer*."

She fought to keep from rolling her eyes at that pronouncement. "Sir, you're mistaken."

"I'd be honored if you call me Grayson."

Thea studied the meticulous boxwoods that framed the area. All these honorifics and titles were confusing enough. She didn't want to make a bigger fool of herself than she already was, especially in front of the marquess. "If I call you Grayson, then how shall you address me? Eanruig sounds too manly, and Theodora sounds too intimate."

He leaned back and chuckled. "I think Lady Eanruig sounds perfect until we become a little better acquainted, don't you?"

She nodded her agreement.

"My lady, I hope I don't shock you, but if you and William don't come to an understanding, I'd like to press my suit."

"You want to marry me?" She couldn't keep the shock out of her voice. "Even with the rumors?"

He nodded. "I don't believe those lies, especially after I've met you. It's common knowledge I need to marry an heiress and rather quickly. I inherited my title, and the coffers are practically nonexistent. I'm not an ideal marriage partner from that standpoint, but I have a lovely estate. I think we'd suit and get along quite well together.

Hopefully, after some time in each other's company, we'd find love or at least a comfortable companionship with one another."

His gaze was sharp but honest.

She was too surprised to answer. With his dark hair, deep brown eyes, and fine features, he was handsome. But his someberness took away from his countenance.

"We could split our time between both estates," he added.

"I see," she said finally. "I—I don't think that would be in my best interests."

"Of course." He smiled slightly. "I understand. I have nothing to offer but a run-down estate."

"No. I have no concerns over that. I have more than enough for both of us." She caught his gaze, hoping she could explain without hurting his feelings. "I couldn't leave Ladykyrk. It's my estate. It needs me as much as I need it."

"Just like mine needs me," he said softly. He took her hand in his and gave a perfunctory kiss in the air over her knuckles. "Sometimes, we all have to make tough decisions to do what's best for those who rely on us."

"Yes, we do." Pride kept her from arguing anymore.

"Will you at least consider my offer? Perhaps we could come up with a compromise." He stood to leave.

"I'll give it some thought," she answered.

Her traitorous heart that wanted Will skipped a beat in defiance.

The sight of Grayson comforting Thea nearly tore Will's heart out of his chest. He should be the one. Grayson kissed Thea's hand, then turned and walked toward him. Will nodded, not bothering to stop. The overwhelming need to reach Thea's side drove him to hurry. However, the marquess stopped him.

"It wasn't my place to follow her out here, but she looked like she'd lost her last friend," Grayson said.

"You have my eternal thanks for seeing after her. My aunt came into the room just as Thea fled." Will extended his hand for a shake.

Grayson's forehead furrowed into neat lines. "You may not want to shake my hand or claim me as a friend after this."

"Why?"

"I asked her to marry me," Grayson said without a hint of emotion. "Go and comfort her. We'll discuss it tomorrow." Without giving Will a chance to demand an explanation, Grayson walked away.

Will exhaled the breath he'd been holding. It seemed it was the only thing he could control in that moment. He cursed to himself, then continued to approach Thea. When he reached her side, she glanced at him then returned to her study of the garden.

"When I first found this spot, I thought it rather sedate and secluded." She spoke with a quiet but desperate firmness. "However, first Grayson found me and now you."

He eased onto the bench seat beside her. Just being close to her caused the angry pounding of his pulse to calm. "Would you rather be alone?"

"No, I'd enjoy your company." She studied the fountain before them. "This part of the park is beautiful."

"Just like you." He brushed a loose wisp of hair from her forehead. She closed her eyes at his touch.

She didn't acknowledge his compliment but bit her lip and turned away. "It was rude and ill-mannered to speak of money. What was I thinking? I embarrassed you and myself."

He scooted closer to her, then laid his hand next to hers. His dwarfed hers. It seemed so small, but he knew that her hand had accomplished amazing things in her short life. She'd used it with her nimble mind to keep her grandfather's duchy and reputation intact while taking care of him throughout his illness.

Without a word, he tangled his fingers with hers. "You weren't vulgar." He struggled to find the right words to take the blame and make her feel better. "I was. I should have planned your introduction to my friends more carefully. I'm here to apologize to you. I had no idea that *The Midnight Cryer* had published that rubbish. I would have been by your side sooner, but Aunt Stella came in immediately after you left. She had a copy of today's edition."

"What did it say?" Her voice trembled a little, betraying her disquiet.

He released a deep breath and studied the garden. It was damn embarrassing, but she had a right to know. "The *Cryer* always refers to me as a failure in love. I quote 'the Damp Squib of Love.'" Every time they published such garbage, he always tried to ignore it, but not now—not when it hurt Thea. "They said I finally found my match made in heaven."

"Your Aunt Stella told me that you didn't like to participate in *ton* events. She mentioned that you had an unfortunate *incident* when you were younger," she gently said.

"Incident?" he asked.

"Your third cousin who broke your betrothal years ago." Her earnest gaze caught his.

"She wasn't officially my betrothed." He tried to keep his voice as nonchalant as possible, but a hot scourge burned his throat at the memory of Avalon's rejection.

He smoothed his palms down his breeches. Thea had a right to know about his past no matter how much it hurt or humiliated him. He never liked to discuss Avalon with anyone, but with Thea, he needed to since the *Cryer* had embroiled her into his past.

"When I was nineteen, a woman rebuffed my suit when she decided to marry a wealthy marquess. Of course, *The Midnight Cryer* mocks me ever since Lady Warwyk jilted me."

She leaned forward and caught his gaze. "Why do they do it?"

"To punish me. Not long ago, they were going to publish a diary of a family member, and it would have destroyed her and others I love. I helped ensure it was returned to the rightful owner by being there when the offices were broken into. Someone from the *Cryer* recognized me, and I've been a target ever since." He turned toward her. "But the real truth is that the *Cryer* loves to publish rubbish about my family."

"Does it hurt?"

He chuckled. No one had ever asked that question before. He'd always acted indifferent about their taunts of his failure. "Sometimes."

"I imagine it does," she said. "What did they say about me?"

"Nothing important."

"William, please. I'm a grown woman." She straightened her shoulders as if preparing for a punch. "Tell me. I need to know what I'm facing at the soirée."

He waited for a moment, debating how much to tell her. But Thea's strength was one of her greatest assets, along with her wisdom. She did need to know what she faced from the *ton* tomorrow when they descended on Langham Hall. "They called you the 'Nemesis of Northumberland.'"

"That's all?" she asked incredulously.

"That's all I read. I threw down the paper without

finishing the article. My first priority was finding you." His gaze caught hers.

Her eyes betrayed her confusion and hurt, and it haunted him. For the world, he didn't want to see her hurt by the nonsense that gushed from *The Midnight Cryer.*

"Of course, the editor thinks he's a cleaver wordsmith. Stella's worried about your reaction to the story." He entwined their fingers again to comfort her. But it also soothed the frustration he felt at their circumstances. "I'm sorry if you're embarrassed. I've felt that way before with their reporting."

Her fingers tightened around his. "She should have worried about me making a mess with your friends. I'm sure you are too."

He dipped his head until their gazes were eye level. "No. My only concern is you. With my friends, you were honest." He grinned slightly and hoped she'd return the favor. "If they can't handle the truth, then they're not worthy of you. However, you don't give yourself enough credit. You're an incredible woman. Any man would be lucky to marry you." He lowered his voice. "I'm sorry too, if you're embarrassed because I didn't tell my friends why they were invited today."

"It makes little difference." She shrugged and turned her gaze to the fountain. "Lord Grayson asked me to marry him just now."

Her voice was so low, he had to lean forward to hear the words.

"He told me he has no money and wants to rebuild his estate. He suggested that we split our time between our two estates." She sighed softly as if the thought pained her. "I told him no as I didn't want to live anywhere except Ladykyrk. He pressed me to give it some thought. I told him that I'd think about it."

She turned and faced him. Her slight grin would have

been endearing if it wasn't for the fact she was discussing marrying another.

"I'm not certain it's a good idea for me to be away from my responsibilities for any length of time. Such a silly thought, isn't it?" Without waiting for him to answer, she continued, "I could hire a land steward, and he could manage the responsibilities as I start a new life with my husband. But I want my husband by my side at Ladykyrk."

He stiffened at the word *husband*. It baffled him that he would respond that way. She'd made it quite clear, she didn't want to marry him, yet the thought didn't sit well with him anymore. Instead, a need, a want even, to change her mind took root inside of him.

"Grayson is a good man but has serious money problems. His father made several bad investments and lost a great deal of money. Instead of accepting his losses and trying to figure another way to return the estate to a flush account, he continued to make even riskier investments, hoping to recoup his losses. He just made it worse. When the old marquess finally passed, Grayson inherited a world of troubles."

"Well, one thing is clear." Her lips pursed in annoyance. "I may be a failure at behaving like a true countess, but I did manage to receive a marriage proposal today." She let out a tortured breath. "Oh God, Will. What am I going to do? I don't want to marry just anyone."

Suddenly, a solution presented itself, one that would help her with the committee and give her some time to find true love too. It would solve her immediate problem but could ruin his reputation forever. At this point he didn't care, as he needed to help her. Without any hesitation, he scooted closer. "What if we were engaged?"

"Engaged?" Her gaze widened which emphasized the blue-green hue of her glorious eyes. "As in marriage?"

"It'll work. I'll be by your side during the hearing. After you secure your title, then you can jilt me." He cleared his throat in hopes his voice relayed his confidence. "That will allow you time to find someone you can fall in love with."

"You would do that for me?" A true smile, one incandescent in brightness, lit her face. "It's a brilliant solution." Suddenly, a few lines of worry creased her brow. "But what happens after the committee makes their decision?"

"We could . . . we'll figure it out," he said. Just then, a gardener came into view, trimming the boxwoods across from them. "Let's go someplace private." He brought her fingers to his mouth, letting his warm breath tease her skin.

She continued to stare at him. "Why?"

"So, we can talk without any interruptions." His throat tightened, but he forced himself to answer as truthfully as he dared. "Because you need to regain the confidence you had before my friends came to visit. You need every ounce of strength you can find to face that committee. I want you to succeed in everything you want in life, Thea."

Because I don't want anyone to kiss you but me.

She released a sigh as if accepting the weight of the world on her shoulders. "All right."

"Come." He tugged her to a standing position. "Let's get a drink. I have the perfect place." He gave her a smile designed to be as intimate as a kiss.

The Countess of Eanruig may have thought she lacked any skill in handling the patrons of society, but she'd developed another talent that was rarer in his opinion.

She'd learned how to turn his world upside down.

Chapter Eighteen

Will escorted Thea from the park into a side entrance of Langham Hall, then through a corridor she'd never seen. When they entered a dark stairwell going down, he preceded her, but took her hand in his.

"Where are you taking me?" Her heart pounded in excitement. There was something forbidden and exhilarating in the adventure, and she was impatient to follow him.

"A secret place that hardly anyone ever visits. Pitts comes down here on occasion. He and I are the only ones who know the location of the key." He led her down a hallway lit by two wall sconces. He stretched and reached to the top of a doorjamb where he retrieved an iron key. Will made quick work of opening the door, then swept his hand in front of him, inviting her to proceed.

When she walked into the room, darkness surrounded her. She turned and bumped into Will.

"Careful." His hands brushed down the sides of her

arms to steady her, and she shivered at his sinfully dark voice. When she moved to step away, he pulled her near. "Stay close for a minute. I don't want you to hurt yourself. Pitts has been known to leave things on the floor."

In seconds, the soft glow from a candle lit the room. She found herself in a small area much like an alcove. Two comfy-looking wingchairs stood guard beside a small table. Behind the cozy sitting area was a massive table where bottles of what appeared to be liquor stood in an orderly fashion. Behind the table stood barrels stacked one on top of another, forming a wall of wooden casks.

"What is this place?" she whispered.

He chuckled. "It's the whisky room. My father stores his vast collection of Scottish whisky, Irish whiskey, and French brandies here. It's his one true indulgence. My great-grandfather started this collection, and my father has kept up the tradition."

"It's impressive. How do you know where to find the key?"

He leaned close as if divulging a great secret. "Besides Aunt Stella, I'm one of Pitts's favorites too."

That he was a favorite of those two didn't surprise her in the least. He was easily one of the most captivating men she'd ever met. A smile tugged at her lips. Of course, she hadn't met many men, but she had a hard time believing that anyone could outshine his brightness. Even Lord Grayson, Mr. Farris, or Lord Honeycutt couldn't hold a candle to Will.

Seemingly nonplussed with her smile, he continued, "Claire's mother's family was known for producing some of the finest Scottish whisky to ever come out of the lowlands of Scotland. We have two casks."

He took her hand and led her to the large table behind the seating area. He picked a bottle and poured some of

the amber liquid into an elegant but short and stocky
leaded crystal glass. "Do you have a distillery on your
land in Scotland?"

He propped his hip against the edge, the stance casual
and confident. Below the main floor of the house, all
sound was absent. Only their voices and breaths broke
the silence.

"No. The excise duties were too high for my grandfather's taste. When he was active in the House of Lords,
he regularly argued that Parliament should eliminate
such unfair taxes. But it was always to deaf ears." For
emphasis, she leaned closer to whisper, though they were
the only ones down there. "There are two large copper
stills on my property. Completely illegal. I refuse to have
them torn down. I think one of these days Parliament
will see the errors of its way."

A roguish smile beamed across his face. "I've never
drunk whisky with an outlaw before."

"There's a first time for everyone." She scooted closer
and mimicked Will's lean. Only a hand's width was between them. With deliberate slowness, she placed her
hand over his and moved his hand with the glass to her
lips.

His smile changed into a deep and rich rumble of
laughter. She wrinkled her nose both from the sound and
the medicinal smell of the alcohol. She sipped a small
amount of the amber liquid and swished it around in her
mouth, savoring the unique taste of peat and malted barley and water. When combined correctly, those three
simple ingredients turned into magic.

Thea carefully swallowed and closed her eyes. The
liquid warmed her throat all the way down to her stomach. She'd seen grown men take a sip without understanding how to enjoy the drink, then cough their lungs
up for not paying proper respect to its potency.

When she opened her eyes, Will stared intently at her.

With an equally deliberate movement, he brought the same glass to his mouth and took a drink.

Thea's gaze never left his, and her hand still covered his. Her breathing had deepened, and the warmth from the Scotch that had filled her stomach moved lower. Her whole body seemed to thrum with each loud beat of her heart. "Sharing a glass of whisky is akin to a kiss."

"How so?" He moved just a tad nearer to her.

But it was close enough that the whisky on his breath and his bergamot fragrance combined into a potion she wanted to lose herself in. "Our lips touched the exact same spot on the glass, and our mouths tasted the same whisky."

"God, Thea, what did my family teach you yesterday? Perhaps I need lessons." He groaned, and without taking his eyes from hers, he took another swallow.

"Let's try to share the whisky in another way." She raked her fingers through his silky hair. The throbbing between her legs grew in strength. She searched his eyes for any hesitation and found none. The intensity of his gaze matched her own yearning for more.

To prolong the moment, she slowly moved her lips to his. In concert, he wrapped his arms around her. The weight of his fingers on the small of her back grounded her, and it felt heavenly. She brushed her lips against his, and she could taste the rich sharp taste of the whisky. Without warning, she licked his lips, delighting in the taste again.

"Where did you learn to do that?" he whispered.

"It's a requisite part of the whisky lesson," she crooned against his lips.

"Who exactly is the teacher here?" he asked.

"You're teaching me how to kiss, and I'm teaching you how to appreciate Scotch whisky." With her whisper against his lips, she pushed a little harder. In response, he pressed his lips against hers, then parted his mouth slightly. She did the same in return. The tart taste of whisky swirled between them as he gently caressed his tongue with hers. He groaned and pulled her tighter.

She gripped his hair, as the room seemed to spin around them. He released another moan, and the sound vibrated through her chest. In response, her heart knocked against her ribs, desperate to break free.

She sighed in answer, and her kiss grew more frantic. In that moment, she realized she'd never grow tired of his kisses. She'd never grow tired of him. This was what men and women were created for—to share moments like this that threatened to consume them.

"*Will*." She gasped for breath and broke away. The smoldering heat in his eyes burned through her. Gently, she kissed him again. "I want more."

"Whisky?" he grunted.

"You," she answered.

Without taking his eyes from hers, he put his hands around her waist and sat her on the table. She wrapped her arms around his neck and kissed him again. As he returned her kiss, he gently caressed her ribs.

"Touch me," she begged. She brought his hands to the undersides of her breasts. She arched against him.

With a light and soothing caress, he cupped her gently then gradually increased the pressure of his hands. When she lifted her head, his hot mouth kissed and licked the base of her neck. All the while, he kneaded her breasts through her silk gown and stays, learning what excited her, driving her mad. She cursed that there were so many barriers between them.

She pulled him closer between her legs. There wasn't an ounce of fat on his lean, fit body. When her skirt restricted her movement, she softly growled in frustration.

With infinite slowness, Will raised her skirts while never ceasing to kiss her neck, the dip of her shoulder, or her jaw. He drew his mouth across her cheek until he reached the tender spot beneath her ear. He tasted her skin with his tongue then soothed his lips over the same spot.

Finally, with her skirts out of the way, his erection nestled in between the valley of her legs. But it still wasn't enough. She moaned his name and tilted her hips, desperate to find relief.

When he drew back, they were both panting. She knew something incredible was waiting for her, but she had no idea what it was or how to ask for it. "Please?"

Their gazes caught and the passion they'd created surrounded them, pulling them together. After a long moment, when she thought he might refuse her, he kissed her like he'd never let her go.

"I'll need to touch here," he murmured as he ran one hand lightly up her thigh to her nether curls.

Without hesitation and too stunned to say a word aloud, she nodded.

His fingers combed through her curls then drifted down. When his finger touched her *there*, she mewled a soft approval and leaned into his touch.

"You're warm. Wet. Soft," he whispered. The words vibrated between them, and the ache between her legs intensified, demanding attention.

He kissed her again, his tongue possessing hers. She was lost in his touch as his fingers caressed and coaxed more from her. She closed her eyes and curled her toes in her slippers seeking purchase. With a soft moan, she pushed against his fingers, desperate to climb to relief.

"You're close, Thea. Let go. I won't let you fall," he whispered.

Slowly he pushed two fingers inside her while he continued to caress her with his thumb. She sobbed a breath.

Wanting relief from this ache, her head fell against his chest. A surge of ice and fire combined, then flew apart inside her. Pleasure rolled in waves through her as she held on to his powerful body, desperate not to shatter into a thousand pieces.

His arms surrounded her. With his mouth against her ear, he repeated her name over and over like a solemn prayer. Never before had she felt so cherished by another.

When her breath came under control, she leaned back and looked into his eyes. He was taking deep breaths as if he'd run an uphill race.

"What's wrong?"

"Nothing," he exhaled. "I'm just trying . . . trying to calm this tempest we've created."

She searched his face, desperate to understand. "What can I do?"

"You've done enough for now." He closed his eyes and grinned.

Then she understood. "You pleasured me, but I haven't done the same for you?"

He trailed one finger down her cheek. "Oh, you've given me pleasure. The memory of you climaxing in my arms will always give me pleasure."

"Really? Did you enjoy it?"

He drew nearer and kissed the side of her mouth. "Immensely, Thea." The sound of her name in his low, gravelly voice sent a thrill through her. "Tomorrow, we stand side by side. I'll not let the *Cryer* defeat you."

Gently, she returned his kiss with one of her own. "I can still taste the whisky."

"So can I." He kissed her lips.

She sighed and nuzzled closer to him. "I think I'm going to enjoy being betrothed to you."

He laughed, and his brilliant blue eyes flashed. "And I with you."

"Which leads me to one conclusion," she said.

"What's that?"

"You're not to taste whisky with any other woman except me."

After Will escorted Thea to her room with the excuse she needed to rest before tonight's soirée, she couldn't stop thinking about their whisky tasting. Was it always like that with a man?

When they kissed, she felt wonderfully free yet at the same time possessed. She closed her eyes, then ran her hands lightly over her breasts that still tingled from his touch. Her breath hitched when she imagined Will kissing her there, suckling her nipples. She continued the caress down her middle over the soft satin of her dress, slowly trailing her fingers over her hips and thighs, careful not to touch her mound that still throbbed from their passion.

She released a deep sigh, willing her body to behave. She could easily see herself always craving Will's touch. But it was best to remember that their intimate moment was a mere speck in time that they'd shared when they both needed comfort and let their guard down. It had been lovely that he'd been worried that his friends had upset her. Though neither of them had changed their minds about marriage, his marvelous solution that they pretend to be engaged would solve some of her problems. Instead of focusing on finding a husband, she could concentrate on Ladykyrk and her interview in front of the committee.

Fortune had smiled on her when she met Will. There was no truer friend than he.

A vision of Lord Grayson pushed into her thoughts. Though tall, dark, and if he smiled, handsome, Grayson didn't have the physical presence Will had. When Will walked into a room, it was as if her body recognized him immediately and practically hummed in appreciation.

But their kissing lesson wasn't the only thing to capture Thea's attention this afternoon. To her utter delight, a box that she hadn't ordered had arrived from Mademoiselle Mignon's this afternoon with the most exquisite gown and matching slippers she'd ever seen. Consisting of a flowing iridescent silk best described as a subtle coral color, the dress was trimmed with seed pearls. Inside one of the matching slippers was a handwritten note from Stella:

Wear this and you'll have Lord Howton magically eating out of your hand.

The rest of the day flew by until a knock sounded on her door. When Thea answered, it was Nancy, Stella's intrepid lady's maid, who stood ready to help Thea dress for the evening.

Within a half hour, Nancy had transformed Thea once again. Adjusting a few loose curls, Nancy sighed. "This dress makes you glow, my lady."

The scooped décolletage was low enough to make Thea feel feminine but didn't overly expose her chest. The capped sleeves perfectly matched the neckline design. With her mother's diamond ear-drops and pearl necklace, she felt like a countess and a fairy princess all rolled into one.

She checked her appearance in the mirror once more, then swallowed, hoping to tame the butterfly flutters that were currently holding court her stomach. They reminded her that tonight she'd meet several members of the House of Lords and other dignitaries that the Duke and Duchess of Langham had invited on her behalf. A successful evening of swaying opinion to her side held the promise that she'd be victorious in front of the privileges committee.

The guests for tonight's soirée would start arriving within an hour, and Stella and Lady Edith had commanded she meet them in the family sitting room for a sherry. Thankfully, Thea had quickly learned to maneuver the labyrinth that consisted of Langham Hall, and entered the sitting room where the two grand dames sat chirping like birds over each other's dresses. When they realized Thea had arrived, they both drew silent.

Lady Edith was the first to stand. "Come here, Thea, and let me see you in the light," she commanded.

As she approached, Stella rose and stood beside Lady Edith. Both ladies looked Thea up and down.

Stella was the first to break the silence. "You're lovely, Thea. I knew that color would suit you when we picked it out, but it's even better than I imagined."

Lady Edith nodded vigorously. Somehow, her red turban set at a jaunty angle stayed put on her head. "You look like a queen."

Stella smiled. "How do you feel?"

"Like a countess." She dipped a deep curtsey, showing her respect. "I have something to tell you." She'd share what had occurred before she and Will came to an arrangement. Instantly, heat flooded her cheeks as she recalled his tender touch and kisses. "I received a marriage proposal today from one of Will's friends."

Edith's thin white eyebrows shot skyward. "Oh, my. That's excellent news, isn't it, Stella?"

"Well done, Thea," Stella offered. "There's always more than one way to reel in a fish. Very creative. Who's the bait?"

"Bait?" This was not the reaction she'd expected. She thought the ladies would have been shocked rather than pleased.

"The one you're using to reel in William," Edith answered.

"The Marquess of Grayson," she said.

"Come, Thea, take this." Stella held out a glass of sherry. "This is to take the edge off the evening." Without a hint of consternation, she continued, "Grayson, you say?"

"Grayson is a good man, but poor as a church mouse," Lady Edith piped up. When she sat down with her glass of sherry, her knees cracked louder than a bolt of thunder. "Must be a storm brewing."

"Don't be dramatic, Edith." Stella winged an eyebrow, then turned her attention to Thea.

Thea took the glass of sherry but didn't take a sip. She wanted all of her wits about her this evening. She took the chair next to Edith, who sat on the sofa.

Lord Fluff entered the sitting room with his nose held high. He glanced at Edith, then Stella before sauntering over to Thea. He gracefully jumped on the arm of her chair, then sat as if taking his rightful place on his throne.

"Thea, dearest." Stella strolled over to stand before her. "Good title, but I'm not certain Grayson is the right one for you."

The hesitation in the grand dame's voice gave Thea pause. She wasn't certain either, but the more she thought about it, the clearer it became that she'd made the right choice. Gently, she placed her glass on the side table beside Lord Fluff whose tail had started to flicker in displeasure. Stella reached for her hands, and in response, Thea stood and faced the older woman.

The love and concern in Stella's eyes touched something deep in Thea's heart. She squeezed their hands together. She could easily grow to love this woman as if she were her own great-aunt.

"I'm so sorry about the *Cryer*'s article today"—Stella took a deep breath and shook her head—"but you can't allow it to bother you this evening. You need to push such drivel aside and concentrate on what is important. And that is Lord Howton. However, don't make a rash decision about marriage. No good would come from marrying the first man who proposes."

"I agree," she said softly. "Will came up with an idea to help me. I won't be forced into marriage just to appease the committee." She tightened her stomach in preparation of the barrage of questions soon to erupt.

"Oh?" Edith took a sip of sherry.

Stella sat frozen in anticipation.

"We're going to announce our betrothal." Thea raised her hand as sly smiles graced the grand dames' faces.

Stella and Edith leaned forward in their seats in anticipation of Thea's next words. Even Lord Fluff halted his meticulous ablutions and gave Thea his undivided attention.

"It's not what you think. We're only pretending to be engaged."

The ladies' eyes grew round like full moons.

"After the committee reaches a decision, we'll announce we don't suit," Thea added.

"Oh." Edith's disappointment was clear in her voice. "Of course, dear," she reluctantly agreed, then a hopeful grin tugged at her lips. "But maybe you both will see things differently . . . after the committee decides."

Thea shook her head slightly to thwart the ladies' thinking that a true betrothal was in Thea and Will's future. "Will and I think it'll work beautifully, particularly after what *The Midnight Cryer* printed about us." She turned to Stella. "You've been such a dear friend to me. I'll try my best with Howton." Thea stepped closer and placed a kiss on the woman's warm cheek. "Whatever happens, we need to accept it."

"You can't fault us for hoping," Lady Edith murmured under her breath.

Stella clasped Thea's hands in hers. "It's going to be quite a night. Mark my words. Marvelous things are going to happen to you this evening."

Thea nodded, but she couldn't help but hope that some of those marvelous things included the attention of a certain fiancé named Will.

Will they, or won't they?
Gentle readers, the church bells have been noticeably quiet.
Isn't that our answer?
Respectfully submitted,
The Midnight Cryer

Chapter Nineteen

Thea stood in between the Duke and Duchess of Langham. They were the only ones greeting the dignitaries and other members of the *ton* who strolled through the receiving line. As the duke introduced her to each guest, her chest and stomach tightened in preparation for a cut direct. Perhaps she should have shared at least one sip of sherry with Stella and Lady Edith.

The duchess leaned her way and discreetly whispered, "We're almost through here, then you should find Will and have him fetch you a glass of punch. It'll help, trust me."

"Thank you, Your Grace," she said.

Somehow, Will had quietly sidled up in between the duke and her. He leaned forward, and his cheek lightly brushed against hers as he bent close to her ear. There was a hint of roughness in his cleanly shaven skin. She took a deep breath as her heartbeat kicked into a jig at his presence.

"No whisky, though," he whispered. He drew back, then winked. "We'll save that for later."

If she hadn't been staring at his face, she'd have missed the wink.

He turned his attention to the next guest, and she took in the sight before her. He was so resplendent in his evening coat and breeches that her breath caught in her throat.

Will turned and smiled. She cleared her throat and pretended not to be affected by his presence. "Lady Eanruig, may I introduce you to Lord Howton?"

The man in charge of the committee was surprisingly young, no more than mid-thirties. He took Thea's hand and bowed over it. "Lady Eanruig, the pleasure is mine."

Though he said the correct words, his reserve was apparent. "The Duke of Langham has told me much about you." He smiled and moved a step closer. "However, I look forward to learning more in the days to come. Congratulations on your betrothal to Lord William. Perhaps we'll have a chance to talk privately this evening."

"Thank you, my lord." She studied his eyes intently and smiled in return. The man and the influence he wielded in his committee held great power over her future. But she would not shrink into a wallflower before him. That was not her destiny. If she believed Stella and Edith, tonight she could prepare the groundwork necessary for having the committee look favorably on her claims to her title. "I look forward to our conversations."

"I'll tell you exactly what happens in our committee. When you appear, you'll know what to expect." He bowed over her hand.

"Howton," a stern voice called behind her.

He released her hand, then turned in the direction of Stella, who stood next to the duchess.

"Madam, it's always a delight to see you in London."

The smile that tugged Lord Howton's lips indicated that he and Stella were well-acquainted with one another.

"I'll see you at the whist table later, young man. Last time I was in town, I promised to let you have an opportunity to win back the hundred pounds I won."

"Howton, you know Aunt Stella's reputation," Will added. He leaned slightly closer to Thea, and instinctively, she moved toward him.

"In other words"—Howton smiled affectionately in Aunt Stella's direction—"I'm doomed."

"Luck favors the bold." Stella lifted an eyebrow and smiled.

The expression reminded Thea of Lord Fluff at his most haughty feline self.

With a brief bow, Howton left with Aunt Stella holding his arm. Whatever she was imparting to him had captured his interest as he'd bent his head close to hers.

"What was that all about?" Thea asked the duchess.

"I have no idea, dear." The duchess sighed. "But whatever Aunt Stella is up to, we should allow her to let it play out."

"I agree," Will said. The blinding smile he gave Thea would have stopped traffic on the busiest London street. "I've learned long ago not to doubt what she's capable of achieving." Will's hand caressed the small of Thea's back. The touch was so unobtrusive that no one had seen him do it, yet she felt the tenderness in it.

The duke laughed at Will's response, then turned to greet the last guest in line. After welcoming the late straggler, the duke and duchess entered the ballroom where the laughs and conversations slowly quieted as they waited for the duke and duchess to start the festivities. The regal couple took the center of the room, and the orchestra struck up a waltz. The joy on the duke's face matched the duchess's. A part of Thea, that speck of optimism that life could be grand, perked to attention. There was only one way to describe them—a couple still in love with one another after all their years together.

Will stood close enough that his evening coat brushed up against her dress. He grew nearer and bent his head to hers. "What's the sigh for?"

She waved her hand at his parents. "Look at them. Their love for one another is apparent to all. They're simply beautiful."

His body stiffened, and his earlier amusement faded from his face. "They've always been in love." He stole a glance around the room.

She tried to find a cause for his sudden shift in mood. "Are you all right?"

"Perfect in every way," he answered. Finally, a wry smile tugged at his lips. "Would you care to dance?"

"I'd be honored," she answered. "But . . ."

"What?" His blue eyes blazed.

"Do you see any women around the ballroom you might be interested in dancing with except me?" He'd been such a dear friend to her, she wanted to help him— even if it would hurt her to see him hold another woman in his arms. She held her breath in preparation for his answer.

"No. There is no one," he enunciated clearly. Without touching her, he leaned closer and the warmth from his body wrapped her in comfort. Those sapphire eyes of his locked with hers. "I only want to dance with my fiancée."

She exhaled gently, and the anxiety of waiting for his answer evaporated. "I don't know if I can dance in public," she said softly. "What if I trip?"

"Do you trust me? I promise I'll take *great care* of you and not let you stumble." He delivered a smile worthy of a rogue, and she'd have followed him to the moon and back if he continued to look at her that way.

With an innate grace, Will escorted her to stand next to his parents. Several others joined them on the dance floor for which Thea was grateful. If she stumbled, hopefully everyone would be so busy watching their own feet, they'd forget to look at hers.

She tilted her head back and regarded Will. With his height, he seemed to be a mile away from her.

As he twirled her with an ease that had to be inborn, she missed a step. With his strong arms around her waist, her slight trip remained hidden from the other dancers. "Remember to think of me as your horse."

"Are you going to take me for a ride?"

He bent his head closer to hers. "The things you say astound me."

"You're the one who wanted me to ride you," she answered innocently.

"I may have to follow you around all night long so you don't say anything inappropriate." He laughed.

"Or get one of your family members to play chaperone," she said. "Speaking of family, do you know what else I've noticed about yours?"

"What's that?" The music slowed, signaling the last bars of the waltz. He gently brought them to a stop.

As Will led her off the dance floor, she leaned close so their conversation stayed private. "Everyone in your family is in love with their spouse, just like your parents. Even Stella was deeply in love with Lord Payne when he was alive. It's an amazing sight."

Before he could comment, Claire stood before them.

"Thea, I'd like to introduce you to a friend of Alex and mine, Mr. Marcus Leighton." The marchioness turned to a handsome gentleman with dark blond hair and shimmering brown eyes. "Marcus, this is Thea, Lady Eanruig, a dear friend of mine."

As Thea greeted Mr. Leighton, Will stiffened and glared at his cousin.

Claire simply smiled in return. "Marcus owns several businesses in the city and is a large contributor to my charities. I thought you both would enjoy meeting each other."

Will lifted a brow in Claire's direction.

"It's a pleasure, Mr. Leighton," Thea said.

He bowed elegantly before her. "Lady Pembrooke convinced me to come tonight just to meet you. It's my good luck I took her advice." His voice rang with a deep resonance, and the smile on his face enhanced his attractiveness. "Might I request a dance for later?"

"I can't promise," she answered politely. "I've saved them all for Lord William."

Claire's green eyes widened.

A sudden sadness dulled Will's brilliant blue eyes, then disappeared quicker than lightning in the sky. But Thea had seen it. Before she could inquire what had upset him, the duke and duchess were by their sides to whisk her away to chat with Lord Howton.

Before Will could explain to Claire his engagement to Thea, Will's parents had interrupted them to escort Claire and Thea to Aunt Stella, who still held Lord Howton entranced in whatever she was discussing.

Thea had her head bent close to Claire's as they left his side. Will would need to inform his cousin on his own that he and Thea were engaged. He'd not divulge that it was an *engagement of convenience*. If Thea wanted to share that with Claire, then it was her prerogative—not his.

He quickly made his way to the side of the room and hoped to hide there until it was safe to retire for the

evening. But that was like wishing for snow in July—
not probable. He'd stay here as long as necessary to get
his thoughts in order. He leaned against a floor-to-ceiling
window and closed his eyes. His unease was more than
Claire's introduction of Leighton as a possible suitor for
Thea.

What ate a hole through him was Thea's comments
about his parents' marriage. Ever since he'd been a little
boy, he'd adored his parents and their relationship. Even
when they handed out some appropriate punishment for
one of his misdeeds, normally involving his sister, Emma,
his parents were fair and loving in their discipline.

He'd been blessed to have such a devoted couple as his
parents. More than fortunate, really. He thought he'd recognize love once he found the right person.

He'd witnessed Claire finding happiness with Alex.
His brother, McCalpin, had fallen head over heels in love
with his March, then married her. Even his sister, Emma,
who had abhorred the idea of marriage, had found true
love with Somerton.

He was truly happy for his family and their marriages.
They deserved nothing less. From these blissful unions,
he had nieces and nephews whom he adored. His family
was multiplying and creating future generations. But
lately, it'd been painful to see his siblings and his cousin
with their spouses. Their deep affection and love for one
another was something he'd always wanted.

He couldn't deny the truth. What he felt for Thea was
changing—growing into something more than friendship. But was it love? He exhaled, hoping it would clear
the confusion that seemed to constantly whirl inside his
head whenever he thought of her.

Through the music and the din of conversation, he
heard a laugh that pulled him from his musings. He
closed his eyes to concentrate on the resonance, so clear

and honeyed. It caused his gut to tighten. He knew who it was before even looking. He drew a deep breath and opened his eyes. Immediately, his gaze found Thea. She was the one making that joyful sound. His father bent low to her ear and whispered something. It caused another laugh, this one sweeter and deeper. It reached inside his chest, straight to his jaded heart, and twisted until he wanted to curse at the pain.

He pushed away from the window to find a drink.

"William, we need to talk." Grayson stood beside him with his somber face. "About Lady Eanruig."

He grunted in answer.

Of all the people he *didn't* want to talk to, it was Grayson. All Will could think about was how perfect Thea had felt in his arms as she found her pleasure. He'd never had a woman be so bold in what she wanted from him.

When she'd seduced him with a lick of his lips, he wanted to take her then and there.

He shook his head, trying to tame his tangled thoughts. What kind of a friend was he to Grayson? The man had asked Thea to marry him.

Which begged the question, what kind of friend was he to Thea? He'd done things to her that only a husband had a right to do. Thank heavens, no one at the soirée had mentioned *The Midnight Cryer* and today's lead article. It gave him time to think of the proper course of action. But all afternoon, his thoughts veered to Thea and their interlude.

"I thought you were going to stop by tomorrow."

Grayson was known for his iron will. Even if the world was collapsing around him, his face never showed it. But the slight narrowing of his eyes and the subtle tic below his right eye betrayed that his extraordinary self-control hung by a thread.

"I arrived before you joined the receiving line, then

milled around the ballroom waiting for Lady Eanruig to finish greeting the guests. I found myself just outside the doors. When I saw the two of you dancing together, I, well"—he ran a hand down his face as if wiping away his discomfort—"I wanted to give you the opportunity to say something."

Will didn't want to say anything. He wanted to scream to the entire ballroom that Thea was his, but miraculously, he kept his composure—barely. Personally, he thought he might have lost his mind in the tasting room this afternoon. That would explain his incredible behavior and thoughts.

"What would you like me to say?" To his own ears, his voice sounded hollow.

"Don't be dense. It doesn't become you." Grayson clenched his teeth together so hard that a muscle in his jaw tightened. "I saw how you two looked at one another."

A wad of cotton seemed to have sprouted in Will's mouth. He cleared his throat twice before he could answer. "We're engaged."

"Really?" Grayson's comment was more of a challenge than a question.

"Yes, really," Will growled. "Come to Langham Hall tomorrow, and you can speak with her."

"Oh, you're giving me permission. I'm grateful," Grayson answered sarcastically. "Now it makes sense your reaction when your cousin introduced Leighton to Lady Eanruig."

"What do you want from me?" The annoyance in Will's voice echoed through the room. In response, several elderly matrons looked their way.

Grayson leaned closer. "I want you to look deep inside that warped heart of yours. Though I'd never want to jeopardize our friendship, I don't know if I'll step aside gracefully."

A footman strolled by with a tray holding sparkling glasses of champagne. Grayson grabbed two and handed one to Will.

"If you don't want her, I do," Grayson continued, completely ignoring Will's declaration. "I promise you I'll give her a happy life. She'll want for nothing."

"Did you not hear me correctly? I'm engaged to Thea. Besides, you don't have anything to give her. She's the one with all the money," he seethed. Immediately, he wanted to recall the words.

Grayson's right eyebrow shot upward. "Is that really what you think I care about? The marriage settlements?"

Will winced at his own behavior. Grayson was one of his dearest friends, and he'd just insulted him. He had little doubt now—he'd lost his mind tonight. Probably, it was still on the dance floor or in the whisky room. "I apologize. I don't know what's come over me."

"I didn't think I needed to say this, but perhaps I do for your sake." Grayson's tone had mellowed. He took a sip from his glass. "Thea is bright, beautiful, witty, amusing, and extremely intelligent. I could see myself easily giving my heart to her."

"You?" Will asked incredulously.

"Yes, me," Grayson said. "I could fall in love with her. I'm confident of it."

He swallowed again. The cotton in his mouth had returned and had grown double in size. He downed his glass, hoping it would relieve his discomfort.

Grayson smiled ruefully. The sight of his lips moving upward for any reason was a rarity. If this was any other circumstance, Will would have teased his friend unmercifully. But not tonight. Not when they were discussing Thea.

Grayson stared with an intensity so great that Will believed his friend could see straight through him. Or at least could see the struggle between Will's illogical heart and his logical mind.

"I know you well, my friend. Don't underestimate me on love. I'd say"—Grayson's gaze grew sharper as if slicing him open so that all of Will's faults and insecurities would bleed on the ballroom floor—"you're half in love, if not completely."

With a slight nod, Grayson took his leave without another word.

There was only one thing to do. That was to find Thea and prove Grayson's theory wrong.

He was not half in love with Thea.

God help him, but it felt like he was *completely* in love with her.

But could he trust his heart this time?

Thea had found herself in a long conversation with Lord Howton, Will's mother, Lady Edith, and Stella. Will's father finally joined the group and begged for his wife's company. Another waltz was set to commence, and the duchess had promised it to the duke. With great fanfare, Lady Edith and Stella had commandeered Lord Howton with each holding one of his arms. They'd demanded he escort them to the card room, leaving Thea alone.

Unbelievably, she relished the break from the guests. Though Lord Howton had been charming and affable, Thea had examined every question and comment he uttered. Always cautious, she had looked for hidden or double meanings. Frankly, it had been exhausting. However, Stella had beamed at her throughout the entire exchange, and Thea finally found her confidence increasing every minute.

Lord Howton had asked about her estate and how she could manage it without directly referring to the Duke of Ferr-Colby's challenge. Thea had taken the opportunity to explain the proud tradition her family had instilled with working together with all of Ladykyrk's tenants to make each working acre profitable. Thea had even expressed her displeasure of the Scottish Clearances of years past where longstanding tenants on profitable estates had been uprooted and moved to the various coasts of Scotland so that their land could be used to raise sheep. Her grandfather had warned her that the new duke might consider such actions acceptable under the right circumstances, particularly if there were minerals rights on the ducal estate that could be sold. The new duke had even told her grandfather that he'd *kindly* relocate the longtime ducal tenants to the coasts so they could earn their keep fishing. But he'd promised that would only occur if profitable mineral veins were found at Dunbar on Ferr.

It was simply despicable that the tenants who came from generations of past farmers were expected to make a living fishing without any equipment or experience. More inconceivable was that anyone could be that heartless to destroy families and traditions all in the name of profits.

Lord Howton had listened intently, then smiled slightly. However, there had been a coolness behind his demeanor that set her on edge.

She gazed around the room. With Howton's conversation finished, Thea relished her first real social event and the fact that she was the guest of honor. She allowed herself to relax for the first time that evening. As she gently tapped her foot in rhythm to the music, she subtly looked for Will in the crowd. She found Claire dancing with her husband. The smile on the marchioness's face made her glow from within. They seemed to be in their own world as they danced and never took their gazes from the other.

In awe, Thea sighed. That was love, and the Cavenshams had it in abundance. Spending time with Will and his family made her believe love could be in her future. For the first time since her grandfather had fallen ill, Thea believed she might deserve that dream—she could have a husband who loved her.

She had no doubt what she and Will had shared this afternoon was something remarkable. Something only the two of them could have created together. She wanted more, and she wanted his company. She glanced around the room again looking for him.

"Lady Eanruig, how delightful to see you after all these years."

With a practiced smile on her face, Thea turned, expecting a guest. Instantly, she took a step backward.

"By the shock on your face, I've taken you by surprise. I apologize." Garrett Fairfax, the new Duke of Ferr-Colby, stood before her.

For a moment, neither said anything. They just stared at one another.

Thea swallowed but never broke eye contact. In that instant, she knew exactly what the hens felt when the fox snuck into the henhouse uninvited. She straightened her shoulders and vowed not to show any fear.

He took her hand and performed a perfunctory bow. When he stood, the smile on his face was pleasant.

Ever cautious, she dipped a slight curtsey. "Your Grace, I didn't know you were invited this evening."

There was no plausible way he'd received an invitation, as the duchess had gone over the guest list with Thea. It was a small gathering of only about a hundred people. Taking in consideration the Cavenshams, that left about ninety or so guests.

"Lord Howton asked if I could attend and explained to the Duke of Langham that he'd only attend if I was invited. He doesn't want to appear as if he favors one of us over the over. Langham graciously agreed." Ferr-Colby clasped his hands behind his back and surveyed the room. "Were you looking for someone?"

"I'm just enjoying the scenery and the lovely couples dancing." Her pulse had quickened. Though he was her family, albeit a cousin thrice removed, he was trying to take her inheritance away. Yet, with his cool air and manners, he stood before her as if nothing was amiss.

"I thought perhaps you were looking for your fiancé." His gaze bored into hers. "I read in *The Midnight Cryer* article that you are betrothed."

She blinked slowly, then smiled without answering.

He glanced away, revealing he was as nervous as she was. "You're aware of his reputation, I take it? I've heard he dallies with widows and women of the demimonde. Never staying in the same spot for longer than a night. It gives a whole new meaning to the *Cryer*'s words 'failure in matrimony.'"

"I don't take stock in rumors, nor do I spread gossip. Whatever you've heard, that's not the man I've come to know."

"I meant no harm," he quickly offered. "You need to know what you can expect if you marry him."

"I'm aware of a hardworking man who knows how to run an estate. He's a man who places his family and friends first." Defiantly, she lifted her chin. "He's a man who would protect his land and his tenants. That outplays any slur you might utter."

"He has a champion in you, I see," he drawled. "Since you've raised the topics of rumors and slurs, I must say they're everywhere, aren't they?" He tapped his chin with his forefinger as if deep in thought. "I wonder what *exactly* happened to my dear great-uncle?" His brow furrowed into neat lines of feigned concern. "I'm sure the committee is curious too. A challenge to a title reeks of drama, particularly when there's a sniff of *unpardonable behavior*."

Her pulse pounded in alarm, and her chest rose and fell as she fought for breath. "Are you threatening me?"

"Of course not. Please, my lady, excuse my own indefensible behavior." Heat flooded his cheeks. "I meant no harm." He exhaled deeply. "I had hoped my comment might lead to a frank discussion between the two of us."

"And that is what? The real reason you're challenging my right to my title and my estate?" she asked.

He shook his head and studied his evening shoes for a moment. The white stockings against the pristine black leather dancing shoes practically blinded her. "I believe that the earldom should go to me. I'm trying to do what's best for my future heirs. You can't fault me for that, can you?"

"No," she answered tersely. "But only if there was a hint of truth in such a claim."

"I understand why you're leery of me. I'd feel the same if you were disputing my right to the dukedom." He smiled. "You never commented about your betrothal to Lord William." He looked around the dance floor once again. "It wasn't announced this evening as expected, which gives me hope."

"Hope for what?"

"Perhaps this is a little presumptuous, but if you aren't betrothed officially, I'd like you to consider marrying me. It would serve both of our purposes."

"Why would you want to marry me?" Thea asked, completely dumbfounded.

"The match would benefit us both. The Eanruig title would be combined once again with the Ferr-Colby dukedom. Our combined family would retain possession of the estates and the titles. I'd dismiss my challenge in front of the Committee for Privileges immediately, and we'd both win." The feigned sincerity on his face contradicted his earlier threat.

A slight breeze could have pushed her over with what the duke had offered her since he'd practically accused her of killing her grandfather.

Thea tightly clasped her hands together. Finally, she forced herself to answer. "Under the circumstances, I think we both need to think about the ramifications."

"Of course," he said. "If you marry me, all rumors about what happened with your grandfather would die a quick death. I'd not let anyone besmirch my wife. It would make your life so much easier. When you're ready to talk, send word. I'll call on you."

She stood still, not answering.

"There you are, my darling," Will announced with an engaging smile, one she was all too familiar with. "I've been looking everywhere for you." He turned his attention to Ferr-Colby. "I think she's done with you, Your Grace. If you'll excuse us? I must steal my *fiancée* from your side."

Thea wanted to run into his arms and never let go.

It was the first time he'd ever acknowledged to someone else that they were betrothed.

Her renegade heart pounded in approval.

Will wanted to challenge Ferr-Colby then and there, before sweeping Thea into his arms and escaping to the farthest corners of Langham Park. Even then, he wasn't certain that was enough distance from the Duke of Ferr-Colby and his threatening marriage proposal.

After his conversation with Grayson, the urge had seized him to find Thea so they could talk. Not about anything consequential, but he just needed to hear her voice.

When Will found her, it didn't take long to understand who was attacking her. With his anger barely under control, it took every ounce of willpower not to knock Ferr-Colby senseless.

But Will decided against such primeval action. He'd not embarrass Thea tonight at her first introduction to society. The duke's insinuations were vile, and he'd meant to shock her into accepting. All of it a bit too convenient for Will's tastes. The duke was desperate for Ladykyrk.

"Thea, may I have the pleasure of your company?" Will held out his hand and waited, not daring to breathe to see if she'd follow him or stay with the Duke of Ferr-Colby, who'd just made an unexpected proposal after trouncing Will's reputation and insinuating that Thea was a murderer.

She took his arm. In that singular moment, he'd imagined what it would be like to have her by his side as they lived their years together. Surprisingly, such a thought calmed his racing pulse.

"Your Grace." Thea dipped a slight curtsey.

Before Will could escort her from the ballroom and up the stairs to the wing that held their rooms, he was interrupted by two elderly ladies who closely resembled wet hens.

Aunt Stella picked up her quizzing glass that hung around her neck and examined the duke from head to toe, the movement designed to intimidate. "Imagine our surprise at seeing you here. Spying on *our* Thea, I see."

"Humph." Lady Edith tipped her nose in the air.

Stella lifted a single eyebrow, and the duke generously bowed. He took his leave without another word.

Will tugged Thea a little tighter to his side, still wanting to protect her.

Edith pried Thea's hand away. "William, your father and brother need you immediately."

"I'll see to them shortly." He exhaled loudly. For once, he didn't relish addressing any business with his family. His only priority was Thea. "Allow me to escort the countess—"

Aunt Stella swung her daunting gaze to Will. "We'll be more than happy to escort Thea while you see to your father and brother." The quizzing glass made her eye look massive as she regarded him. "Glad to see you've come to your senses. Thea told us about the engagement. There is no sense in playing games, is there my boy?" she asked with a rigid aplomb.

Not waiting for an answer, she wheeled around and led Thea and Lady Edith away.

Will ran a hand down his face. He didn't think he was playing a game, but if he was, he wished he understood the rules.

One thing was becoming clearer.

What he and Thea shared was becoming all too real.

Chapter Twenty

❦

Will could hear Thea pacing on the balcony next to his. Each bedroom in this wing had double doors that opened to a private balcony with massive stone balustrades. His doors were wide open so the outside sounds swept in along with a cool evening breeze. Though her individual steps were muffled, he could clearly make out the gentle movement of her gown each time she turned. Her rhythm was steady and as regular as the second hand on a longcase clock.

After tonight's soirée, he'd entered his room and thrown his evening coat and waistcoat aside. The formal eveningwear had grown uncomfortable and hot. But before he could completely undress, he'd heard her sigh, the sound poignant as if she carried the weight of the world on her shoulders. Quietly so as not to startle her, he made his way onto his balcony.

"Thea, can't you sleep?" He kept his voice low. Though they were the only ones in this wing of Langham Hall, their balconies faced the other family wing across a small courtyard that led directly to Langham Park. Festive lit

lanterns placed for tonight's soirée adorned the edges
of the walkways and surrounded the three fountains in
the courtyard. There were smaller ones hanging from
the various ornamental trees, giving the entire courtyard the appearance of a fairyland.

She stared wordlessly across at him, then smiled. It
caused her eyes to brighten in the soft light from the
moon and the lanterns. She was happy to see him, and
the sight caused his chest to tighten.

"No. I've much on my mind," she said, matching his
tone. Her smile stayed, then she looked across the courtyard. "It's beautiful, isn't it?"

"Not as beautiful as you." He kicked off his shoes,
then quickly pulled his stockings from his legs. He lifted
one leg, then straddled the balustrade.

"What are you doing?" She rushed to her railing as if
to stop him.

He quickly stood, then stepped over the two feet that
separated the balustrades. With her hand over her heart,
she took a step back so he could jump down.

When he leapt to the stone flooring, she grabbed his
shirt in her hands and pulled him to her. "You, foolish
man. What were you thinking?"

"I was thinking you were too far away from me to
have any real conversation." He embraced her and exhaled his breath. He'd wanted to touch her all evening.
With her in his arms, the wobbles in the Earth and moon's
orbits around one another felt settled in their paths. "I've
wanted to talk to you ever since Ferr-Colby cornered you.
Then when Lady Edith and Aunt Stella whisked you
away, I didn't have another opportunity."

Her rapid breath signaled she'd truly been scared for
him. "Did the thought ever occur to you to knock on the
connecting door?"

He frowned at the door in her room. "You wouldn't

have heard my knock if you were out here." He pulled her tighter against him, and she latched on to him as if she'd never let go. It felt perfect. "If I jumped, it was quicker. Were you worried?"

"A little."

"McCalpin and I used to jump these balconies all the time as young boys."

Her eyes had grown wide. "Did your parents know?"

"Well, I don't think my mother ever did, but our father caught us one day. He couldn't be too angry as he and his brother did the same thing when they were our age." Gently, he rubbed his lips against the top of her head. Her sweet scent gently filled the air. For the first time all evening, he relaxed.

"Did your father have any other siblings?" she said.

"No. Just Claire's father, the previous Duke of Langham. After my uncle and Claire's mother died in a carriage accident, that's when Claire came to live with us."

"She was lucky she had you." The empathy for Claire shown plainly on her face, and with the evening's gentle light, she looked like a fairy queen ready to protect her fey subjects.

"We were lucky to have her with us." He leaned back and looked into her eyes. "She's always had a talent to steer me down a straight and narrow path."

"I didn't realize you needed such guidance," she answered.

"Always." Even though his darling cousin aggravated him at times like tonight. Will ran his hand gently down Thea's back. The fabric of her gown felt like a silken waterfall. "What are you wearing?"

"My dressing gown." She twirled away from him. "Your mother had it made for me and surprised me with it after our visit to Mademoiselle Mignon's. Look, it even has pockets."

Thea slipped her hands into the slits hidden in the sides of the gown and held the skirt away from her. It appeared to be a light apricot silk that had been printed in a delicate turquoise-and-red floral print. It tied around the waist with a red satin sash that highlighted the floral patterns. Even in the dim light, she looked radiant.

"Look at the shoes to go with it." She stuck out one dainty foot from beneath the dressing robe. Her foot was covered in a low-heeled backless slipper in a red silk that matched the sash. Crystals and small pearls adorned the top of the buckle. "I've never possessed such elegant but frivolous shoes." She put one hand to the side of her mouth then looked both ways as if about to impart a grand secret. "I adore them."

Will stepped closer and took her into his arms once again. He wanted to say he adored her. Instead, he murmured, "You deserve those shoes and so much more."

She nestled close, and the entire universe seemed to be in perfect harmony. "What did your father and brother need?"

He let out a silent sigh of exasperation. His family, whom he loved dearly, thought he was at their beck and call. All the rest of the night, he'd wanted to find Thea, but their conversation about the family estates had turned into his father and brother wanting his opinion on an upcoming vote regarding a bill his father was sponsoring. When other members of the House of Lords had joined them for a brandy, Will's father had taken the opportunity to lobby for their votes.

That meant that both McCalpin and Will had to help with his lobbying efforts. Afterward, their father had paced with worry whether he'd succeeded in getting the support necessary for a win. For over three hours, Will had listened and offered his advice.

It was a routine he'd become very familiar with over

the years, but for the first time in his adult life, he'd resented the time commitment. Tonight, his only thought was finding Thea.

"They needed my help with several estate matters and then my opinion on several political matters." One wisp of hair had fallen from her chignon. Her hair always seemed to be falling, tempting him to touch her. Gently, he pushed it back behind her ear. He let his fingers linger over the soft skin.

She gazed at him, and a line creased the skin between her eyes. "They depend upon you, don't they?"

"More than they should." This woman called to him like no other.

"It must be nice to know you're loved and valued." She tilted her head back a little farther, and a slight grin tugged at her lips. "Do you know how fortunate you are to have such a loving family?"

"I do," he murmured while he ran his hand gently up and down her back. He couldn't quit touching her. Even in the moonlight, she seemed to glow. "Now, why were you pacing?"

The worry that marred her brow hit him square in the chest. "I was thinking about the two marriage proposals I received. I don't want to make a mistake. Everything that's important to me, my estate, my tenants, not to mention my happiness and hopes for a family, are dependent on me making the right decision."

The need to roar that she was *his* reverberated through him. Without thinking, he pressed his lips to her forehead. Warm and soft, it summoned him to sample and taste her luminous skin. "Thea, with our engagement, you don't have to do anything you don't want to do."

"You're right." She bit her bottom lip, then turned her gaze to the courtyard. "Truthfully, I don't want to marry either of them."

The familiar simpering nag that wouldn't leave him alone reared its obtrusive head, always ready to point out the flaws in his thinking. He didn't want to examine too closely whether his motives were pure. If they were, he'd encourage her to marry Grayson. He was a good man.

In a straight path, bitterness scourged its way from Will's heart to his mind. He didn't like the vision of Thea with Grayson's children and definitely not the Duke of Ferr-Colby's heir. It sickened him to think of her with any other man than himself.

"Let's go inside and sit by the firelight." Thea shivered slightly in his arms. "Your father sent up a few shortbread biscuits and orange marmalade for my evening treat." She took his hand and led him into her bedroom where two cozy chairs were strategically placed in front of the fire. He'd never really spent much time in this guest room, but the large floral design of the chair's upholstery fabric matched the bedcover and the canape above the bed. It was feminine and bold at the same time—and it reminded him of Thea.

"My father is corrupting you with his sweet tooth?"

She nodded. "Ever since the first night, he sends me sweets."

Before she could lift the silver lid over the shortbread and marmalade, Will sat in a chair. They still had their hands clasped so he gently tugged her toward him. "Sit with me."

"On your lap? Is this another kissing lesson?" The gleam in her eyes caused his body to tighten.

"Would you like that?"

She nodded.

Though he tried to be deceptively calm, his heart pounded, knowing he'd be holding her again.

She had the uncanny ability to decipher his every thought before he could even express them. She settled facing forward on his lap. The feel of her back against his chest felt natural, as if they'd been made for one another. Hopefully, their positions hid his raging erection that refused to behave. Ever since he'd had a glimpse of her slipper, he'd lost control of his body. Such was the effect of Thea on him.

She leaned against him, with her head resting against his chest. In response, he wrapped his arms around her waist. The moment was perfect. Moonlight streamed through the open doors, and the small fire before them crackled every moment or so. Neither of them said a word, both content to be in each other's company.

After several minutes, Thea broke their peaceable silence. "I didn't tell Ferr-Colby we were betrothed when he asked. Why did you tell him I was your fiancée?"

"Would you rather I not say you're mine?" He waited the agonizing seconds for her answer.

She tilted her head slightly to gaze at him. "Truthfully, I rather liked it."

Her words seemed to caress his cheek, and he silently sighed. Having her in his arms like this tonight was akin to heaven on earth. The position of her neck gave him the perfect angle to explore her soft skin. With his lips, he trailed light kisses from the indentation at the bottom of her neck up to her ear where he gently bit then tongued her earlobe.

"I didn't like that he had cornered you at a soirée held in your honor. Then when he'd brought up your grandfather and asked you to marry him in exchange for dropping his claim, I became angry. He was coercing you to do his bidding." With the lightest touch of his fingers, he caressed one cheek. The softness of her skin mesmerized him. "I wanted him to know that my family supported you. But more importantly, I wanted him to know that he'd have to deal with me if he wanted you." His lips trailed a path to her temple, and he lightly pressed a kiss against the tender skin.

"He said if we married, then we'd once again be combining our legacies just like my grandfather had." The huskiness in her voice pleased him to no end, but when she again lifted her neck in offering, he knew then and there she wanted him as much as he wanted her. "I don't trust him."

Her pulse visually pounded in the very same indentation that'd he'd just kissed. He tasted her skin there again, her pulse driving his hunger for more. The subtle musky scent of her arousal wafted toward him and added to her unique fragrance. He wanted to taste her everywhere.

"I don't trust him either. Now, let's not talk about him anymore," he said, as he kissed a tender spot on the back of her neck. He pulled her tighter against him, causing his member to swell at the contact. In response, he ground his hips against her backside.

She moaned softly, then took his hands in hers. "Untie my sash."

"Thea," Will whispered. "We should have a conversation before we do anything."

"No," she groaned. "No talking. Not now." Not waiting, she pulled the tie of her sash.

The air around them seemed to electrify.

Slowly, he helped her, and soon, the robe was open. She took each of his hands and placed them over her breasts. The silk of her nightgown was soft, but thin. Her hard nipples seemed to tighten more with each caress of his hand. He gently bit the side of her neck, then soothed it with his tongue. The need to touch her and taste her became overwhelming. He wanted to suck her nipples until she cried out his name.

Though a hot ache burned his throat, he managed to growl, "You're so beautiful."

In response, she arched her back, giving him greater access to her magnificent breasts. With his fingers, he explored every angle from the tender sides of each breast to the sensitive nipples. Not one inch of her soft, sweet skin was left unattended.

She took one of his hands and trailed it down her stomach. He adoringly caressed each crevice and bump, letting his hand linger on her hip. He gently squeezed, and she moaned while tilting her hips in offering. He trailed his fingers across the silk. "Thea, are you certain?"

"More than anything else in my life," she whispered as her fingers gently entwined with his. She pushed his hand farther down until he found her mound, where her curls pushed against the fabric.

He had little doubt if he had her in bed, neither of them would leave for a week.

He groaned and pushed himself against her again.

She gracefully stood and took his hand in hers. "Come, let's have another lesson."

"Who'll be the teacher?" Will asked as he stood.

"You will this time," she whispered. She dropped his hand, then shed her robe, revealing the translucent gown that showed practically every inch of her body.

He chuckled as his engorged cock ached for relief. "I see I have a very clever pupil."

"I'm a fast learner."

He fisted his hands at the huskiness in her voice. With her hand, she drew him toward the canopied bed.

At the foot, they faced each other as the firelight danced between them and over them. Neither seemed to want to move as the desire grew even more heated.

"Thea, I want to kiss you." The passion in his voice made it raspy.

She barely nodded, then stood on her tiptoes, giving

him easier access to her delectable lips. Slowly he lowered his mouth to hers. She opened to him on a whimper as if he were the only one who had the key to unlocking her heart. His tongue met hers, and he explored every inch of her mouth. He moaned in answer, and she pressed her body against his. The silk hid nothing as his hands traced every inch of her body. The perfect curve of her bottom and the silky smoothness of her straight back made him want her more.

Gradually, he pulled away, then picked her up in his arms as she kicked off her slippers. Tenderly, he lay her on the bed. She reached for him, and he mounted the bed to cover her with his own body. It was another first moment of intimacy for them as he took her in another blinding kiss.

In two tugs, she'd freed his shirt from his breeches. With a curse, she tried to pull it over his head. He broke the kiss, then rested his weight on one elbow as he helped her complete her task. She tossed the shirt aside, not watching where it landed. She was panting as hard as he was as they stared into each other's eyes.

Her eyes searched his face before her gaze traveled the length of his bare chest. Softly, she traced the muscles, then ran her fingers through the slight smattering of hair at the center of his chest. He closed his eyes briefly as her touch teased then coaxed him. He straddled her hips to distribute his weight evenly. When he opened his eyes, her tender gaze was latched to his.

"Will, I never knew a man's body could be so perfect." Her fingers tangled in his hair, and she brought his mouth to hers where she kissed him senseless.

Her words had emboldened him. Resting on his elbows, he moved his mouth down her neck, his lips trailing kisses. At the base of her neck, he worshipped the slight indentation of skin with his tongue.

When he pulled the sleeves of her gown down her shoulders, she lifted herself to help him. Thankfully, it was a loose garment, and the sleeves floated down her arms until she could free herself.

With her chest completely exposed to him, she captured his gaze. "Teach me."

He swallowed and prayed that he'd survive the lesson. Shaped like round apples, her breasts fit perfectly in his hands.

Her pink nipples puckered delectably, tempting him to suck. Never one to forgo a sweet treat, he kissed his way down her chest until he found one perfect bud. He lightly nipped the hard peak, then soothed it with his tongue.

"Do it again," Thea gasped.

"I knew you were my star pupil," he whispered against the other breast. He ran his tongue around her areola. "You learn quickly."

"I have a marvelous teacher," she purred.

"I want to kiss you more."

She ran her fingers through his hair. The smoldering heat in her eyes would melt ice in January.

He inhaled her sweet sensuous fragrance and fell deeper under her spell. As he nuzzled her breasts, he slowly raised her gown to caress her leg. The soft skin of her thighs made him groan softly, and he placed a kiss on each. He coaxed her to open her legs, then hooked them over his arms so he could pleasure her the way a man treasures a woman. Gently, he separated her folds, and the scent of her arousal enveloped him. He took a moment to savor it and her.

His gaze locked with hers. She was so trusting, and he realized how unique, how truly spectacular she was. She deserved all the happiness that life could offer. In this moment, everything had aligned perfectly in their universe. He'd been given the gift to provide her with pleasure, a sensual delight she'd never experienced before. Slowly, he lowered his head, ready to enrapture, please, and possess her. At the same time, he let go of one of her legs to unbutton the fall of his breeches. His cock sprang free as if released from prison. He took himself in hand as he swept his tongue around her perfect pearl.

She tasted of bliss and rapture, and with his tongue and lips, he worshipped her. So pink, so wet, and so perfect. Just like her.

She propped herself up on her elbows. "What are you doing?"

"I'm showing you another type of kisses, one that I think you might enjoy." He leaned back and stroked himself. His cock leaked as if crying for attention.

Her eyes widened as she studied his member, then her gaze softened. The desire on her face made her even more beautiful. "I want to learn."

Again, he bent to kiss and stroke her, and she shuddered and tilted her hips toward him, demanding that he attend her. Thea needn't worry. There was no place else he wanted to be. Bliss was in her bed. Ecstasy was having his mouth learn every sensitive spot she possessed. She moaned, then writhed against him. Her fingers dug into his hair, demanding more.

She was close to coming as her moans had turned to breathless pants. As her body tightened underneath his, he continued to kiss and suckle her. When she mewled his name, he thrust his tongue inside her. If this was the only way to have her, possess her, and make her his, then he'd be damned if he'd forgo such pleasure. Her muscles tightened around his tongue as she came, and he stroked himself harder and faster. Raw hunger swirled through him, congregating in his swollen member and bollocks until finally exploding. His release seemed to go on forever as come spilt over the bedcovers.

Never had he experienced such a shattering orgasm, one that robbed him of his senses. He rested his head on her torso, struggling to regain his breath. When he reclaimed his strength, he took her in his arms and kissed her thoroughly, letting her know he was as affected as she was by the power of what they'd shared.

"Will," she whispered, as he nuzzled her neck.

"Hmm?" he murmured, as he trailed his lips over the curve of her cheek.

"Will you stay with me?"

Forever. His heart beat the word into his mind. She'd come for him and *only him.* He'd been the first to witness such a sight.

"I've never slept with anyone in a bed before. I'd like you to be my first."

Her softly spoken words stole his breath. Finally, he inhaled deeply. "You've never slept with anyone? Not even a nurse when you were little?"

She shook her head gently.

She'd been so alone all her life. How could he deny her such a simple pleasure?

"I like being your first," he whispered. With the utmost care, he gathered her in his arms and tugged a cotton throw around them both. She sighed, and the sound reminded him of the gentle beat of a hummingbird's wings. He settled close and rested his chin on the top of her head. "Thea, after what we shared tonight, we should marry."

He waited for a response, but there was nothing. Gently, he pulled away and gazed at her soft features. Her breathing had grown even and deep.

With their naked bodies entwined, Thea had fallen

fast asleep in his embrace. At that moment, he knew what he had. He held his own piece of heaven in his arms.

His heart warred with his mind, keeping him from joining her in sleep.

He'd never let her go.

Attention!
If any man is absent from your family, you should investigate
their wardrobe for missing clothing.
In a macabre ritual, Lady Man-Eater collects
pieces of clothing from her victims as trophies.
Your faithful reporter,
The Midnight Cryer

Chapter Twenty-One

❧

T hea." The voice turned urgent, pleading.

Desperate, Thea turned, trying to find Will. He stood across the meadow next to her folly, with his hand out.

"Hurry, Thea." The closer she got to him, the more distant he became, until he disappeared like a plume of smoke.

"Will." Startled, she sat up in bed. Not knowing where she was for a moment, she reached out her hand, desperately searching for him. He lay beside her, warm and large.

Relieved, she bent her head and took a deep calming breath.

He murmured her name as he reached for her.

"Theodora, Nancy says your door is locked, and you're not answering when she knocks. She's worried and asked if I could rouse you." Brisk banging on the door commenced. "Theodora, are you in there?"

"Are you all right, Thea?" A softer, more mellifluous voice carried into the room.

Will sat up like a ball shot from a cannon. "Aunt Stella," he hissed. "With Claire."

Thea scrambled from the bed. "Hurry," she whispered. Frantic, she searched for her robe which somehow had ended up in a ball of silk between the two chairs flanking the fireplace.

"Is someone with you?" Stella boomed.

"I'm fine," Thea called out. "Give me a moment."

Will rushed to her side while buttoning the fall of his breeches. "We'll speak later." He kissed her on the mouth soundly, then exited through the connecting door.

Smoothing her hair which felt like a bird's nest of tangles, Thea made her way to the door, then opened it.

In midstrike, Stella lowered her fist. Claire and Edith stood beside her.

"I overslept. I apologize." Thea's heartbeat slowed to a gallop as she tried to head off an inquisition. What she really wanted was to go back to bed and lie in Will's arms. Her body still thrummed from their kisses and sweet caresses from last night. When he'd kissed her in her most private part, she'd felt herself change into a different being, much like a caterpillar into a butterfly. She blinked slowly, wanting to lose herself in the wonderful memories.

"Thank goodness," Stella exclaimed with a sigh. "I was beginning to worry myself. Nancy is practically beside herself."

"Dearest, would you like me to send Nancy to you?" Claire asked.

"No, thank you. I'll dress myself." She'd managed the task for years on her own. "I'll hurry."

"We'll see you downstairs." Claire took Lady Edith's

hand and tugged her away from the door. "I'll have tea waiting for you."

The trio turned to leave, and Thea started to shut the door. Before she could close it completely, a small, bony hand shot out.

"You forgot something," Stella whispered.

Thea blinked as the grand dame pushed open the door, bent down, then retrieved an object off the floor just inside Thea's room. When she rose, a blinding smile lit her face. By her thumb and forefinger, she held out Will's shirt.

Heat scorched Thea's cheeks.

"Or should I say, did William forget something?" One of Stella's graying eyebrows shot up. Without another word, she handed the shirt to Thea.

"I—I—" Her thoughts reeled as she struggled with something to say.

Stella affectionately patted her on the cheek. "*Shush* now. You're the Countess of Eanruig. You answer to no one." Will's great-aunt leaned forward, then gently kissed her on the cheek. "Never forget that." She closed the door.

Thea rested her head against the massive mahogany frame and closed her eyes, willing her cheeks to cool. She brought Will's shirt to her face and breathed in, filling her lungs with his scent. The sweet memories flooded her thoughts, washing away her embarrassment. Last night in bed with Will was the most incredible evening she'd ever spent in her entire life.

And she wanted more.

But as Stella said, she was the Countess of Eanruig. With that dignified title, she carried responsibilities. She took another breath, then went about the business of her morning ablutions—brushing her teeth, washing her body, and finally dressing. She chose a green-turquoise silk dress this time with a coral spencer trimmed with crepe ribbon dyed to match the turquoise in her dress. But as she tamed her unruly mass of hair, her thoughts never tarried far from Will.

Though she washed herself thoroughly this morning, she could still smell his scent on her body, marking her as his. It was the sweetest perfume, and she wanted to bathe in it. With a sigh at her silly musings, she left her room, but not before she'd hidden Will's shirt in the bottom of her wardrobe. She would give it back to him tomorrow. She'd sleep in it tonight, so she could at least have a piece of him with her in bed again.

She practically floated as she made her way to the blue salon but stopped on the landing to gaze at the picturesque view of Langham Park in the distance. The lush green lawns were reminiscent of the vast fields of her home, but the perfectly manicured bushes with elaborate fountains and massive hothouses were signs she didn't belong in London.

She missed home and her tenants. Work waited for her at Ladykyrk. There were servants she wanted to hire. That's what she needed to focus on. She couldn't afford her wayward thoughts to constantly veer onto Will. She needed to concentrate on her visit with Stella, Edith, and Claire. Lord Somerton and his solicitor, Mr. Odell, who would represent her in the hearing, would attend. They were here to help her prepare for the committee interview. Nothing was more important than that. She had to crush Ferr-Colby's claim.

Or did she? She stopped midstride. If she accepted the duke's offer of marriage, then the title would remain hers, with no risk of losing it. But she'd be married to a man who thought the worst of her.

More important, she'd have to give up Will. Her heart stumbled, and her lungs refused to take a breath in protest. Thea had seen enough men in her short time in

London to know the truth. She couldn't see herself with any other man than Will, particularly after last night.

With her thoughts churning, she entered the blue salon. Claire rushed to her side and hugged her as if this was the first time she'd seen Thea today. Stella and Lady Edith waved her forward as if nothing were amiss. As she made her way to the sitting area and tea service, she stopped in her tracks as if she'd hit a glass wall.

Before her stood Will, freshly shaved and elegantly dressed in a navy broadcloth coat, brown waistcoat, and doeskin breeches. He was stunningly handsome, but the look in his eyes stole her breath. Will held a baby boy about two years of age in his arms who was pulling Will's immaculately tied cravat.

Thea stared, speechless. There was no denying what she was seeing. The expression on his face could only be described as love. The tenderness around his eyes and joyful smile on his lips would make the heavens stop everything to witness the scene before her. Will's laugh and the accompanying giggles would make angels harken. It was unbelievably breathtaking.

Such thoughts would not help her situation, and her traitorous heart needed to behave.

"Oh no, young man, you'll not untie all my hard work." Will threw the baby in the air, then caught him. Unable to contain his giggles of glee, the boy grabbed at his cravat again.

"William, stop that," Claire pleaded. "Nurse will never get him to sleep this afternoon if you keep wrestling with him."

"When Liam turns irritable because he didn't sleep, we're sending him straight to you," Stella announced, as she studied the papers before her.

Claire took the baby from Will. "Why does your Uncle

William insist upon playing so rough?" She patted the boy on his back.

"Liam, tell her that we men learn to fight from such play. That's how we protect our own."

Lady Edith rolled her eyes. "He sounds like he's from some ancient clan of Highland warriors."

"Why, thank you for the compliment, Lady Edith." Will bent and kissed her on the cheek. "I always knew you were sweet on me."

She batted him away. "Off with you now. I don't have time for your shenanigans."

"Thea," Claire said. "Come meet my son, Liam."

At the sound of her name, Will's focus turned to her. Suddenly, he lost a little of the levity he had shared with his family. "Good morning, my lady. I trust you slept well?" Then he winked at her. No one else could see it except for her. In response, a blast of heat pressed her cheeks.

His smile grew even brighter, as he realized she was blushing because of him. Before she could approach Claire, Will scooped Liam into his arms and brought him to Thea. "Lady Eanruig, may I have the honor of introducing you to the handsomest man in all of England besides me? This is Lord William Hallworth, but his family calls him Liam."

Will's gaze captured hers, and his eyes were the brightest she'd ever seen. The glorious sight made Thea's heart tumble in a free fall. She'd always considered Will handsome, but with the baby in his arms, he was dazzling to behold.

The boy stole her attention with a wave in her direction, and she took the small hand in hers. Immediately, he grabbed her fingers and placed them in his mouth.

"Lord Liam, I can tell you're a lady's man, just like

your uncle." She gave a slight shake of her head to clear the fog.

Claire had joined her and Will.

"Claire, he's beautiful." And in that instant, Thea felt a spark of longing. It wouldn't take much for it to turn into a blazing fire of want. She wouldn't call it envy or jealousy, as Claire deserved every happiness that life would give her. But Thea couldn't help but want a baby. To share such an experience with Will would be her heart's desire. It'd be the answer to what was missing in her life—a family, love, belonging.

"Thank you. He's a good baby, and the twins adore him." Gently, Claire took him from Will. "Let me take him to his nurse, then we can get our work done."

On impulse, Thea leaned in and gave the boy a kiss on the cheek. "It was my pleasure to meet you, Lord Liam," she whispered. She was rewarded with a big grin and a short giggle.

The grand dames waved Claire and Liam over to say their goodbyes. While the two ladies cooed and played with the baby, Thea took the opportunity to talk to Will.

"Liam's a beautiful baby." The Cavensham family had riches that paled in comparison with their material wealth. What made them dear to Thea was they knew what was important in life and didn't take it for granted. If only she'd had such examples when her grandfather was ill.

"I'll admit, I'm a little partial to him as he's named after me, and I'm his godfather." Will took a step closer to her and lowered his voice. "We had a near miss, didn't we? I wish I could have kissed you goodbye properly this morning. Last night was something out of a dream."

"For me too," she answered softly.

"We need to talk, Thea," he murmured.

"About whisky lessons?" she teased.

When he smiled, his eyes flashed, and matching twin dimples appeared on his cheeks, giving another reason for why he was breathtakingly handsome. "Among other things," he said softly. "I have an appointment with the stewards for Falmont and McCalpin Manor after this. This evening, we need to get things settled."

The seriousness in his tone was unexpected. "What do you mean *settled*?"

"Come, you two. No time to dawdle." Stella glided gracefully to the sitting area and the tea service. "Theodora, I'd like you to serve."

"Later." Will offered his arm, and she linked hers with his, gently resting her hand on the muscles of his forearm.

The simple touch had her senses spinning as he escorted her to Stella and Edith. Would it always be like this with him? When she glanced his way, she discovered he studied her with an expression she'd never seen before, one that left every inch of her craving him. An impish grin tugged the corner of his mouth as if he could portend that she was unbalanced because of his effect on her. Then, she made the mistake of stealing a glance at his lips, the same ones that had kissed her until she felt he cherished her above all others.

Without thinking, she released a tremulous sigh—such was the impact of Lord William Cavensham on her wayward emotions.

He leaned close and whispered, "If you keep looking at me like that, I'll have to kiss you in front of everyone."

His sinfully deep voice heightened the desire that thrummed through her. Never had she felt so unsettled about her emotions, but at the same time, experiencing a perfect alignment in her world.

All too soon, they reached Stella's and Edith's side and sat down. With a slight smile on her face, Thea started serving tea as instructed. Shortly, Claire joined them, and as a group, they proceeded to discuss what was required for the hearing that would take place tomorrow, all the while munching on fairy cakes and finger sandwiches.

The salon door opened, and Lord Somerton in the company of a man in his sixties with thick, white hair that resembled snow drifts came into the room.

"Good morning, everyone." Somerton strolled to Thea's side and bowed elegantly. "Countess, I'd like you to meet Mr. Samuel Odell, my solicitor. He'll represent you tomorrow."

Mr. Odell bowed briefly and nodded at her with a confident smile. "Good morning, Lady Eanruig. I'm looking forward to tomorrow."

The confidence he exuded immediately put her at ease. "Thank you, Mr. Odell. Frankly, I'll be relieved when tomorrow is over."

"He's the best in the land when it comes to peerage law, Thea," Stella announced. "You made a wise choice retaining him."

Somerton and the solicitor sat, then without batting an eye, Mr. Odell started giving directions for Thea's final preparations in front of the committee. It was as if he were sending troops into battle, and he expected the military maneuvers to be performed perfectly. "Countess, the committee expects the counsel for the claimant— that's you—and the counsel for the challenger—that's Ferr-Colby—to appear on their behalf with any witness. They normally don't entertain such appearances from the people who are claiming or disputing the title. However, Howton has his own way of doing things. He wants to see you both in front of the committee. See if anyone is nervous and will back down."

Thea froze. "Will I have to speak?"

"Not if you don't want to." Mr. Odell shook his head.

"Thank you." Thea tried to tamp down the nervousness that twisted her insides.

Stella smiled fondly. "We all know how important this is for you, dearest. You'll be brilliant." She turned to Mr. Odell. "Any word on where the charter might be?"

"No. We'll just have to rely on other evidence. The proof of your ancestry and the tracing of the title through birth records, marriage registers, death records. It's a long and tedious process but must be done." Mr. Odell turned toward Thea. "Frankly, my lady, the charter would make tomorrow much easier. We'll present our best arguments and hope for the best. Now, the questions will be direct. Howton will ask me how you come by the title. I'll explain that based upon the lineage history that you provided to the committee, it proves you are the direct descendant of Alexander Gordon, who was first granted the title from King Alexander of Scotland in the year 1012."

"What happens then?" Thea asked.

"He'll offer any additional evidence you've gathered, including parish registers, entries in Bibles, and written declarations," Somerton added. "Then Odell will prove why Ferr-Colby's arguments fail."

"But how do you know these things for certain?" Thea asked.

Mr. Odell's sharp focus came to rest on her. "Simple. All the Earls of Eanruig can be traced through your direct line."

"Let me interrupt for a moment." With his turquoise eyes flashing, Somerton turned to Thea and Will. "I have some rather disturbing news."

"What is it?" Will leaned closer to Thea, and his thigh touched hers, the simple contact comforting, yet it awakened that all-too-familiar hunger.

Somerton's gaze never left hers. "I have an informant,

a Mr. Goodwin, whose vast knowledge about London and the various echelons of society helps me make decisions about my shipping business. He came across information today that isn't in his usual line of business."

"Goodwin is a snitch," Stella offered helpfully. "A marvelous one, at that."

Somerton's gaze shot to Will's. "It was Ferr-Colby who took the story that Thea had something to do with her grandfather's death to *The Midnight Cryer*. He's also the one that spread the tale about her with footmen. He planted those lies to hurt her credibility." Somerton's voice turned guttural. "He'll stop at nothing to win his challenge tomorrow."

"Including ruining my reputation." Thea gripped her clasped hands tightly to keep herself from jumping up and pacing. Why was she not surprised by the news? Ferr-Colby had created a perfect storm to destroy her.

Will placed his hand over hers. "We'll stop him."

"I don't care about my reputation, but I'll not allow him to defame my grandfather." Thea's voice grew stronger. "Whatever he plans on doing tomorrow, I'll thwart his every move. Mr. Odell, I want to speak on my own behalf tomorrow. Any accusation leveled at me, I want to address head-on."

The solicitor tilted his head and regarded her. "My lady, that's highly unusual."

"That's appropriate in this case, sir," Thea said. "I'm a highly unusual peer."

He studied her as if trying to decide whether she was up to the task. Finally, with a single nod, he agreed.

"That's the right attitude for a countess," Edith said.

"Excellent." Stella turned her hawk-like gaze to Will. "Now, your part in the interview is simple. You'll sit beside Thea. You're there in a show of support. The committee will look favorably on Theodora with all the

Cavenshams sitting behind her. Plus, once they realize you and Thea will be married, it'll make their decision easier to make. If they ask you anything, just identify yourself and answer their questions honestly."

"It'll be my pleasure *and honor* to sit beside Thea," he answered, then turned to her. "Whatever you need." His gaze was kind, even affectionate. He lowered his voice until it was a whisper between the two of them. "I'll be there for you." Discreetly, without anyone seeing, Will squeezed her hand, offering his strength, giving her courage. "Ferr-Colby will not sully you—not if I have anything to do with it."

"Hear, hear," Edith and Stella chimed together.

Claire captured her gaze. "You can do this, Thea."

Miraculously, Thea didn't feel nervous anymore. Whatever happened tomorrow, she'd be prepared. Whether she was called a cold-blooded killer or a countess, she'd fight with everything she possessed to protect her grandfather and his legacy. With Will and his family behind her, her determination soared. It truly was a magical day after meeting Liam, listening to Stella and Lady Edith, and most important, having Will's support.

She didn't even spill one drop of tea when she served it this morning.

Proof that miracles really did occur.

For the rest of the day, Will didn't have an opportunity to see Thea, as he'd been called to his brother's house for some Langham estate business. What should have only taken a couple of hours, turned into an all afternoon and evening affair.

Finally, Will left for Langham Hall. As he walked the short distance back to his home, his thoughts drifted to his brother and sister-in-law. They'd discussed an addition to McCalpin Manor for their expanding family. McCalpin's excitement over the project was contagious. If it were Will's wife who was having a baby, he'd want the same thing—everything perfect and in place.

He stopped beside a park across the street and let his gaze wander. Another lovely vision of Thea with their child propped on her hip flooded him with warmth.

Claire's warning—*be careful what you wish for*—pounded in his head. He closed his eyes and inhaled the stale London air. It was in direct contrast to Thea's natural clean scent, the one he'd become accustomed to.

No matter what, last night wasn't a mistake. What they shared was something incredibly tender and honest, and he'd never experienced it with any woman before in his life. He shook his head. After pleasuring Thea, he wanted to marry her. Not only was it a matter of honor, but he cared for her deeply. He'd not ruin her, then let her go.

She was passionate and wasn't afraid of her own body or his. She knew what she wanted. And she wasn't afraid to go after her dreams either.

With a renewed determination to convince her he was the right man for her, Will continued his way home. When he entered Langham Hall, Pitts failed to appear. Will wouldn't let another second tick by without talking to Thea. He asked an attending footman where she was and discovered she'd spent the night preparing for tomorrow's hearing.

Before Will could ascend the staircase, Pitts miraculously appeared. "Lord William, a moment, please. The Duke of Ferr-Colby is in the duke's salon. He says it's a matter of urgency and asked for Lady Eanruig." Pitts was always a consummate English butler who guarded Langham Hall and its inhabitants from unnecessary interruptions. However, even he appeared to be under a little stress about tomorrow's hearing, if the dark circles under his eyes were any indication.

The affliction seemed to be shared by all of them.

"I'll see him." Will started down the hallway to the sitting room with Pitts right beside him.

Soon they arrived outside the salon. Without his usual fanfare, the butler opened the door and announced Will.

"Ferr-Colby," Will drawled as he strolled into the room. "What could possibly bring you here this evening? Are you dropping your claim?"

"Unfortunately, not," the duke said. He turned from his study of the fireplace and faced Will. "I wanted to see Theodora. Not *you*. She needs to know that I'll still be her friend." He smiled gently and glanced at the floor, as if he really were sorry it had come to this between the two of them. "No matter what—"

Will interrupted him. "No matter what lies you spread to hurt Lady Eanruig, you want her to know that you'll still marry her? What happens if you prevail? Will you still want to marry her then?" He continued to stare at Ferr-Colby. The tension between the two men could have been severed with a sword. "That's what I thought, *Your Grace*. No suave or ready answers to my questions. Just empty threats."

"I'll do whatever is necessary, and in my power, to win, including marrying her," the duke said, as if he were commenting on the dreary London weather. Then his visage visibly tightened. "Do you know what exactly happened at Ladykyrk? Why wasn't the duke seen in all those years? Why did the invitations to visit cease?" He leaned close and stared into Will's eyes. "I'll bring charges against her if need be."

"Ducal charm at its finest." Ferr-Colby's true agenda had started to emerge, proving what Will thought was true. The man had no morals. "What happened to wanting to be her friend?" He didn't wait for an answer as it wouldn't be worth listening to. "What charges would you bring against Lady Eanruig?" Will demanded.

"Murder."

"Be my guest," Will taunted, then stepped forward, ready to challenge the duke. He lowered his voice to a growl. "Where were you all those years Thea was taking care of her ill grandfather? If it had been me, nothing would have kept me from visiting my great-uncle, particularly if I was his heir. I wouldn't have waited for an invitation."

Ferr-Colby's eyes widened.

"Your threats are meaningless. Thea's grandfather was a great and fair man. I wonder what he'd think of you, his default heir, if he could see you trying to steal Ladykyrk from his only granddaughter."

"What the old duke would think now is immaterial to your *countess*," Ferr-Colby mocked. "The only thing that matters is tomorrow." Without waiting for a reply, he strolled from the room.

Standing guard, Pitts nodded to Will, then followed the duke. The sound of their footsteps faded as they made their way to the entry.

Without losing a second, Will headed to Thea's room. Tonight, they'd get their future settled. When she didn't answer after his brisk knock, he entered his room and headed for the balcony.

The structure was empty, and the balcony door was shut. No soft candlelight glowed through the window. She had to be asleep in preparation for tomorrow.

Though he didn't regularly pray, he whispered one tonight.

Dear God, let her win tomorrow so Ferr-Colby and his threats will be out of her life forever.

*The latest edition of the **Cryer** will be delayed this morning.
We're waiting for the
Committee for Privileges—or as Lady Man-Eater likes to
call them—a bunch of 'white-wigged men' to make a formal
announcement as to who is the true head of the Eanruig
earldom. A bit of news we did pick up this morning—one
member of the committee divulged that he sits on a dais to
keep Lady Man-Eater from attacking.
Sounds like a traveling circus, doesn't it, gentle readers?
Fair and honest reporting always,*
The Midnight Cryer

Chapter Twenty-Two

Thea smoothed her hands down the elegant but sub-dued blue-and-silver Italian crepe gown that Mademoiselle Mignon had crafted for her to wear today. Even the fine leather gloves that had been dyed to match couldn't keep her palms dry. Her hands had become watering pots, and the hearing hadn't even started. Her future and the fate of all the people that depended on her would be decided today. It would be a blessing to just have it over with. Living in limbo was hell.

Beside her sat Will, who looked impressive in a dark-navy double-breasted morning coat with black wool breeches. His silver silk waistcoat almost shimmered in the light, the material was so fine. A sapphire sparkled in the small stickpin he'd used in the intricately tied mathematical knot of his cravat. Every time she glanced at him, the thing appeared to wink at her, and she prayed it was a good omen.

Behind her, the entire Cavensham family had come to support her. The Duke and Duchess of Langham sat directly behind them, with Stella and Lady Edith directly behind. Claire and Pembrooke, McCalpin and March, along with Emma and Somerton sat directly behind the duke and duchess.

Even with all this support, the uncertainty of today's outcome twisted her stomach into a knot that she didn't think would ever become untangled. It didn't help matters that Mr. Odell hadn't arrived yet. His seat sat empty, and the table depressingly bare. Across the aisle, massive piles of papers were carefully sorted and laid in precise order in front of the duke's solicitors.

She turned to Will, but he was talking to his father. She caught his eye, and he smiled in return. Just then, the door opened behind them, and the Duke of Ferr-Colby entered with his entourage. With his blond hair and blue eyes, he cut a striking figure. His straight posture and confident smile made him appear at ease—almost as if on a stroll in the park.

After he greeted the Duke and Duchess of Langham and the rest of the Cavensham family, he turned his attention to her. "Lady Eanruig, you look especially beautiful today." He bowed slightly.

"That's where you're wrong, Ferr-Colby," Will drawled. "She looks this way every single day."

The duke winged an eyebrow, then returned his attention to Thea. "No solicitor? That's a novel approach. Good luck."

Thea didn't answer.

As soon as the duke settled at the table directly across from Thea, three members of the committee in full ceremonial robes and wigs took their seats. Following behind them, another man entered.

Will leaned close. "That's the attorney general. He's here to listen and take notes for the Prince Regent. He'll not ask any questions."

Lord Howton called the hearing to order. "Is the claimant ready to procced?" He looked around the chamber. "Where is Mr. Odell?"

"I'm afraid Mr. Odell hasn't arrived yet." Thea rose slowly and faced the dais. Her pulse pounded, but she refused to sit. "Lord Howton, if it would please the committee, I'd like to say a few words first," Thea announced with a strong and steady voice. Thankfully, no one knew her knees were knocking gently.

His eyes widened. "It's out of the ordinary, but of course you may. Please proceed."

Will also rose to stand beside her. He took her hand in his. His whisper only loud enough for her to hear. "Odell will be here. Just remember you are the true Countess of Eanruig, and your confidence and commitment are in rare form today." He squeezed her hand gently. "Countess, you've never been more beautiful in my eyes than you are now."

She squeezed his hand in acknowledgment.

When Will sat, his chair squeaked, the only sound in the chamber besides the pounding rhythm of her heart. She forced herself to ignore the stares of the committee members and glanced at the Cavenshams behind her. When her gaze settled on Stella and the Duke of Langham, she nodded. Slowly, she drew a deep breath for courage. The Daniels family flashed before her. Ladykyrk and its future depended on her succeeding today. She drew her shoulders back and faced the committee. Silence reigned through the chamber, but she'd not allow it to quiet her.

"I'd like to start with why the original Earldom of Eanruig was created in the first place." Thea cleared her throat so her voice would carry through the room. "My ancestor, Alexander Gordon, who was named after King Alexander II, fought against the British repeatedly. In honor of his bravery for those battles long ago, Alexander Gordon was given the title of Earl of Eanruig and the land that is now called Ladykyrk by charter in the year 1012. The king decreed that the title would pass to the heirs of the marriage, not the male heirs of the marriage."

Without a single note, Thea traced her entire ancestry, everything she'd learned from her grandfather, including his relentless lessons on the history of her family. Finally, she came to her mother. "I am the only heir from the marriage of my father, James Monmouth, the Earl of Northcross, to my mother, Lady Janet Worth, who was the only child of the previous Earl of Eanruig, who also held the title of the Duke of Ferr-Colby."

Though she didn't dare look, she felt Will's warm gaze. Her confidence continued to strengthen, knowing he was by her side.

"My grandfather was a fair and just man. His loyalty has always been to the crown and the responsibilities he bore with his titles. One of those responsibilities entailed ensuring my readiness to assume my duties as the Countess of Eanruig, which I've been performing for years. There is only one decision that this committee can make today—the only decision that is fair and in the best interests of the estate and the people of Ladykyrk. That's to declare the title of the Earldom of Eanruig as my birthright. Today, I stand before you and declare that my claim is true."

Her last words echoed through the chamber. When they finally faded, silence blanketed the room. Lord Howton and the other members squirmed in their chairs.

She might have been too passionate, too loud, but she would never forgive herself if she didn't speak on her own behalf.

"Before I sit down, there's another matter to be addressed, the rumors and allegations that have been printed about me and my grandfather." She turned to Ferr-Colby. The spineless coward refused to look at her. With a slight shake of her head, she continued, "My grandfather was ill for seven years before he passed. When he started failing, his doctor and his most loyal servants came to me. It was in my grandfather's best interests if his duties could be simplified. That's when I took over the administrative and secretarial duties for him. With the help and support of Mr. John Miles, the butler for the ducal estate, Dunbar on Ferr, along with his brother, Mr. Charles Miles, the butler of Ladykyrk, we provided the best care possible for my grandfather and assistance in the management of his estates to the best of our abilities."

Will's steadfast presence gave her strength as Thea stared at the three committee members, daring them to question her.

"Barely at the age of eighteen, I took all responsibility for my grandfather's well-being and the responsibilities of Ladykyrk and Ferr-Colby. Not once did his ducal heir make an effort to see about my grandfather's welfare or the status of the ducal estate. Not once," she repeated. "If anyone believes I'd do my grandfather harm, then they don't know me nor do they know the loyal servants in my late grandfather's employment." Thea inched her chin upward. "If anyone"—she turned toward the duke—"would like to examine the account books for Ferr-Colby or the Earldom of Eanruig, then they are welcome. If they'd like to interview the servants, I'll make the arrangements. I have no secrets to hide."

Will rose from his chair and stood beside her. "I'd like to add to what the Countess has said today."

Lord Howton nodded.

"I've had the opportunity to become familiar with the tenants of Ladykyrk. Every single one of them praises the Countess of Eanruig's efforts. Under her management, the estate and the Ferr-Colby duchy have prospered. Lady Eanruig's tenants respect her for not only her business acumen but her kindness and her willingness to work hard for them." Will turned toward her and smiled. "For anyone to besmirch her integrity is a travesty. I can attest to that. All the rumors and innuendoes that have been printed or bandied about are utter hogwash."

The smile on Will's face hit her square in the chest, and she stood a little taller, basking in the warmth and pride of his gaze.

"Gentlemen, I find myself in the most fortunate position of being betrothed to this amazing woman. I can only come to one conclusion. Jealousy and pettiness are the source of such ugly rumors and the utterly ridiculous challenge to her claim."

Lord Howton cleared his throat. "That's all well and good, and we appreciate your candor and observations. However, your conjectures regarding the reasons for the rumors aren't relevant here."

"Oh really?" Will drawled. "Well, when my fiancée is threatened with a capital crime, I think it best to be on the offensive." Tenderly, he took her hand. "I'll not allow her reputation to be ruined because of someone's greed."

Ferr-Colby stood. "Now see here!"

"Gentlemen, both of you sit." Howton banged a gavel. "This hearing will not be turned into a spectacle." He turned his attention to Thea. "Outside of your oration about your family's lineage and the few papers that have been submitted on your behalf, you've presented no evidence against the Duke of Ferr-Colby's challenge to the title nor have you presented the title's charter. Do you have any other evidence?"

A suffocating silence surrounded her as the room grew quiet. If someone dropped a needle, everyone would surely hear it. Thea's stomach fell in a free fall along with all her hopes for success. "That's all I have, my lord."

Howton leaned back in his chair and stared at her as if making a decision. After a grueling moment, he addressed her. "It's the claimant's responsibility to prove their claim. I can't advise the attorney general and the Prince Regent you are the rightful heir without irrefutable evidence."

Will stood abruptly, followed by the Duke of Langham.

"Howton, we're all aware that once a title is granted, it can't be taken away," Will practically growled the words.

"Please, Lord William. Treason and murder are reasons for titles to be revoked." Howton sighed. "If I need your instruction about the granting of titles, I'll ask you the question directly. I don't need a lecture."

"No, but you'd better listen to me," demanded the Duke of Langham. "Do not make a mistake that can't be undone."

Clearly irritated, Lord Howton regarded both Will and his father.

Stella and Edith were fretfully whispering behind her.

Someone from the duke's table said, "She's going to lose."

Thea's vision blurred, and she gripped the edge of the table tightly in hopes she'd not faint into a heap. This was her day of reckoning for all her misdeeds in the care of her grandfather and his ducal estate. Silence roared in her

ears, portending she would lose Ladykyrk and the chance
to protect her grandfather's legacy.

The crack of the gavel shattered the uneasy quiet that
had surrounded her. Fate had slapped her in the face.

"Since the claimant has no other evidence except her
oral history, the committee will take the matter under
advisement—"

"I apologize, my lord, for my tardiness," Mr. Odell
called out as he practically ran down the aisle to stand
next to Thea. "I was detained by an important matter."

"More important than the hearing?" Howton queried.
His anger clearly hadn't abated.

Mr. Odell turned to Thea and whispered, "I'm certainly sorry if I caused you any worries, my lady." Then
he addressed the dais. "Lord Howton, just now a courier
from Ladykyrk arrived with documents. We're hopeful
it's the charter, and if so, it's crucial evidence that the
committee must see."

As the other committee members whispered amongst
one another, Howton scowled. "Please proceed."

Thea sat. Only then did she start to tremble. Will sat
too, but discreetly took her hand. Gently, he rubbed his
thumb against her hand.

Mr. Odell retrieved documents from his leather portfolio, then turned his attention to the committee. "My
lord, it's simple really. The Duke of Ferr-Colby's argument is that King Charles II made a mistake in granting
the title to descend to 'heirs of the marriage' which would
have allowed females to inherit instead of 'male heirs of
the marriage.' In 1660, John Worth, the fifteenth Earl of
Eanruig, returned the title and the deeds of land to King
Charles II as a show of support for his majesty. In return,
the king reissued the patent for the title to the earl. The
language in the charter received this morning will clearly
state, the title would descend to the 'heirs of the mar-

riage' not the 'male heirs of the marriage' as is customary for English titles."

Lord Howton glanced at Ferr-Colby, who raised an eyebrow.

Mr. Odell didn't wait for a signal to continue. "Respectfully, the Duke of Ferr-Colby argues that since an English king granted the title, it should have provided that the succession of the title passed to the oldest 'male heir of the marriage' as the English law of primogeniture provides." Mr. Odell leaned forward as if divulging a grand secret. "But this is a Scottish title, and Charles II was also the King of Scotland, which has a long tradition of allowing titles to pass to females. Since the reign of Robert the Bruce, female succession has been prevalent. The king knew exactly what he was doing. There was no mistake."

The entire room went silent. Ferr-Colby slowly pushed his chair back and stood. "If that's the language of the charter, then I agree. But I want to review the document for myself."

The three committee members nodded. The attorney general was frantically whispering to his scribe what to write down.

With Will by her side, Thea allowed herself to embrace with open arms a spark of hope that it was over. She squeezed Will's hand, and he returned the gesture.

Mr. Odell opened the leather portfolio and pulled out a stained parchment. He quickly read the document, then bent his head and closed his eyes for a moment. Finally, he turned to her. "I'm sorry, my lady."

Ice threaded through her veins, and she sat there frozen, unable to move or feel.

"May I?" Ferr-Colby stood and extended his hand.

Odell slowly handed the document to the duke, then exhaled painfully.

For an eternity, Ferr-Colby examined the documents. He passed the documents to his solicitor, Mr. Blaze, who nodded.

The duke leaned over and gave the documents back to Mr. Odell. "Thank you, sir." He turned his attention to the dais where the members of the committee sat. "It's the original charter which became null and void on the issuance of the second charter by King Charles II. It isn't relevant to my claim. Based upon Lady Eanruig's statements and what I've learned today, I'm more certain than ever that the earldom should be awarded to me." He looked over to Odell. "By Lady Eanruig's own recitation of the title's passage through the family, it has always descended through the firstborn males."

Lord Howton nodded.

The attorney general stood and addressed Thea. "Lady Eanruig, it's my duty to advise the Prince Regent that you have not proven you are the rightful heir, and as such you are not to be admitted to the peerage with all the rights and dignities associated with the Earldom of Eanruig."

With little fanfare, the attorney general left the room.

"This hearing is adjourned." Howton pounded his gavel, then exited after the attorney general, followed by the other members of the committee.

A soft cry of disbelief broke from her lips. She covered her mouth with her hand at the outburst. In the span of less than an hour, she'd lost everything. Slowly, she brought her hand to her forehead while a suffocating sensation crowded her chest.

"Where did they find this charter?" Will closed the distance between them, then leaned close to Mr. Odell.

"It arrived by special courier." Odell shook his head slightly, then lowered his voice so they couldn't be overheard. "Mr. Miles sent it. His note said he'd found it in the henhouse."

Mr. Blaze asked to speak with Mr. Odell, and the two gentlemen stepped away.

"Mr. Miles doesn't read Latin," Thea murmured. She had no energy to speak any louder.

"Thea, darling, look at me." Will's voice broke the spell that encased her, and she finally turned to him. "Your grandfather hid it there?" He spoke softly so others couldn't hear.

"Most likely," she answered.

"It stands to reason that he hid the other charter there too." Will's eyes searched hers as if willing her to fight. "We have several trustworthy solicitors that can leave for Ladykyrk within the hour to search for you. They have associates who can accompany them."

"No," she whispered. "It needs to be me."

"I'll go with you." Just then Ferr-Colby laughed and drew Will's attention from her. "I'll kill him," Will said as his furious gaze bore into the duke's back.

Thea placed her hand on his arm. "It's over."

His hands tightened into fists. "No, it's not."

"No," she said firmly. "The only thing important now is to leave this room."

Will's intense blue eyes stared into hers. "All right."

His words were a promise, and inside, Thea's heart pounded in agreement. But her mind told her to let it go. Such efforts for retribution wouldn't help Ladykyrk or its tenants right now.

The Duke of Langham came to their side. "I'm on my way to see the Prince Regent." His gaze locked with hers. "Thea, I'll make him promise not to decide anything at least until we can think of a plan to right this wrong."

Will took her hand in his. "Shall I go with you?"

His father shook his head. "Take Thea home."

"Thank you, Your Grace." All the earlier tumult in her brain had disappeared, only to be replaced by despair.

She closed her eyes. She had spoken from the heart to the committee, and her grandfather's wishes hadn't prevailed.

Thoughts of the tenants, Mr. and Mrs. Miles, and the folly crashed through her. She'd failed them, just as she'd failed her grandfather. A sob welled inside, but she refused to allow it to escape.

An hour ago, she thought of herself as the true Countess of Eanruig, with all the responsibilities that it entailed, and she'd relished every part of it.

Now, she was simply Theodora Worth, a woman without any place to call home in the world.

Will hadn't had much of a chance to talk to Thea alone since his entire family had swept her into Langham Hall to offer their support and love after the hearing. While he spoke with McCalpin about the day's event, Thea had stolen away to her room, then sent word she wouldn't attend dinner. Not wanting her to be alone, Will had asked that a tray for two, a bottle of whisky from the Langham cellars, and two glasses be delivered to his room.

After today, his decision had become clearer. He wanted to marry her. The overwhelming need to have her forever in his life felt right—for both of them. He never wanted her to hurt again.

Always ready to shed his uncomfortable evening clothes, Will had put on his favorite pair of doeskin breeches with his silk banyan tied around his waist. Before he could make his way through the dressing room between their chambers, a knock sounded on the connecting door.

He opened the door within seconds. Immediately, Thea's expression caught him off guard. He'd known she'd be despondent from the results of today. Who wouldn't be? But the haunted look on her face broke his heart.

With his gaze, he caressed her, then held out his arms. "Thea, I'm relieved you're here."

At the sound of her name, she rushed into his embrace. "I needed to see you."

He wrapped her tightly to him. "And I you."

For how long they stood locked together, he couldn't tell. But he'd hold her forever like this if it gave her comfort. Never had he wanted to take the pain from someone as much as he did with Thea. Gently, he pressed his lips to the top of her head. She exhaled painfully.

She leaned back, and her mystical eyes met his. "I've thought about your suggestion to go to Ladykyrk together, and I agree. But I want to go to Lady Prydewell's soirée tomorrow."

Of all the things she would say, her wish to attend a society event surprised him. "I'll escort you. Is there a reason?"

She nodded once. "I want to show society that I'll not give up. If I leave for Ladykyrk tomorrow, then London will think I'm running away. But if I make an appearance tomorrow, they'll realize I'm still fighting for my title. I can't allow the *Cryer* or Ferr-Colby to taint my reputation any more than they already have."

"That's wise in my opinion." Her determination to continue to fight thrilled him. She'd not back down after this setback, proving his Thea was impressively strong.

She pressed her lips together. "I thought . . . if you're still willing . . . we could leave the day after."

"I will always be willing." He brushed the back of one finger across her cheek, the skin silken soft. "I'm ready to tear apart a henhouse."

She grinned, then reached up and kissed his cheek.

"What do you have there?" She left his embrace and walked to the tray with the food, whisky, and glasses. "Are we having another whisky lesson?"

"I thought you might be hungry. And thirsty." He came to her side and lifted the bottle in his hand as if she were a goddess and he was making an offering for her pleasure.

"Just thirsty," she answered. "I couldn't eat a bite."

He moved closer and stood directly behind her. "Maybe after a drink?"

With his free hand, he gently trailed his fingers across her cheek, and she leaned into his body. She felt so perfect in his embrace. He ran his lips up the tender slope of her neck until his mouth rested against her ear. "Though you didn't get the result you wanted today, we'll not give up without a fight. You were simply magnificent today, Thea. You took my breath away."

She inhaled deeply, and her breasts rose as if demanding to be admired. Her beauty could make men fall to their knees in praise, and he held that perfection in his arms. He'd do everything he could to comfort her.

"Will?" The whisper of his name across her lips sent blood pulsing through his body.

"Hmm," he murmured, as he teased and kissed the tender spot below her ear.

She leaned her head sideways, so he could have greater access. Without kissing her, he trailed his lips down her neck this time.

"I want to stay with you tonight," she answered.

London, your men can rest easy.
The Northumberland Nemesis has chosen her latest victim.
He's no stranger to our pages.
It's ~~the Damp Squib~~ Lord William Cavensham.
Respectfully reported,
The Midnight Cryer

Chapter Twenty-Three

〜

Thea briefly glanced at the massive canopied bed against the wall. Covered in a regal blue velvet with a spring-green ribbon trim, the coverlet was masculine and welcoming at the same time. A sitting area at least twice the size of Thea's flanked the fireplace. The upholstered chairs matched the stool and the bedcover.

His gaze never left hers as he came to her side and handed her a glass of whisky. His sole focus was her. "I want you to stay with me too."

For the first time in her life, Thea believed she might have all she ever dreamed, including the man in front of her. The soft throbbing in her stomach was a call not to let another day vanish without taking what she wanted—to be in Will's arms and in his bed.

They raised their glasses to one another.

"To the true Countess of Eanruig. Today was just a test of your endurance. Your fairness and brilliance will bring bountiful rewards to Ladykyrk and all who reside there."

Her pulse quickened at the deep thrum of his voice. But it was his words that took her breath away. Indeed, that was what she wanted for Ladykyrk—to increase the prosperity of the earldom and become the best estate owner in all of England.

"Thank you. I know my grandfather would not want me to rest until I secure Ladykyrk for both me and my tenants." She lifted her glass a little higher. "To you, William, the man who taught me confidence and made me feel beautiful. Thank you for the lovely things you said about me in front of the committee."

"I merely spoke the truth," he said softly.

They each took a sip. Sensations of smoke, peat, and strength ran across her mouth and tongue.

"You are beautiful." He dropped his tone. "Inside and out. You grow more exquisite every day." The sweetest smile tugged at his lips, one that made her heart pound against her ribs as if trying to reach him. "But I'm of a mind you always had confidence, and it mesmerizes me."

Since she'd arrived in London, her grief and the accompanying guilt had slowly faded like an ink stain on a hand. It was still there but had grown fainter and fainter. She had Will to thank for that. Just having someone to talk to about those horrible, wretched days had lightened her burden.

"I want to thank you for being patient with me . . . and allowing me to talk honestly about my grandfather. You were like a shelter during the darkest storm." She waved her hand in the air. "Forgive my bad metaphor. I never had much talent at being a poet."

"Don't thank me for sharing your losses with you. I wanted to do it, and I'm honored that you confided in me." He strolled to her side.

She took his glass from his hand. With a slight turn, she placed it next to hers on a writing table close at hand.

With tender ease, he slid his arms around her waist, pulling her tightly to his chest. Heat from his body radiated through his banyan straight into her dressing gown. The silk covering his body was only slightly thicker than the thin silk covering her own. The friction of the fabric against breasts was sweet torture as they were already heavy, and her nipples had hardened in sharp peaks. She closed her eyes and leaned against him, desperate for more of his heat, more of his body, and most of all, more of him.

She'd never have enough of him.

Ever.

In an infinitesimal amount of time, one that could not be measured in minutes or seconds, she understood what had just happened to her. In between the beats of her heart and the time it took her to blink her eyes, she realized that she loved him—fully, completely, and decidedly.

That small, minuscule moment would impact her life for all eternity. Such overwhelming feelings didn't come from a place of logic and reason or even despair. Her foolish heart did what it wanted when it came to Will.

He pressed his lips gently to hers as if worshipping her. "What are you thinking about?"

"Time," she answered, then pressed her lips against his, learning the shape and every curve of his lips.

"Why time?" He whispered the words against her lips.

"Because I want to remember every moment I have with you."

He pressed his forehead against hers. As intimate as a kiss, the movement caused their noses to touch. Not breaking the caress, she moved her lips to his, begging for more.

He groaned, not loudly, but with a rumble that vibrated through his chest to hers. He parted his lips, letting her in, and she didn't hesitate. She tilted her head and deepened their kiss, tenderly dancing her tongue with his. His arms tightened around her as if he'd never let her go. He needn't fear. As long as he wanted her, desired her, she'd stay by his side forever. His thickened cock lay rigid against her stomach, but every other part of his body flexed and coiled with a restless energy she was learning to associate when he was aroused. He canted his hips toward hers as if offering himself to her.

That part of her, hot and wet, wanted all of him. A sweet ache throbbed between her legs as if searching for him. She loved him and wouldn't waste this opportunity to experience the physical aspect of sharing everything with him. His nearness kindled a fire of need and want within her. To feel him close to her would at least make her feel alive again.

"Will, I want—" She shuddered in his arms at the feelings he aroused within her. "No, I *need* to take you to bed."

He broke the kiss and searched her eyes. His gaze was tender but at the same time apparent to both of them that he was questioning, deciding.

He slid his hands up her arms, then stared at her. "Are you sure?" Desire made his husky whisper even rougher. The sound sent another surge of awareness through her.

"Yes." She grabbed the lapels of his robe and pulled him close. "I want to make love to you."

He studied her as if trying to divine a truth or perhaps find a solution. Slowly, he exhaled, and a slight roguish smile broke across his lips. "I'm certain too."

He cupped one of her breasts and teased her tightened nipple. The sensation tingled, and she wanted more. She leaned in to him to give him greater access without breaking their incendiary kiss. He slid his hands down the lines of her waist and hips, exploring her. Desperate for more, she moaned in response. He was the one who broke the kiss when he trailed his mouth down her neck, tasting and nipping as if starved.

After she placed the lightest of kisses to his lips, Thea pulled him toward the bed. "I need you. Come."

"Oh, I plan to." With a grin, he swept her into his arms and carried her to his bed. "And I'm going to make certain you do also."

She was beyond blushing at this point. Gently, he sat her on the edge. As he untied her dressing gown, she was pushing his banyan off his shoulder. He brushed his lips against her. "*Countess*, there's no hurry. We have all night."

Tell that to her heart and the wild desire pounding through her veins. "If we have all night, then I don't want us to waste a second."

He chuckled softly, then finished undressing her by pulling the gown gently down her shoulders, tenderly worshipping her body with his lips. The sweep of his mouth across her skin set a fire through her that could only be extinguished by him.

She stretched out on the bed like a cat waking from a nap. The luxurious velvet cocooned her in its softness, and she wanted to purr at the feel. Every inch of her body felt primed, intense, like the air before a bolt of lightning struck. His eyes widened, and she found it remarkably easy to get lost in the heat of his gaze.

"Theodora, I shouldn't have called you beautiful," he growled. "You are stunningly magnificent." His robe fell from his shoulders to reveal his chest, and with several flicks of his fingers, he'd undone the fall of his doeskin breeches. He hitched his thumbs into the low-slung waistband and his gaze locked on her toes, then slowly inched upward.

The hunger on his face caused a delightful shiver to

run through her. It reminded her of diving into cool water on a hot day. She willed her heart to slow its erratic beating. But it refused to listen when she discovered his gaze anchored with hers.

She waved her hand at his falls as she scooted to the edge of the bed. "Now, are you attempting a dramatic reveal, or would you like me to do the honors?"

"Be my guest." He laughed. He stood close, and she tilted her head to peer up at him. Then—just as he'd done with her—she allowed herself a long, unfettered examination of his body. From his wide shoulders down his muscled chest, her gaze lingered. Gently, she traced each rib and smoothed her hand over the taut muscles that tightened under her touch.

He gasped while placing his hand over hers.

"You're torturing me," he said.

She lifted an eyebrow in protest. "I didn't stop you when you examined me."

He took her hand in his and rubbed his lips against her knuckles. "I didn't run my hands over your body, driving you wild either. I daresay, you're trying to make me fall on my knees and promise you fealty forever."

"I'd take it," she said softly.

"Let me give it to you," he answered in the same sotto voce.

She pulled her hand away from his lips and continued her slow meandering touch until she traced a circle around his navel.

He inhaled sharply. She trailed her finger down the thin coarse hair that ran in a straight line from below his navel to disappear under his waistband.

She reveled in the power that she could elicit such a response from him. It made her burn hotter. He was all male—bigger, stronger, and harder than her. But now, she had him entreating for her next touch.

With her hands, she pushed his breeches over his hips, and her own stomach tightened. His turgid cock leaned toward her as if trying to reach her. It was huge, thick, and if such an organ could be proud, his was—reminding her that it was swollen just for her. A vein extended from the base where it resided in a thick nest of curls then twined around its engorged length. She traced it with her finger. He hissed, and the muscles in his legs visibly contracted as if her touch was too much to bear.

"Thea," he whispered. Her name sounded like a prayer on his lips.

A pearly drop of his essence sat like a jewel on the center of the tip, glistening as if tempting her to taste. She swirled her thumb against the fluid, then rubbed it across the crown.

He groaned but let her continue her exploration as he watched her every move. He trusted her, and in return, she trusted him. This was the man who had stood beside her when it seemed as if all the world was conspiring against her. She wanted to celebrate him and all his goodness. Without hesitating, she licked the length from the base of his cock up to the tip, then took him in her mouth and sucked. He tasted of musk and Will, and it was heavenly.

"Sweetheart, what are you doing?" He cupped her cheeks, then tilted her head slightly to look at him.

With a soft *pop*, she released him. "Kissing you?" she ventured. Her cheeks heated, whether from embarrassment or the warmth of his hands it was hard to tell. "I thought since you liked to kiss me . . . perhaps I could kiss you there."

"I adore it but not as much as I adore you." He brushed his fingers across her cheek. "I want us to make love to each other. I want this to be special for you, more so than me. We'll have plenty of time later to explore how to pleasure each other."

He bent and kissed her, then with infinite care, he helped her scoot back on the bed. She wanted to ask if he meant tonight or some other night but held her tongue. She wouldn't let the future intrude on their time together. She wouldn't waste this beautiful night with him.

His hand tightened around one of her hips, then he settled between her legs. It was a perfect angle for him to kiss her again. Their lips met in a tender kiss. He trailed his mouth down her chin, her throat, and chest. When he took one of her breasts into his mouth and started to suckle, she thought she'd fly off the bed. His tongue teased her nipple, as his hand fondled her other breast. He was a master at ensuring that no part of her was ignored.

White-hot flames of heat burst through her. Looking for purchase, she grasped his shoulders tightly. But the need to learn his body was stronger. As she ran her hands over the muscles and contours of his back, she bent her legs, giving him a better angle to position his body.

"Is that comfortable?" he whispered.

She nodded, loving him more that he was worried about her. Carefully, he positioned his member between her folds. His kisses grew bolder, more demanding, and she ran her hands through his hair, scratching his scalp.

"Thea, darling, are you sure?"

She stared into his eyes as she gripped his hips, urging him closer. "I've never been more positive of anything in my life."

He was above her, then dipped toward her for a gentle kiss that lingered. His breath grew deep and his arms were flexed to bear his weight. "Do you have any idea how much I want you?"

"As much as I want you." Tentatively, she wrapped her hand around his hot length. "No, I want you more."

"We shall see." He chuckled as he wrapped his hand around hers. "Let me show you how to touch me. I'll not break."

Together, they pushed up and down. His member reminded her of hot, silken steel. His hand left hers, and gently, he caressed her folds. With his fingers, he found her sensitive nub and started the sweetest torment by gently rubbing in mesmerizing circles.

He crushed his mouth against hers and deepened the kiss. It grew bolder and more demanding. His tongue invaded her mouth as if he were possessing her. She moaned her approval. He continued to stroke her, and she rolled her hips over and over, taking all the pleasure he offered. Pinpricks of sensations raced through her. She needed to possess him as much as he was possessing her.

She was close to climaxing from his strokes, but then he entered her with two fingers, pumping gently, stretching her. It caused another riot of sensations to careen wildly through her body. He used three fingers to prepare her even more, all the while coaxing her to climax with his intoxicating kisses and the stroke of his thumb against her clitoris. She closed her eyes as everything within shattered at once. Her nerves tingled, and light exploded behind her eyelids.

"Will," she sobbed. "Oh God, Will."

"I'm here," he soothed. "I'm not going anywhere."

She moaned his name again and arched into his hand. Her release continued to pound through her. Slowly, her body floated back under her control. He cradled her in his arms and nuzzled her neck.

But still it wasn't enough. She wanted all of him. She ran her hands down his back, over his hips, and caressed the tight muscles of his buttocks. Her skin tingled where his body touched hers. She tilted her hips toward him. "I want you inside me."

He reared back and stared into her eyes, their breathing in concert with one another. The tenderness on his face was almost her undoing. He took himself in hand and rubbed the crown of his cock up and down her folds, sliding through her wetness with ease. He positioned himself at her sex and gently inched his way inside.

It was heaven and hell at the same time. Though he'd tried to prepare her body for this, she hadn't anticipated such pressure and fullness. He pushed more, and her body tightened. She gasped for air as she threw her arms around his neck as if to hide. He took her into his embrace, then kissed her.

"Try to relax. Take a deep breath. I promise I'll make it feel good for you."

She nodded and did as he asked. With a thrust of his hips, he was seated inside her. She froze momentarily as her body fought to accommodate the girth of his member.

"Breathe, Thea," he coaxed as he nuzzled her neck.

She concentrated on her breathing. *In. Out. In. Out.* Finally, her body relaxed.

"That's it, sweetheart." He possessed her mouth with his, then started to move within her, his rhythm mimicking her breathing. *In. Out. In. Out.* The slow and even thrusts of his hips were hypnotic, and she moved with him, raising her hips to match his movements.

"You're so lovely, Thea." His tempo increased slowly at first until he was pounding into her. Sweat glistened on his brow and his face looked like a man possessed.

The sight caused her own body to heat. She mewled his name, and in answer, he moved his fingers to her center and started pleasuring her again. But instead of slow meandering circles on her clitoris, this time he caressed her with a frenzied touch, demanding her to come once again. She locked her legs around his hips and matched his movements, flesh pounding flesh. Her breathing accelerated. She closed her eyes, and her release sped through her body until it shattered into a million points of pleasure. She cried out his name again.

He grunted her name and drove into her one final time. He pulled out, then took her in a blinding kiss as he released his seed on her belly. The bucking of his hips decreased, until they lay holding on to each other, as if desperate to calm the tempest they'd created.

"Thea," he whispered her name like a prayer.

Gently, he rolled off her, and the cool evening air rushed over her heated body. They both stared at the canopy overhead, not saying a word. She needed to touch him to make certain that the moment was real—that what they shared was real. Before she could turn to him, his hand found hers, and he interlaced their fingers together.

Their breathing grew gentle, and he raised her hand to his lips where he pressed a gentle kiss to her knuckles. He released her hand, then got up from the bed. When he returned, the mattress dipped slightly, and he sat beside her with a wet linen cloth. "Let me clean you."

She started to protest, but he put a finger to her lips, followed by a kiss on her cheek. He took the cloth and gently wiped her thighs, then between her legs. Licks of embarrassment flamed her cheeks, but she did her best to push such feeling away. After what they'd just shared, it would be tantamount to closing the barn door after the horses had escaped.

When he moved the cloth to her stomach to wipe away his release, she sucked in a breath. "It tickles."

"I wish I had warm water for this," he said as he kissed her stomach. He sat up and made quick work of cleaning himself. When he'd finished his task, he lay sideways in bed with his head resting on her abdomen. He reached for her hand again as if needing to touch her.

She definitely needed to touch him. While she rested against the headboard, she combed her fingers through his hair, letting the silky locks trail across her skin. This moment between them was both soothing and unnerving. What did one say after sharing their body with another? *Thank you. I'll see you at breakfast.* Or perhaps, *That was a bully of a try for a first time. Shall we give it another go?*

She let out a sigh but continued to play with his hair.

"We should marry," he murmured. "For real."

Her eyes widened, and she stopped playing with his hair. She didn't trust herself to speak as her thoughts came to a skidding halt. Her traitorous heart refused to stay quiet as it pounded against her ribs, trying to break free. If she could hear the rattle in her chest, then so could he. This was everything she'd wanted from the beginning, a true marriage proposal. What made it more magical was the fact it was from him. He was the man she loved with every fiber of her being.

Yet she couldn't summon one word. She wanted to cry out *yes*, but something told her to stay quiet. She was on a precipice without any guidance for the right response. One wrong move or word could lead to her ultimate fall, one that promised no soft landing. Only the hard, stone-cold fact of heartbreak.

Perhaps her appearance in front of the committee had transformed her into a meek person, afraid of taking the chance for happiness and love. All she could think about was the effect of a marriage to Will on Ladykyrk. When she'd told Grayson she wouldn't split her time between his estate and hers, should the same apply to Will? He didn't own an estate, but his commitments to his family were substantial.

But what good was any of this thinking? She may not even have an estate anymore.

He turned on his stomach and took her hand in his. "Will you be my wife?"

Silence descended between them as his gaze captured hers. His blue eyes blazed with an emotion that reminded her of hesitation or perhaps uncertainty.

As if trying to convince her, he continued, the words spilling free. "We should announce our official betrothal at Lady Prydwell's soirée tomorrow. As you said, society will see that you still consider yourself the countess, and you'll continue to act as such. I believe it'll have the effect of silencing the *Cryer*. Another factor in our favor is that it'll be a small affair of no more than eighty or so people. Of course, my parents will attend since they're close friends with Lord and Lady Prydwell. I'll make certain the rest of the family is there. I want you to have support around you when we make the announcement. Devan, Grayson, and some of my other friends will be there."

At the mention of Lord Grayson, she blinked slowly. Will was the third man in a week to actually offer for her, but not a single one had said it because of anything they felt for her. Both the Marquess of Grayson and the Duke of Ferr-Colby wanted her for her assets. Only the marquess's offer held a promise that love *might* be in their future. Now Will was a member of the collective group that wanted her. Only he hadn't told her why he wanted her.

She wanted to laugh at the absurdity of it all, but at this tender moment, it was too painful.

"I can secure a special license at Doctors' Commons." His devilish grin appeared. "We can marry whenever you want, here in London, or if you prefer, we could have the banns called in Northumberland. I'll let you make the choice."

"Why do you want to marry me?" she asked. She forced herself to breathe as she waited for her answer.

He grew quiet as he studied their entwined hands for a moment.

"I guess I jumped ahead of things, didn't I?" Slowly shifting his gaze to hers, he continued. "Well, I thought it would be the best thing for us after the other night when we pleasured each other. I wanted to talk about it then, but we never seemed to have the opportunity until now. After what we just did, I think the answer is obvious." He lifted her fingers to his lips. "It's the honorable thing to do." Still holding her hand, he looked down at the velvet blue of the spread underneath them as if trying to divine what to say next. "Thea, it's the right thing for us."

"Oh, I see," she said tersely. "A matter of honor." She nodded slightly as if understanding, when the exact opposite was true. The only thing she understood was that she gave herself to him because she loved him. A small part inside her withered away to nothing. "Another reason is you'll be sure to inherit your great-aunt's estate."

"There's that too." He nodded.

Hearing his agreement, she was ready to slide off the bed and don her dressing gown.

Then he lowered his voice, the gentle sound like a lover's touch. "Thea, isn't the real answer obvious?"

She stayed still, then shook her head.

"I want to spend the rest of my days with you." His voice softened. "I want to hold you, comfort you. I want to wake up beside you every morning and lie down beside you every night."

His lovely words guided her like a beacon into his arms where she felt cherished. Her marvelous Will thought of her as his own. It was a precious gift, one she never thought to have—one she never thought she deserved, but one she vowed to treasure all of her days.

"Oh, Will." She cupped one of his cheeks as tears blurred her vision.

"Everything in my life had dulled to gray until I met you." He placed a hand over hers where she cupped his cheek. "You make my life bright again with brilliant joy and color that's unique to you."

She didn't answer him. Instead, with every emotion of hers bared, she kissed him and pulled him to her where they made love again and again.

In the early morning hours, emptiness crept into the room and stole all her newfound happiness. How could she marry Will while her future was in limbo? What about her promise to protect her grandfather and Lady-kyrk? If she possessed any virtue whatsoever, she'd tell Will that she couldn't marry him until her future was settled. Until someone said otherwise, she was still the Countess of Eanruig with sole responsibility for a great estate and tenants who depended upon her for their safety and livelihood, not to mention their future.

What would she do if she lost her title? Marry Will and ride toward the sunset while leaving Ladykyrk and all its people in the hands of Ferr-Colby?

Those people were hers to protect.

She settled under the covers and stared at Will's face, hoping to find some comfort. A wisp of sable hair had fallen across his forehead as he slept and threatened to fall into his eyes. Gently, so as not to wake him, she brushed the errant lock back.

What a fool she'd been to think she'd be satisfied with one night in Will's bed.

She wanted forever, but she couldn't see how, not when Ladykyrk's future still sat undecided.

It's been reported that Lady Man-Eater is a Scottish witch,
a fact we can support.
If you need proof, here it is. She's conjured yet another
proposal.
What man in their right mind would want to marry such a
creature?
Only our very own Damp Squib.
What more advice can we impart?
You can show a horse the barn door when the hay catches fire,
but the poor creature won't heed the advice if he doesn't
possess common sense.
Respectfully submitted,
The Midnight Cryer

Chapter Twenty-Four

When Thea woke, she found a single red rose, perfect in color and shape with a note from Will on her pillow.

> *My darling, I have an early meeting with*
> *McCalpin. When I return, prepare to be ravished.*
> *I'll be counting the seconds until I can hold you*
> *in my arms.*
>
> W.

With a contented sigh and Will's rose for company, Thea broke her fast in her room, then bathed and dressed with Nancy's help. Indeed, she'd be counting the hours, minutes, and seconds until Will returned. Last night had turned one of the worst days of her life into the most magical evening she'd ever experienced. But the morning brought a new reality that couldn't be swept under the bed like a piece of lint.

As Nancy was tidying up her room, Thea reread the note from the Duke of Langham. The missive was delivered with last night's treats. In it, the duke shared that he'd called upon the Prince Regent as promised, only to discover that Prinny had taken a trip to his palace in Brighton. The duke immediately wrote a detailed letter describing what had happened with the committee with a request that Prinny not take any action until Thea and Odell could have an opportunity to deny Ferr-Colby's arguments. He'd sent a Langham Hall footman as courier to deliver the message with specific instructions not to return until the Prince Regent responded. He promised to keep Thea apprised of any news he received.

What she wouldn't give to have the entire matter resolved. Then she could concentrate on her future with Will. After they'd made love last night, she'd practically paced a hole in the carpet in her room trying to decide the best course of action with him and his beautiful declaration that they'd marry.

She wanted to marry him with all her heart. Perhaps the best decision was to see about a special license and marry immediately. As Will had said, there were several advantages. Society and the committee would see her settled and part of their community.

But most importantly, she'd have in Will in her life forever.

When an unexpected knock sounded on the door, Nancy had raised her eyebrows, then went to find out who would call at such an early hour of the day. Nancy returned with a calling card.

The Duke of Ferr-Colby waited for her in the duke's salon.

As she made her way to meet him, thoughts rushed and tangled together. Whatever he wanted, she'd listen politely, then ask him to leave. She had nothing to say to him. When she entered the salon, Ferr-Colby had his back turned and stood staring out the window at Langham Park.

Even she had to admit that he cut an impressive figure. Many a lady would welcome his attentions. However, she was not one of them, as all she felt for him was wariness.

Without acknowledging her, he continued his study of the park, then broke the silence. "Amazing beauty here, wouldn't you say so, Miss Worth?"

Thea bristled. He was baiting her by not addressing her as Lady Eanruig. If he came here to gloat over her loss, he could enjoy it by himself as she would determine the reason for his visit, then make it short. "Why are you here?"

He elegantly turned, then came to her side. With a graceful bow, he greeted her, then surveyed her from head to toe. "London agrees with you, Thea. You've become a proper young woman."

She didn't answer.

In response, his cheeks flushed. Another person might have missed his unease, but she watched him like a hawk would defending its territory from a rival.

"May we sit?" he asked.

"Of course." She led him to a sitting area in front of the fireplace. He waited until she was seated, then sat across from her.

"Would you like for me to ring for refreshments?" Thea asked.

He chuckled slightly. "I understand you are now quite adept at serving tea."

"If you're here to mock me, I must ask you to leave." Though the urge to flee was fierce, she stood her ground. "I have work."

"Ladykyrk matters?" he asked as if he were genuinely interested.

"Until someone officially usurps and takes away my title, I'm still responsible for it." She swallowed her trepidation but continued to stare at him.

"Thea, I've made a poor impression on you. Shall we start anew?" Without waiting for her to answer, he continued. "I want to discuss Ladykyrk. I'm here to make you an offer."

"And what is that?" Her confounded hope started to flutter in her chest. If he wanted money to drop his challenge, she'd pay him to settle this once and for all.

"I'm offering you marriage once again."

"Out of the question," she answered without hesitation.

His gaze intensified, then he slowly thrummed his fingers on his leg. Each tap against the wool fabric jabbed her composure. Finally, after making some sort of decision, he leaned back against the sofa. "I still want to marry you. It's only fair. I don't want you homeless."

"I wouldn't be homeless," she countered. "Particularly, if you dropped your challenge."

"I won't do that," he answered with a feigned impatience as if talking to a child. "You wouldn't be homeless in the physical sense but in the heart. You belong to that land and those people. I don't want to rip you away from the only home you've known. I'm not that cruel." He smiled gently. "By the by, the twins, Rose and Iris, send their regards. They're asking when you're coming home."

She swallowed. Ferr-Colby knew exactly how to unnerve her by bringing up the Daniels family. "It's Ivy and Fern," she said gently.

His eyes flashed as if he'd aimed and hit a target dead center. "See, that proves my point. They're your people." He straightened his coat sleeves, then rested his elbows on his knees. The full force of his gaze settled on her. "Your situation is untenable. My servants have searched every inch of Ladykyrk Hall and all the outbuildings. There is no charter to be found."

"You had no right." She stood in protest.

"I have every *right*." He stood in response as his words echoed through the room. "I have no idea what happened up there, but tell me why the entire house looked like a storm had ripped through it before my men arrived? My man of affairs posted that Mr. and Mrs. Miles were systematically scrounging through every nook and cranny in that house, trying to find the charter. Where or why did your grandfather hide it?"

She refused to answer, so they stared at each other with neither of them ready to give in.

"It's not there," he said softly. "I have no interest in dredging up your grandfather's death nor do I want to manage the estate outside of the mineral rights. I'll allow you to continue with the estate and the tenants as long as they don't interfere with my business."

"What happens if they do?"

He ran a hand down his face. "If you don't marry me, then I'll not bother with any of it. I'll have the tenants relocated to another estate, or I'll buy their leases out."

"You can't do that. It'd be abominably cruel to uproot them from the only home they've ever known."

He let out a long-suffering sigh. "Thea, don't you see? I've won. Now, I'm trying to do what's right for all of us, including your tenants."

Her heart pounded in her chest. He would destroy the lives of those families who'd given so much to Ladykyrk, all in the name of wealth. For generations, these people had lived there. "Why are you doing this? Don't you have enough money?"

He lifted an eyebrow in challenge. "Think of what I'm offering with marriage to me. All the rumors will be put to rest. You can return to your old life, one you love and cherish. You'll still have your earldom."

"But I don't love you," she said softly.

"Love isn't a good ingredient in these types of matters." He narrowed his eyes as he studied her.

Inside, her stomach roiled in revolt at his scrutiny. To put distance between them, she chose to stand next to the fireplace.

"Decisions like these should be made on what's in the best interests of the estates." He followed her. "Thea, I'm giving you everything you want."

"I'm afraid the answer is—"

"Before you refuse, consider this." His voice softened. "Your grandfather would be so proud if he knew you were the next Duchess of Ferr-Colby." He reached for her hand, but she pulled away. "You promised to protect Ladykyrk, and I'm giving you that chance. You won't lose anything."

Except for Will, her heart pounded in answer.

"The people of Ladykyrk need you." He stood tall and his gaze had captured hers.

Those six simple words gutted her, and they both knew she was running out of options. Though her guilt had diminished with Will's help, it now sidled up to her once again. She'd made the promise she'd protect her home the day her grandfather had passed. She'd protect his legacy. It was the only way she could live with the guilt that he'd died with no one but her by his side.

"Why do you want to marry me?" Thea's willful heart pounded against her ribs, rebelling against her decision.

"Because you're worth a fortune." He looked her up

and down as if appraising her value. "You'll make a fine duchess, Thea."

Her heart stuttered in protest. Why did she ever think she could hope for love? Her dream for a life with Will evaporated before her eyes. She had no other choice but to accept.

The longcase clock marked the seconds passing, but for her, time stood still. She felt like a queen on a chess board in a famous move called the smothered mate. On her own, she could move in any direction she wanted with unlimited power. However, the queen's ultimate role meant she'd forsake everything in a forced checkmate for the sake of the game. Once captured, she lost all power. The king piece could and would continue without her. She'd always wondered how the game would be played if the queen could choose a king who would be a true partner. Each defending the other, united in their cause.

That's what she wanted—a true, loving partnership. Will offered such a life, but the cost would require she sacrifice Ladykyrk.

The truth refused to stay silent as it clawed its way out into the open. Love had never been her fate, as she didn't deserve it. It was best to accept her lot in life and go home.

"All right," Thea whispered. She concentrated on her breathing as her grief swelled, but she'd not allow a single tear to escape in Ferr-Colby's presence.

"I'll make the arrangements." Without another word, the duke bowed, then took his leave.

She let out a gasp as a sob escaped along with all her hopes and dreams for a life with Will.

For the rest of the day, Will didn't have an opportunity to see Thea. He'd been called away to his brother's house again on the expansion. What should have only taken a couple of hours, turned into an all afternoon and early evening affair.

He hurried home to dress for the Prydwell's soirée. Along the way, he couldn't help but laugh at Claire's warning: *Be careful what you wish for*. Though he and Thea hadn't wanted to marry initially, their betrothal felt perfect, as if all the planets had aligned on his behalf. Though he'd be loath to admit his vulnerability to anyone, he could only be thankful that he'd set aside his fear Thea would reject him when he asked her to be his wife.

Last night, they shared something incredibly tender and honest, and he'd never experienced it with any woman before in his life. He shook his head. Without a doubt, marrying Thea was his destiny.

He'd quickly dressed into his evening attire, then started for Langham Hall's entry where he'd meet his family and Thea. His body practically hummed with the need to see her again. As soon as they were alone together, he'd take her in his arms for another sweet, passionate kiss.

When he first saw her standing by Pitts, he couldn't help but smile. She'd always been beautiful to him, but tonight in an ivory gown, she looked like Venus in Botticelli's *Primavera*.

This was the start of a new life for both of them. He couldn't wait until they married. Whatever their future held, he'd do his damnedest to make her happy and would gladly share her grief and hardship. She was his, and he was hers.

Without wasting another second, he sidled up to her. "I'm sorry I didn't get to see you today," Will said softly for only Thea to hear. "I was detained at McCalpin's all day."

He stood close with his hand on the small of her back and peered down at her with a smile. Once again, she devastated him with her beauty, and her ball gown only enhanced the aura that seemed to glow around her.

My God, the things this woman did to him. If he didn't know himself better, he'd think he was a fool in love.

"Thea and I will drive to the Prydwells' separately from the rest of you," Will announced to everyone gathered in the entry.

"Perhaps we shouldn't go this evening," Thea murmured as her gaze lifted to his. "We must speak."

"Thea, I think we should go. It's perfectly understandable you're nervous." He gently caressed the small of her back. "We'll take a separate carriage and talk privately. Will that suit you?"

The duke and duchess turned their attention to them, and, in tandem, their eyebrows peaked into perfect arches.

Thea nodded reluctantly.

"Is something amiss?" A tinge of alarm resonated in the duchess's normal honeyed voice.

"Of course not," Will answered. "Thea and I have some private matters that need to be discussed. Since I was completely absent from the house today, I thought we'd take this opportunity to be alone."

Stella and Lady Edith looked at one another with shock clearly written on their faces, then Stella turned to Will. "Anything you want to announce to us now, William?"

"Not yet." He took Thea's gloveless hand and raised it to his lips. "But hopefully, by this evening, we'll have some news to celebrate."

Now, it was Thea's turn to raise her eyebrows.

Pitts opened the door where the carriages that would take them to Lady Prydwell's soirée stood ready in the circular drive of Langham Hall. The massive black carriage with the Langham seal and four black horses was the first in line. The duke and duchess, along with Stella and Lady Edith, entered it. Will escorted Thea to a smaller, unmarked black carriage with two matching bays. He helped her into the carriage, and then followed, closing the door behind him. He settled in the rear-facing seat across from her, and with a slight jerk, the carriage was in motion.

"Imagine how lost I've been today. I made wild passionate love to my fiancée last night, then was forced to leave her bed. When I craved her company, envision the stinging disappointment I've had to bear when I was called away to my brother's home."

"I'm sorry, but after last night . . ." She swallowed. "After we . . . hmm . . ."

"Made love?" He rested his elbows on his knees, leaning close to her. "That's what it's called. That's what we did." He grinned. "You seduced me, remember?"

"Yes. Well, after that . . ." She twisted her fingers together as if struggling to find the right words. "I found I needed to sort some things out for myself."

"Did I hurt you last night?" God, he should have stayed home today and made certain she was fine. He'd much rather have held her in his arms than talk finances with his brother and sister-in-law. After today, he vowed to change his priorities. He valued his work, but Thea was priceless.

"Do you mean physically?"

He took one of her hands and squeezed. "Tell me the truth, Thea. I would never purposely hurt you, but if I did . . ."

She shook her head.

"Then what is it?"

"Ferr-Colby stopped by Langham Hall today." Hesitantly, she shifted her gaze to his.

His ire rose, ready for a fight. If that reprobate had

upset her again, he'd personally call the man out and beat him to a pulp. Everything within him snapped to attention. He shifted closer, ready to protect her like a wolf who would do anything to protect his mate. Ferr-Colby would never cause her anguish or pain again if he had anything to do with it.

Before he could ask Thea what the duke wanted, her next words drove a wedge straight through his heart.

"He asked me to marry him, and I agreed."

The speed with which Will leaned away resembled a man who'd just been shot at close range.

"Pardon?" he asked incredulously.

"He told me he'd throw my tenants off Ladykyrk if I didn't marry him." The words were swirling in her mind, and she knew if she didn't get them out quickly, she'd lose her nerve.

"I'm at a loss here." He ran his fingers through his meticulously combed hair. "Help me understand. After what *we* shared last night, today you told Ferr-Colby that you'd marry him?"

"Yes. I should have said something earlier. . . ." She ceased talking once she saw the dumbfounded look on his face.

He suddenly seemed to recover his senses as he scooted forward with his knees framing hers. He took both of her hands in his, and the empathy in his eyes didn't hide his underlying shock. She felt ashamed at her own cowardice and wanted nothing more than to hide in the farthest corner of the carriage.

Such a shame they'd taken one of the smaller ones from the Cavensham stables. You couldn't hide a flea in here, much less a grown woman.

She chided herself for such thinking. This was the man she loved with all her heart, and she was setting him free. "But you should know . . . I love you," she said softly. "I always will."

"Oh my God, Thea." The creases around his eyes marked his pain, and he tilted his face to the roof of the carriage. "Do you want him?" he asked, his voice suddenly wooden.

"No. But I have no choice."

"We can find another way. You don't have to marry Ferr-Colby." His gaze held hers. "You don't even know if you've lost the title. There's been no decision on Eanruig. You can't marry him."

"He told me that his servants searched Ladykyrk and never recovered the charter. It's not there." A single tear escaped, and he gently wiped it with his thumb. "For all I know, my grandfather could have thrown it in the fire."

"Or Ferr-Colby's men could have done that." He continued to caress her cheek with his thumb, ensuring that any other tears that fell would be swept away. If only he could do the same with her heartache.

"You could still marry me, and we'll live with Aunt Stella until we find out for certain what happens to the earldom. Your tenants could come live there too. We'll buy more land and build homes for them. I have money."

"Will—" Her voice cracked betraying her pain. "They all just renewed their leases with me. They've committed to Ladykyrk for five more years. Ferr-Colby would seek damages against them." She wanted to scream to the heavens at the insufferable circumstances before all of them. "He told me if I didn't marry him, he'll ruin them."

"He'll ruin you."

The agony in his voice cut her to the quick.

He spoke the truth. She'd be nothing but chattel as Ferr-Colby's duchess. Her gaze dropped to her hands where she could see the whites of her knuckles. She was clenching Will's hands so hard, she had to be hurting him.

There was no use holding on to him. Everything inside of her stilled, then slowly cracked into a million pieces and fell into nothing. For a moment, she wished she could recall every word from this evening. She closed her eyes, desperate to find some type of equilibrium.

Gradually, she let go of his hands. "I'm sorry. I didn't have any idea I was holding on so tightly."

"Thea," he whispered as he cupped her cheek. "Marry me, and we'll build a wonderful life together."

She leaned away from him purposely and summoned every ounce of courage she possessed and prayed it would be enough to do the right thing. "I can't let those people suffer."

His eyes widened, then he shook his head as if disbelieving what she was saying.

"I made a promise, Will. I couldn't live with myself if I cause my people harm. We'd both suffer, and I love you too much to put you or me through that." She fought to maintain control over her grief while wretchedness crept in like a thief stealing all her previous happiness. "I'm sorry."

The simple words were inadequate for the pain she had created for both of them.

He shook his head vehemently. "What about last night?"

"No harm came from last night. We were two people who shared something profoundly special." This time, she bent forward and cupped his cheek. He leaned into her touch. "I wouldn't change a thing. I'm grateful that my first time was with you."

"Thea." He placed his hand over hers, holding it to his cheek. "I'll not let you go."

"My sweet darling." Never before had she used such

a tender endearment. She swallowed, in hopes it would give her strength. "Remember when I said I didn't think I deserved love? I was right."

"No. I beg to differ." He leaned forward and swept his lips against hers.

His gentle touch was a bittersweet reminder of all they'd shared over their short time together. Memories she'd keep for the rest of her life. Another rebellious tear fell.

Gently, he wiped it away with his thumb. "Don't cry. Every tear stabs me."

"It stabs me too." Determined to maintain restraint, she closed her eyes. Every touch of his became another haunting memory. "For seven years, I took care of my grandfather, Ladykyrk, and the ducal estate. I was so lonely through that time, then I met your wonderful family. Thank you for sharing them with me. It was a dream of mine to have a family like yours welcome me, accept me, and make me feel as if I was one of their own. All because I met you. . . ." She shuddered inwardly as the pain lashed through her, but she forced herself to continue. "You gave me everything. You're everything in this world I want, but I can't have." Though the pain ripped her heart into shreds, she forced herself to smile. "It's the right thing for me to do. I have to do this. It's who I am."

There. She'd said it.

However much it hurt, she had to let him go. The insufferable pain made her want to double over and cry like a baby. Never had she felt as if her insides were being ripped out of her.

The carriage had come to a slow stop outside the Prydwells' stately home. The entire building was alight in merry lights and the soft sounds of music and conversation filled the air. Such gaiety appeared almost garish when compared to the sorrow inside their small corner of the world.

By now, he'd pulled away from her. Though the distance was a mere foot, it felt as if miles were between them. He rested his elbows on his legs, legs that she'd caressed last night. He held his head between his hands. Those same hands had worshipped her body hours ago. Oh God, she had to stop torturing herself with such thoughts. There was already enough pain inside the carriage from both of them.

He wiped one hand across his face, but it did little to hide the hurt and agony there. "Thea, give me a chance."

"Will, I can't." She swallowed, desperate to find the courage to finish this between them. "But one more thing. I'll make certain Stella understands why I can't marry you. I'll ask her not to disinherit you." She said it as gently as possible, but his nostrils flared as he clenched his jaws tightly.

"She never would have. It was an argument in her arsenal to bring us together. She didn't think I had it in me to fall for you." The edge in his voice made her lean back. "She was wrong. I fell off the cliff for you."

He leapt from the carriage and held out his hand for her to take. "If you truly love me, give me a chance."

Chapter Twenty-Five

❧

"G ood lord"—Devan examined Will from head to foot—"you look as if you just lost your best hunter."

If he wasn't in shock, Will would have snorted. He felt as if his best hunter had just kicked him in the teeth, then to add insult to injury, kicked him in the bollocks for good measure.

She'd jilted him.

He was still reeling like a top, desperate to land someplace. He hadn't even seen it coming. He clenched his fists by his sides. He should have never left her side today. He should have made love to her again and again. That would have kept Ferr-Colby from forcing her into marriage.

"I've a lot on my mind," he answered. Anger welled inside him faster than water collecting in the hull of a sinking ship. What was the use of hiding anything from Devan? He was a vicar, and if anyone needed consoling at this particular moment, it was Will. "Thea told me on the way over that she didn't want to marry me. She's marrying Ferr-Colby to secure her rights to Ladykyrk."

Devan's mouth gaped open. "When did you actually ask her to marry you?"

Will stared at his friend. That damnable horse kicked him again. "Last night."

"I'm sorry, Will." Devan shook his head. "Even I, who have never courted a woman or even sniffed at marriage outside of performing the services, know this must be tearing you up inside."

Gutting him was a more appropriate description. Devan had no idea the devastation that had ripped through him. Everything had been perfect thirty minutes ago, and now his whole world had been torn apart.

"Don't say you're sorry." If anyone should say they were sorry, it was heaven above. How could fate and God combined be so cruel to allow him to fall in love with her then snatch his happiness away? Having his heart ripped from his chest would hurt less than this.

His gaze constantly tracked her movements. Currently, Thea was talking with Lord and Lady Prydwell. Her mellifluous voice cut through the din of the other conversations and flew straight through him, piercing his slim thread of sanity. He still couldn't quite understand exactly what had happened. How had something so clear and perfect last night turn into a nightmare?

His chest tightened in revolt. Grayson had arrived and stood by Thea's side. Will took a deep breath to ensure that he wouldn't march across the ballroom and plant a facer on one of his best friends.

"What will fix the problem?" Devan asked.

"Hmm," Will absently replied.

Devan snapped his fingers in front of Will's face. "Hello, I'm over here."

Will pivoted on one foot and turned slightly so he could look at Devan, but out of his peripheral vision still see Grayson and Thea.

Devan genuinely smiled. "What will fix your problem with Lady Eanruig?"

"Only finding the second charter will convince her to marry me," Will snapped. None of this was Devan's fault, but at the moment, he didn't give a damn whether he was civil.

Devan's eyes grew wide. "Oh God, William. You've got to find it."

He shook his head slightly. "I think it's never going to be found. Apparently, the entire estate has been searched without any luck. Devan, I want her to have everything she wants in life. Ironically, I thought she wanted me, but she wants Ladykyrk more." He looked his friend in the eye. "Is it wrong of me to say that this whole situation reminds me of Avalon?"

"It's not the same." Devan shook his head. "Thea wants you but can't shirk her commitment to her estate. You understand that," he said gently. "You've done the same thing with your family's estates your entire life." He clasped his hands behind his back and rocked onto his heels, a sure sign a lecture was about to ensue. "Do not compare Thea with Avalon." His eyes grew wide. "Speak of the devil."

Will turned, fully expecting to see Thea. Instead, it was a nightmare from his past.

The Marchioness of Warwyk, the former Avalon Cavensham, the woman who had laid him to waste all those years ago, stood directly in front of him. He hadn't seen her since that fateful day ten years ago. Time had been somewhat kind to her. She was still fetching, but there was a coldness about her that diminished her beauty.

"*Lady Warlock*. Of all the nights for her to make an appearance, she chooses tonight," Devan mumbled.

But Will heard every word. Indeed, why on all nights

would she make an appearance like a witch swooping into the room on her broom to torment him after he'd lost Thea? Fate could only be described as cruel with an evil sense of humor. But he'd show fate and Avalon who could be even more heartless.

Devan bowed. "Lady Warwyk."

"Mr. Farris," she acknowledged without a smile.

"Lord William." Her strong clear voice did little to mask the dread in her eyes.

That she would show such weakness in front of him didn't faze him in the least. Every hair on his arms stood at attention. What little was left of his civilized mind told him to take heed. It wouldn't serve either of their interests if he caused a scandal now.

Even if she deserved it.

He took a deep breath. It was such a childish reaction, one he desperately tried to tame. He took another breath, but the beast inside him thrashed and twisted, anxious to lash out at her. Refusing to calm, it demanded retribution. All the agony of his humiliation from years ago came back to haunt him, while reminding him of the pain of losing Thea.

He narrowed his eyes and examined her more carefully. There was a brittleness about her; he could see it in the lines around her eyes. A sharp wind through the ballroom would likely break her in two pieces.

Really, how appropriate that she chose tonight to taunt him? He'd doubted he had the capacity to bear any more pain—not after Thea cut all ties to him.

But he was wrong.

Will didn't hide the fact that he watched Thea's every move. Even when she had her back turned to him, she could feel his stare as if he'd actually touched her. Suddenly, it stopped, and for the life of her, she missed it.

Discreetly, she turned from Lord Grayson and stole a peek Will's way.

The most beautiful woman Thea had ever seen stood before Will. She was dressed in a satin lilac gown with Belgian lace as an overlay. Tall and thin with hair as dark as the night, she stood perfectly still, not batting an eye, like an automaton. The sight reminded Thea of a rare lavender rose she once saw at her grandfather's conservatory.

Lord Grayson immediately stiffened beside Thea when he saw the woman with Will. "Oh God, it's *Lady Warlock*."

"Who?" Thea asked.

He shook his head quickly. "Forgive my crass comment. That is Lady Warwyk."

"The woman who broke Will's—"

"Heart," he growled. "Yes. The one and only, Avalon, the Marchioness of Warwyk."

Thea looked at Will's back. The stiffness in his posture and his clenched fists meant one thing. He was livid and most probably hurting. She'd seen in his eyes the wounds he suffered when he'd shared how the woman had jilted him.

And she'd just done the same to him. All her earlier suffering and shame flooded her once again with numbing pain. With every ounce of strength she possessed, she forced herself to go to him. Without taking her leave of Lord Grayson, Thea went to stand by his side. She had to save him before he lost himself in anger.

She'd not allow the man she loved to be decimated in front of her.

"Lord William, would you introduce me to the Marchioness of Warwyk?" Thea's honeyed voice instantly soothed the beast inside him. Reluctantly, the lashing monster retreated into its chains but still continued to rattle them in warning.

Before he could bite out the word *no*, Grayson did the honors for him.

"Lady Eanruig, it would not be appropriate under these circumstances," Grayson announced in a steel, cold voice designed to cut Avalon in two with a single swipe.

This whole evening had turned into a bloody mockery. The two women whom he'd wanted to marry stood before him, and neither of them wanted him—then or now. While he didn't want anything to do with Avalon, he wanted Thea desperately. With his calm reserve in shambles, he wanted to sweep her up in his arms and take her to the carriage. He'd kiss her, then make love to her. Afterward, they would go home, and he'd take her to his bed and make love to her again and again until she realized that she belonged to him and he belonged to her— even if it took a week, a month, a year, or a decade.

As Thea was wont to do, she did as she pleased. She ignored Devan, Grayson, and himself to do her own bidding. While still holding on his arm with her left hand, she extended her right. "How lovely to meet you, Lady Warwyk. I'm Lady Eanruig."

Avalon's cheeks flamed red, but she didn't shy away from any of them. "It's a pleasure, Lady Eanruig." Her eyes widened when it dawned on her who Thea was. "You're the Countess of Eanruig, William's fiancée. I read about you in *The Midnight Cryer.*"

"Lud, not everything you read is true, my dear lady," Thea answered gaily as she squeezed Will's arm. "It's true that I'm husband hunting in London. Alas, I'm afraid that I'm not as fortunate as some lucky women who've snagged a loving husband." She pursed her delectable red lips into a pout. "Lord William's heart isn't mine to keep."

She playfully batted his arm. "Perhaps I'll have to try harder."

Darling Thea. She was giving him an out to save him from losing face over another jilting.

The men around him chuckled uncomfortably and shuffled their feet. Will was intrigued and frankly, terrified at the same time as to what Thea would say next.

Thea looked at Avalon with a coy smile. "If I'd ever been lucky enough, I'd have never let him go." She batted her eyes twice. "Wouldn't you agree, Lady Warwyk?"

Her gaze softened as her eyes met his. Those mystical irises wove a spell around him. He was speechless and didn't have a clue as to what to say.

Neither did Avalon. She stood in front of them with a look of abject shock on her face.

"You aren't still chasing after Lord William, my lady?" Devan inquired of Avalon in a soft lilt. "Or are you looking for different prey this time?"

Thea reached for her fan that dangled at her wrist, then lightly tapped Devan on his arm in a lighthearted rebuke. "Silly man. I'm the one looking for prey."

Duly chastised, Devan smiled and bowed his head. "Excuse my error, Lady Eanruig."

Avalon straightened her shoulders at Devan's cutting remark, then directed her attention to Thea. "I'm certain you've heard all about me then. I'm not chasing anyone. I'm a widow." Finally, she turned to Will. "I wanted to express my sincere apology for how I treated you. It was wrong and cowardly. If I had the opportunity, I'd do it all so differently."

Thea's playful flirting evaporated. "Meaning you wish you would have married him?"

"No, but I wish I had never treated you that way, William. Please say you'll forgive me. I'd like to introduce my sister into society next year, and I hope if I expressed my heartfelt apologies, you'll accept it. I don't want my sister's reputation in tatters before she even arrives in town because of my previous bad behavior."

The movement of the footmen, the chatter of the guests, and the music wilted around them. Everything seemed suspended in time. Only the feel of Thea's arm clasped around his kept him grounded. He still stared at Avalon but put his hand over Thea's and squeezed gently—*thanking her, needing her.*

Her actions freed him from any remaining anger he held for Avalon. She stood before him, sincere in her apology, making him realize that she'd been a girl just like he'd been a young man, both too immature to know the ramifications of what they were doing.

Avalon stood welded to the floor, ready for his rebuke or cut direct. After what must have been agonizing moments for her as she stood before him, she turned to walk away.

"Forgive her." Thea squeezed his arm again and whispered, "If not for her peace of mind, do it for you."

He continued to grip Thea's hand tightly, taking her strength for his own. "Lady Warwyk?"

Avalon turned toward him, and her lips trembled, the first sign she was crumbling before them.

"You and your sister have nothing to fear from me. Let's forget the past," Will offered.

"Thank you," she murmured. Without another word, she left the ballroom.

Whispers grew in volume as she left. Guests' heads bobbled from Avalon's retreating figure to Will. He growled low in his throat. "Vultures looking for the fresh kill."

"Then smile and laugh with your friends. Show the

vultures they need to find something else to satisfy their appetite for carrion," Thea said softly.

Devan nodded, then told some silly joke. They all laughed. Relief thrummed through his veins. Thea had done more than save his reputation from a second jilting. She made him believe in second chances.

His need became overwhelming to hold her. He wanted to thank her and see if she'd walk with him in the gardens outside. Perhaps he could convince her to change her mind. He turned, only to discover she was gone. He swallowed in a panic and swept his gaze through the ballroom and back. There wasn't a trace of her.

Pain took hold like a rabid beast and ripped through him. What he'd experienced with Avalon had never felt like this.

Thea had stolen something valuable from him—his heart.

And there was one thing as certain as the moon rising in a midnight sky, he'd never get it back.

A cool breeze swept past him, and his cousin Claire's words came back to haunt him.

Be careful what you wish for.

He wanted to tilt his face to the ceiling and howl in pain. He should have known better than to wish that Thea would be his forever.

Thea quickly stole away from the Prydwells' soirée. After seeing Will and Avalon reach an understanding, or at least, the beginnings of an understanding, she had to leave. Standing close to Will and touching him had resurrected the vexing doubt of whether she'd made the right decision to set him free. Of course, when she told him she wouldn't marry him, she fully expected he would someday pursue another. But it was a shock that she'd come face-to-face tonight with the woman he'd asked to marry years ago.

The Langham coach had brought her home, and she listlessly wandered to her room where a note from Ladykyrk awaited her. Mr. Miles had sent word that no other documents had been found on the property.

Blowing a piece of loose hair from her forehead, Thea collapsed in one of the matching wing-backed chairs that framed the fireplace. The time had come to return to Ladykyrk, and she wanted to leave now. There was no other reason to stay in London except to marry Ferr-Colby. Immediately, she penned a note telling him of her plans. She added that she wanted to marry in Northumberland.

Thea leaned back and released a soulful sigh. It was dreadful business when her heart screamed there was only one man it desired. She forced herself to stand, then called for a maid to help her pack. She'd leave in the morning. When she turned to her wardrobe to start the packing, the Duke of Langham's nightly tray of sweets stood waiting for her on the small flat-top secretary desk in her room.

She lifted the domed covering, then sampled a little of the creamy lemon syllabub that he'd sent this evening. Such personal touches from the Cavensham family had made her feel welcome. Her eyes burned, and her throat tightened. She would miss every single one of them, particularly Claire and the duke and duchess.

But she'd miss Will the most. Even when he moved to Stella's estate, she'd miss him. It'd be painful since she'd probably see him regularly. Deep inside, she knew it would take a monumental effort on her part to act as if they were just friends.

An efficient knock on the door brought her out of her reveries. When she opened the door, Stella and the duchess rushed in, still in their evening gowns from the soirée.

"Thea?" Stella exclaimed. "What's this that you're leaving us? Pitts told us as soon as we arrived home."

The duchess took Thea's hands in hers. Though the duchess's hands were small like Thea's, they were strong but gentle at the same time. "Did Lady Warwyk upset you? Was it William?"

"No, it's nothing like that." Thea's voice hitched. "I must return to Ladykyrk." She handed the note to the duchess who, after reading it, gave it to Stella.

"Sweetheart, I thought we were going to plan a wedding." The duchess pulled her into her arms, and Thea rested her head on the duchess's shoulder.

It was wonderful to have someone who cared for her and offered comfort. The warmth of the duchess surrounded her, and Thea closed her eyes, soaking up every sensation. This was what it felt like to be held in a mother's arms—no judgment, just unabashed love. Thea wanted to bottle it up and keep it for all the lonely times ahead of her.

"Theodora, let's sit." Stella gently lowered herself into one of the floral wing-backed chairs.

The duchess released Thea from her embrace, but still held her hand as she brought Thea to the other chair. Instead of taking the chair, Thea pulled up a footstool and sat between the two women, facing them.

Thea's chin quivered, but she bolstered her resolve by wrapping her arms around her waist. "My attention is needed in Ladykyrk."

She almost fell to her knees at the kind regard on the faces of both the duchess and Stella. Deep inside, she knew she was saying goodbye to the duchess. Once she returned to Ladykyrk, her friendship with Stella would change as the grand dame's loyalties would lie with Will, as they should. Still, she was thankful for everything they'd taught her, but most importantly, she relished the friendships they'd given her.

She addressed Stella first. "I appreciate all you've done for me, Lady Payne."

Stella's eyebrows contracted at the formal address.

Thea smiled, but inside she felt like crying. "You should know that I've decided that Will and I won't suit. I told him this evening."

"Why?" Stella softly asked.

"Aunt Stella," the duchess gently chided, then turned her attention to Thea. "My heart's heavy with your news. If you can't share with us, we'll understand. But I want you to know that you're welcome here anytime. Both the duke and I have grown so fond of you." The duchess's eyes glistened.

Thea nodded, and her own eyes grew blurry with unshed tears. She pinched her fingers over her eyes to squelch any tears from dropping. After a moment of quiet, she could talk again. "You see, I agreed to marry Ferr-Colby."

Stella started to sputter a protest, but Thea raised her hand. "Please, Stella, this is hard for me. If you'll allow me to finish, I'll answer any questions you have. I promise."

"I apologize." Stella's voice cracked with emotion. "Go ahead, Thea."

Hearing her name on Stella's lips resurrected all her memories of her grandfather, both good and bad. Now was not the time to dwell on them. She had to make the two women in front of her understand her decision.

"I wanted to marry Will. I've fallen hopelessly and ir-retrievably in love with him," she said softly, as she studied her hands. "I have no doubt he'd be a wonderful husband to me and the perfect father to our children. Yet,

I can't jeopardize my home, nor can I trust to leave the responsibilities to someone else. I made a promise to myself and my grandfather that I'd protect and cherish Ladykyrk. The only way I can keep from losing it is to marry Ferr-Colby. He'll destroy everything otherwise." Her chest tightened as her sorrow grew. "Now, will you both promise something?"

The duchess and Stella barely nodded.

"I need you both to look after my Will," she murmured. Deep sobs racked her insides, but she sat rigidly, denying their escape. Once she felt able to continue, she took a breath. "I've hurt him deeply tonight, and there are no adequate words to express my sorrow. I wish there were some way I could take his pain as my own." Despising the pain she had inflicted upon them all, she forced herself to continue. "Please, I beg of you both, take great care of his heart." A small cry escaped, but Thea clenched her eyes shut. "He deserves so much in life and most importantly, he deserves someone he can entrust his heart to along with all of his love. They're grand gifts." She shook her head in denial. "I was a fool to think I deserved him."

Sadness had softened the duchess's countenance, and Stella wiped her eyes.

"But there's someone out there worthy of him. Whoever she is, she must be a woman of great character with a giving heart like Will. Someone who is free to love him in return." She fought her tears by swallowing hard. "She must be someone who loves him . . . as much as I do."

Her heart shattered into pieces that would never be repaired, and though her words cut like a knife, Thea continued. "Now you know."

"Can't you stay in London and we'll fight Ferr-Colby and the committee?" Stella asked.

"If I stay here at Langham Hall, all I will think about

is Will, and I'm not certain I'll be able to do the right thing." One renegade tear fell. Thea bit her lip, willing them to stop. "Besides, Ferr-Colby had his men search Ladykyrk. There's no charter. Mr. Miles verified it. My business here is finished. I've lost the title. But the Cavensham family has been a gift beyond my wildest dreams. Claire has become the friend I've always dreamed that I find. She and Pembrooke have generously offered a carriage for my return to Ladykyrk." She looked at Stella and smiled gently. "Once I return to Ladykyrk, I plan to hire a proper lady's maid."

"Good for you, Thea," Stella said favorably, with a nod of her head. "Does Ferr-Colby love you?"

Thea shook her head. She exhaled slowly, desperate to maintain a calm façade but failing. Everything inside hurt.

"But why would you forsake Will for Ferr-Colby if he doesn't love you and you don't love him?" Stella asked. "Do you really want to forsake your own happiness for Ladykyrk?"

The fire cracked as if demanding her answer, and the duchess leaned close.

Thea glanced at the connecting door to Will's dressing room. Had it really been only yesterday when they'd made love, and he'd teased and flirted with her to her heart's joy? So much had changed in such a short period of time.

Another tear escaped, and she quickly brushed it away. "You see"—she dropped her voice in an attempt to keep her emotions contained—"when the committee makes its recommendation, it's the only choice I have to protect Ladykyrk."

"Oh, Thea." Tears fell down the duchess's face. She gently wiped them with her handkerchief. "You don't think we can find another solution so that you and Will . . ."

"No," she answered with what she hoped was a smile, though her heart was torn to shreds. "And I want him to find happiness and someone to love. He's a marvelous, giving, and honorable man. He deserves every wonderful thing that life offers. I'm lucky he shared so much of himself with me."

The grand dame shook her head in denial, and the duchess closed her eyes and sighed tremulously.

"Spending time here in your home and seeing the family you've created has shown me that a perfect marriage should be two people who are committed completely to each other." Thea put her hand over the duchess's and squeezed. "It's a marvelous thing. Thank you for sharing so much of your family with me. You've taught me about love. And so has your son. I'm grateful to have had a chance to fall in love with him. Please, never doubt that I love Will more than any other in this world." She shook her head once. "But I can't marry him. It's not to be."

"I think I understand," the duchess murmured. "Sometimes we don't get what we want because we have a higher responsibility to others."

Stella straightened her spine and tilted her chin in defiance.

"Don't disinherit Will. He didn't do anything wrong." She went to Stella and hugged her. "Please say you understand." She kissed the grand dame on her cheek, then whispered loud enough for the duchess to hear. "Your great-nephew loves you beyond all reason, you lucky girl."

They laughed through their tears.

"Of course, I'd never disinherit him." Stella sniffed

and wiped her nose. "What do you need from us to help make the way home easier?"

"I'd like to leave at first light tomorrow." Thea forced herself to hold the duchess's gaze. "I plan to write a note to Will, as I don't think I could bear to say goodbye in person. Would you see that he gets it?"

The duchess nodded gently.

Thea stood and grasped both the duchess and Stella's hands. "I haven't had a lot of family in my life, but I consider you both like my fairy godmothers. Thank you for . . ." Her tears won the war and started falling.

The duchess took her in her arms and rocked her. Thea allowed herself to be consoled, as she wanted to remember every moment of this pain. She'd recall this time with the duchess and Stella and hopefully find comfort when her tears came again.

And again.

Lady Warlock vs. Lady Man-Eater
A true cat fight broke out at the Prydwells' soirée, where
biting and nail scratching were rampant.
This morning, Lady Man-Eater escaped to Northumberland
to lick her wounds.
Good riddance.
The Midnight Cryer

Chapter Twenty-Six

Thea had left her slippers in Will's room.

Who knew that delicate footwear could be such an efficient torture device.

Every time Will saw them on his night table, it gutted him. It would have hurt less to be drawn and quartered than to gaze upon her shoes. But he couldn't help himself. It was the only thing that tied her to him. Because when he glanced at those petite shoes, it reminded him of that bloody letter she wrote. If he'd read it once, he'd read it a thousand times. By now, he could recite it from memory.

> *Dearest William,*
>
> *I hope you don't think I'm a coward, but I decided it would be best if I not say goodbye in person. I'm not certain I could have told you all the things I needed to say without embarrassing either of us with my emotions.*
>
> *I will always be grateful for everything you*

*did for me while I was in London. Your strength,
kindness, and friendship are precious gifts I'll
cherish forever. Your generosity in sharing your
family is something I'll treasure always. But what
you said when you stood in front of the committee
with me is engraved on my heart forever.*

*Thank you for teaching me about love. I feel
honored to have fallen in love with you. Please,
it's not my intent to make you uncomfortable, but
you know me well. I do say outlandish things
from time to time, as it's who I am. For if I hadn't
fallen in love with you, I don't know if I would
ever have experienced how sweet and tender love
can be. With your warmth, caring, and attention,
you fed my heart and soul and allowed me to
grow as a person. I now have courage to move
forward and hopefully find peace with my
decision.*

*Please know that you'll always have my heart,
and I hope you'll always consider me a friend. If
you ever need me, I would drop everything and
come to you—day or night, winter or summer. I
only ask that you not be surprised if I not seek
your company when you return to Payne Manor.
I'm still trying to mend the pieces of my broken
heart.*

*It's my most fervent wish that you find a special
someone who will hold your heart forever and
tenderly give it great care. It's my deepest
disappointment that it couldn't be me, but I have
faith you'll find her. Whoever she is, I have no
doubt she's spectacular.*

*I have no right to ask, but please forgive me.
You'll always be my best friend.*

Theodora

She'd been gone for exactly two days, twenty-two hours, six minutes—he pulled out his timepiece and flipped the enameled covering to reveal the clock's face— thirty-four, thirty-five, thirty-six—

Bloody seconds. He snapped the cover so hard, it cracked in protest. He didn't give a tinker's row if he broke the damnable piece. Perhaps then he'd have something else to concentrate on besides the fact that she'd left London and him behind.

Last night, when he woke in a sweat, his first thought was that Thea had abandoned him just like Avalon. Once they both had found a way to secure their titles, they'd left him like dust under a carriage wheel. But once his heartbeat had slowed, he'd understood that wasn't the case. Thea had told him honestly why she was setting him free. Still, it didn't placate the ache in the middle of his chest every time he thought of her. He rubbed a hand over his face and stared at the plate of food in front of him. He couldn't recall eating for the last two days. He wasn't even certain he was hungry.

McCalpin leaned over and placed his hand on Will's shoulder. "That's the fourth time you've looked at the time since you've arrived for our breakfast."

"Is there a law against checking my timepiece?" Will snapped.

Devil take him. He'd been short of temper for the last two days. He'd hardly slept at all, and when he did, all his dreams turned into nightmares—Thea leaving him on the side of the road, or she'd just disappear from sight. When he woke from his bad dreams, he'd be covered in sweat. To find relief, he'd get up to wash his face, only to stare at her slippers, the constant reminder that she was gone.

"I'm not myself."

"You're hurting. We all understand. Go to her."

McCalpin leaned back in his chair. "Talk to her. See if you can come up with a solution that will solve both your heartaches."

"And say what?" He played with a piece of toast on his plate. "Come back to London. I can't sleep. I can't eat." He threw his serviette to the table. "I'll sound like a child."

"Will, we're worried for you," Claire said. Her alto voice normally soothed, but nothing would give him comfort. "Tell her how you really feel."

"I have," Will admitted. "I begged her to choose me." There was something wrong with him. Either that or everything was wrong in the world. The only thing he knew was that he felt like an untethered balloon drifting aimlessly in the sky without a driver. Only if he crashed to the ground, then burned to oblivion would he find relief from the pain.

McCalpin heaved a sigh. "What can we do to help?"

"Will," Emma said softly. "Mother said that Thea expects Ferr-Colby to arrive within a fortnight. She wants Lady Edith to stay as a chaperone before they marry. Aunt Stella is beside herself."

He slammed his fist on the table, and the silverware flew off the plates as if to escape his wrath. "He's not good enough for her."

Leaning close, McCalpin put his arm around Will's shoulder. "Listen to me, Brother, and listen well. She jilted you, and it hurts. We can see the effect on you, and it's completely deplorable. But she didn't do it because there's something missing in you. It's because of her circumstances."

"What difference does it make?" Why hadn't he paid heed to his vow when he was jilted the first time? He blindly allowed himself to fall in love again with no thought to the consequences.

The sad truth was, he knew better.

"You're a fighter and always have been," McCalpin said. "You need to act before you drive yourself mad, or worse, before you run out of time."

He just stared at his brother, unable to physically move or say a word.

Emma placed her hand on his arm. "Will, do you hear what he's saying?"

He turned and stared at her hand, then shook his head in denial. What the hell was happening to him? He couldn't let Thea go, nor could he let her marry Ferr-Colby. Anger, or more likely fear, kept him from taking action. Even leaving McCalpin's house seemed too much of a challenge. He was pinned in place, unable to move, like a beetle smashed under a boot.

Claire placed her cup on the matching saucer, then fixed her gaze on Will. "Alex and I talked last night. What if I give you my Lockhart estate? It has enough acreage for Thea's tenants, and I'll buy more land for you if need be."

"That's very generous, Claire, but it won't work."

"I'll lease it to you," she offered.

"No. Thea's emotionally tied to Ladykyrk." Just as he was to her, but she would never leave the people of Ladykyrk. "The tenants have new leases, and she's concerned Ferr-Colby would pursue all legal remedies just to hurt them."

"I see." Claire let out a soulful sigh. "Will, I hate to say this, but McCalpin's right. You're going to lose Thea forever if you don't come up with something quickly."

He shook his head in a desperate attempt to clear this miasma that held him in chains, unable to think. He stood and left the room without taking his leave. In a daze, the only thing he remembered was clenching his fists by his side.

He couldn't lose her, but the truth haunted him.

He'd already lost her, and there wasn't a damned thing he could do.

Will stood on his bedroom balcony, yearning for some great burst of energy to break him out of the paralysis that kept him locked in place. It had been five days since the weekly breakfast with his siblings and Claire. Since then, he had shunned his family and friends, while managing to hide inside Langham Hall. His company was his own misery. Thankfully, his anger had dissipated. Yet he didn't even have the fortitude to see Grayson and Devan when they called at Langham Hall. Every harried breath and painful sigh came from a place so deep inside him, he didn't recognize himself.

Simply put, he pined for Thea. He missed her smile and teasing. He missed her fretfulness when worried.

He missed holding her.

No other woman had ever caused him so much pain.

He studied the pretty and delicate slipper he held in his hand. When he tightened his grip, it didn't bend or give at all, much like the woman the shoes were made for.

The door to his bedroom opened, but Will ignored the intruder.

Will had practically become a recluse since Thea left. Always before, his thoughts were consumed by work, family, and friends. Now, he was consumed with a fairy countess who was hundreds of miles away.

A hand grasped his shoulders and squeezed. Will closed his eyes, savoring the human touch. His father always knew when Will needed him.

"I'm lost," Will murmured.

"I know, son." His father stood beside him overlooking the view of Langham Park. "Come inside. I brought some whisky and food."

He followed his father to the sitting area and plopped into the chair where a wave of memories washed over him. Thea lying across his lap. Thea under him as they made love. Thea in the throes of passion. The sensual memories licked at his senses, but what truly overpowered him was how much he missed her presence. He still held her slipper, afraid to put it down for fear he'd lose all connection with her.

His father made a plate of ham, cheese, and bread, then handed it to Will. "Eat this first."

He set two glasses with a fingerful of whisky on the table between them.

The food tasted like dust, but Will forced himself to eat it. When he finished, he took a sip of Claire's family brew, then leaned back into his chair. He let out a breath with a woeful sound.

"What's holding you back from going to Thea?" His father's deep voice reminded Will of highly polished mahogany—dark, smooth, but with an inherent strength that was unbreakable.

Will took another sip, then set the glass down. "I can't find a reason for her not to marry Ferr-Colby." He slowly shook his head.

"What do you mean?"

Will ran a hand down his face and hoped it'd wipe away his confusion. If anyone could help him see clearly, it was Father. "Thea is Ladykyrk. Her heart and soul are in that place. I don't know how I can beg her to marry me when I can't see a way to give her what she wants." He stared into his father's blue eyes so like his. "What she needs."

His father nodded, encouraging him to continue.

"I'm so proud of Thea's accomplishments. Single-handedly, she managed her grandfather's estates and took care of him while he was ill. She never resented him. If anything, she thought she'd failed him when he passed." Will studied his father. "She went through hell taking care of him. He didn't even know who she was at the end." He pursed his lips. "While other young women were making their introductions to society, Thea was caring for her grandfather, much like a newborn. He couldn't do anything for himself. She was feeding and cleaning him daily."

"Oh, Christ." His father shook his head. "I can't imagine that type of responsibility would be easy for anyone, especially a young girl."

"There's more, Father. After he passed, she didn't mourn for herself. Her every thought and action were to protect his memory and his estates. She's fighting for her birthright the only way she knows how." He smiled for the first time in days. "Look at her now. She's changed in the time I've known her. She's changed into this incredible woman who has the loyalty of a lion and the fierce convictions of a lioness. She's committed to her tenants and not afraid to do what's right."

His father smiled in return. "She sounds like your mother."

Will nodded. "I think we helped one another. I think I gave her confidence, and she encouraged me to become a better person. She taught me how to love."

He rested his elbows on his knees, then studied the glass that dangled between the fingers of one hand. The amber liquid caught the light, and it reminded him of Thea's golden-red hair. He wanted to see it again and run his fingers through it to determine if it was as soft as he remembered.

God, he was making himself sick with such memories.

"Now, I ask myself how Thea might handle a situation where I must make a decision. I find I want to ask her opinion on things such as estate business and legal matters. I want to spend time with her, enjoying simple things like walking through Langham Park. If she's reading, then I want to sit beside her and read." He examined her shoe that he held in the other hand. "I want her in all other parts of my life. I want to share my family and friends with her. She had so little company growing up. She deserves love."

His father nodded knowingly. "How did it come about that you have a pair of her shoes?"

Heat crawled up Will's neck like a band of marauding pirates. "I found them in my room. . . ."

"Is there a chance she could be carrying your child?" his father asked softly without judgment.

"Probably not. I want her so badly, yet I don't know how or even if I should convince her to marry me." He frowned as he regarded the shoe. "I want her to be happy." His chest twisted into a painful knot, as if wringing out every emotion he'd felt over the last several days. Tears welled in his eyes, and he blinked rapidly to clear them. "More than anything, *I want her happy*, but I'm scared I'll make us both miserable if I convince her to marry me. She'll lose Ladykyrk."

It was his father's turn to rest his elbows on his legs. He leaned forward. "Son, do you realize how incredibly fortunate you are to have found her?"

Abruptly, Will nodded in annoyance at himself. "I love her so much that she haunts my dreams and every waking moment of my days."

His father leaned back in his chair and blew a breath out of the side of his mouth, a tell that he was completely lost for words. His brown eyebrows tapered into a scowl. After a few moments, he broke the silence between them.

"The type of love you have for Thea is worth more than any fortune you could ever hope to acquire in this lifetime or next. You're too intelligent not to realize that."

"I know."

"Now, when has a Cavensham ever been afraid of a challenge? If the first charter was found at Ladykyrk, it stands to reason the second one is there also. Do you think you might help her find it?" his father gently coaxed.

He sat still, waiting for the old emptiness and fear of inadequacy to burn through him.

"Tell me, son. Why are you scared to fight for Thea?"

Will shook his head. There wasn't any use in hiding his fears. His father was the most astute man he knew. Undoubtedly, he'd figure out Will's reluctance.

"I've always known love. You and Mother loved our family unconditionally. Growing up around such security made my childhood wonderful."

His father nodded with a smile.

"But the greatest gift you gave all of us was the sterling example of how true love could make each of you stronger, which in turn made your love for each other stronger." He struggled to draw a breath, as the pain was suffocating. "She's my perfect love, just like you found with Mother."

His father's eyes grew misty. "Your mother is my everything."

Will nodded, then forced himself to hold his father's gaze. "What if we can't find it? What if I convince Thea to marry me, and she's heartbroken by the loss of Ladykyrk? I know heartache. I could never do that to Thea. If Thea resented marrying me, I don't think I'd forgive myself. Perhaps the *Cryer* is correct. I'm a failure at love."

His father scooted to the front of his seat. "Let me tell you about my courtship of your mother. She wanted nothing to do with me, but we had to marry." He looked to the ceiling and shook his head. "I can't tell you the number of times I thought it was a lost cause. But I continued to work hard to earn her love and respect. She did too. That's what marriage is—it's work. Hard work. Every single day. Remember when I once said that love is like a shooting star? Something spectacular?"

"Yes." He recognized that tone. His father always used it when he was about to impart a wise piece of advice.

"I was wrong. I wouldn't change how I fell in love. A shooting star is easy to see. It's brilliant and rare, but I'd much prefer having my own star right above me in a crowded sky of other stars. I may have had to work hard to find the right one for me, but I wouldn't have it any other way. If it's cloudy or raining, I still know my star is there guiding me in life. It's constant, and it shines brightly just for me." His father's warm gaze was reassuring. "Your mother is that star."

"Ferr-Colby will arrive at Thea's home soon." Will ran one hand through his hair. "I don't have time to go star chasing."

His father humphed. "Tell me what you are going to do to save this gift you've received?"

Will blinked several times as he struggled for an answer.

The wall around Will's heart started to crack. He straightened his shoulders. He did want to spend all his moments with Thea. There was no one in the world more important to him than her. He wanted to make her happy and devote every day of his life to her. He wanted children with her. He wanted to eat orange cream with her on the banks of Ladykyrk's pond. He wanted to make love to her under the stars as they planned their life together.

In his heart resided the simple truth. He would love Thea forever.

"I love her," he whispered. "I'll cherish her forever. I'm going to race up to Northumberland and tear apart every inch of Ladykyrk Hall, then I'm going to dig through every outbuilding on the estate. I'm not quitting until I find that charter for her."

"Your mother loves Thea and so do I. We were concerned you weren't going to fight for her." His father enveloped him in a hug. "Whatever you need, you'll have the entire family support."

Will grinned in a real smile that came from within for the first time since Thea had left his side. He picked up her slippers and waved them in the air. "I'll start by returning these to her as quickly as I can."

The Northumberland Nemesis has returned to her cave.
Finally, London is safe and happy again.
An edict has decreed she is never to return.
(Or at least, there should be an edict that says that.)
Humbly reporting the facts as always,
The Midnight Cryer

Chapter Twenty-Seven

When Thea arrived back at Ladykyrk, she couldn't tell if her exhaustion was from the haste to return to her estate or all her emotions being tangled together. Perhaps it was the fact that every inch of her home had been torn apart as people had looked for the charter.

Ferr-Colby had sent a post stating he'd be there in two weeks. When she thought of marrying him, a black cloud descended that she couldn't seem to dismiss.

However, there was one bright spot in her life. All of Ladykyrk's tenants were delighted she'd returned, and some reluctantly congratulated her on her upcoming marriage to Ferr-Colby. Many had brought her small gifts in celebration. Mrs. Daniels and her twin girls had come to the house with fresh breads and preserves. Fern had proudly said that they'd helped their mother bake and prepare the treats.

Before they left, Ivy had shyly asked if the *candy lord* was returning. Her innocent question had caused Thea's heart, which was patched with the slimmest of threads, to break anew. The constant weight of missing Will had taken its toll on her. She'd cried every night since arriving at Ladykyrk.

Without Will around, she felt lost and wondered if she'd ever find her way again. It took every ounce of strength she had to complete her estate work. Even surrounded by her tenants and new servants, Thea had experienced the loneliest week of her life. Finally, she took an afternoon to herself. She saddled Follow, then went for a long ride.

Without a thought as to where she was going, Thea found herself at the House of Four Directions. If there was ever a time in her life when she needed guidance, it was now. She dismounted, then walked into the folly from the south entrance. She opened all four doors. A gentle wind embraced her, bringing with it the sweet smell of barley from a nearby field. She sat on the sofa and stared at the pond outside the window, not really seeing anything.

The idea that she would marry another man while she loved Will kept her from moving forward. Deep down, she realized she needed to accept the fact that she had to marry Ferr-Colby to save Ladykyrk. Perhaps she'd be blessed with children. They'd fill a void in her life for the family she craved, but there would always be a heartache that would never mend. She had no doubt that her heart would always belong to Will.

Another breeze blew in from the north, this time stronger than the one from the south. It brought a faint sweet smell that was pleasing and familiar. Leaning her head against the sofa, she closed her eyes, trying to remember where she'd smelled it before. Slowly, she opened her eyes and breathed deeply. The scent reminded her of her grandfather's favorite citrus cologne.

She shook her head to clear such nonsensical thoughts. There were no citrus trees or fresh fruit around. Another gust of wind, somewhat stronger, rushed through the folly. This time, the breeze whistled as it came through the door. Though brief, it was powerful enough to knock over a bird's-eye maple urn. The lid fell off, and a stack of papers spilled onto the floor. Thea quickly retrieved them before they flew out the open doors.

As she collected them, she read through the documents. They were the original architectural drawings for the folly. All of the pages had handwritten notes from her grandfather. He'd not only had it built, but he'd also designed it himself—just for her.

Lovingly, she pressed the pages smooth, and studied each drawing. Elevations, directions, roof design, ceiling plans, door openings—every aspect of it he'd created himself and had his vision brought to life by master builders and craftsmen. But it was the last page that stole her breath.

To my darling Thea,

  This building was created in love for you on your eighth birthday. I hope you never tire of me saying this, as it brings me great joy and peace. Remember, outside these windows our mighty oak guards your folly and you. Some say it's over a thousand years old, one of the rarest trees in Northumberland. That, my darling girl, is a testament to its strength and endurance. Just like my love for you will withstand all time and tribulation.

  Whether it is the universe or time that separates us, you'll always have my heart. You deserve all the happiness in the world that life has to offer. It may take a while, but it will find you. Only accept it on your terms.

                          Always and forever,
Theodore Ferr-Colby, the luckiest grandfather in
                                    the world

Her heart squeezed, and tears pricked her eyes. In her hand was the first note she'd ever received from her grandfather. A tangible piece that proved he loved her forever. She strolled to the south entrance and gazed at the mighty oak with the swing still attached that her grandfather had lovingly built for her. As she studied its massive trunk, she inhaled the sweet smells of summer and memories of their days together floated into her thoughts.

He'd held her when she cried after skinning her knees while trying to climb their oak tree. He'd played chess with her nightly, always encouraging her to take riskier moves, then explaining why they did or didn't work. He'd taught her how to ride and had given her Follow right before he'd started to show signs of his illness. He'd taught her how to care for the land and the tenants that were so vital to the estate's success.

But most importantly, he loved her. Having his note in her hand brought a closure that she'd desperately sought. The cost of the last seven years diminished because of today. Because without them, she would have never met Will or gone to London. She'd never have learned what she was capable of achieving without having to step out into the unknown. London and appearing in front of the committee taught her that no matter the obstacle, she could rise to the challenge.

Though she still mourned losing Will, she'd have to find a way to mend her broken heart.

Thea took one last look at their tree, then turned to gather the architectural drawings. Suddenly, she stopped. If he'd hidden the first charter in the henhouse, could he have picked another more special place for the second?

What if her grandfather had hidden the charter in the large knothole of the tree?

She rushed to the swing, then with her heart pounding against her ribs, she stood in front of the knothole.

Slowly, not daring to hope, she reached inside. Her fingers touched the smooth inside sanded perfectly by the rough Northumberland weather that had battered the tree through the centuries. Carefully, her hand skated down, then up.

Nothing.

She said a prayer, then with a deep breath for courage, she reached all the way down the knothole. Her fingers collided with something round and cylindrical in shape. Slowly, she pulled it out.

In her hand, she held a molded leather map case. With trembling fingers, she untied the strap, then lifted the top. Inside was a rolled-up piece of foolscap. With her heart galloping like a runaway horse, she gently pulled it out and unfolded it.

Her hands started shaking as tears welled in her eyes. It was in Latin.

The edges were torn from age, but what took her breath away was the bottom of the page. In the center was a large wax seal. Will had told her that she'd recognize the charter because of the monarch's seal.

She didn't dare hope she'd found it, but she couldn't help herself. There was only one way to find out. She had to find the village vicar immediately and have him read it for her. She rushed into the folly to gather her things, then stopped. She blinked twice to make certain she wasn't imagining things.

Atop the center of the desk, one of the slippers that she'd forgotten at Langham Hall sat facing her. Her gaze flew around the room until she found him.

More handsome than she remembered, Will leaned against the door of the east entrance, holding the other slipper in the palm of his hand. She drank in the sight of him. The broadcloth coat he wore made the breadth of his shoulders even greater than she remembered. His doeskin breeches emphasized the muscular strength of his legs. When her gaze met his, she just stared. She'd always known she'd see him again, but she never imagined it would be this soon.

"How long have you been standing there?" It was inconceivable that he was here before her.

"Not long enough." The smile on his face was one that she'd never seen before—cautious, almost tentative. "You've grown more beautiful since the last time I saw you. I could stay in this spot all day and gaze at you, but we have work to do."

His voice was tender, but the uncertainty in his blue eyes made her want to take him in her arms and relieve whatever burden he carried. She shook her head slightly. She would do well to remember she should also be cautious, as her heart was still fragile. "What work? Why are you here?"

He pushed away from the door, then approached with slow, controlled steps. His gaze never left hers as he placed the other slipper on a side table. He stopped no more than a foot away from her. "Remember when you asked me to be your friend? We were standing here. You told me you'd help me in any way you could. That is what friends do for each other."

"Yes. I'd do anything for you."

"Then let's find that charter, Thea," he said tenderly. "I can't lose you. I want to search every inch of this place for the charter. Let us try to find it together."

Without a word, she handed him the document. "Will you read this for me?" Her voice shook. "I'm afraid I still haven't mastered Latin."

His eyes skated down the page. "You found it! Oh God, Thea, this is it. You are the true Countess of Eanruig." He pulled her next to him with one arm as the other held the charter. His eyes blazed with emotion, and if she wasn't mistaken, tears had gathered. "Where did you find it?"

"In the oak tree." Without hesitating, she stood on tiptoe and pressed her lips to his.

Without breaking away from her, he placed the charter on the table next to the shoe, then wrapped both arms around her and deepened the kiss. Once she was surrounded by the strength of his arms, she surrendered all her heartache and loneliness.

"My love," he said softly. "You're forever mine."

All she could do was nod.

Will picked up the slipper for her inspection. "I've taken a shine to these. Do you know they're almost an obsession for me? I found myself unable to let them go. Whenever I wake in the middle of the night because I'm thinking of you, I reach for them." He examined the shoe carefully, then held it out to her. "But it was selfish of me. I had to return them to you."

Gingerly, she accepted it. She found it difficult to breathe. She willed herself to stay calm. She closed her eyes, desperate not to cry in front of him, but the tears kept welling in her eyes.

"I took great care of them for you. There's not a single thread or pearl missing."

"Thank you." She opened her eyes, and a single tear fell. Before she could brush it away, Will did the honors with his thumb. The gentle touch against her skin reminded her of how much she loved him.

"Don't cry, sweetheart." He kept rubbing his thumb gently across her cheek. "If you'd give me the opportunity, I'd like to personally show you my talent for good stewardship. I plan to do it by taking great care of your heart."

"You can't." His touch made her want to lean against him and take some of his strength for her own.

"Why? Are you still going to marry Ferr-Colby?" His rushed words sounded desperate, and his eyes searched hers.

"No. But I left my heart in London . . . with you." She grabbed tight to the lapels of his jacket, never wanting to let him go. "I'm sorry, Will. . . ." Her voice choked on a sob. "Do you think you could ever forgive me for causing you so much pain?"

"My love, always and forever." He lightly pressed his lips to hers. "Never doubt that."

She buried her head against his waistcoat where his familiar fragrance rose to greet her. Surrounded by his strong arms, Thea knew comfort for the first time since she'd returned to Ladykyrk. She was truly home.

Thea leaned back slightly and withdrew a piece of paper from her pocket. "Now I have a question to ask you." With a tremulous smile, she handed it to him. "I actually made this for you when I met your friends. I wanted to give it to you then, but I was afraid you'd say no. But I learned from you not to be timid about what I want."

Will took the paper and read it. A smile brighter than all the chandeliers in London lit his face. "This is the one you held in your hands that day, isn't it?"

She answered with a slight nod as all her emotions threatened to burst free. "Yes, I prepared it especially for you." She pointed to the heart she'd drawn on it. "Only on yours, would I promise my heart. It's yours forever."

"I learned some things myself too. I discovered what it is really like to be in love." He bent and brushed his lips against her forehead. "I've been such a fool since I met you. A fool in love. I was so afraid of taking the risk of falling in love when happiness was right in front of my eyes, I ignored it. I was scared I'd failed you. You taught me to be brave." He tilted her chin and searched her eyes. "I'm in love with you, Theodora." He pulled her tighter against him. "Give me the chance to prove it to you every day."

Her knees felt weak, and she forced herself to take measured breaths. Otherwise she'd faint. Her euphoric heart pumped wildly in her chest. "Always. Will you give me the same chance?"

"You don't need to ask. I love you. Completely." He kissed her nose. "Decidedly." He kissed her cheek. "Thoroughly." He kissed her other cheek, then crossed his heart with a finger as if making a solemn pledge. "I'll love you forever."

She couldn't find the right words. It was unbelievable that this morning she woke up certain that her life wouldn't include Will, and now, he stood in front of her vowing his love for all eternity. "I don't know what to say."

"You don't have to say anything." Little by little, he lowered his lips to hers. "But may I start forever today?"

She didn't answer. Instead, she wrapped her arms around his neck and kissed him. Her lips moved gently against his. A week was too long to go without his kisses, and she vowed then and there, she'd never forgo such pleasures for longer than a day.

His heart pounded against hers in the same rhythm, as if the two were already joined. On a groan, he parted his lips, and she swept inside to show him all the love she had for him. It was a kiss that pledged their troth to one another, declared their faith in each other, and promised they would love one another for all time.

Gradually, he pulled away and took her hands in his. "Let's leave for London tomorrow. We'll send one of Aunt Stella's footmen to ride ahead and inform Odell and Howton that you found the charter." He kissed her nose.

"Will you join me for dinner at Payne Manor this evening? I have a present I want to give you."

"A present?" Surprised, she drew back and searched his eyes. "What is it?"

"You'll see." He grinned. But there was nothing innocent or cautious in this smile.

"You are a tease."

"I learned it from the best." He grabbed her, and she squeaked in protest before he kissed her again. "I learned it from you." Tenderly, he cupped her cheek in his hand. "I love you. I don't think I'll ever tire of saying those three words."

"I don't think I'll tire of hearing it."

"Good, because I plan to tell you that again tonight." He brought her hand to his mouth and smiled.

"Welcome, Lady Eanruig," Mr. Brandon, Stella's butler, enthused. "You look lovely this evening."

"Thank you." Thea smoothed her gloved hands down her peach-colored silk and satin gown. It was not only beautiful, but it was her favorite. She wanted to look her best tonight for Will. She still couldn't believe he was here in Northumberland. She'd pinched herself to ensure she wasn't dreaming when she returned home from the folly this afternoon. "Where might I find Lord William?"

"He's in the dining room already, ma'am." One side of the butler's mouth inched upward. "Jeffry and James will escort you to him."

Two of Stella's Adonis-like footmen nodded. For the first time ever, she saw them actually smile. They were extraordinarily gorgeous when they weren't so stern, but neither could hold a candle to Will's stunning masculine handsomeness. She nodded her agreement, and the two men slowly walked her down the hall.

"My lady, we've been instructed to announce you this evening," Jeffry said.

Truly, she was uninterested. All she wanted to do was find Will and feel his arms around her once more.

Simultaneously, the two footmen opened the double doors to the dining room so Thea could make a grand entrance.

"The Countess of Eanruig," James announced.

Thea wanted to roll her eyes at the formality of the evening. It was keeping her from Will's side. But as a countess was expected to do, she thanked the men, then entered.

"I don't believe it," she murmured.

Will closed the small distance between them and took her hands in his.

"What is this?" she asked incredulously. "What are they doing here?"

"They came to help us search for the charter because they love you, Thea. This is my present for the love of my life," he announced.

The entire Cavensham family stood before her. The duke and duchess, Claire and Pembrooke, Emma and Somerton, and March and McCalpin, along with Stella and Lady Edith. They all possessed the most breathtaking smiles on their faces.

Will dropped to one knee before her. His eyes flickered with an intensity that took her breath. He grasped her hands tightly, and she returned the gesture.

"Theodora, I want to share my life and my love with you for all my days." He swept one hand toward his family. "I want to share everything that's important in my life. I can't think of anything more precious to give you than my family. I want to share them with you. My family is your family."

Thea raised her hand and rested it against her heart

as tears streamed down her face. She glanced at Claire whose own eyes glistened with tears. The duchess's mouth trembled. Even Stella was wiping her eyes. It was the most beautiful and poignant moment in her life. But when Thea looked to the duke, that's when she sobbed.

A single tear fell down his handsome face. "We'd be so honored if you'd join our family."

She turned to Will. "Thank you," she whispered.

"No, it's I who should thank you. You taught me to trust my heart again." He squeezed her hand.

From his touch, she could feel his love pouring into every inch of her and patching the holes that loneliness had worn through her heart.

"My darling, Thea . . ." He cleared his throat, but tears welled in his gorgeous blue eyes. "Will you make me the happiest man in all of Britain, and do me the honor of becoming my wife? I promise I'll protect you and your heart by loving you forever."

She nodded, unable to speak. He stood and took her in his arms and kissed her in front of his entire family.

As the cheers rang out, Thea lost herself in the kiss. She was so blessedly happy. Everything she'd ever wished for in life had come true because of Lord William Cavensham, her true love. He'd given her his family, the one that she'd wanted for so long. But most importantly, he'd given himself to her—heart and soul.

When they finished kissing, Will cupped her cheeks with his hands, then gently wiped her tears with his thumbs. "You're breathtaking."

"How can I be? I'm crying, and I'm sure my face is red."

"It makes you even more beautiful in my eyes. I'm the luckiest man in all of England," he whispered.

"Everyone, may I have your attention?" Stella cleared her throat. She stood by an easel covered with a brocade cloth. "I finished this while I was at Langham Hall. It's Thea's engagement present." She nodded at Jeffry.

With an obvious flare for the dramatic, he whipped the cover from the painting.

Undaunted by the gasps that erupted from the room, Stella stood a little straighter with a wry smile gracing her lips. "It's magnificent if I do say so myself."

The room grew silent, and Thea had to blink several times. She couldn't believe what she was seeing.

Finally, McCalpin broke the spell. "Oh my God, Will. That's you."

Emma snorted. "Are you scowling in it, Will?"

Claire buried her head in Alex's chest, but it didn't hide her mirth. Though she was laughing quietly, her shoulders were shaking. While Pembrooke smiled, he kissed the top of his wife's head, then shot a glance at Somerton.

As soon as their gazes collided, they started laughing.

Will's face turned beet red as he stared at the picture. "You didn't—"

"I most certainly did," Stella countered. "I had Pitts bring the armor to my room so I could paint the texture of the breastplate correctly."

Lady Edith chimed in. "She almost painted you in chain mail, but I thought it too old-fashioned. I talked her out of it."

While the others giggled and laughed over the painting, Thea was in awe. It was a perfect likeness of Will dressed in armor with the Ladykyrk seal painted on his breastplate. He looked straight on with a medieval helmet under one arm. Every feature was perfect, but the smoldering gaze on his face caused her heart to flutter in her chest. Just looking at it caused her insides to go squishy. She leaned a little closer to him. They needed to have the banns read as soon as possible.

"It's glorious," Thea whispered. "You're glorious."

Will's eyes narrowed as he stared at the picture.

"I'm going to burn it," he growled.

"No, you're not." Thea playfully tapped his arm. "She gave it to me. I have the perfect place for it. I'm going to hang it in my dressing room."

The duke and duchess had sidled up to them and admired the portrait.

"She did one for me of Sebastian when we became betrothed," the duchess whispered to Thea. "I have it in my dressing room too."

"Let Thea hang it where she wants." The duke winked at his son. "Trust me on this. You can thank me later."

Epilogue

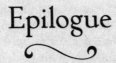

Three months later
London

Will and Thea had finally arrived at Langham House. After having the banns read three times in the local village church, they'd married in Northumberland. All of Ladykyrk and Payne Manor's tenants attended, along with the entire Cavensham family. However, Will's mother wanted a special wedding breakfast in Langham Hall when they arrived back to town for Thea's investiture as the new Countess of Eanruig. The Committee for Privileges had ruled quickly in her favor once they saw the charter, then recommended that the attorney general inform the Prince Regent.

They were also in town for Will's investitures as a baron.

In the past three months, Aunt Stella had been extremely busy. She convinced the Prince Regent to re-create her darling Payne's title of baron and give it to Will. In return, Stella would forgive the monstrous gambling debt Prinny owed her. Will would now be called Lord Cavensham. Of course, his darling wife, would still be called Lady Eanruig.

Will had also been as busy. He'd fed *The Midnight Cryer* all the lurid details of the Duke of Ferr-Colby's deception against Thea. Will almost—*but not quite*—felt sorry for the duke. The *Cryer* hounded Ferr-Colby daily. Word had it that a bevy of marriageable heiresses had snubbed him repeatedly. This week, his fifth marriage proposal had been refused, just like the other four.

Will sat in his usual spot at the Langham Hall dining room table. He rested his arm on the back of Thea's chair. He stole a kiss from his bride in front of all his family—correction, *all of his and Thea's family and friends.* "Are you happy?"

The brilliant smile on her face made him fall in love with her all over again. "Can't you tell?"

"Just making certain." Underneath the table, he held her hand. Craving to touch her, he trailed his thumb gently over her knuckles. "I love you so," he whispered.

"And I love you," she said.

Claire sat to Thea's right and asked her a question. While his darling wife spoke to his cousin and Pembrooke, Will's gaze trailed down the table. All their family were in attendance, including several of Will's friends. Grayson was seated next to his mother, and Devan was sitting across the table from them with Avalon on his right and Aunt Stella and Lady Edith to his left.

Thea had specifically asked his mother if Avalon and her little sister, Lady Sophia Cavensham, could attend since they had no family except for themselves. That was another reason why he loved his wife dearly. She didn't hold grudges and could see when people were hurting. She was truly magnificent in every way.

When she returned her attention to him, he raised her hand to his lips and pressed a kiss against her soft skin. "I think we need to see how your slippers are faring in our bedroom. Not only do I take great care of your shoes, but I give you *great care.*"

"Hush, you rogue," she murmured.

"If I recall correctly"—he lifted a brow—"I gave you *great care* three times last night."

"If you keep talking like that, someone might overhear. Your family—"

"They're yours too," he interrupted.

"And I thank you every day for such a special gift." Her mystical eyes flashed.

"I adore the way you thank me with *great care,* I might add." He waggled his eyebrows.

"They'll think we're acting like field rabbits." Her tone may have hinted at chastisement, but the smile on her face belied any real disapproval.

Thus encouraging him to continue. Will lifted an eyebrow. He leaned close, then rubbed his lips against her ear. "They'll discover we do act like field rabbits when we tell my parents that you're carrying their next grandchild."

All of a sudden, Avalon whipped her head to Devan. "What did you call me?"

Though she whispered, Will could hear the ire in her voice.

Devan took another sip of champagne, then in a nonchalant manner, turned her way. "I called you 'Lady *War-Wick.*'"

"Spare us, Mr. Farris, your sanctimonious, not to mention smug, attitude." Avalon rolled her eyes.

"A poetess in our midst," Devan mocked with a wicked smile.

"I heard it, loud and clear, you pious prig," Avalon hissed.

Thea's eyes widened. "Should we do something? They're getting quite heated."

Before Will could answer, Avalon continued, but lowered her voice even more, "You called me 'Lady Warlock.'"

With raised eyebrows, Stella looked across the table at Thea and Will. "Did you hear the good news? Mr. *Spare Us*, I mean, Mr. Farris, has been assigned to the Warwick Hall parish."

Avalon's eyes grew as round as the breakfast plates in front of them. "No," she whispered to herself.

"All your dreams are coming true, my lady," Devan soothed. "I'll be right next door to you. Perhaps you have a friend or two you could introduce me to. I'm still looking for an heiress."

Avalon's hand skated to her stomach. "You're vulgar."

Devan caught Will's gaze and winked. "And entertaining, my lady."

Lady Edith chimed, "Perhaps there will be wedding bells."

"A match made in heaven." Stella chortled. "Or hell."

Before Will could intervene in the squabble between Avalon and Devan, his father stood with a raised glass by Will's mother. The guests immediately quieted down.

"Everyone, please join me and my duchess in welcoming our daughter-in-law and son as they celebrate their marriage with us today." Holding Will's mother's hand, the duke tilted his head slightly with a smile that spoke of love. "I've borrowed a few words from Shakespeare and added a few of my own for our celebration. Thea and Will, we wish you both all the joy and love you can wish."

After the *hear, hears* and *huzzahs* subsided around the table, Thea gracefully stood and lifted her glass to his parents. Her gaze caught his, and Will's heart fell in somersaults. It was always that way when her face softened with love for him.

He once thought he was the luckiest man in all of England. He was wrong.

He was the luckiest man in the world.

With her glass raised, Thea took Will's hand—her husband's hand—the hand of the father of her children. At that thought, her eyes grew misty, but she refused to allow her tears to interrupt their celebrations. Will gently squeezed her hand in encouragement.

"Your Grace." She nodded at Will's mother. "And Your Grace." She nodded at Will's father. "You fell in love with my husband first. You held him first. You protected his heart first. For all of that, I'm forever grateful. I pledge to you this day that my life and my love are dedicated to your son forever."

Several of the guests dabbed at their eyes, but Thea was determined to finish her toast. She'd been working on it in private for the last two days.

She cleared her throat while tamping down the tears that threatened to fall. "I've always believed in fairy tales, but someone wise once said, 'Be careful what you wish for.' I took that lesson to heart. I was *very, very* careful what I wished for. And my wish was granted."

Will brought her hand to his lips, and his strength allowed her to continue.

"Thank you for being the most wonderful parents I've ever known." Finally, she turned to Will with tears in her eyes and a smile on her face. "Because of you, I found my fairy tale."

As the guests erupted in another round of cheers and well wishes, William stood and they toasted each other.

"Because of you," he whispered, "we both found our fairy tale. I promise to love and cherish you. And a Cavensham never breaks a promise. When we find love it's completely, decidedly, and *forever*."

Author's Note

❦

Suo jure is a Latin phrase meaning in his/her own right.

The idea for Thea as a countess in her own right and the challenge to her title comes from the real Elizabeth Leveson-Gower, the 19th Countess of Sutherland. In 1771, the countess had to defend her rights against a male relative, Sir Robert Gordon, 4th Baronet, who claimed the Scottish earldom should be his.

An infant when she inherited, Elizabeth had not one, but six stalwart guardians, including the Duke of Athol and the Earl of Elgin, along with her solicitors, who helped defend her title in the House of Lords. Typically, only the solicitors were present making the claims and defenses. However, to make the story more interesting, Will and the entire Cavensham family had to be in attendance because there was no way they would let Thea face this alone. She was one of them.

Like Thea's charter, the original "patent of the honour" bestowing the Earldom of Sutherland couldn't be found, so the entire history of the title's passage had to be resurrected and presented. Why did Elizabeth's challenger lose? His family trees consisted of several bastards. The original patent of the Earldom of Sutherland stated that it went to "Heirs of the Marriage," meaning any titleholder had to be legitimate.

However, not everything in the Countess of Sutherland's life was a storybook romance with a happy ending. In September of 1785, Elizabeth married George Leveson-Gower, Viscount Trentham, the son of the 1st Marquess of Stafford. In 1833, he was named the Duke of Sutherland. They are best remembered for the Highland Scottish Clearances where they uprooted over fifteen thousand tenants and subtenants from their lands and relocated them to the coasts of Scotland. Elizabeth and her husband wanted more pasture for sheep, as did many of the landowners in the highlands and the outer islands of Scotland. It's been reported that over 150,000 tenants were forced from their ancestral lands during the hundred years when the Scottish Clearances took place. A devastating fact when you consider that number meant that over fifty percent of the area's population was uprooted during that time. Elizabeth's name was forever tainted when her land steward faced murder charges after he set fire to one of the cottages with an elderly woman inside.

One can easily see why Thea was adamant that the Duke of Ferr-Colby not succeed in removing the Ladykyrk tenants. Thankfully, in *Rogue Most Wanted,* the charter is recovered. Lucky for Will, Thea found the charter, so they could live their fairytale. Lucky for Thea, she had Will's heart *completely, decidedly,* and *forever.*

For more information on Elizabeth's defense of her title, see the transcript and the evidence presented to the House of Lords in *The Additional Case of Elisabeth, Claiming the Title and Dignity of Countess of Suther-*

land, by her Guardians, Case of Sir Robert Gordon, bart. (claiming the title, honour, and dignity of) Earl of Sutherland, and *Peerage Law in England: A Practical Treatise for Lawyers and Laymen*. With an Appendix of Peerage Charters and Letters Patent. By Frances Beaufort Palmer.